JON HOEBER & ERICH HOEBER • WERTHER DELL'EDERA • ARIANNA FLOREAN

THE MISSION™

COLLIDER

JON HOEBER
ERICH HOEBER
WRITERS

WERTHER DELL'EDERA
ARTIST

ARIANNA FLOREAN
COLOR ARTIST

DAVE SHARPE
LETTERER

FONOGRAFIKS
DESIGN

AUBREY SITTERSON
EDITOR

MARC GUGGENHEIM
ALISA TAGER
PRODUCERS

THE MISSION
created by
JON HOEBER & ERICH HOEBER

Image Comics, Inc.

Robert Kirkman
Chief Operating Officer
Erik Larsen
Chief Financial Officer
Todd McFarlane
President
Marc Silvestri
Chief Executive Officer
Jim Valentino
Vice-President

Eric Stephenson
Publisher
Todd Martinez
Sales & Licensing Coordinator
Sarah deLaine
PR & Marketing Coordinator
Branwyn Bigglestone
Accounts Manager
Emily Miller
Administrative Assistant
Jamie Parreno
Marketing Assistant
Kevin Yuen
Digital Rights Coordinator
Tyler Shainline
Production Manager
Drew Gill
Art Director
Jonathan Chan
Senior Production Artist
Monica Garcia
Vincent Kukua
Jana Cook
Production Artists

www.imagecomics.com

International Rights Representative: Christine Meyer (christine@gfloystudio.com)

THE MISSION TRADE PAPERBACK. Volume 1. First printing. Published by Image Comics, Inc. Office of publication: 2134 Allston Way, 2nd Floor, Berkeley, CA 94704.

ISBN: 978-1-60706-463-3

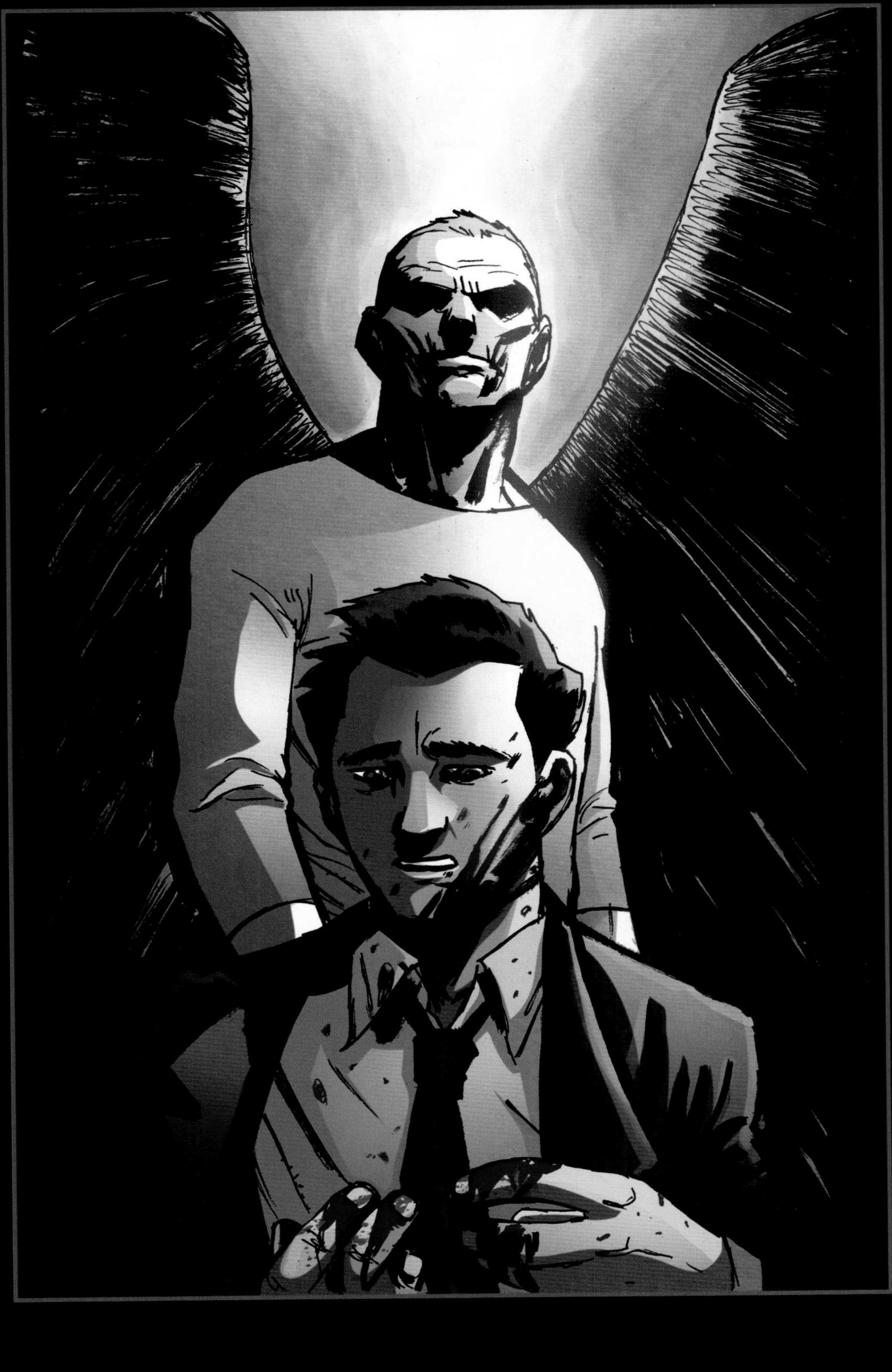

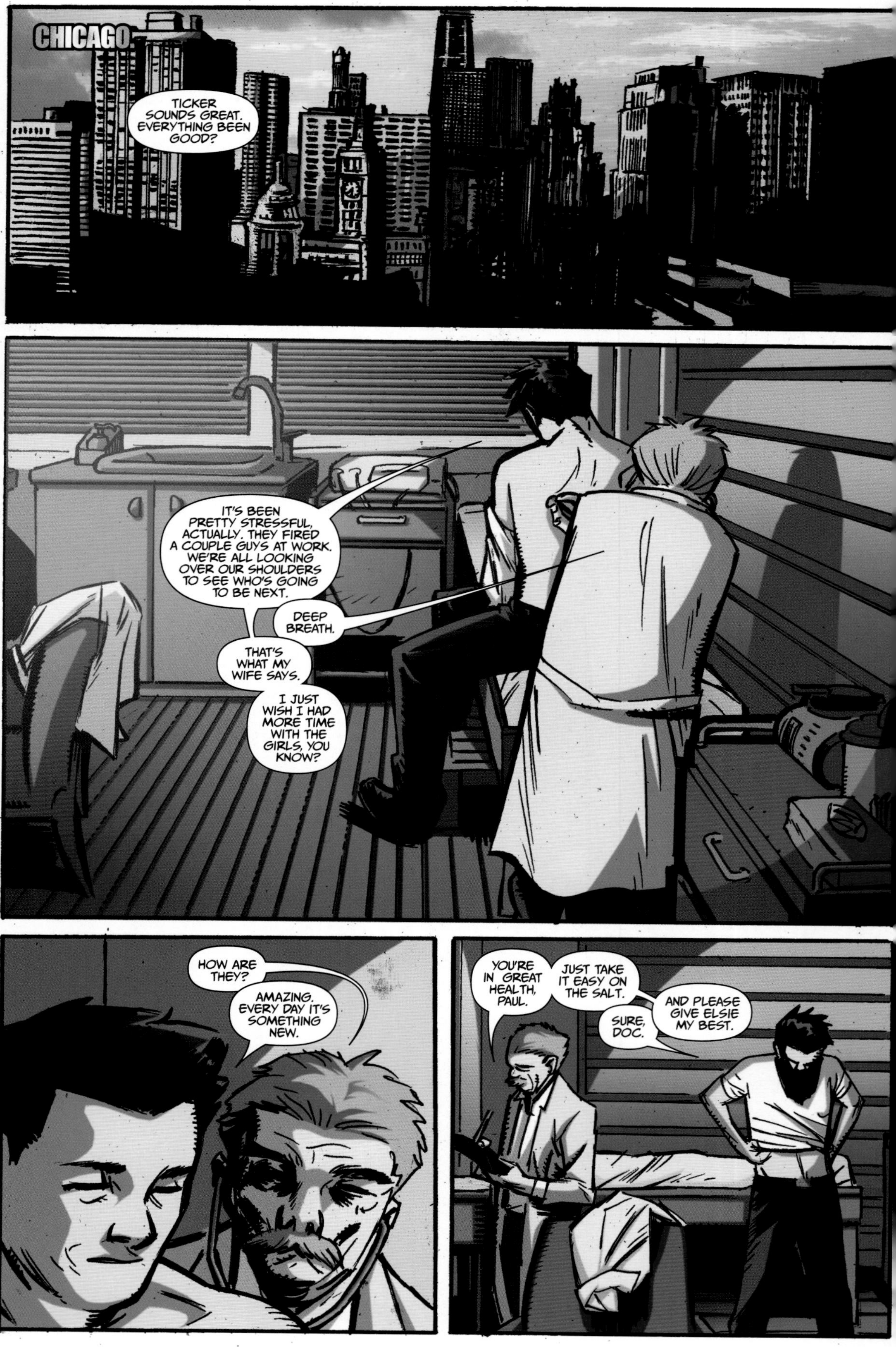
CHICAGO
TICKER SOUNDS GREAT. EVERYTHING BEEN GOOD?
IT'S BEEN PRETTY STRESSFUL, ACTUALLY. THEY FIRED A COUPLE GUYS AT WORK. WE'RE ALL LOOKING OVER OUR SHOULDERS TO SEE WHO'S GOING TO BE NEXT.
DEEP BREATH.
THAT'S WHAT MY WIFE SAYS.
I JUST WISH I HAD MORE TIME WITH THE GIRLS, YOU KNOW?
HOW ARE THEY?
AMAZING. EVERY DAY IT'S SOMETHING NEW.
YOU'RE IN GREAT HEALTH, PAUL.
JUST TAKE IT EASY ON THE SALT.
AND PLEASE GIVE ELSIE MY BEST.
SURE, DOC.

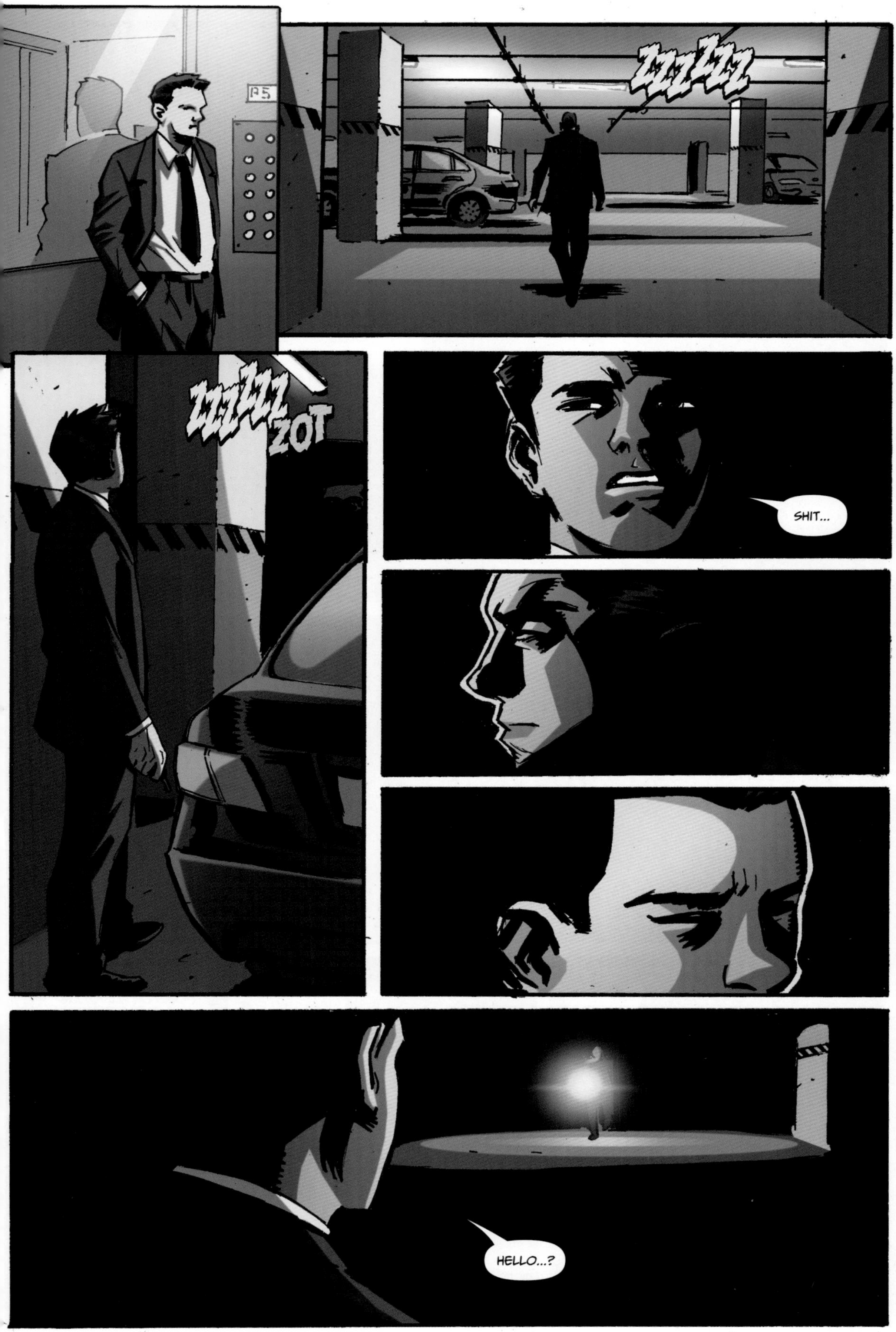
ZZZZZZ
ZZZZZZ
ZOT
SHIT...
HELLO...?

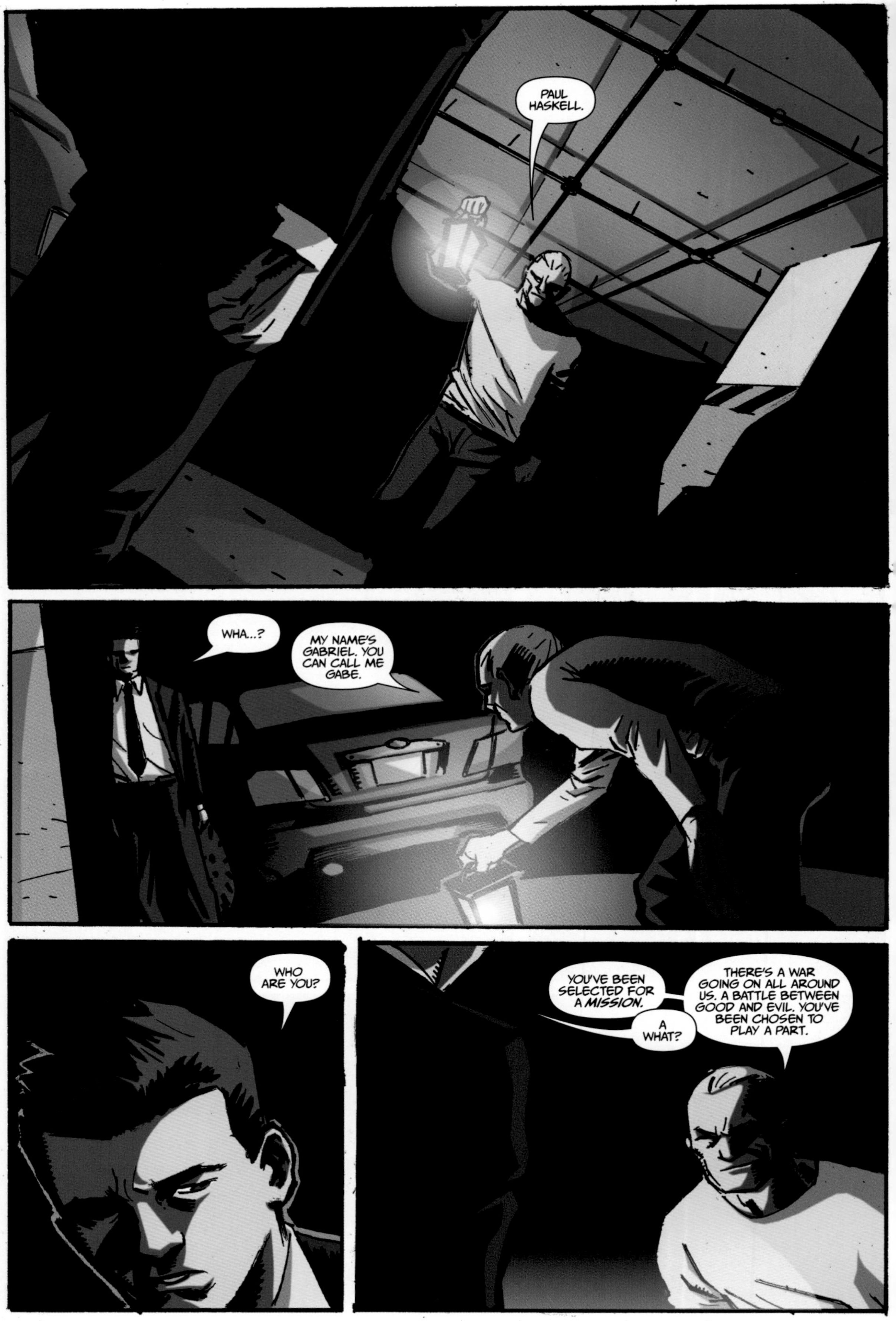
PAUL HASKELL.
WHA...?
MY NAME'S GABRIEL. YOU CAN CALL ME GABE.
WHO ARE YOU?
YOU'VE BEEN SELECTED FOR A *MISSION*.
A WHAT?
THERE'S A WAR GOING ON ALL AROUND US. A BATTLE BETWEEN GOOD AND EVIL. YOU'VE BEEN CHOSEN TO PLAY A PART.

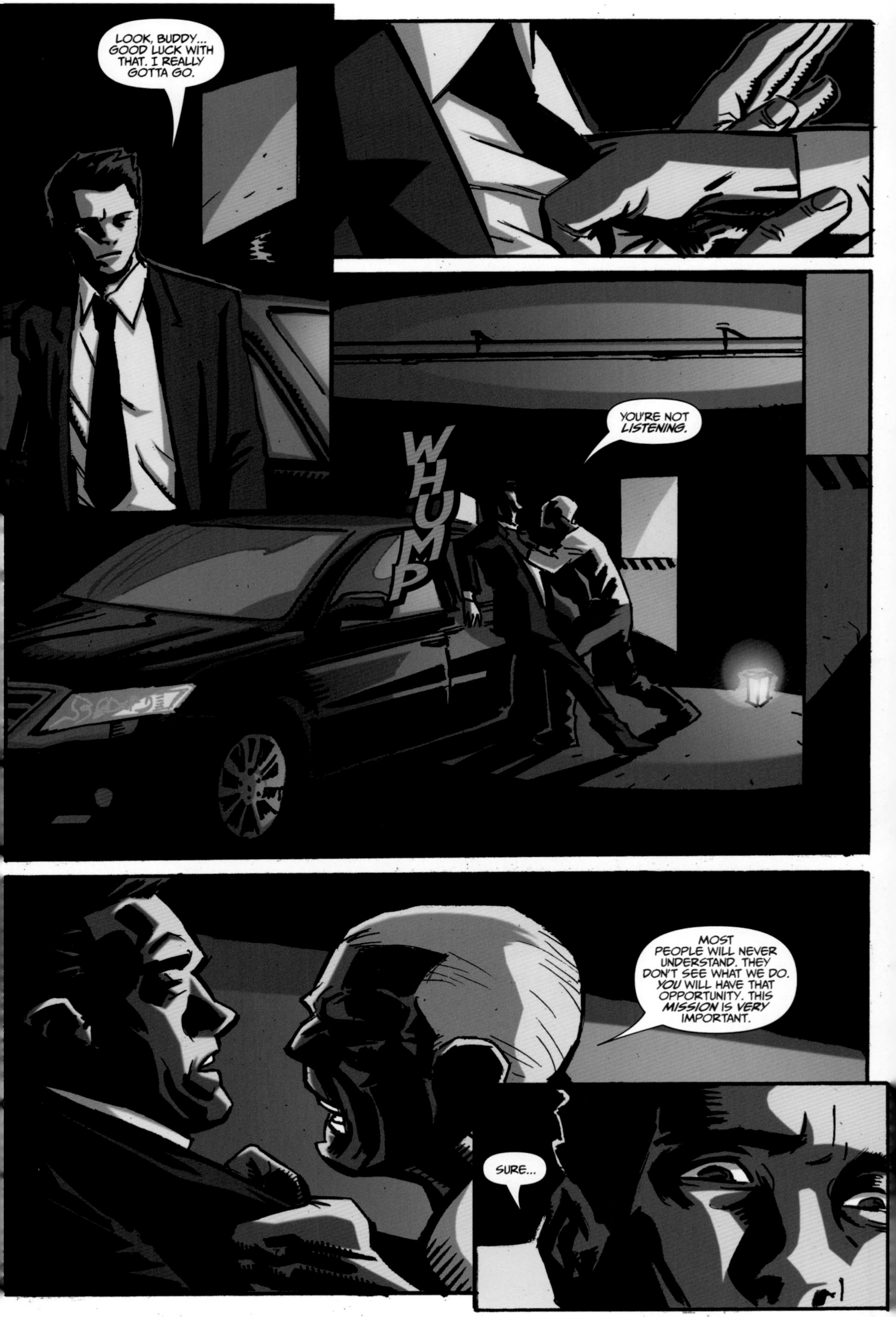
LOOK, BUDDY... GOOD LUCK WITH THAT. I REALLY GOTTA GO.
WHUMP
YOU'RE NOT *LISTENING.*
MOST PEOPLE WILL NEVER UNDERSTAND. THEY DON'T SEE WHAT WE DO. *YOU* WILL HAVE THAT OPPORTUNITY. THIS *MISSION* IS *VERY* IMPORTANT.
SURE...

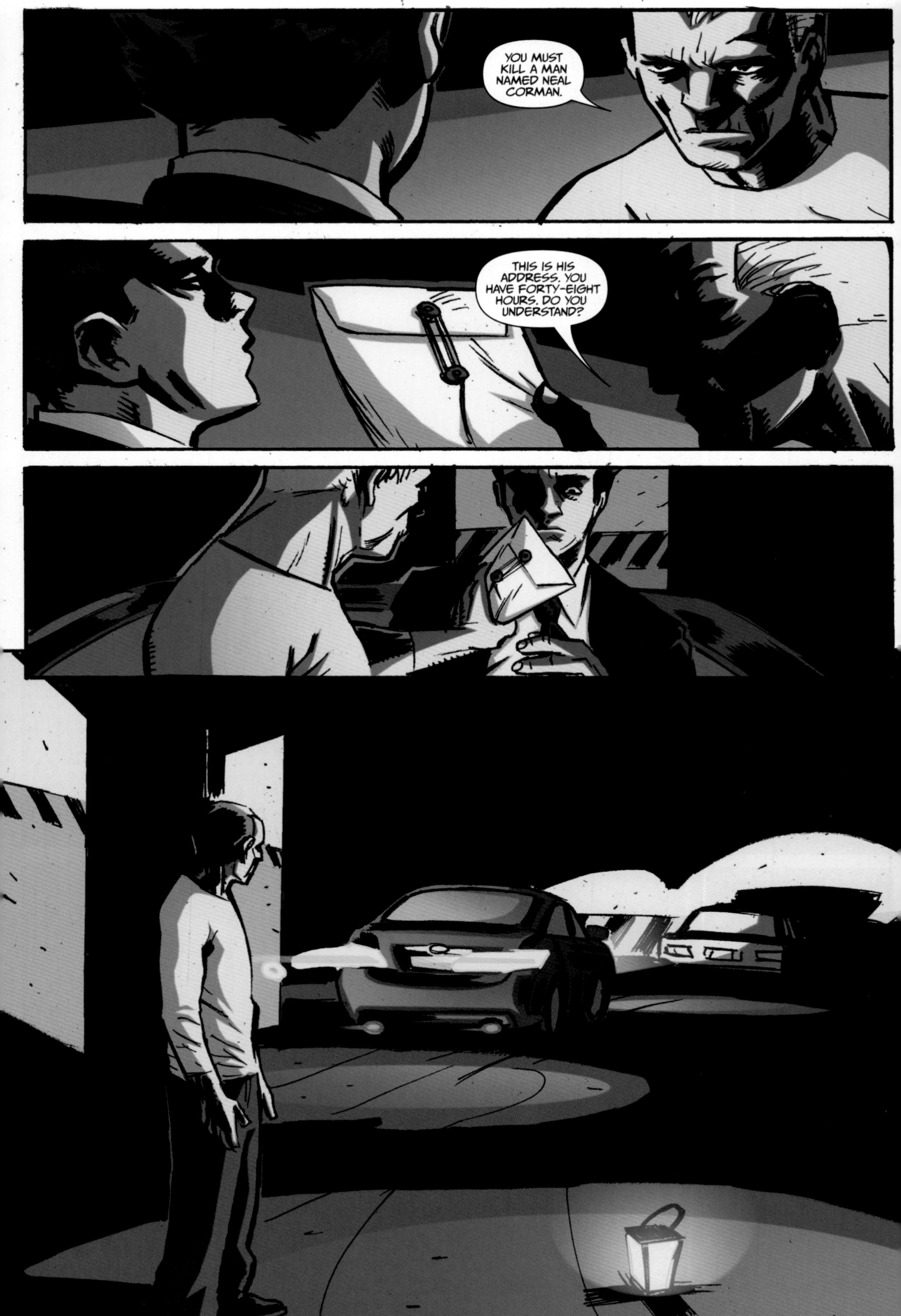
YOU MUST KILL A MAN NAMED NEAL CORMAN.
THIS IS HIS ADDRESS. YOU HAVE FORTY-EIGHT HOURS. DO YOU UNDERSTAND?

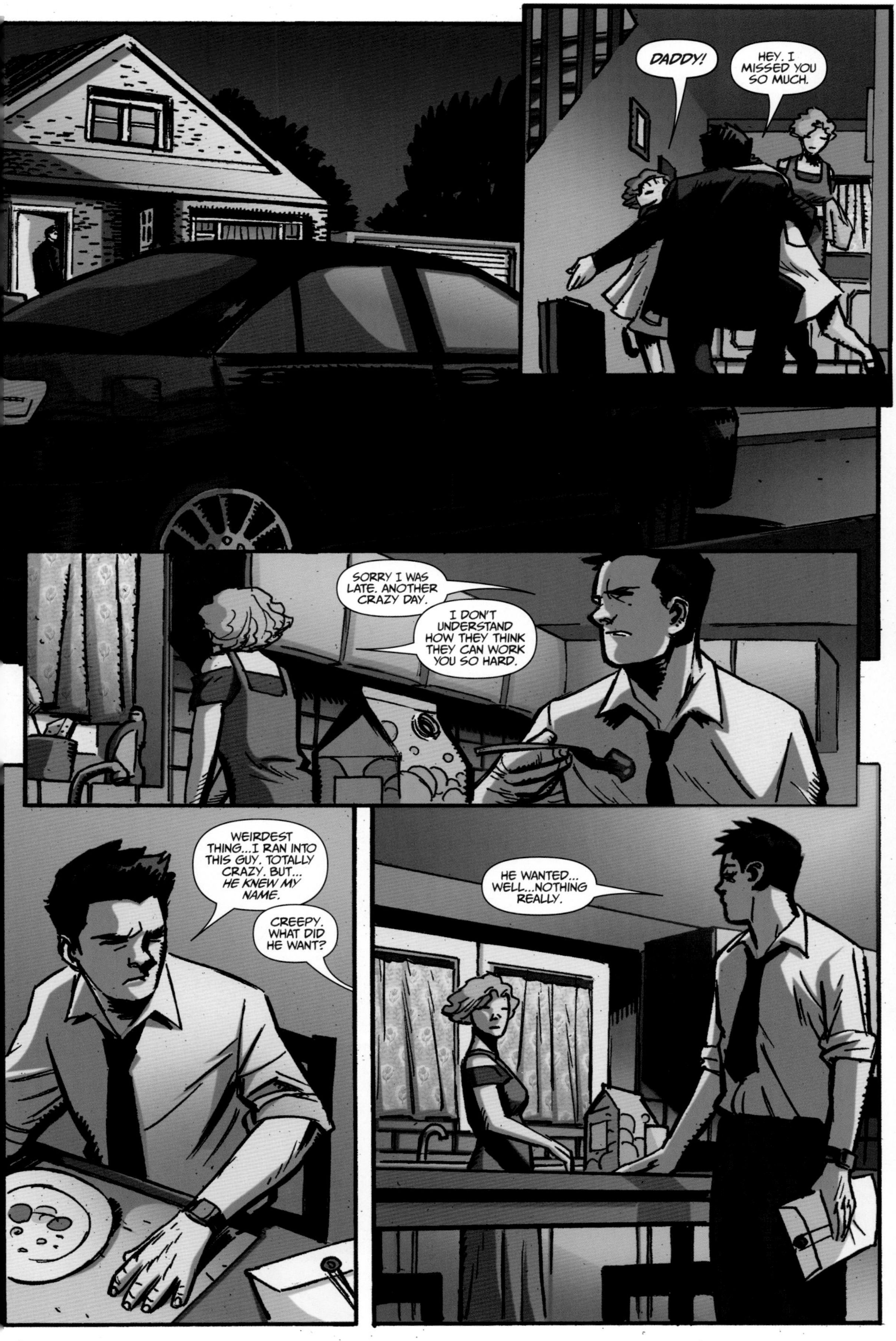
DADDY!
HEY. I MISSED YOU SO MUCH.
SORRY I WAS LATE. ANOTHER CRAZY DAY.
I DON'T UNDERSTAND HOW THEY THINK THEY CAN WORK YOU SO HARD.
WEIRDEST THING...I RAN INTO THIS GUY. TOTALLY CRAZY. BUT... *HE KNEW MY NAME.*
CREEPY. WHAT DID HE WANT?
HE WANTED... WELL...NOTHING REALLY.

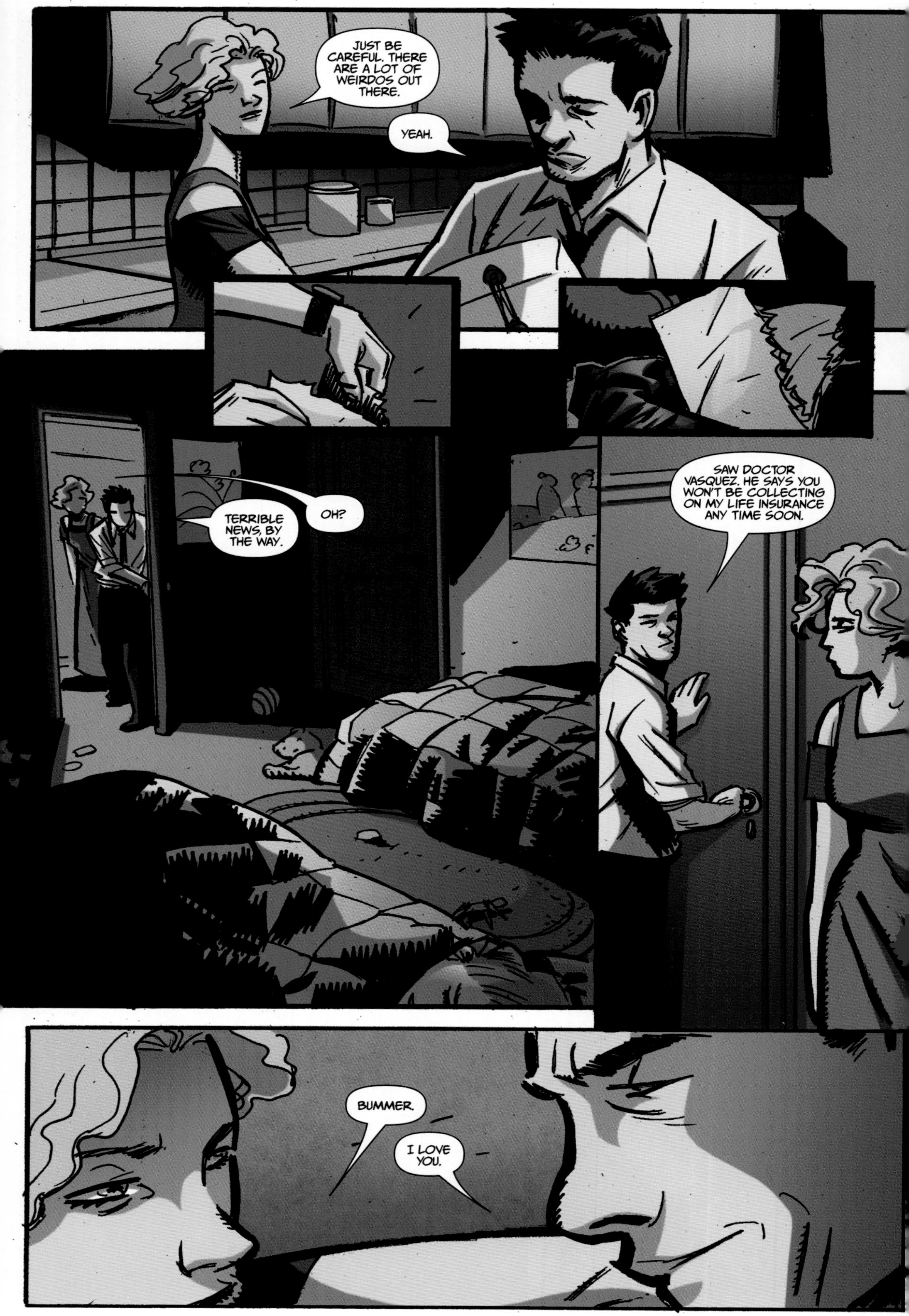
JUST BE CAREFUL. THERE ARE A LOT OF WEIRDOS OUT THERE.
YEAH.
TERRIBLE NEWS, BY THE WAY.
OH?
SAW DOCTOR VASQUEZ. HE SAYS YOU WON'T BE COLLECTING ON MY LIFE INSURANCE ANY TIME SOON.
BUMMER.
I LOVE YOU.

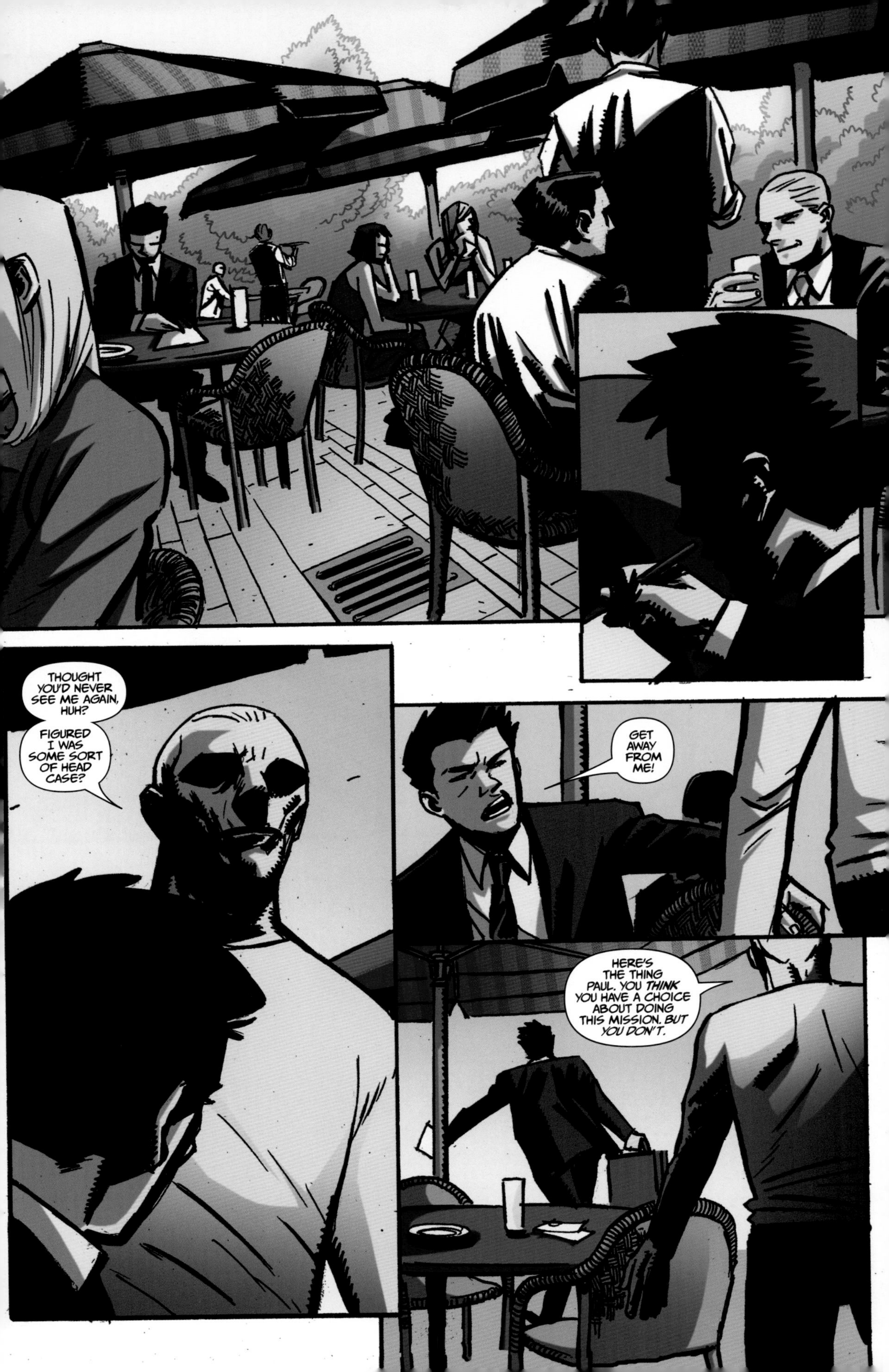
THOUGHT YOU'D NEVER SEE ME AGAIN, HUH?
FIGURED I WAS SOME SORT OF HEAD CASE?
GET AWAY FROM ME!
HERE'S THE THING PAUL. YOU *THINK* YOU HAVE A CHOICE ABOUT DOING THIS MISSION. *BUT YOU DON'T.*

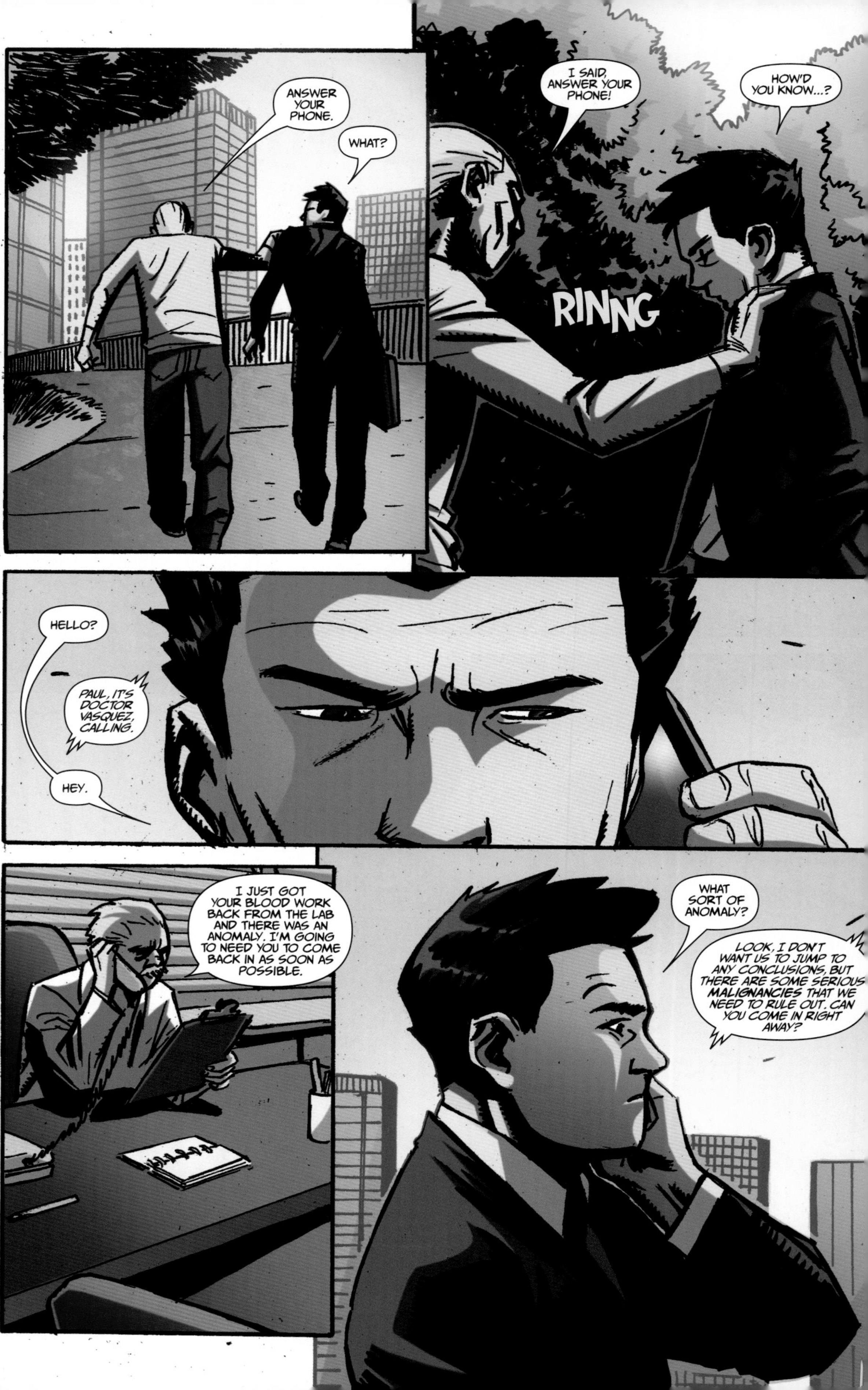
ANSWER YOUR PHONE.
WHAT?
I SAID, ANSWER YOUR PHONE!
HOW'D YOU KNOW...?
RINNG
HELLO?
PAUL, IT'S DOCTOR VASQUEZ, CALLING.
HEY.
I JUST GOT YOUR BLOOD WORK BACK FROM THE LAB AND THERE WAS AN ANOMALY. I'M GOING TO NEED YOU TO COME BACK IN AS SOON AS POSSIBLE.
WHAT SORT OF ANOMALY?
LOOK, I DON'T WANT US TO JUMP TO ANY CONCLUSIONS, BUT THERE ARE SOME SERIOUS MALIGNANCIES THAT WE NEED TO RULE OUT. CAN YOU COME IN RIGHT AWAY?

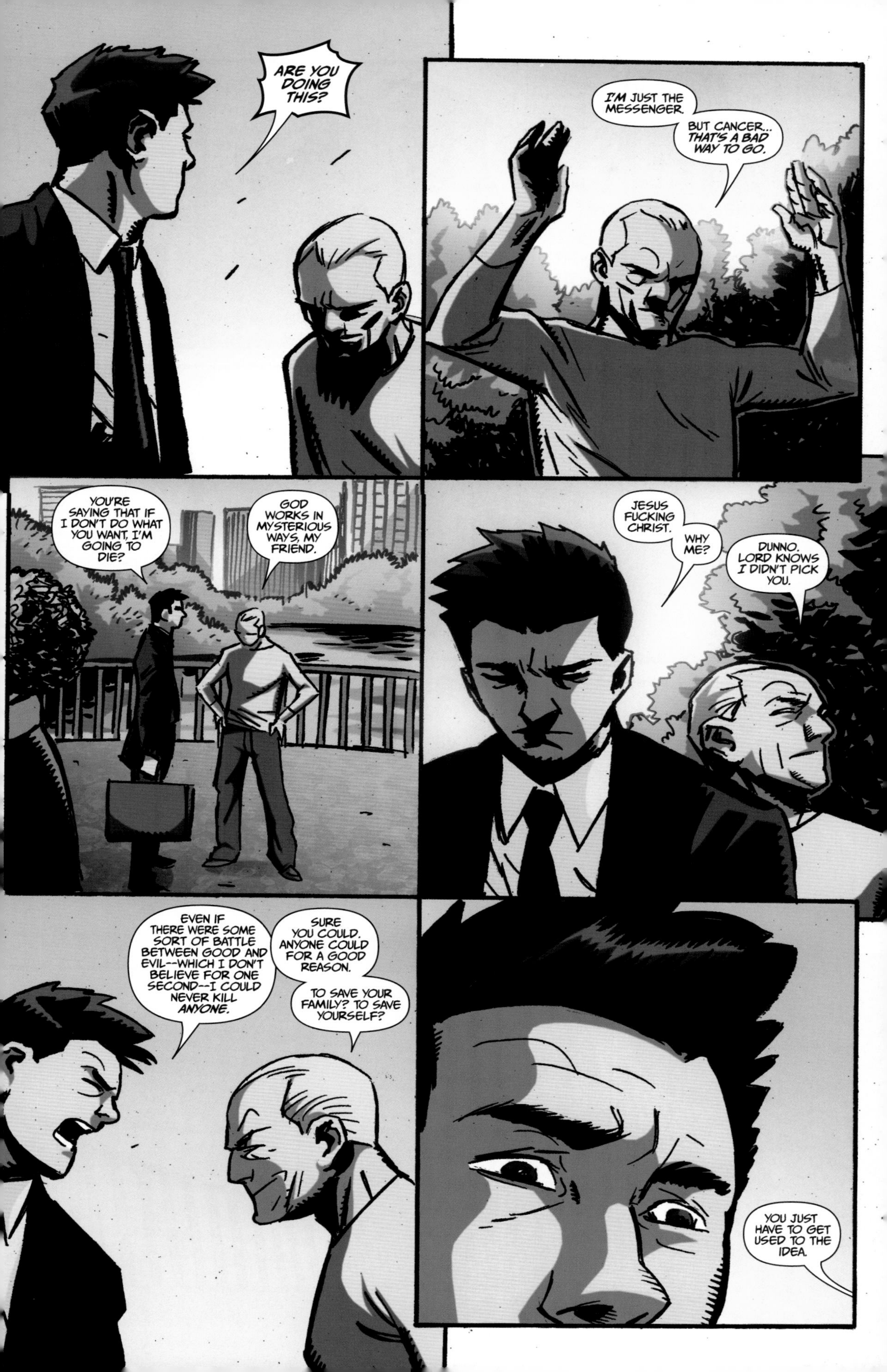
ARE YOU DOING THIS?
I'M JUST THE MESSENGER.
BUT CANCER... THAT'S A BAD WAY TO GO.
YOU'RE SAYING THAT IF I DON'T DO WHAT YOU WANT, I'M GOING TO DIE?
GOD WORKS IN MYSTERIOUS WAYS, MY FRIEND.
JESUS FUCKING CHRIST.
WHY ME?
DUNNO. LORD KNOWS I DIDN'T PICK YOU.
EVEN IF THERE WERE SOME SORT OF BATTLE BETWEEN GOOD AND EVIL--WHICH I DON'T BELIEVE FOR ONE SECOND--I COULD NEVER KILL ANYONE.
SURE YOU COULD. ANYONE COULD FOR A GOOD REASON.
TO SAVE YOUR FAMILY? TO SAVE YOURSELF?
YOU JUST HAVE TO GET USED TO THE IDEA.

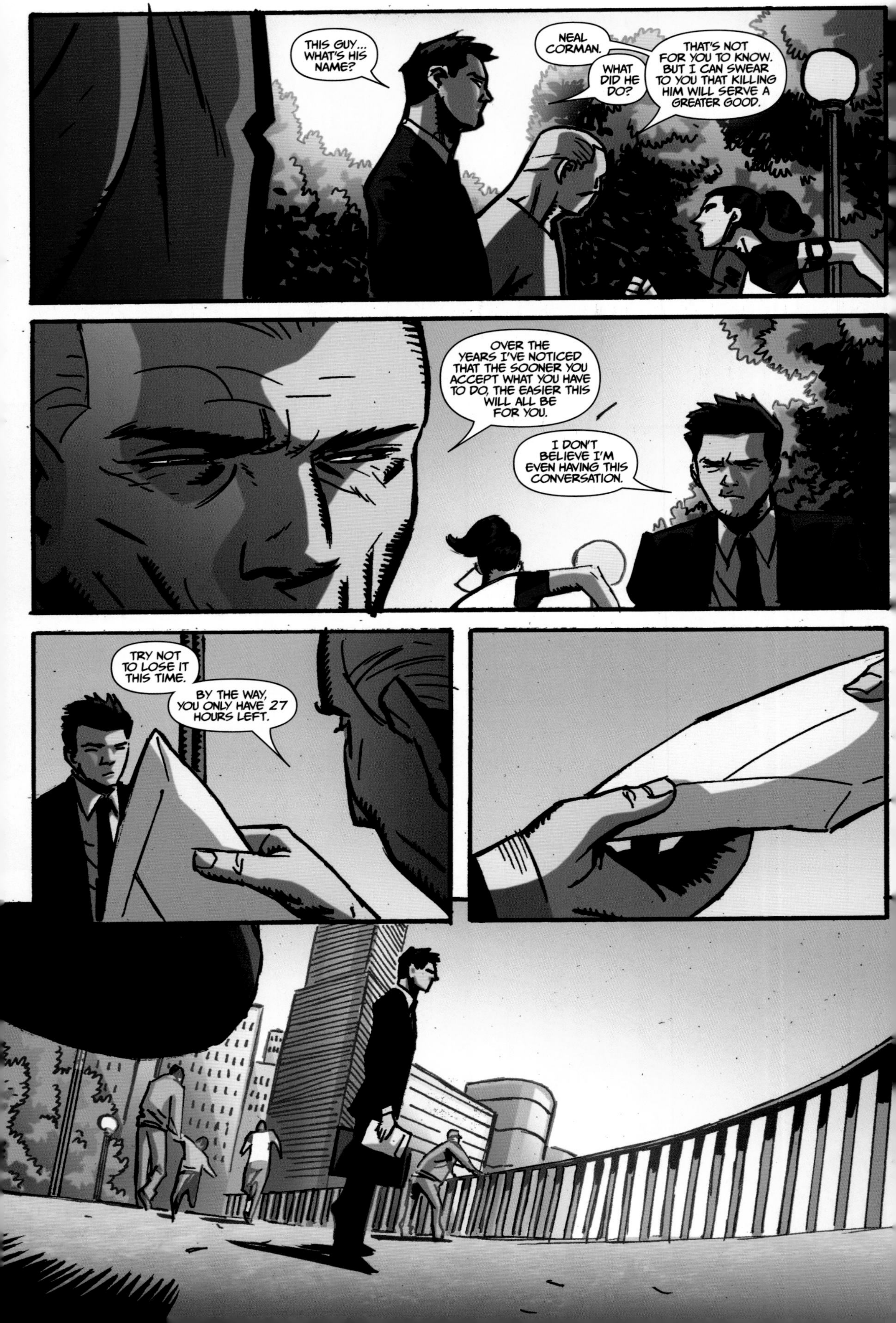
THIS GUY... WHAT'S HIS NAME?
NEAL CORMAN.
WHAT DID HE DO?
THAT'S NOT FOR YOU TO KNOW. BUT I CAN SWEAR TO YOU THAT KILLING HIM WILL SERVE A GREATER GOOD.
OVER THE YEARS I'VE NOTICED THAT THE SOONER YOU ACCEPT WHAT YOU HAVE TO DO, THE EASIER THIS WILL ALL BE FOR YOU.
I DON'T BELIEVE I'M EVEN HAVING THIS CONVERSATION.
TRY NOT TO LOSE IT THIS TIME.
BY THE WAY, YOU ONLY HAVE 27 HOURS LEFT.

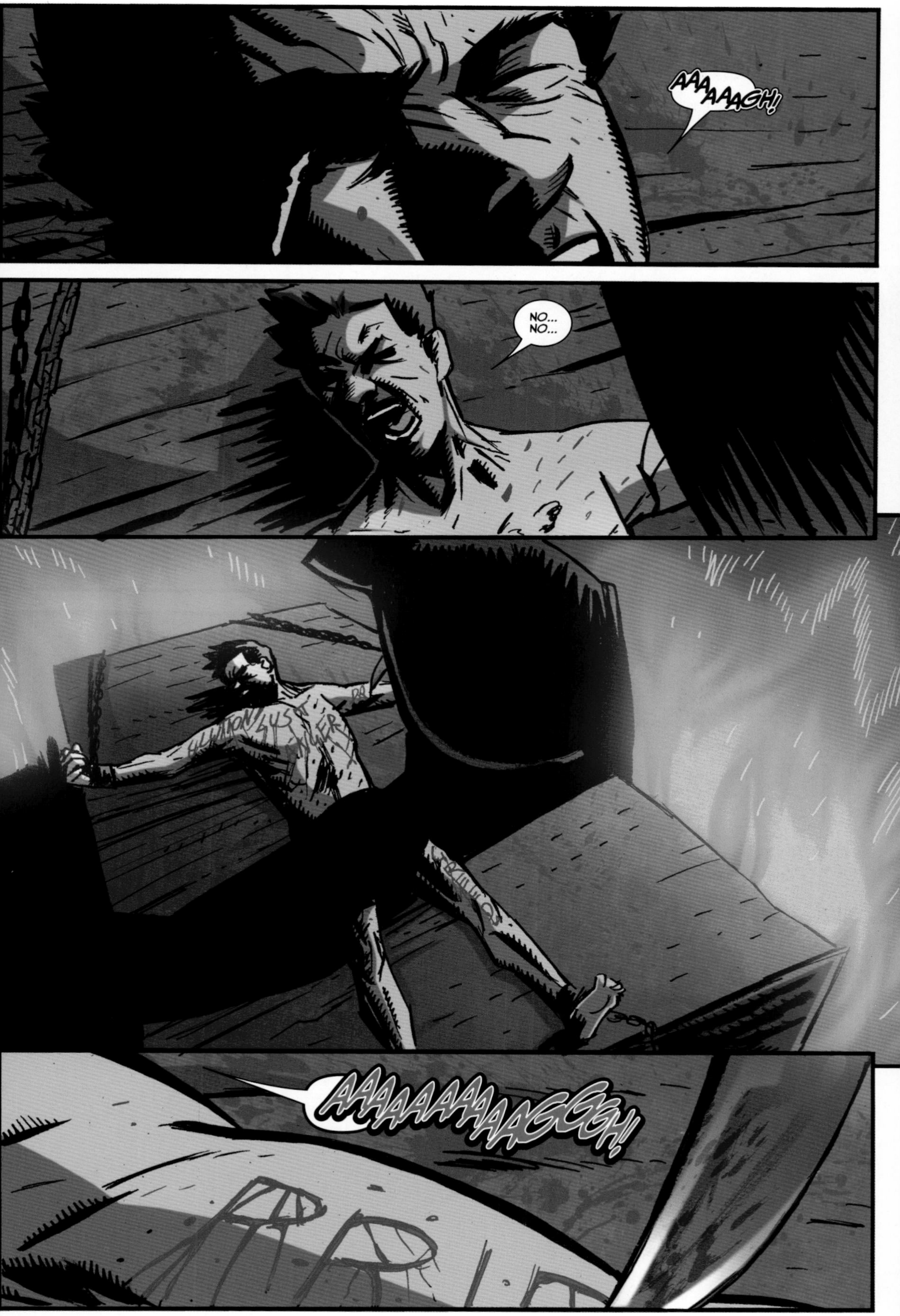
AAAAAAGH!
NO... NO...
AAAAAAAAAAAGGGH!

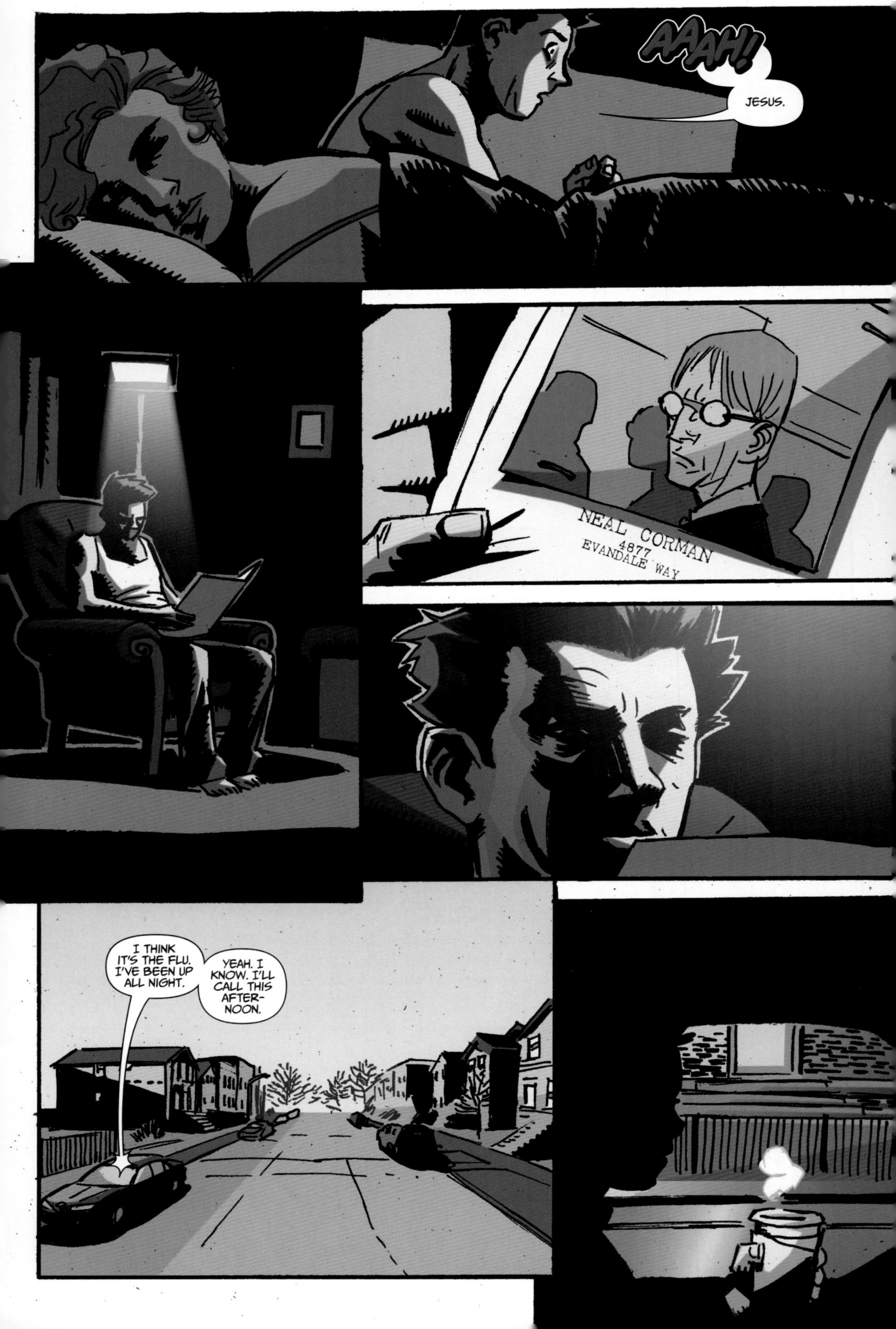

AAAH!
JESUS.
NEAL CORMAN
4877
EVANDALE WAY
I THINK IT'S THE FLU. I'VE BEEN UP ALL NIGHT.
YEAH. I KNOW. I'LL CALL THIS AFTER-NOON.

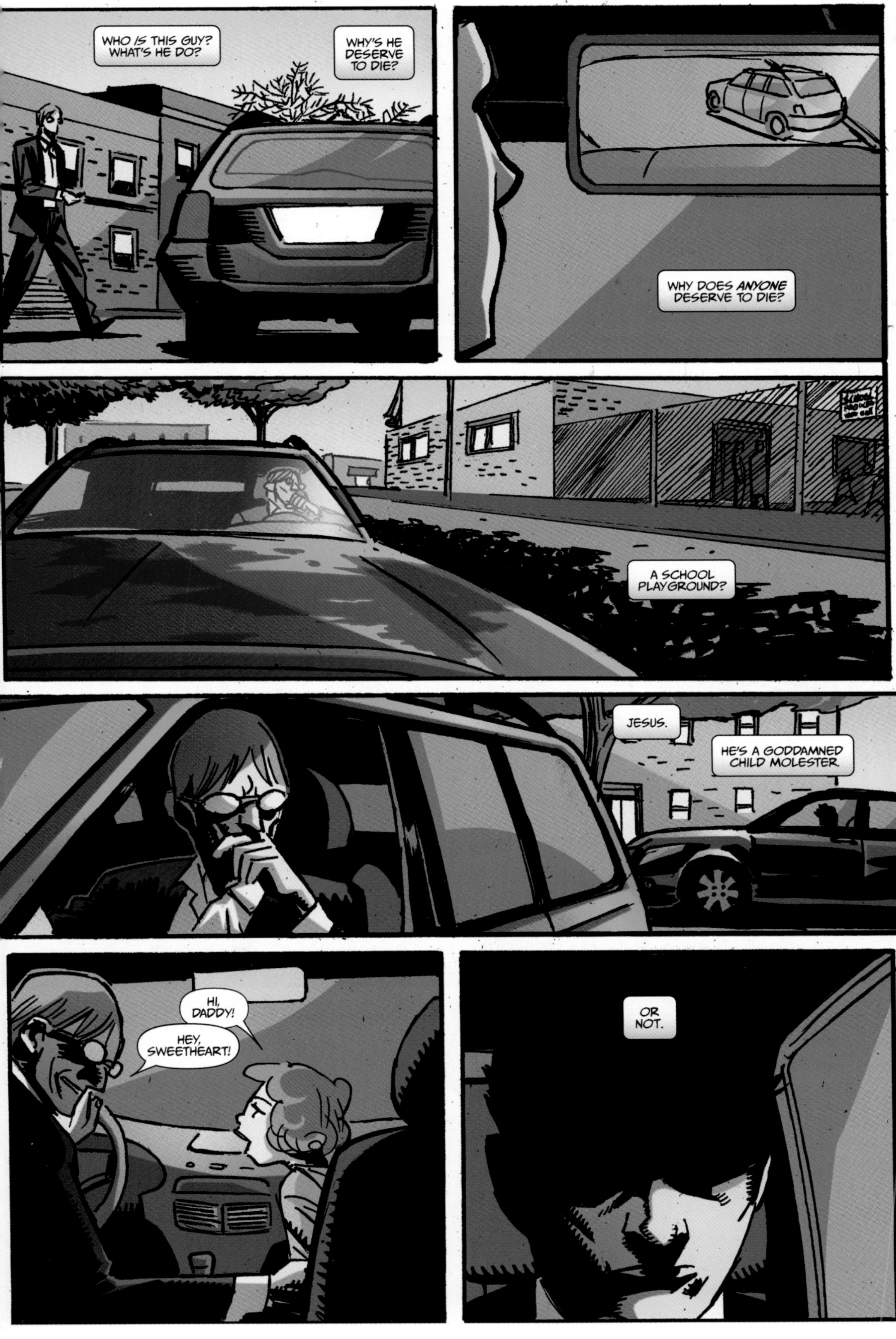
WHO IS THIS GUY? WHAT'S HE DO?
WHY'S HE DESERVE TO DIE?
WHY DOES ANYONE DESERVE TO DIE?
A SCHOOL PLAYGROUND?
JESUS.
HE'S A GODDAMNED CHILD MOLESTER.
HI, DADDY!
HEY, SWEETHEART!
OR NOT.

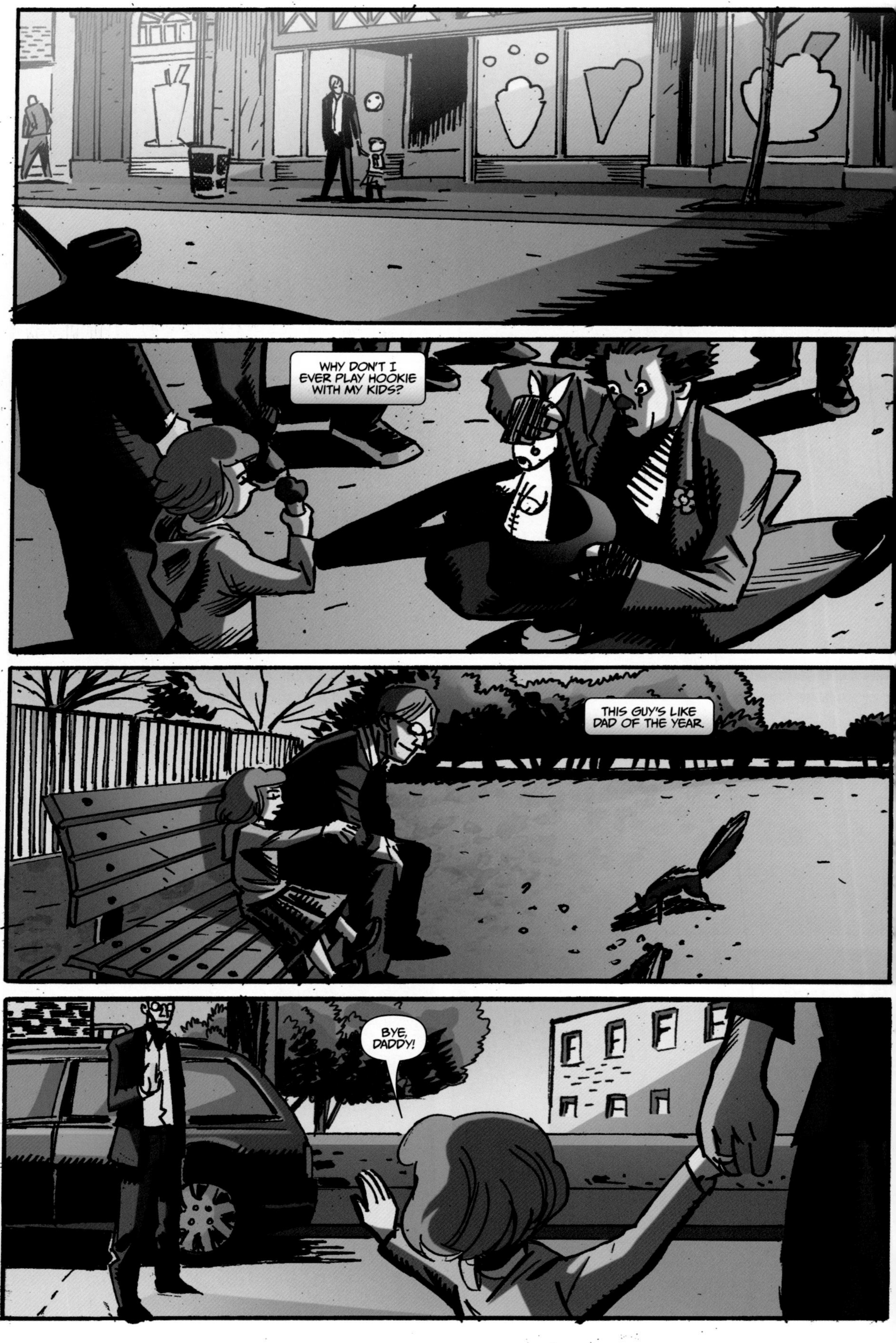
WHY DON'T I EVER PLAY HOOKIE WITH MY KIDS?
THIS GUY'S LIKE DAD OF THE YEAR.
BYE, DADDY!

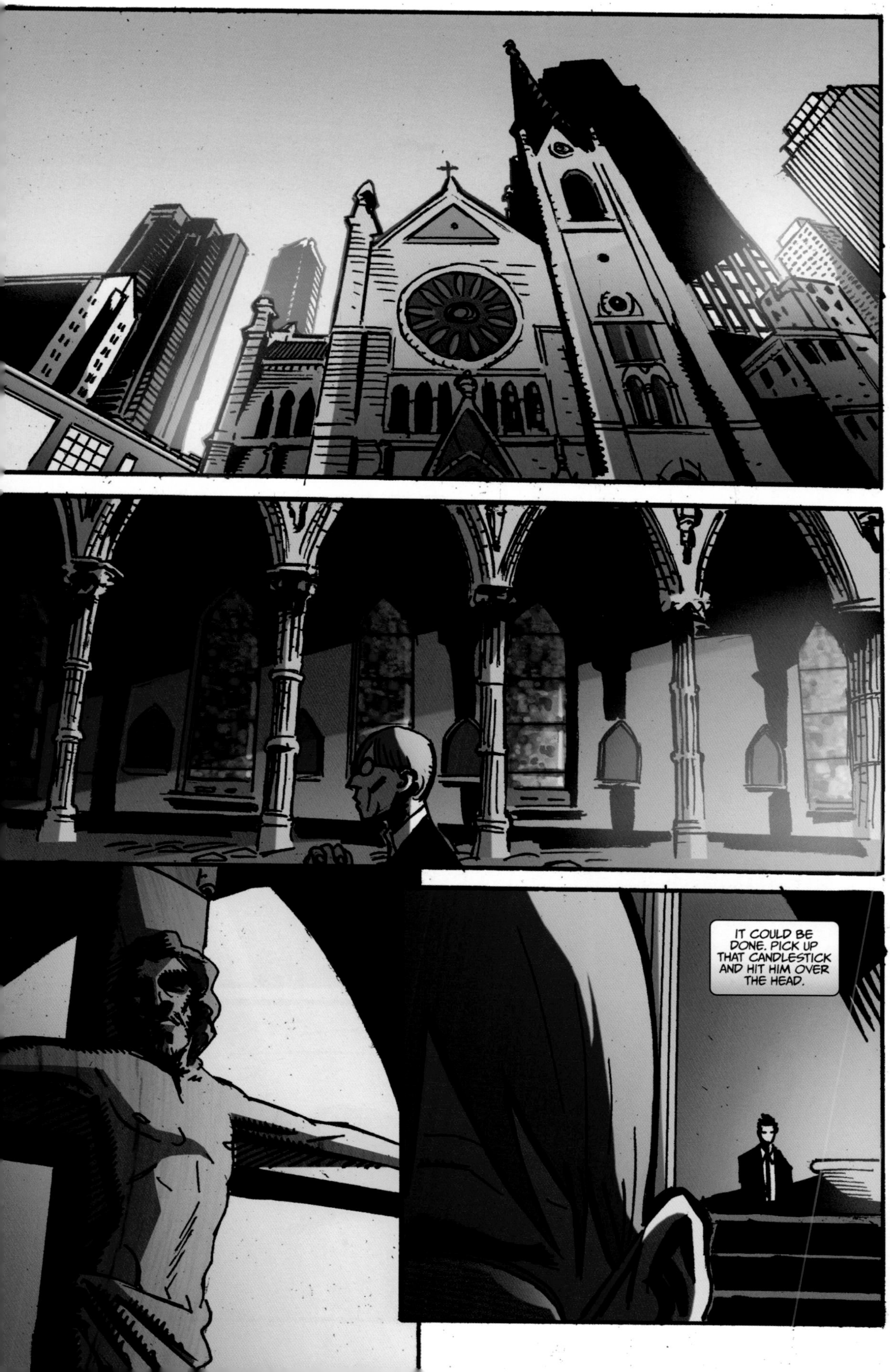
IT COULD BE DONE. PICK UP THAT CANDLESTICK AND HIT HIM OVER THE HEAD.

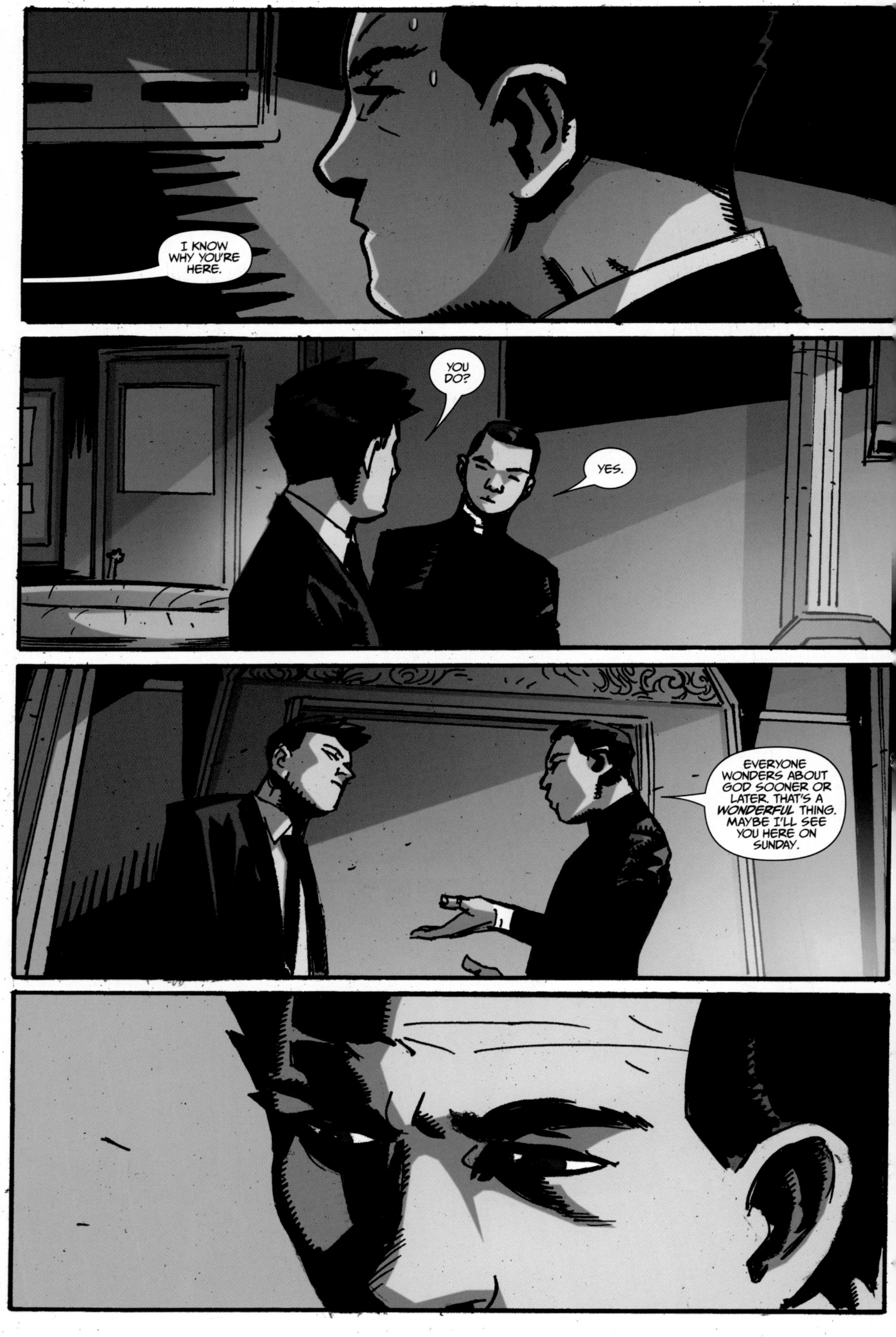

I KNOW WHY YOU'RE HERE.
YOU DO?
YES.
EVERYONE WONDERS ABOUT GOD SOONER OR LATER. THAT'S A *WONDERFUL* THING. MAYBE I'LL SEE YOU HERE ON SUNDAY.

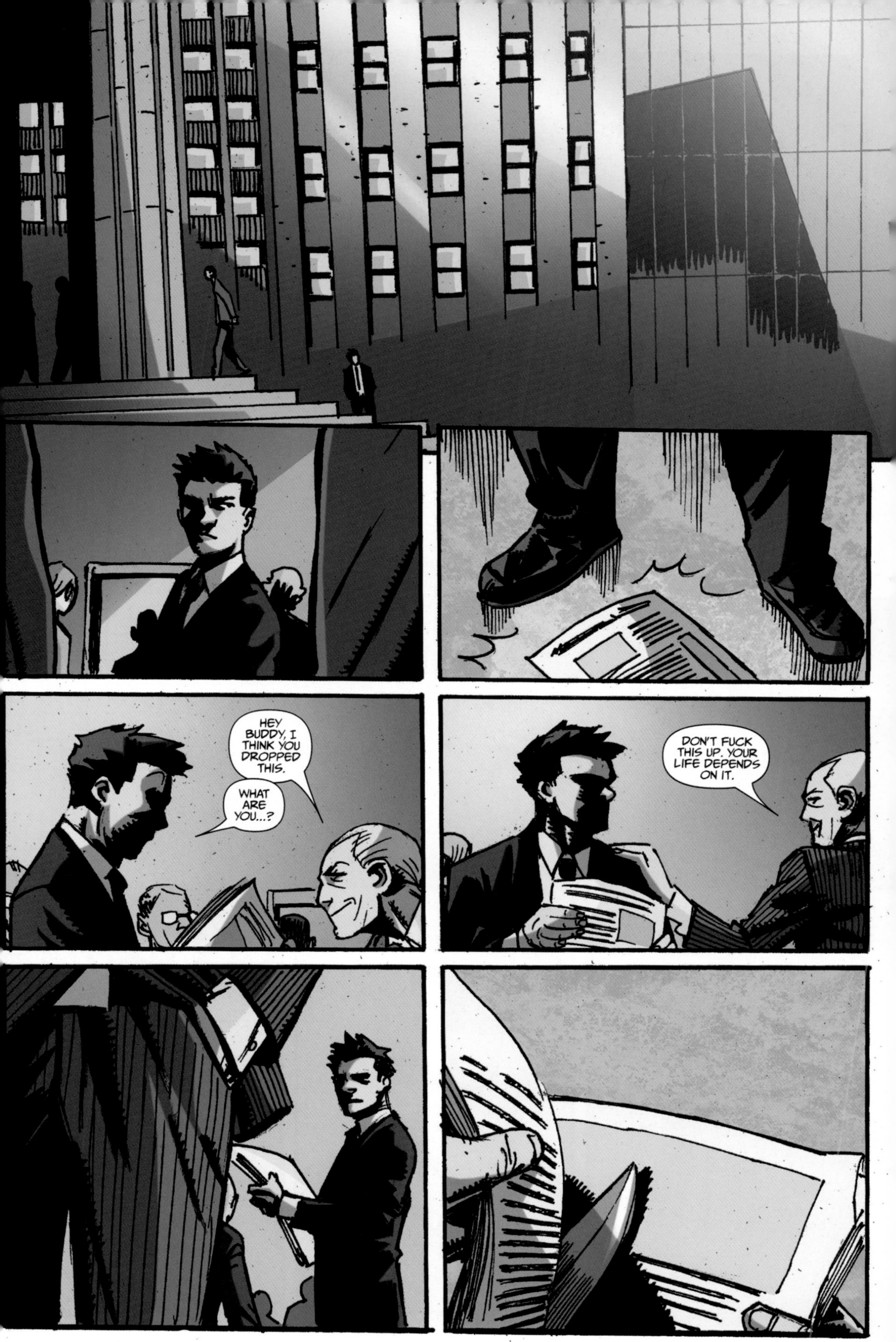
HEY BUDDY, I THINK YOU DROPPED THIS.
WHAT ARE YOU...?
DON'T FUCK THIS UP. YOUR LIFE DEPENDS ON IT.

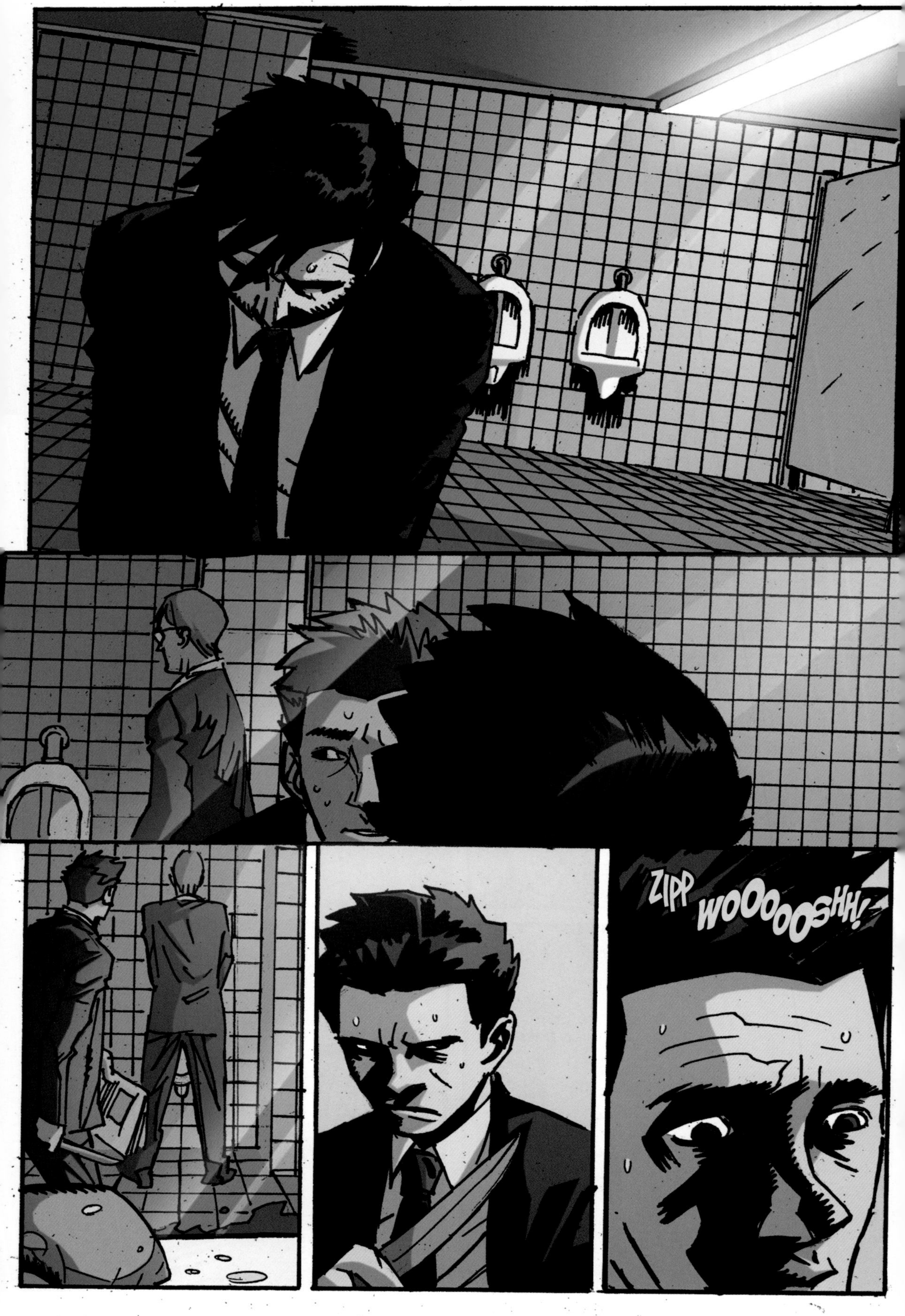
ZIPP
WOOOOOSHH!

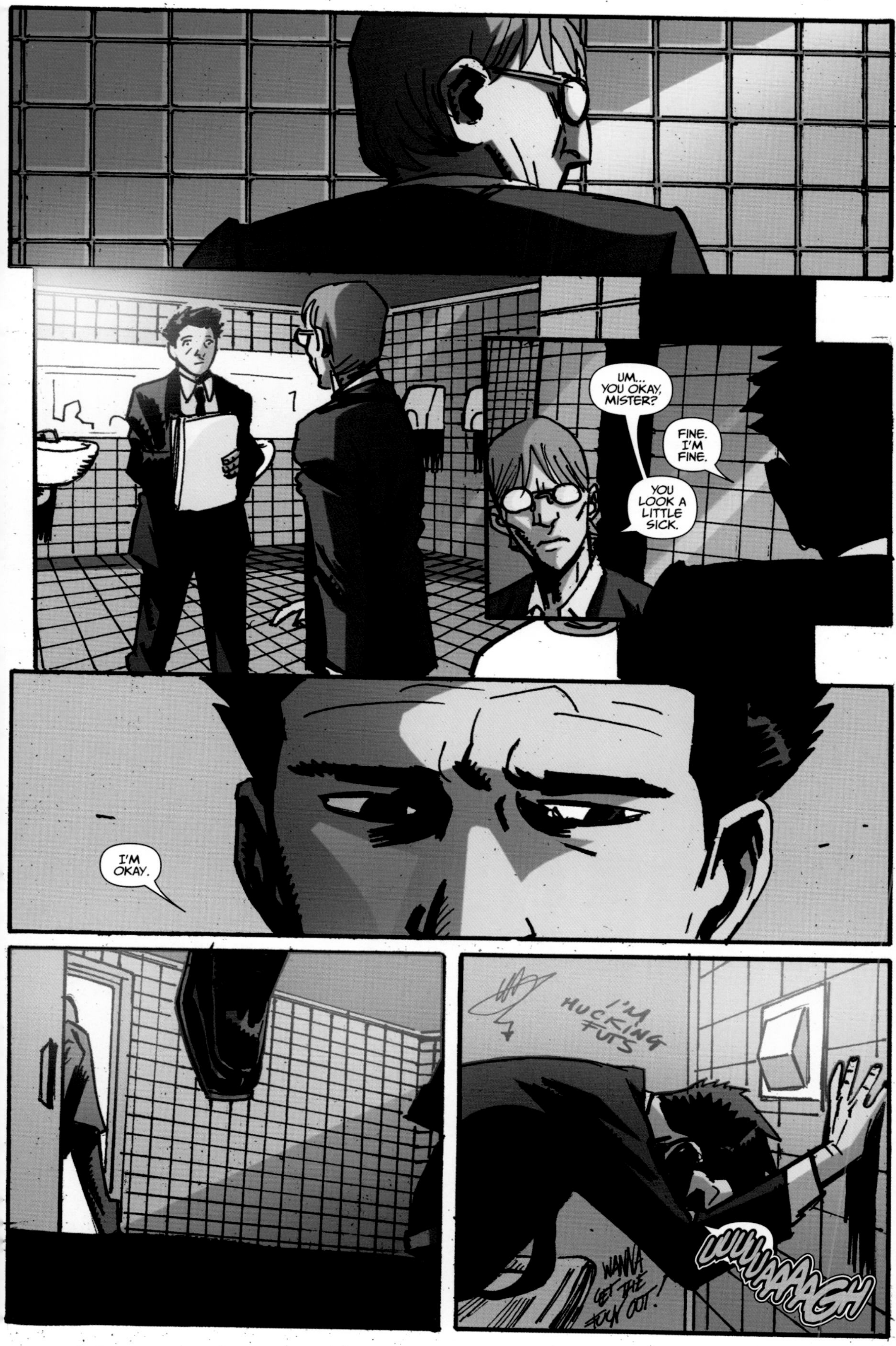
UM... YOU OKAY, MISTER?
FINE. I'M FINE.
YOU LOOK A LITTLE SICK.
I'M OKAY.
I'M HUCKING FUTS
WANNA GET THE FUCK OUT!
UUUUAAAAGH

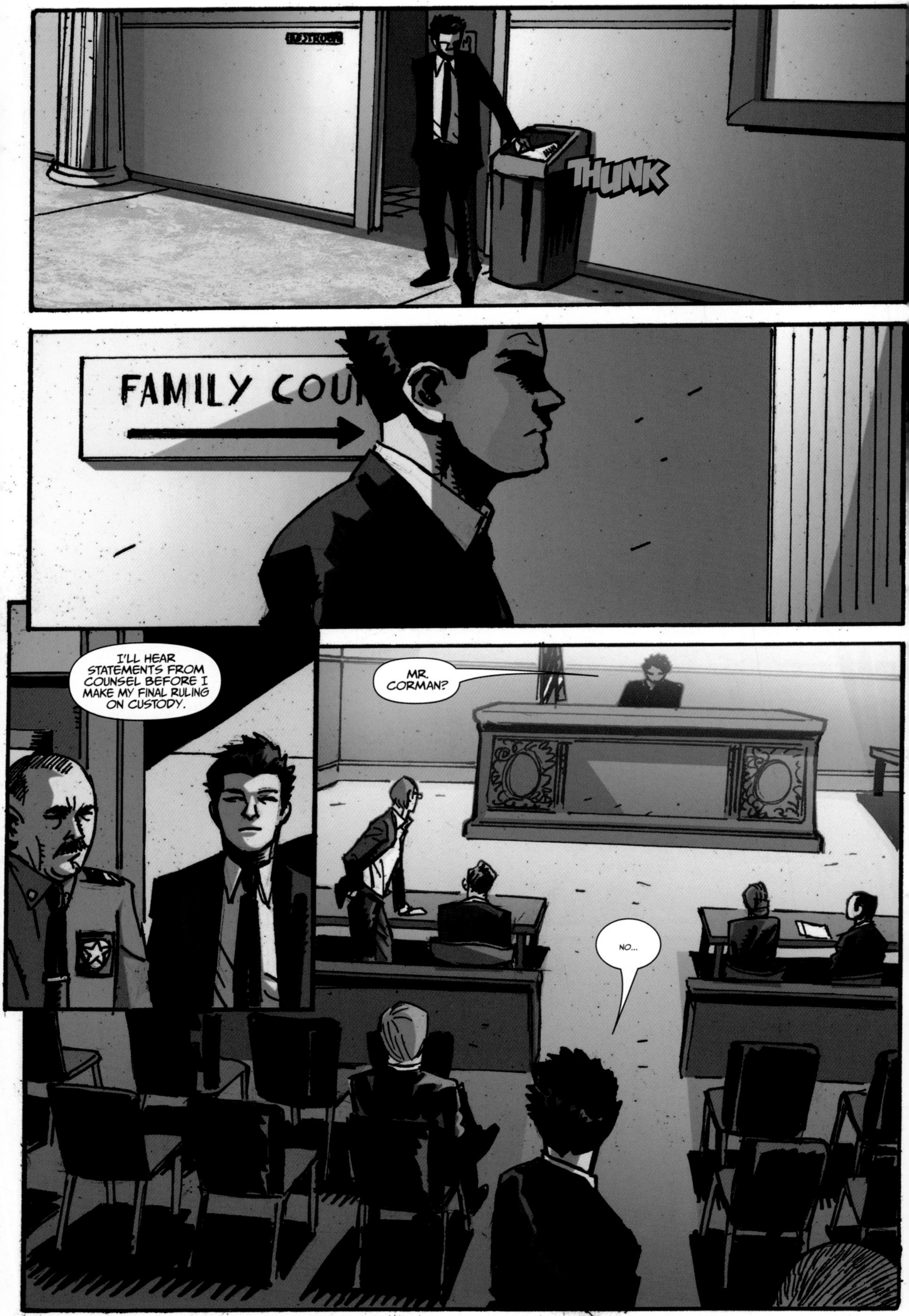
THUNK
FAMILY COU
I'LL HEAR STATEMENTS FROM COUNSEL BEFORE I MAKE MY FINAL RULING ON CUSTODY.
MR. CORMAN?
NO...

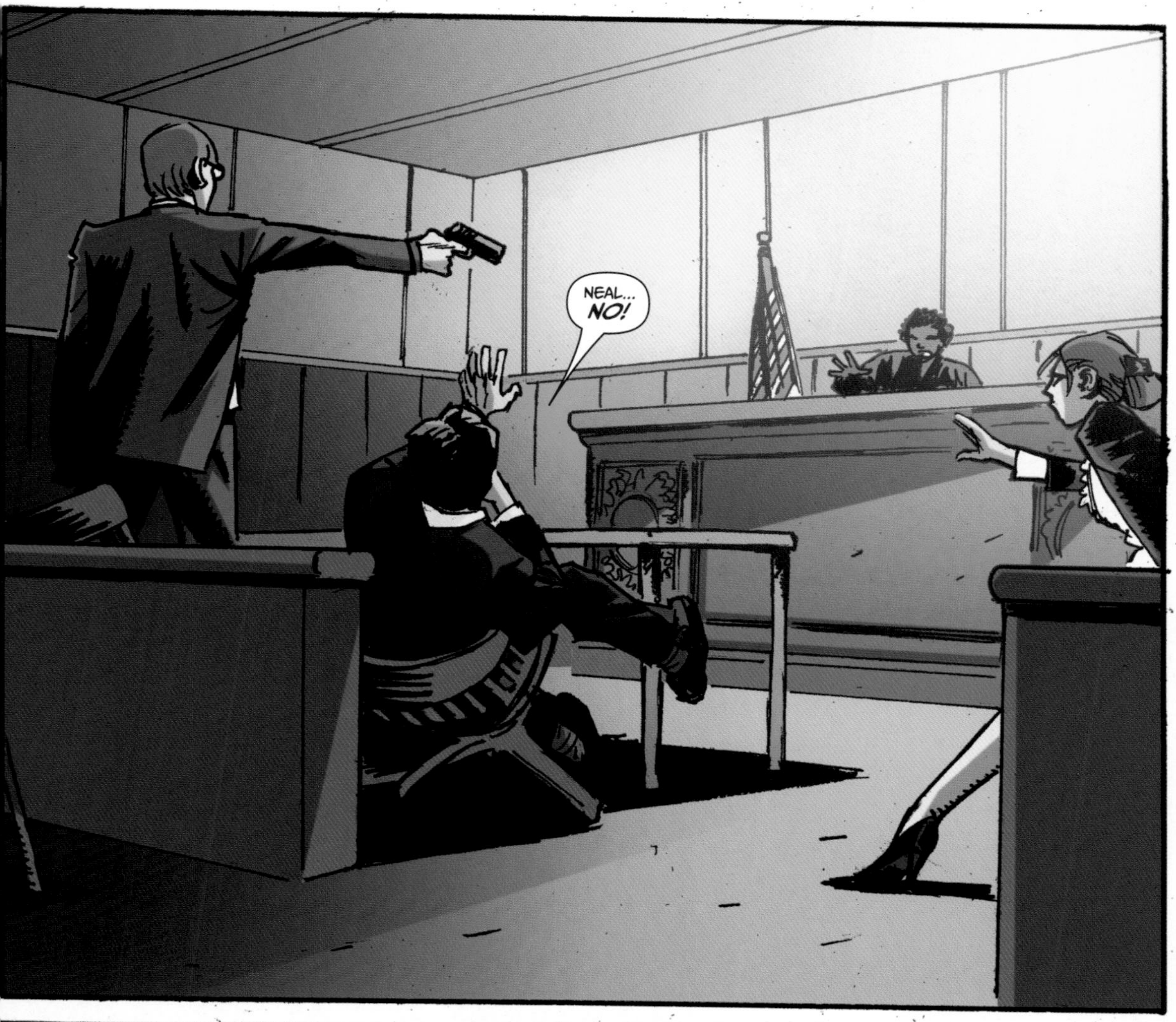
NEAL... NO!

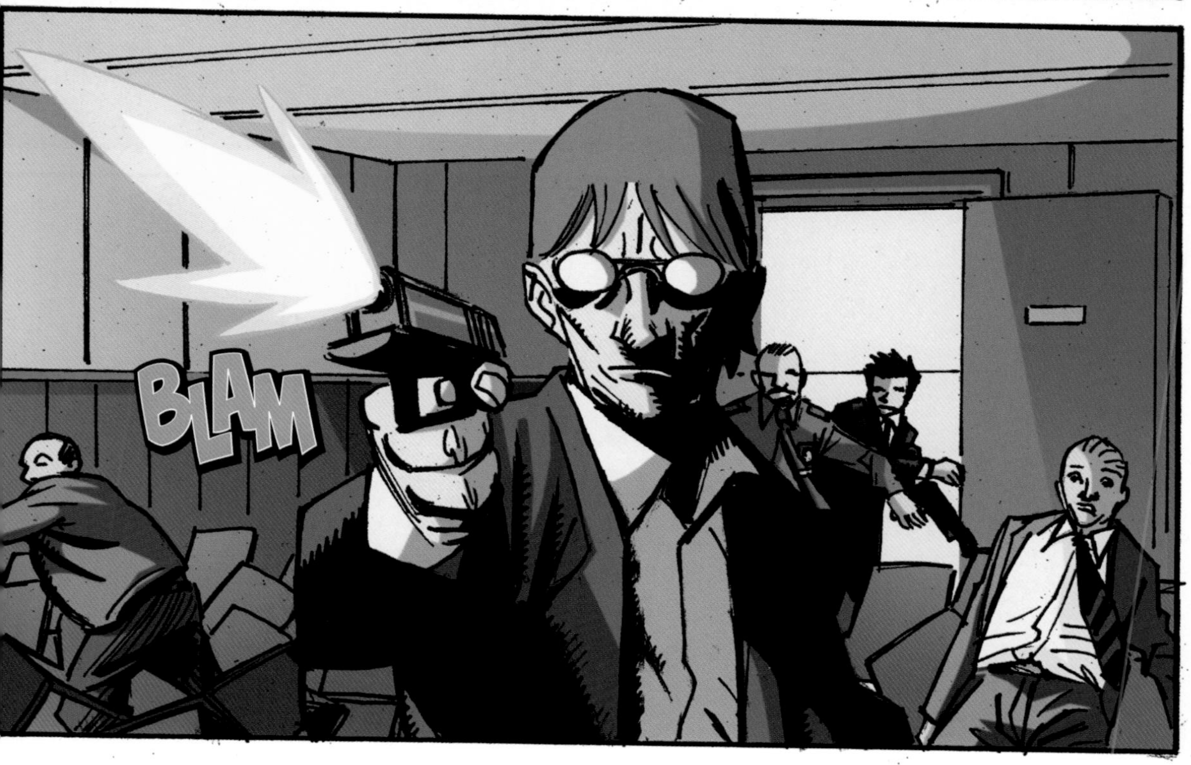
BLAM

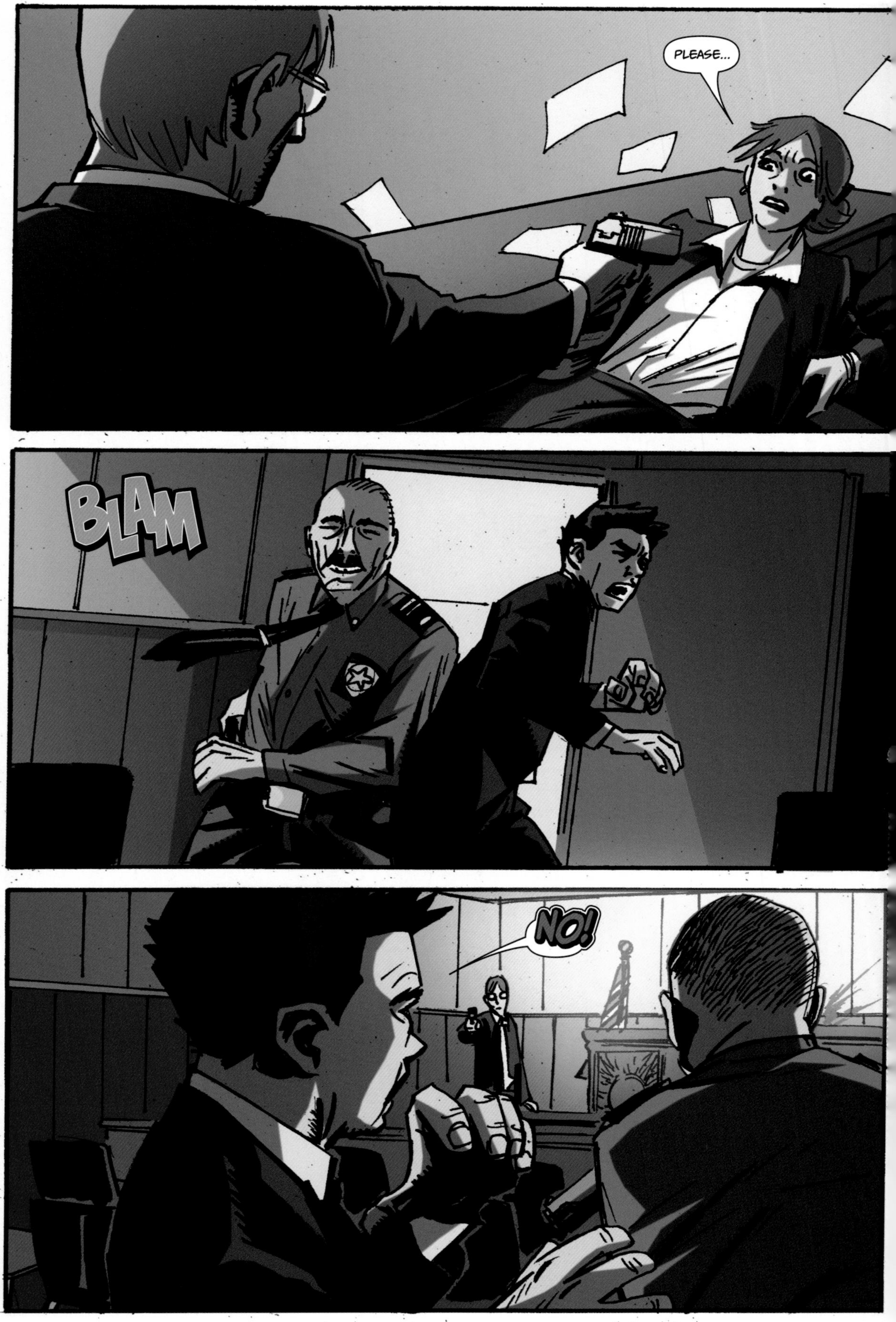
PLEASE...
BLAM
NO!

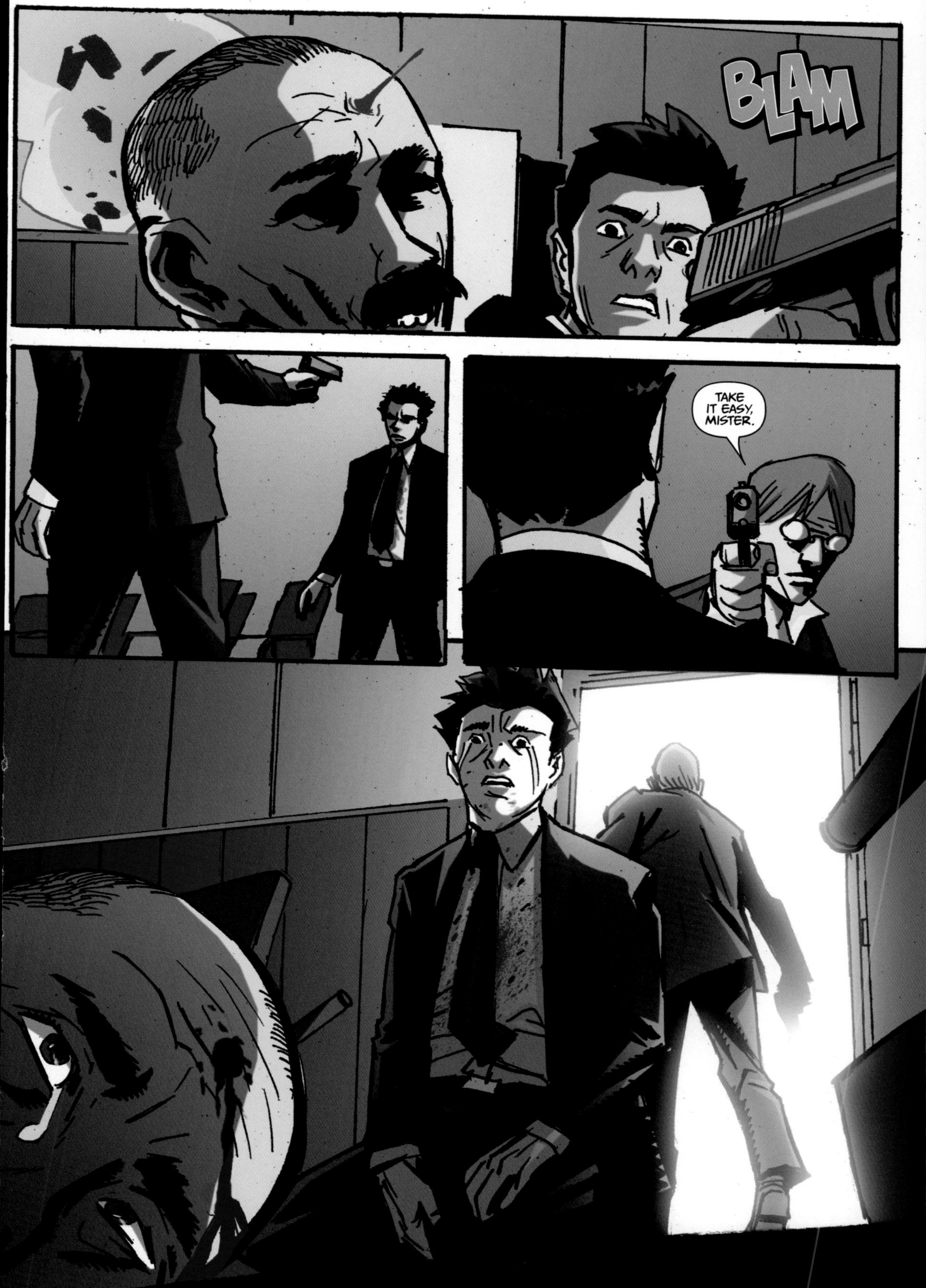
BLAM
TAKE IT EASY, MISTER.

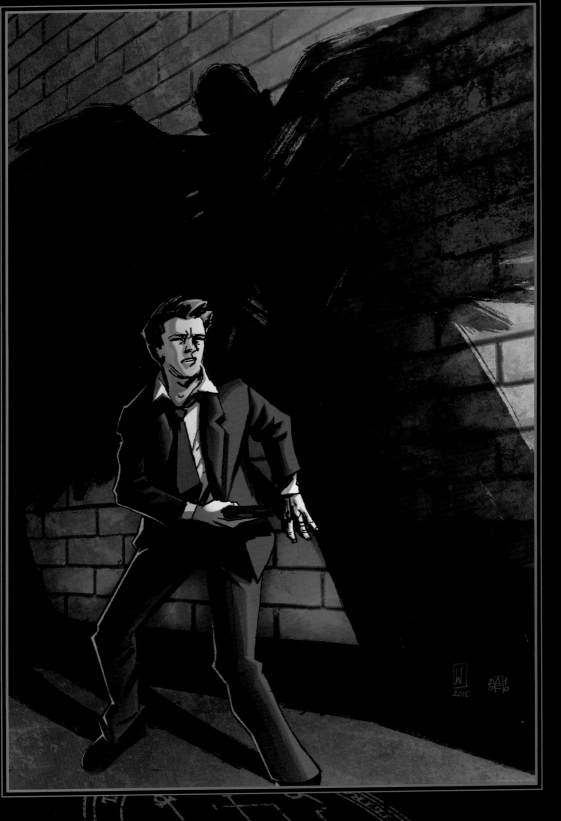

CHAPTER 2

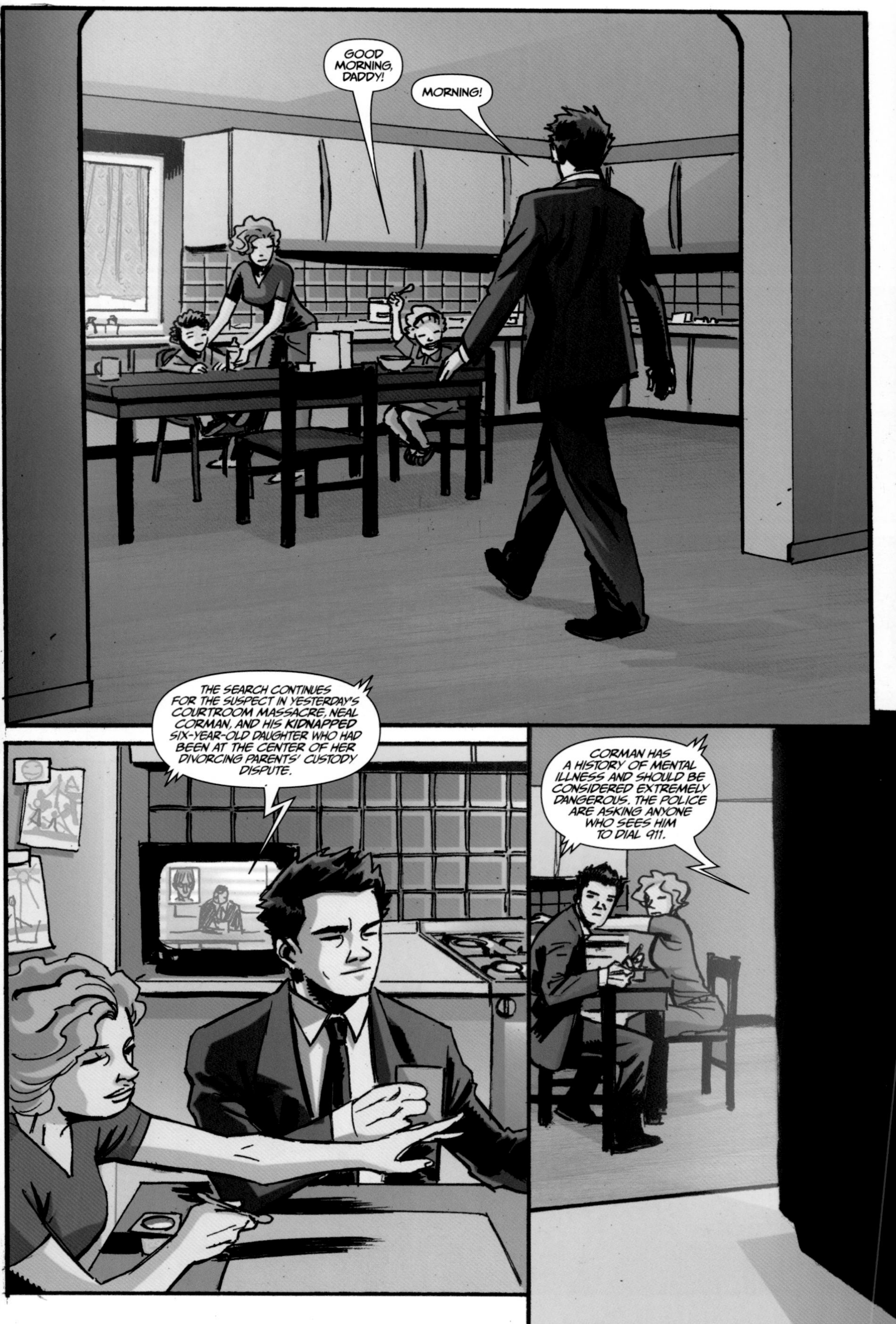
GOOD MORNING, DADDY!
MORNING!
THE SEARCH CONTINUES FOR THE SUSPECT IN YESTERDAY'S COURTROOM MASSACRE, NEAL CORMAN, AND HIS KIDNAPPED SIX-YEAR-OLD DAUGHTER WHO HAD BEEN AT THE CENTER OF HER DIVORCING PARENTS' CUSTODY DISPUTE.
CORMAN HAS A HISTORY OF MENTAL ILLNESS AND SHOULD BE CONSIDERED EXTREMELY DANGEROUS. THE POLICE ARE ASKING ANYONE WHO SEES HIM TO DIAL 911.

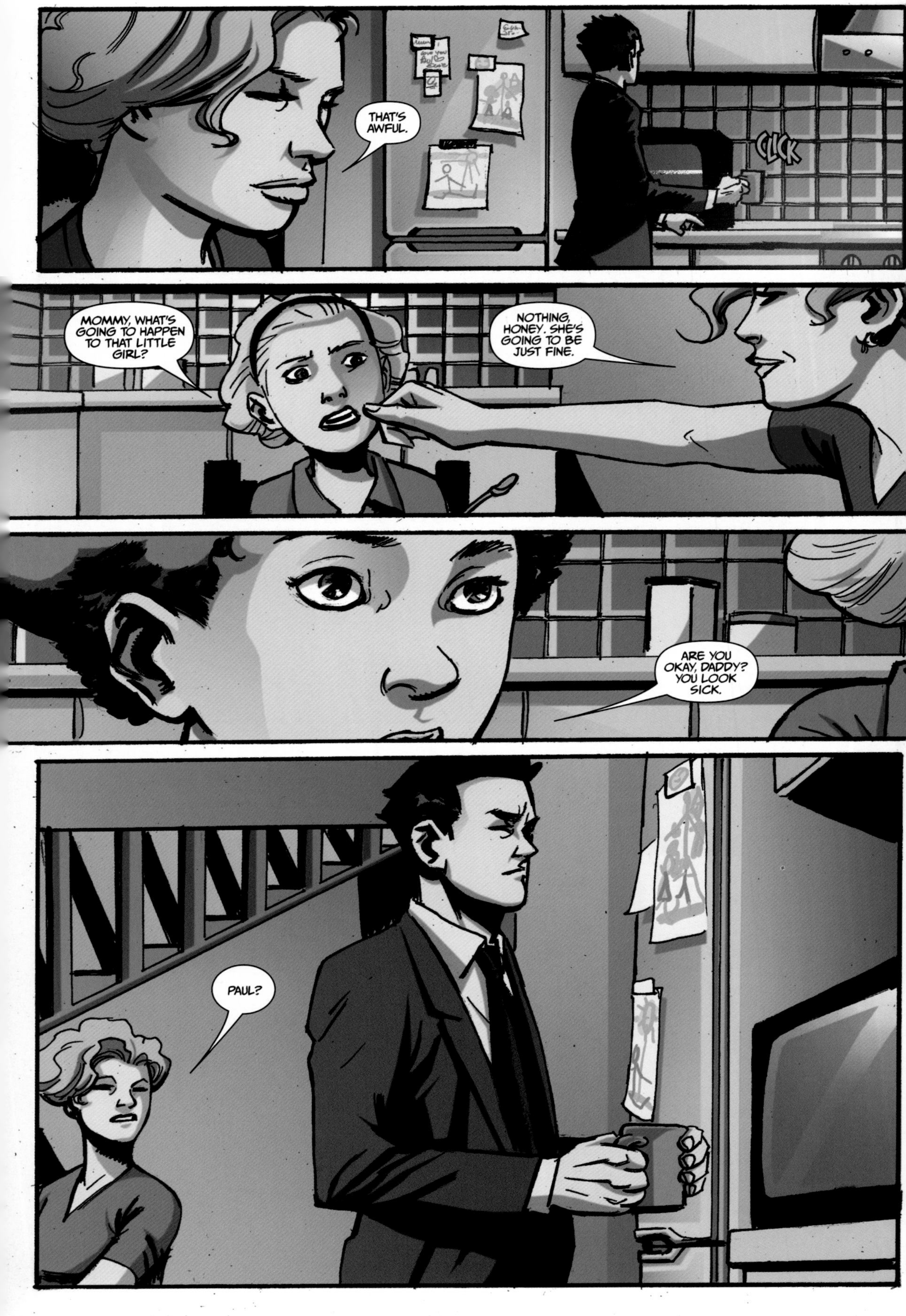
THAT'S AWFUL.
CLICK
MOMMY, WHAT'S GOING TO HAPPEN TO THAT LITTLE GIRL?
NOTHING, HONEY. SHE'S GOING TO BE JUST FINE.
ARE YOU OKAY, DADDY? YOU LOOK SICK.
PAUL?

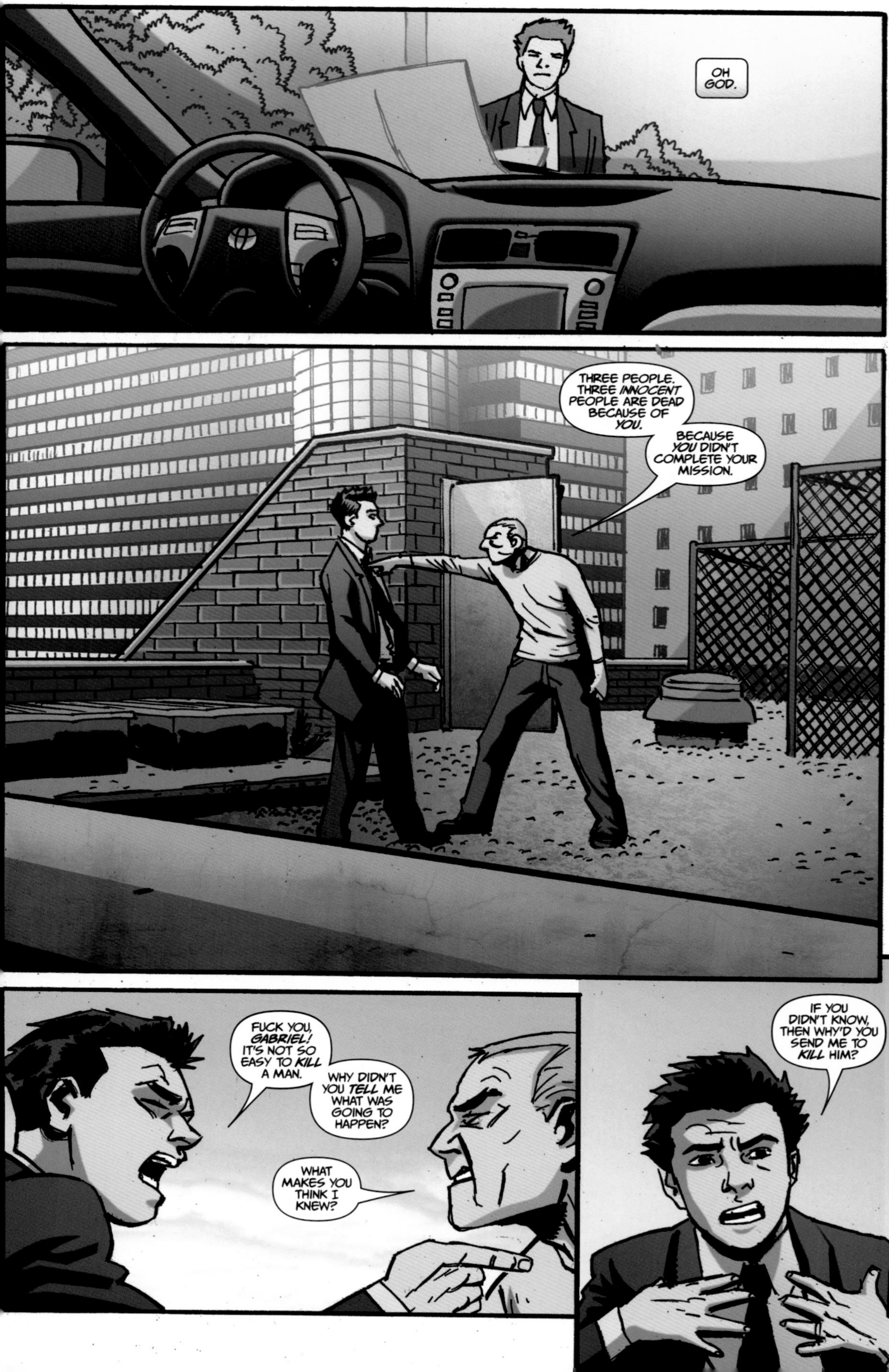
OH GOD.
THREE PEOPLE. THREE INNOCENT PEOPLE ARE DEAD BECAUSE OF YOU.
BECAUSE YOU DIDN'T COMPLETE YOUR MISSION.
FUCK YOU, GABRIEL! IT'S NOT SO EASY TO KILL A MAN.
WHY DIDN'T YOU TELL ME WHAT WAS GOING TO HAPPEN?
WHAT MAKES YOU THINK I KNEW?
IF YOU DIDN'T KNOW, THEN WHY'D YOU SEND ME TO KILL HIM?

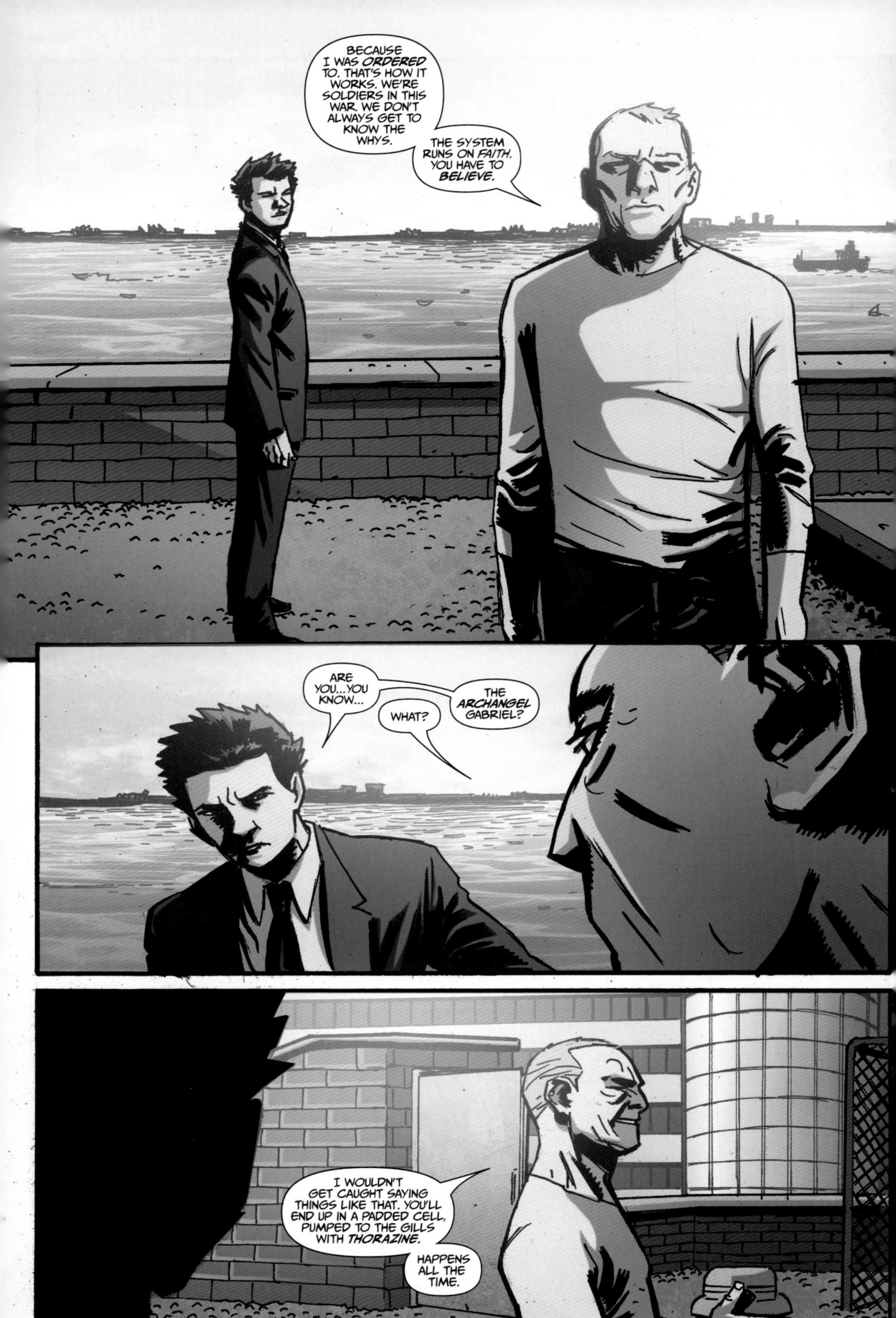
BECAUSE I WAS *ORDERED* TO. THAT'S HOW IT WORKS. WE'RE SOLDIERS IN THIS WAR. WE DON'T ALWAYS GET TO KNOW THE WHYS.
THE SYSTEM RUNS ON *FAITH.* YOU HAVE TO *BELIEVE.*
ARE YOU...YOU KNOW...
WHAT?
THE *ARCHANGEL* GABRIEL?
I WOULDN'T GET CAUGHT SAYING THINGS LIKE THAT. YOU'LL END UP IN A PADDED CELL, PUMPED TO THE GILLS WITH *THORAZINE.*
HAPPENS ALL THE TIME.

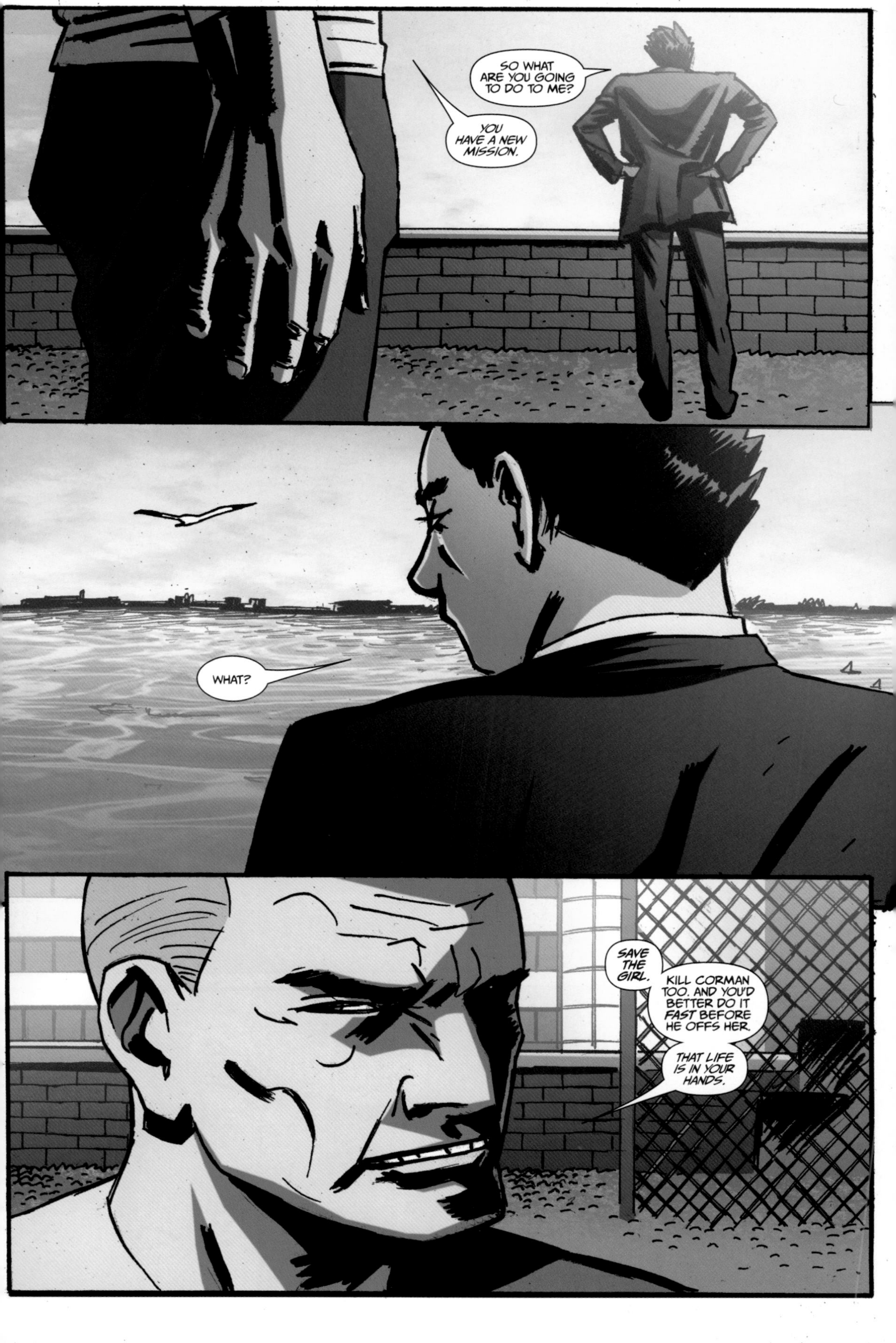
SO WHAT ARE YOU GOING TO DO TO ME?
YOU HAVE A NEW MISSION.
WHAT?
SAVE THE GIRL.
KILL CORMAN TOO. AND YOU'D BETTER DO IT FAST BEFORE HE OFFS HER.
THAT LIFE IS IN YOUR HANDS.

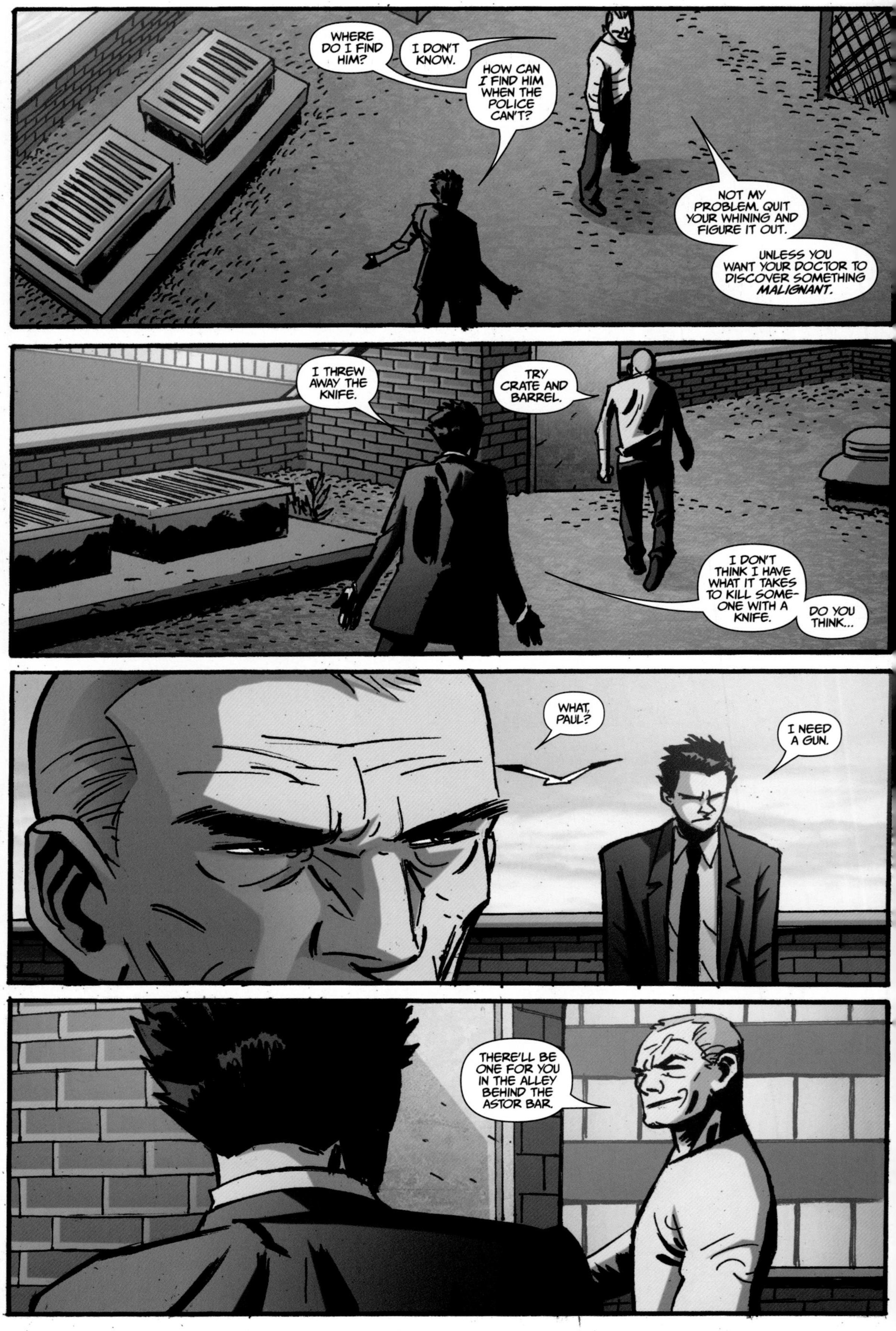
WHERE DO I FIND HIM?
I DON'T KNOW.
HOW CAN I FIND HIM WHEN THE POLICE CAN'T?
NOT MY PROBLEM. QUIT YOUR WHINING AND FIGURE IT OUT.
UNLESS YOU WANT YOUR DOCTOR TO DISCOVER SOMETHING *MALIGNANT.*
I THREW AWAY THE KNIFE.
TRY CRATE AND BARREL.
I DON'T THINK I HAVE WHAT IT TAKES TO KILL SOME-ONE WITH A KNIFE.
DO YOU THINK...
WHAT, PAUL?
I NEED A GUN.
THERE'LL BE ONE FOR YOU IN THE ALLEY BEHIND THE ASTOR BAR.

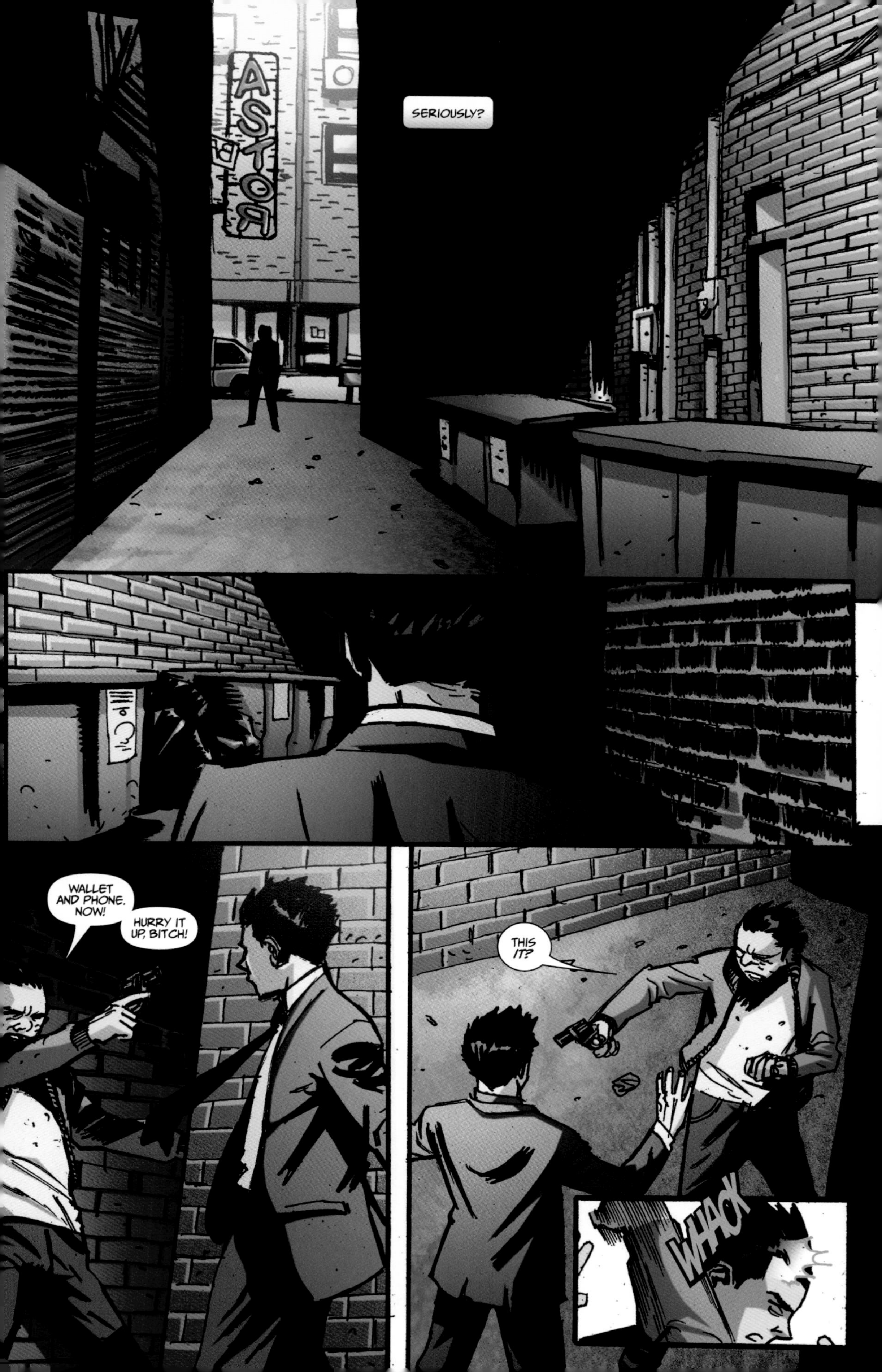

ASTOR
SERIOUSLY?
WALLET AND PHONE. NOW!
HURRY IT UP, BITCH!
THIS IT?
WHACK

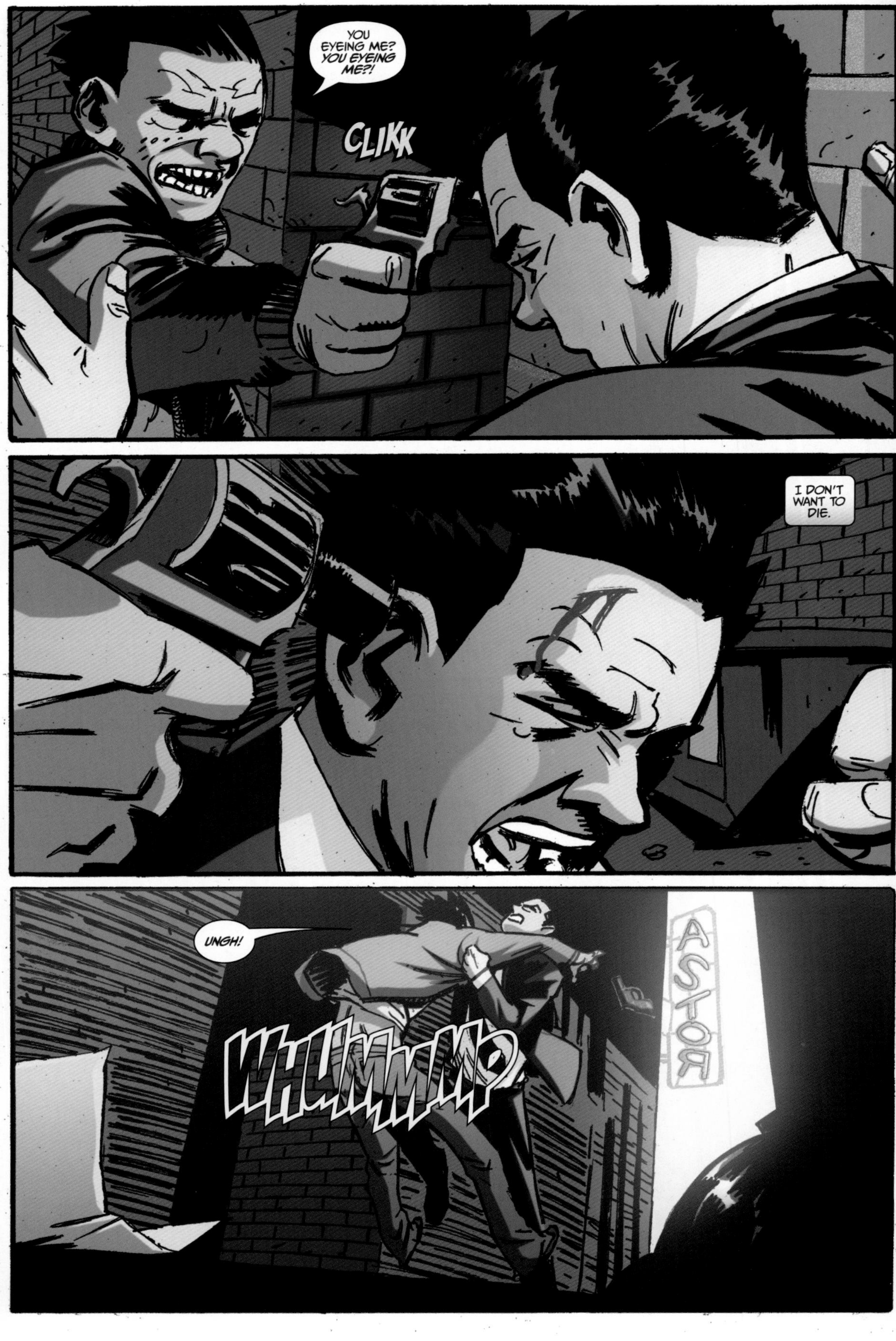
YOU EYEING ME? YOU EYEING ME?!
CLIKK
I DON'T WANT TO DIE.
UNGH!
WHUMMMP
ASTOR

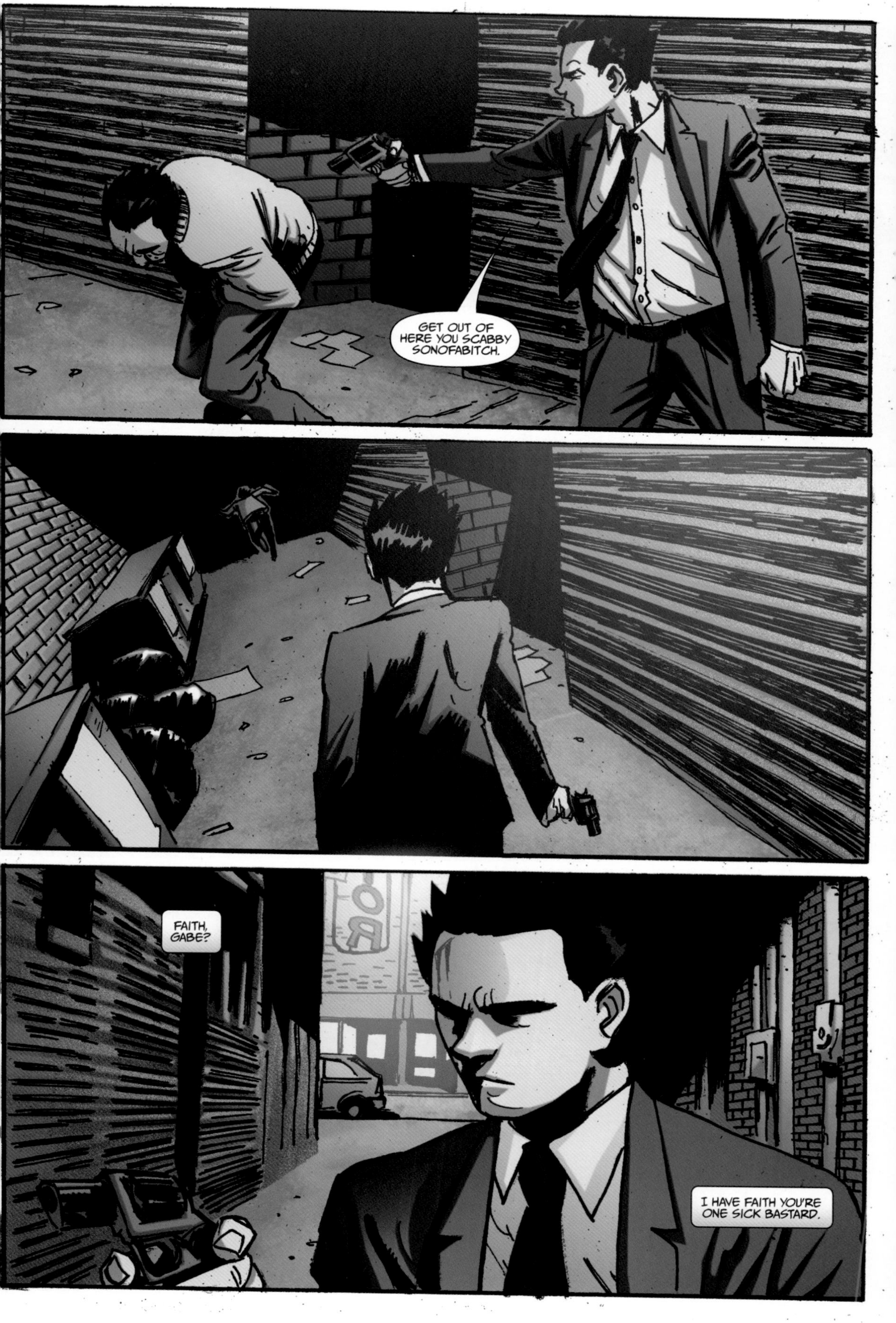
GET OUT OF HERE YOU SCABBY SONOFABITCH.
FAITH, GABE?
I HAVE FAITH YOU'RE ONE SICK BASTARD.

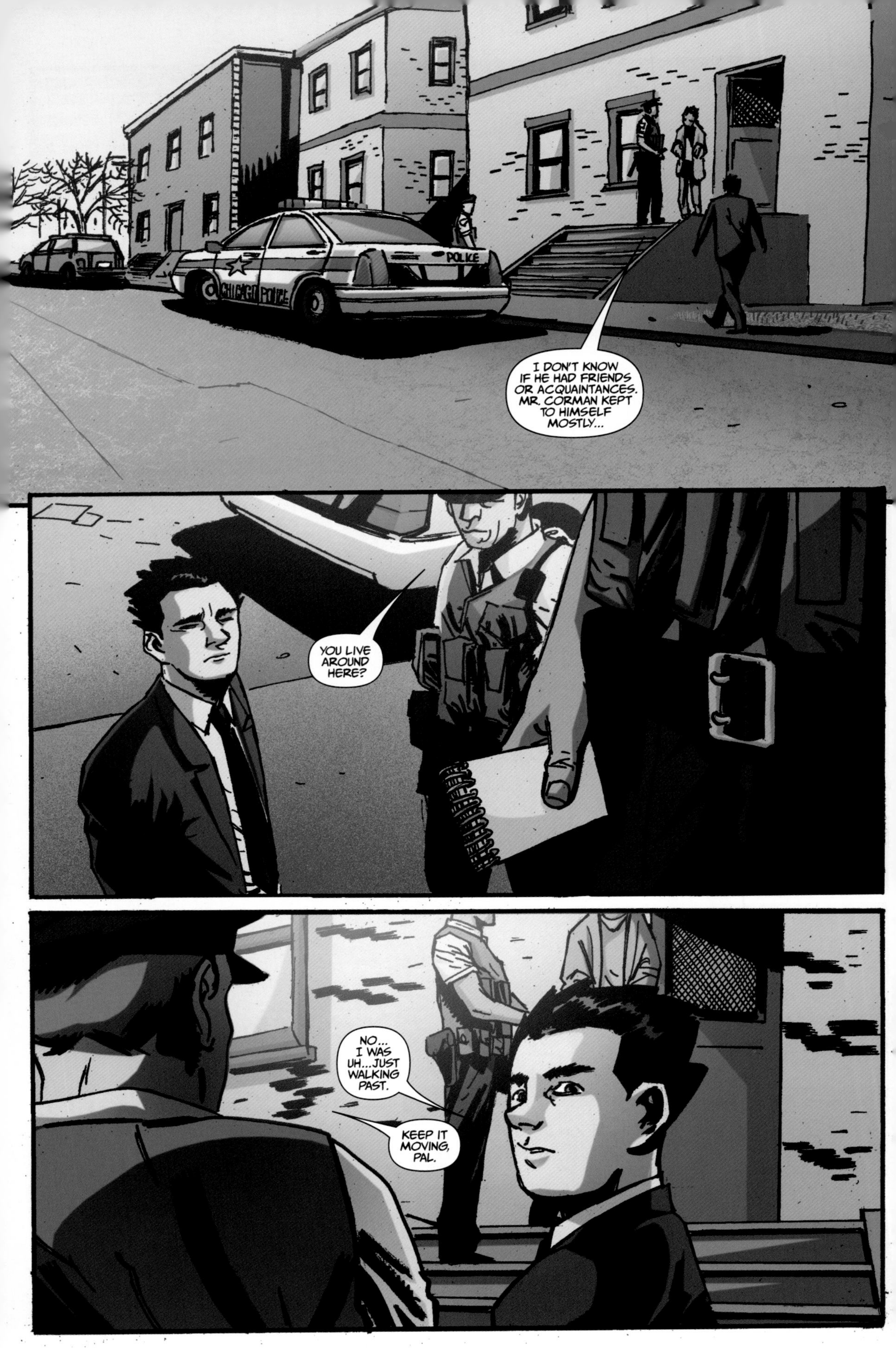
POLICE
CHICAGO POLICE
I DON'T KNOW IF HE HAD FRIENDS OR ACQUAINTANCES. MR. CORMAN KEPT TO HIMSELF MOSTLY...
YOU LIVE AROUND HERE?
NO... I WAS UH...JUST WALKING PAST.
KEEP IT MOVING, PAL.

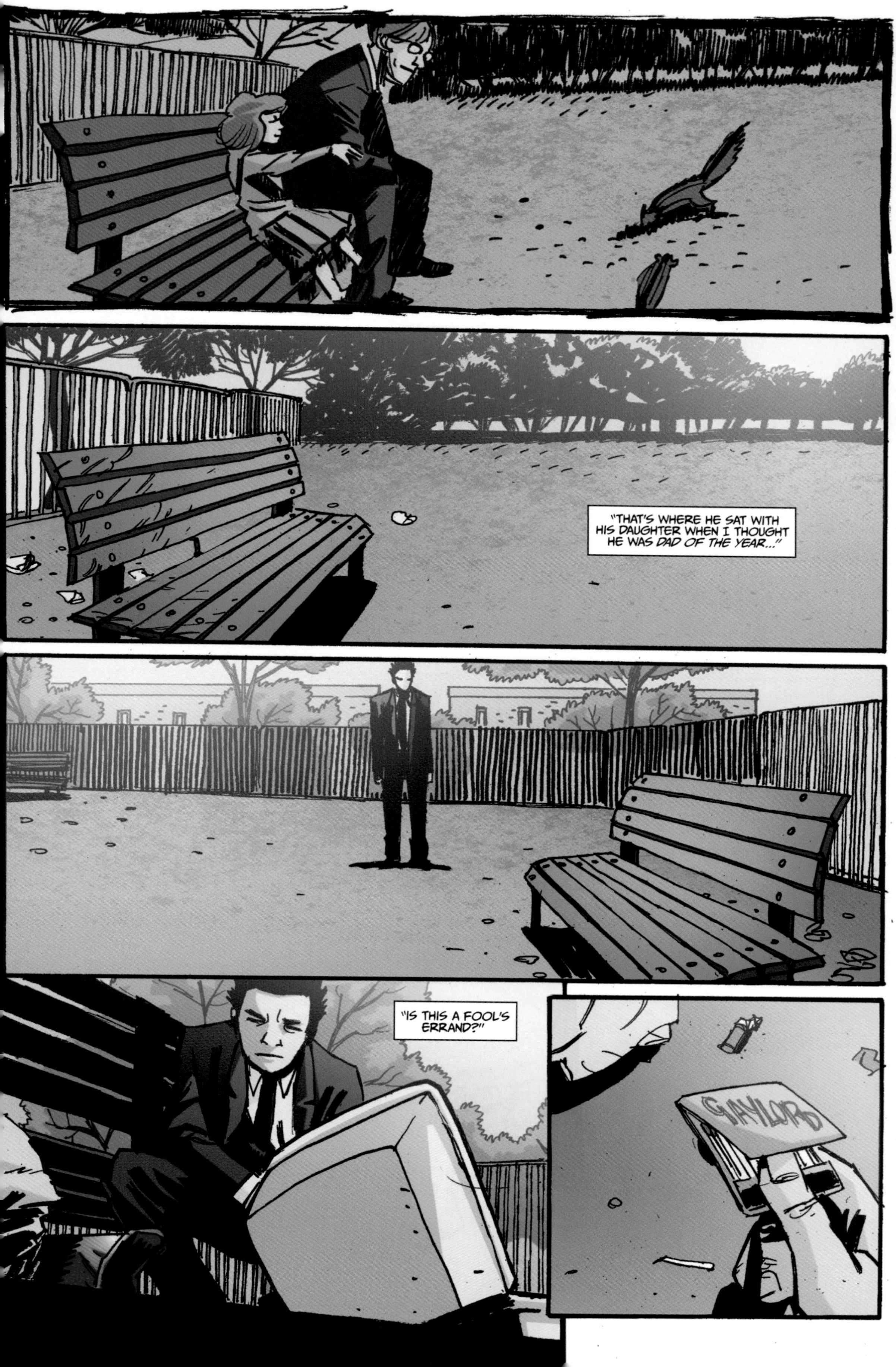
"THAT'S WHERE HE SAT WITH HIS DAUGHTER WHEN I THOUGHT HE WAS *DAD OF THE YEAR...*"
"IS THIS A FOOL'S ERRAND?"
GAYLORD

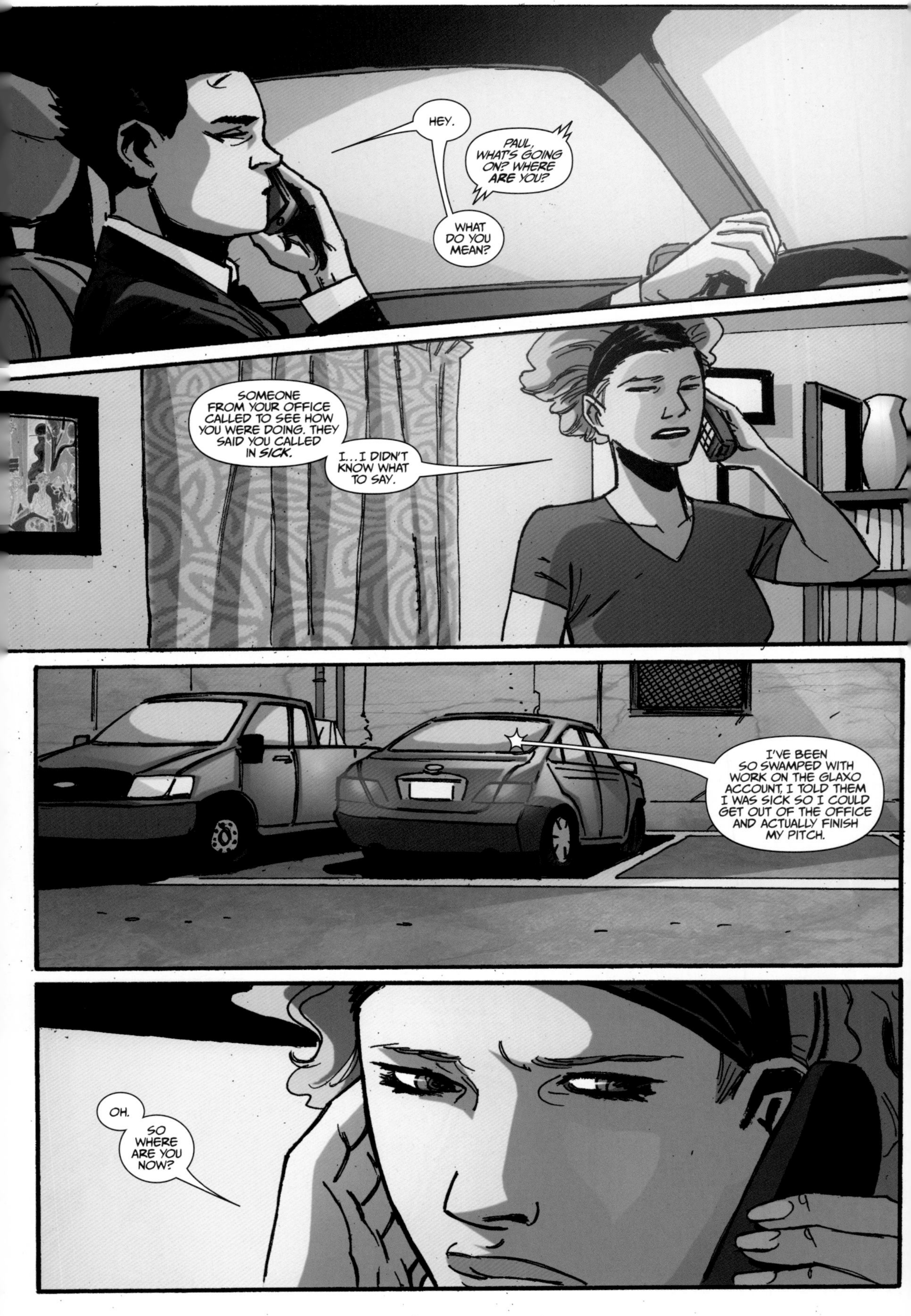
HEY.
PAUL, WHAT'S GOING ON? WHERE ARE YOU?
WHAT DO YOU MEAN?
SOMEONE FROM YOUR OFFICE CALLED TO SEE HOW YOU WERE DOING. THEY SAID YOU CALLED IN SICK.
I...I DIDN'T KNOW WHAT TO SAY.
I'VE BEEN SO SWAMPED WITH WORK ON THE GLAXO ACCOUNT, I TOLD THEM I WAS SICK SO I COULD GET OUT OF THE OFFICE AND ACTUALLY FINISH MY PITCH.
OH.
SO WHERE ARE YOU NOW?

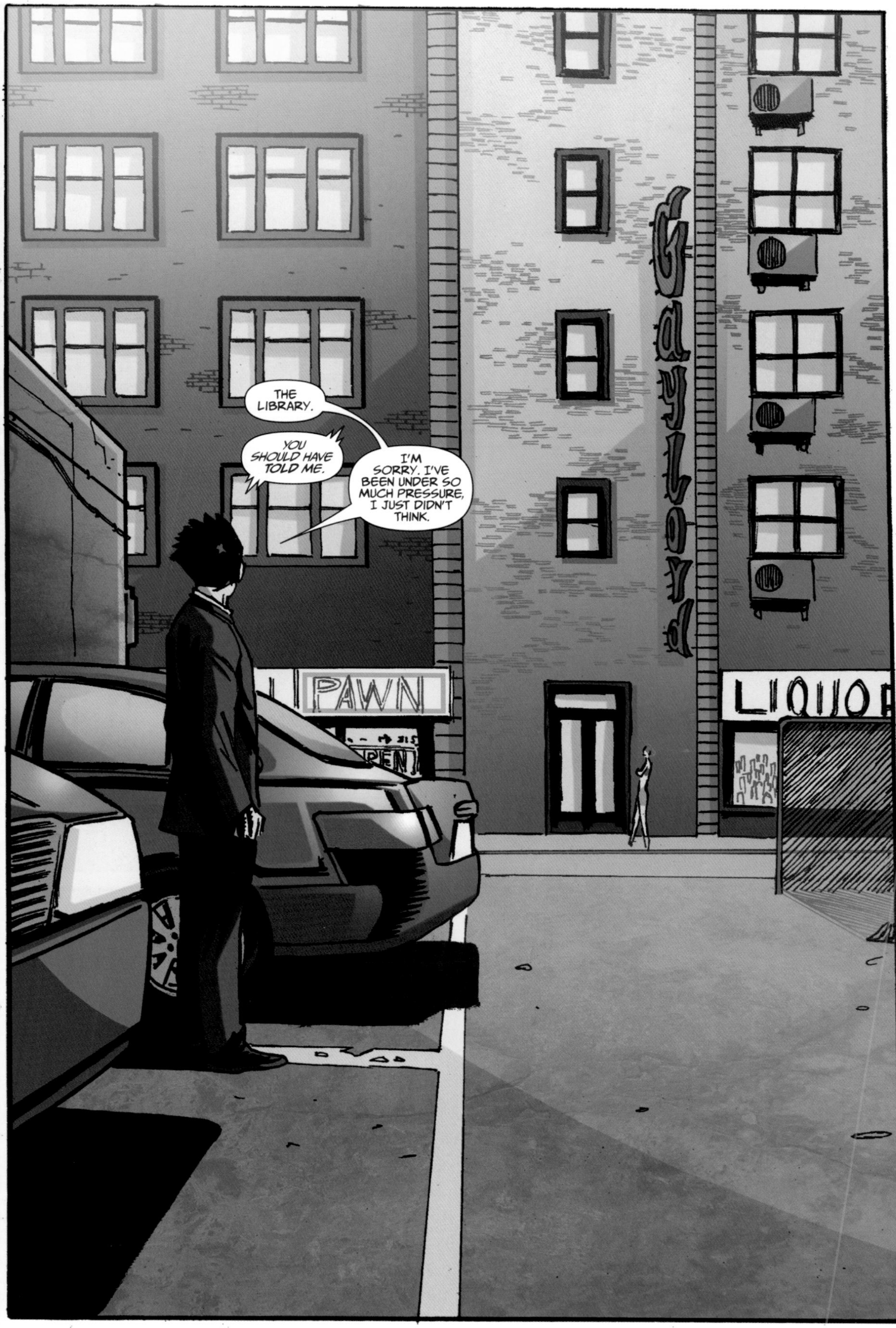
THE LIBRARY.
YOU SHOULD HAVE TOLD ME.
I'M SORRY. I'VE BEEN UNDER SO MUCH PRESSURE, I JUST DIDN'T THINK.
Gaylord
PAWN
LIQUOR

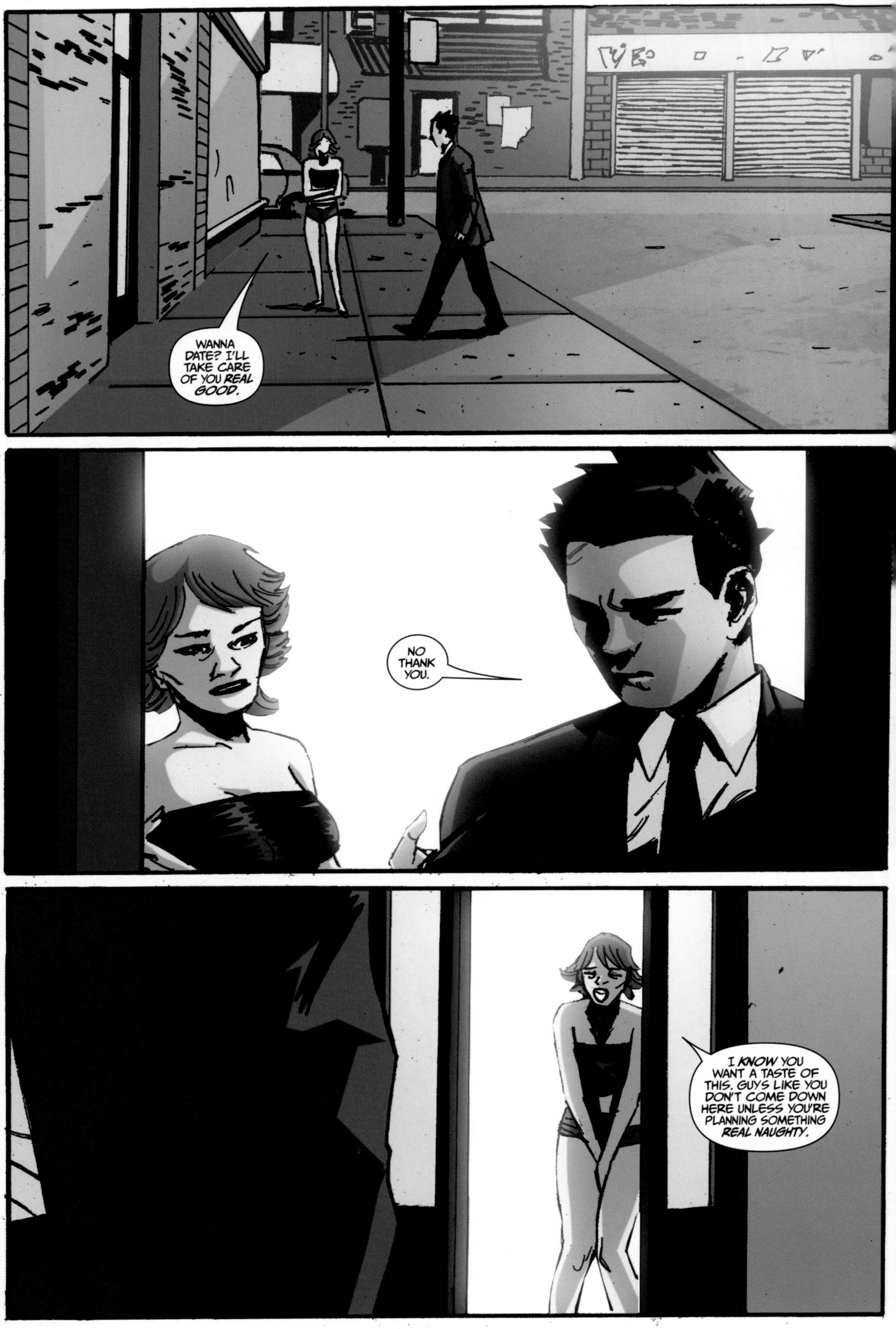

WANNA DATE? I'LL TAKE CARE OF YOU *REAL GOOD*.
NO THANK YOU.
I *KNOW* YOU WANT A TASTE OF THIS. GUYS LIKE YOU DON'T COME DOWN HERE UNLESS YOU'RE PLANNING SOMETHING *REAL NAUGHTY*.

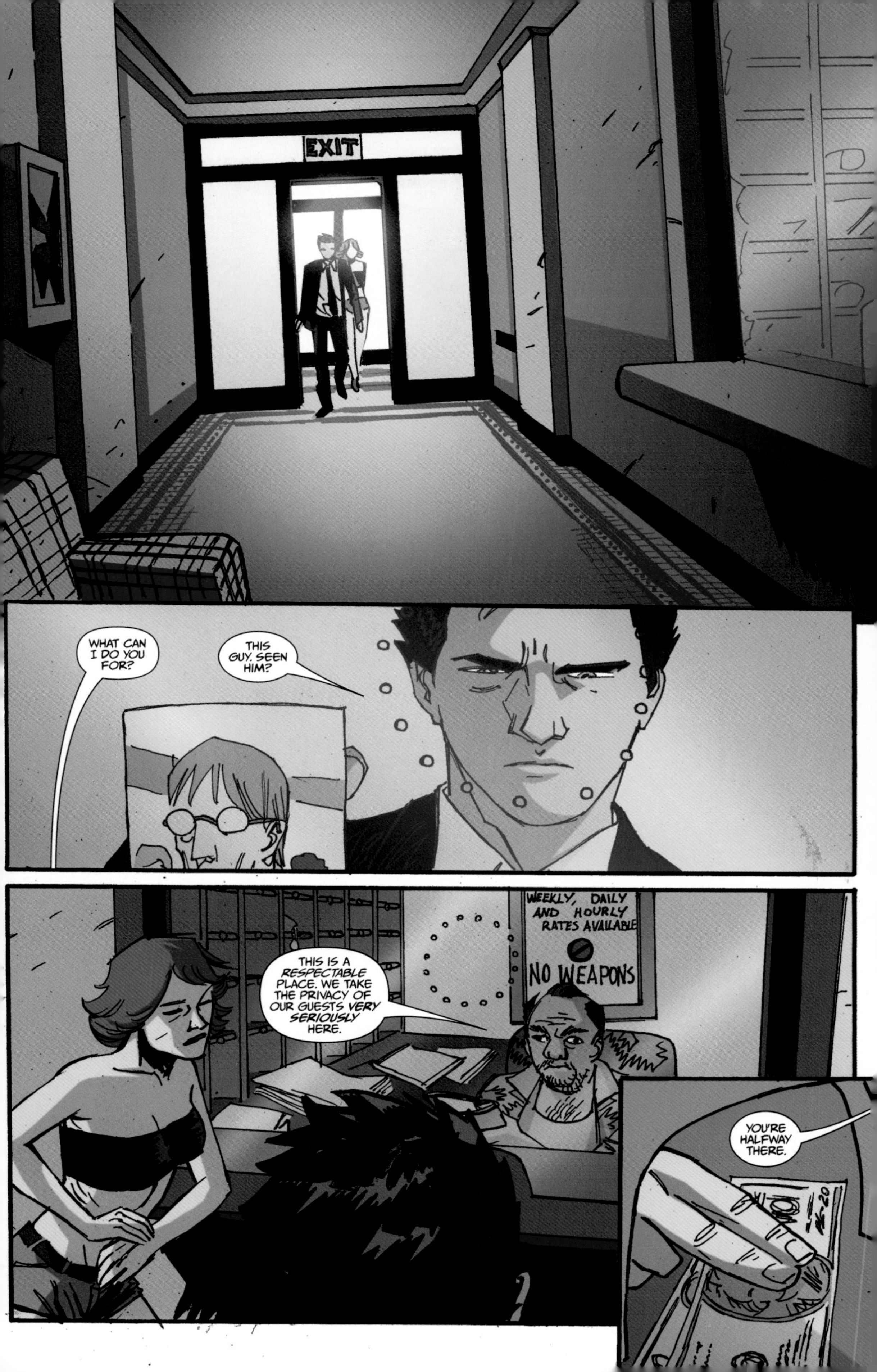
EXIT
WHAT CAN I DO YOU FOR?
THIS GUY. SEEN HIM?
WEEKLY, DAILY AND HOURLY RATES AVAILABLE
NO WEAPONS
THIS IS A RESPECTABLE PLACE. WE TAKE THE PRIVACY OF OUR GUESTS VERY SERIOUSLY HERE.
YOU'RE HALFWAY THERE.

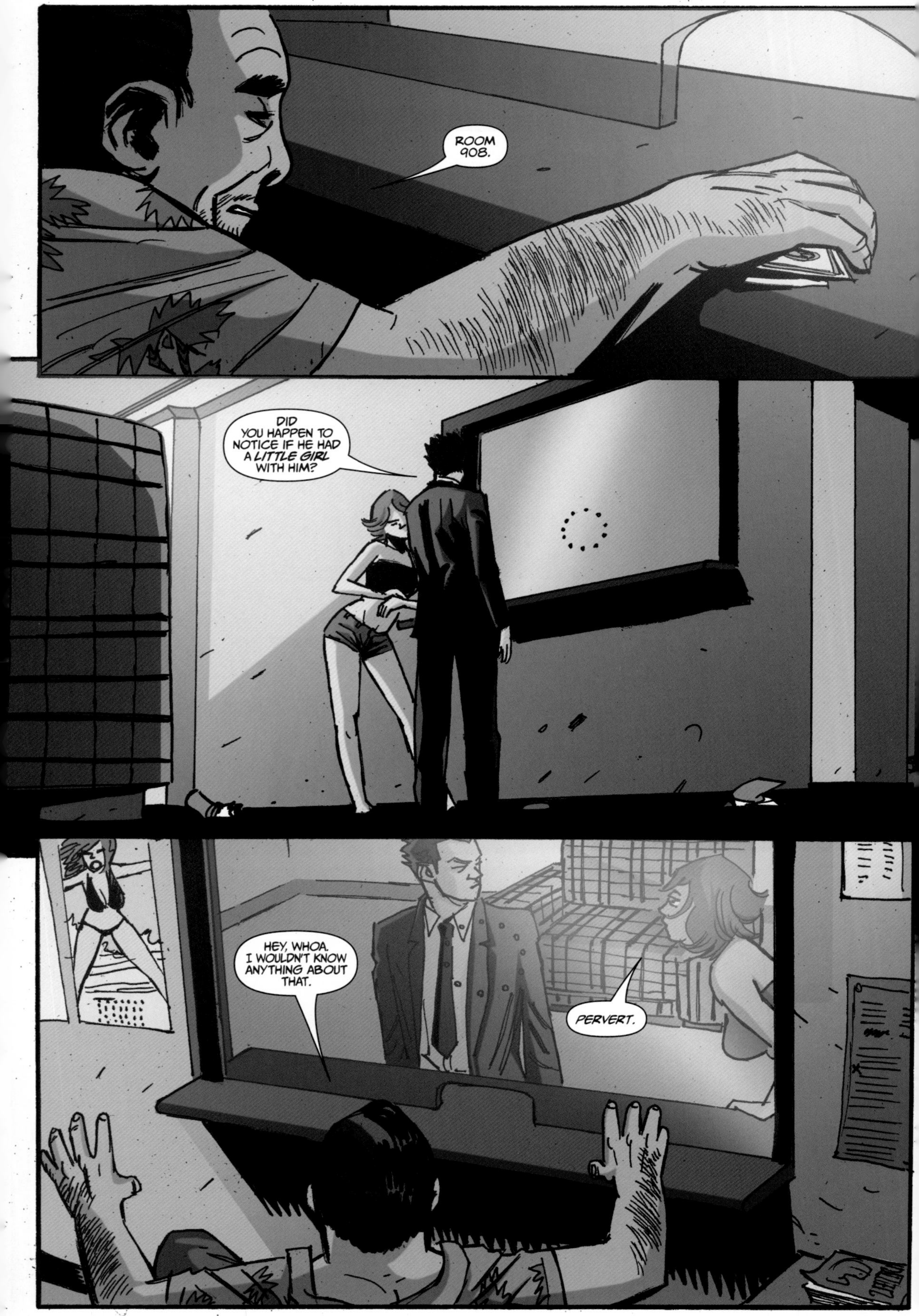
ROOM 908.
DID YOU HAPPEN TO NOTICE IF HE HAD A *LITTLE GIRL* WITH HIM?
HEY, WHOA. I WOULDN'T KNOW ANYTHING ABOUT THAT.
PERVERT.

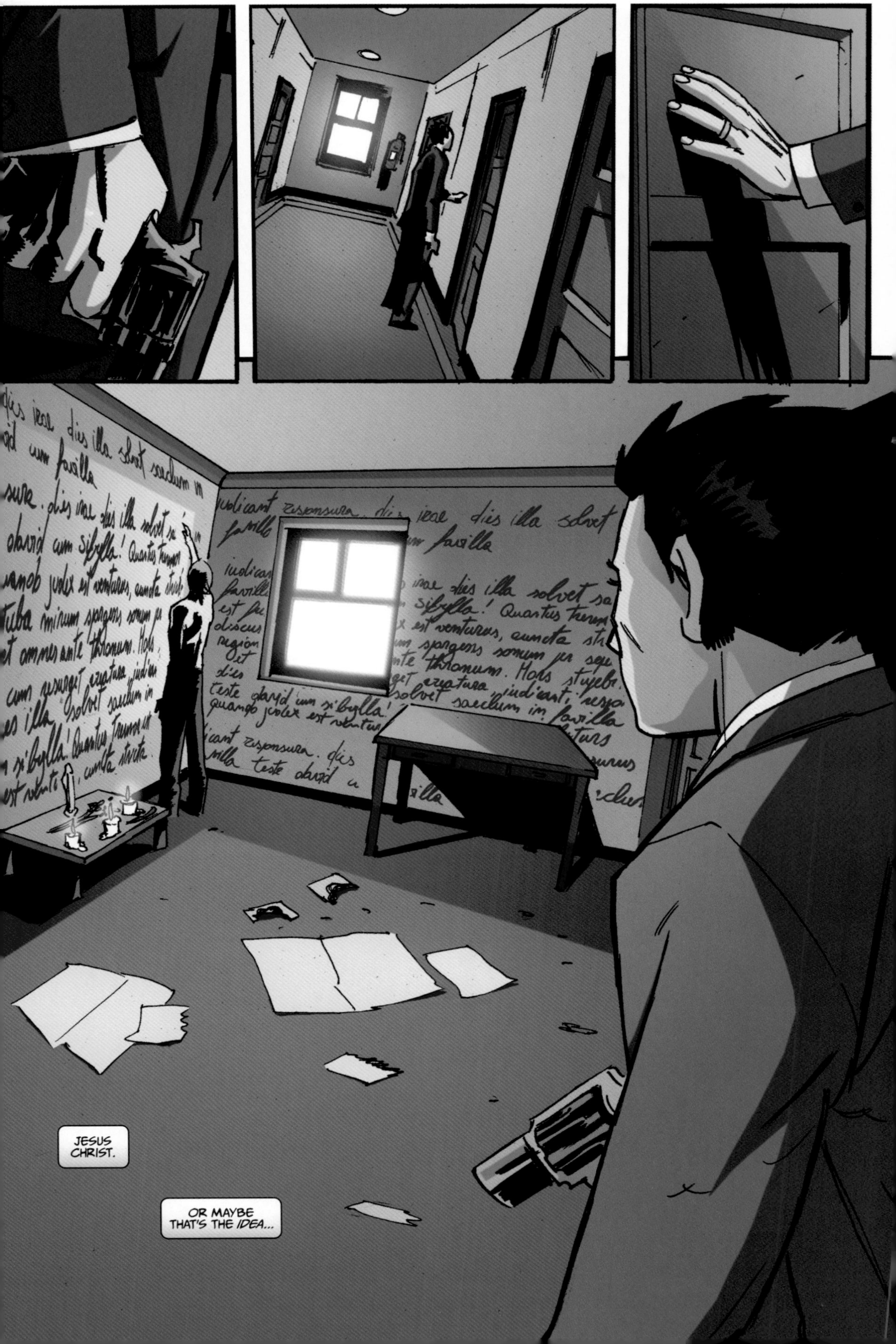
JESUS CHRIST.
OR MAYBE THAT'S THE *IDEA*...

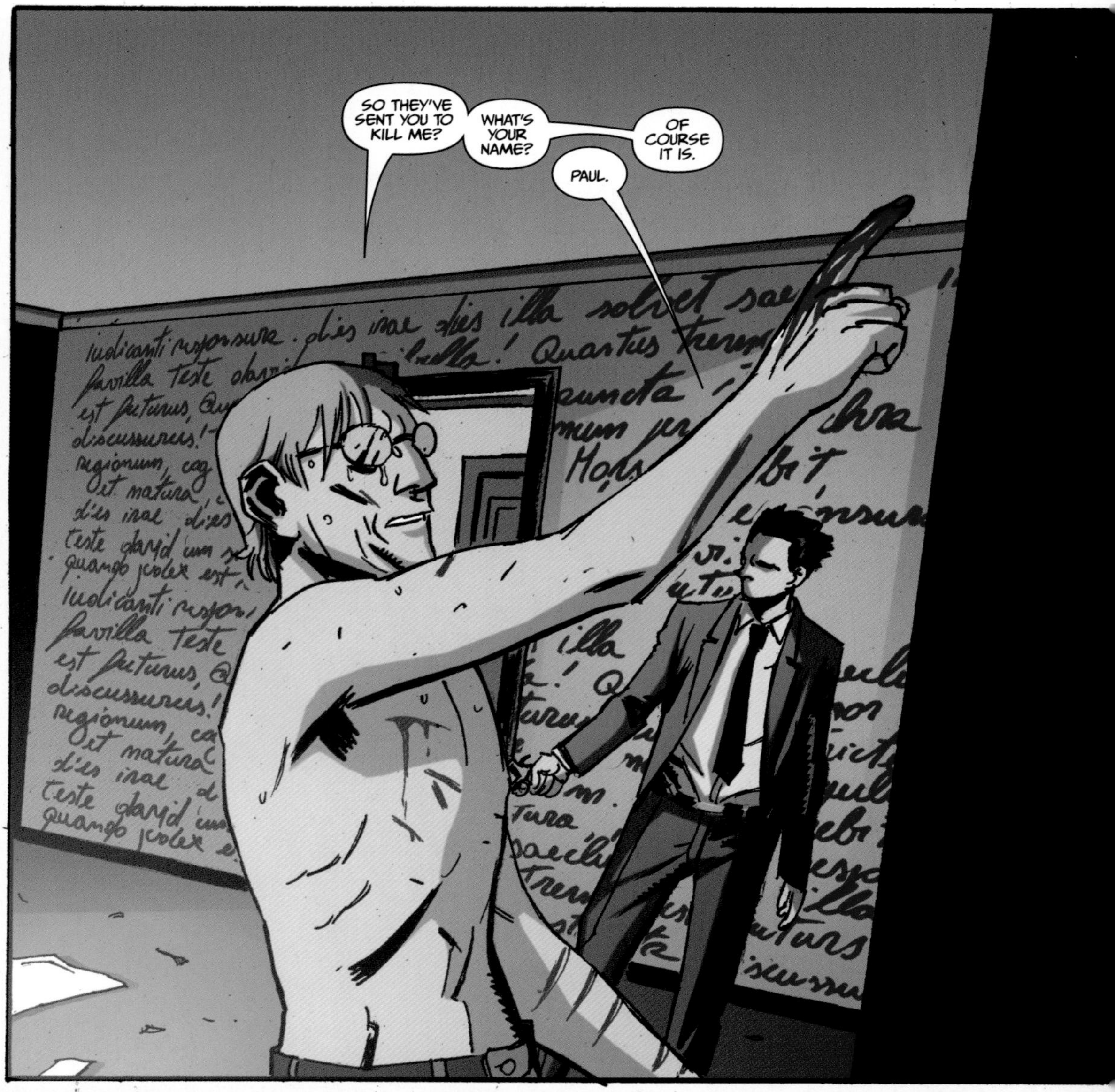
SO THEY'VE SENT YOU TO KILL ME?
WHAT'S YOUR NAME?
PAUL.
OF COURSE IT IS.

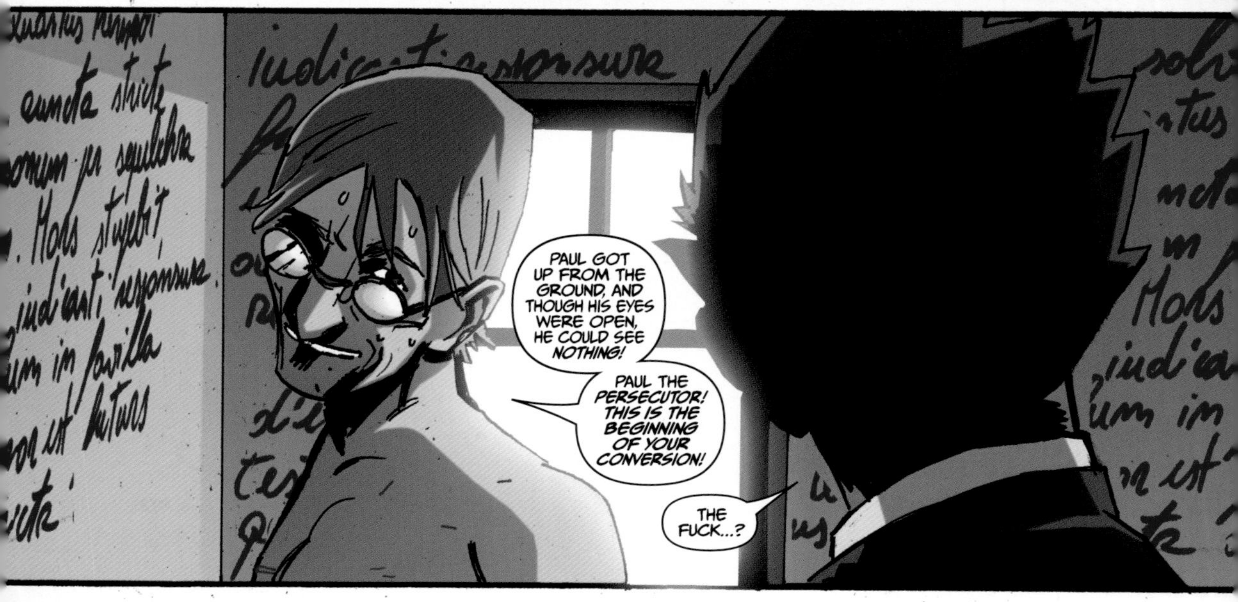
PAUL GOT UP FROM THE GROUND, AND THOUGH HIS EYES WERE OPEN, HE COULD SEE *NOTHING!*
PAUL THE *PERSECUTOR! THIS IS THE BEGINNING OF YOUR CONVERSION!*
THE FUCK...?

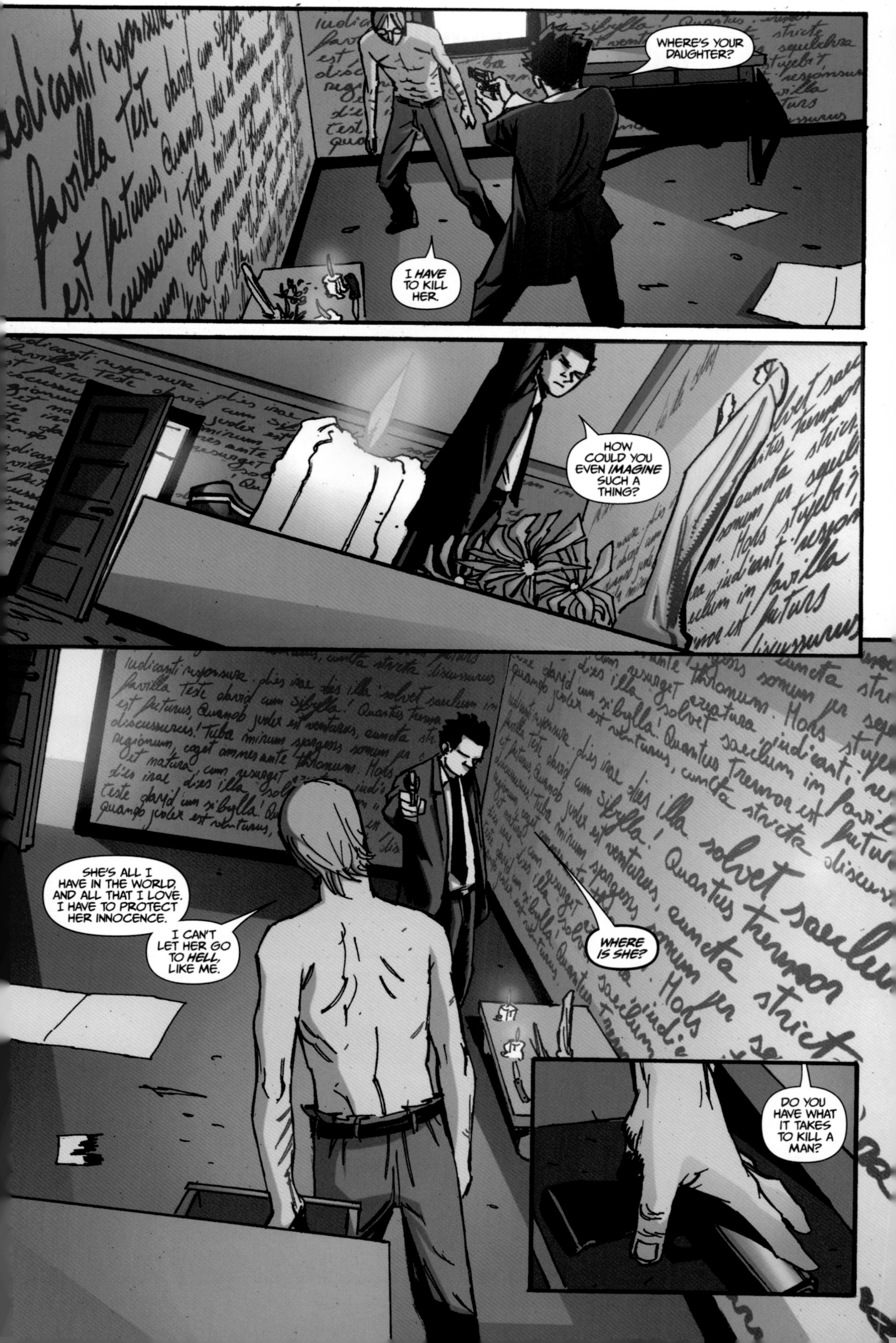
WHERE'S YOUR DAUGHTER?
I *HAVE* TO KILL HER.
HOW COULD YOU EVEN *IMAGINE* SUCH A THING?
SHE'S ALL I HAVE IN THE WORLD, AND ALL THAT I LOVE. I HAVE TO PROTECT HER INNOCENCE.
I CAN'T LET HER GO TO *HELL*, LIKE ME.
WHERE IS SHE?
DO YOU HAVE WHAT IT TAKES TO KILL A MAN?

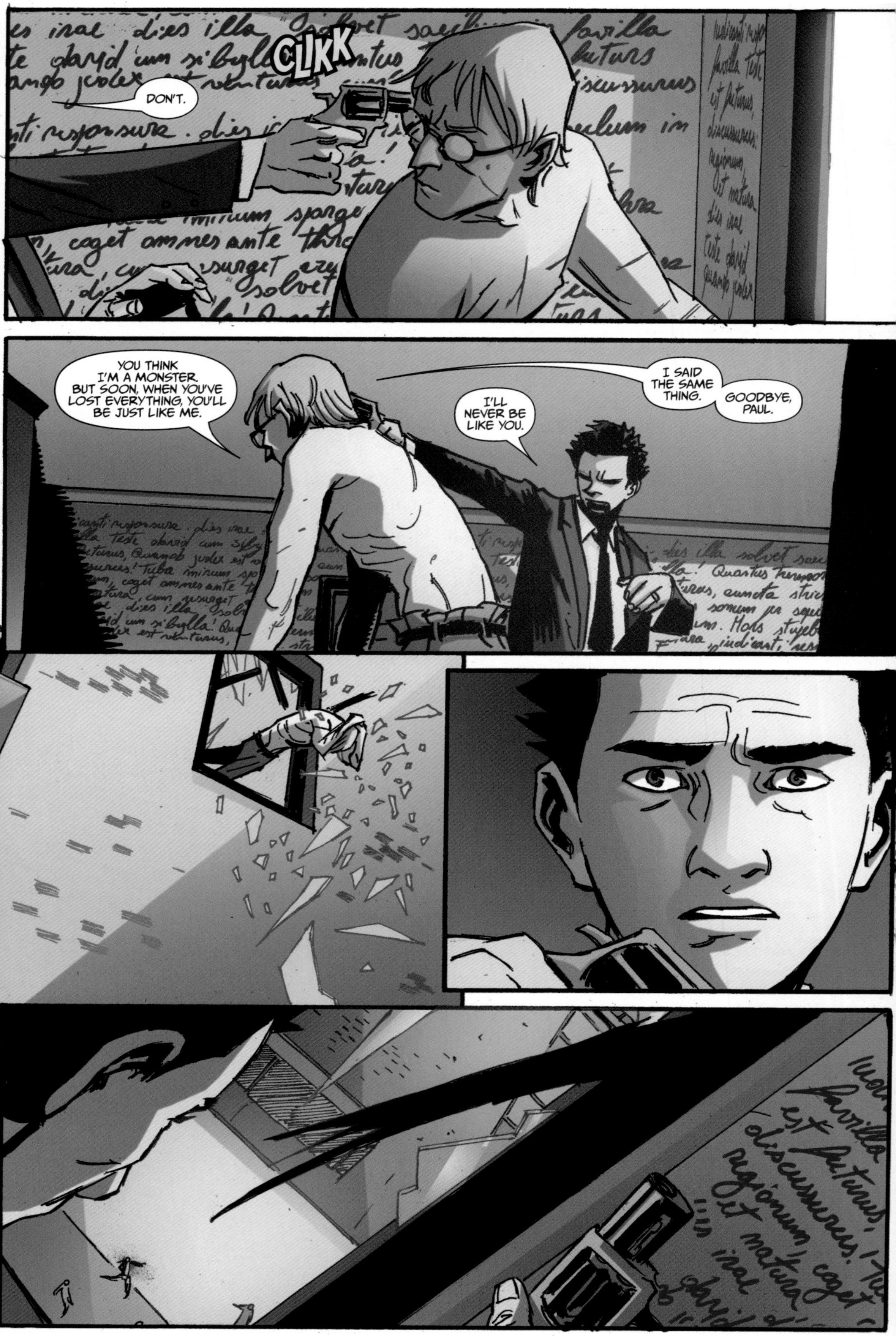
CLIKK
DON'T.
YOU THINK I'M A MONSTER. BUT SOON, WHEN YOU'VE LOST EVERYTHING, YOU'LL BE JUST LIKE ME.
I'LL NEVER BE LIKE YOU.
I SAID THE SAME THING.
GOODBYE, PAUL.

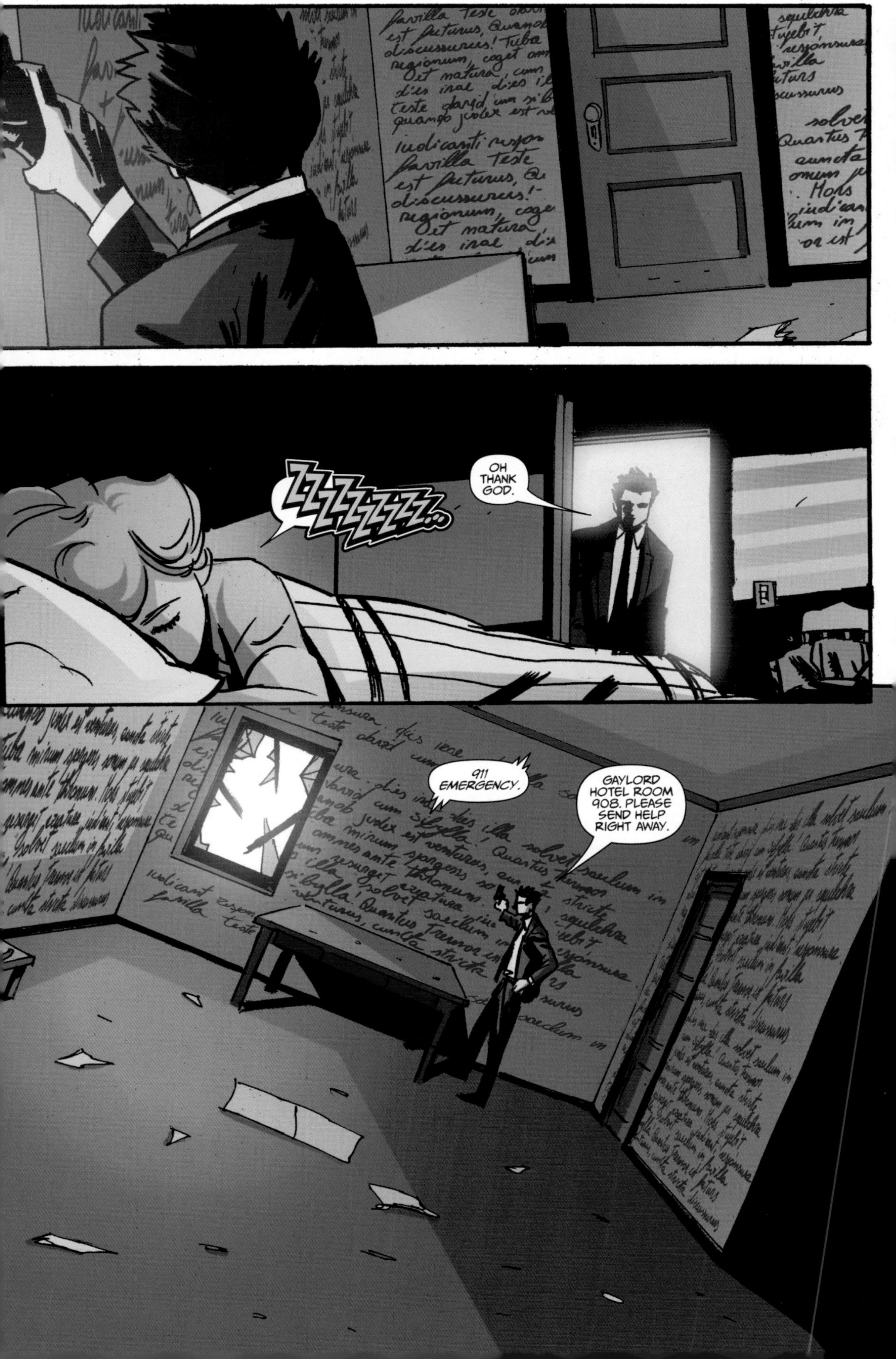
ZZZZZZZZZ..
OH THANK GOD.
911 EMERGENCY.
GAYLORD HOTEL ROOM 908. PLEASE SEND HELP RIGHT AWAY.

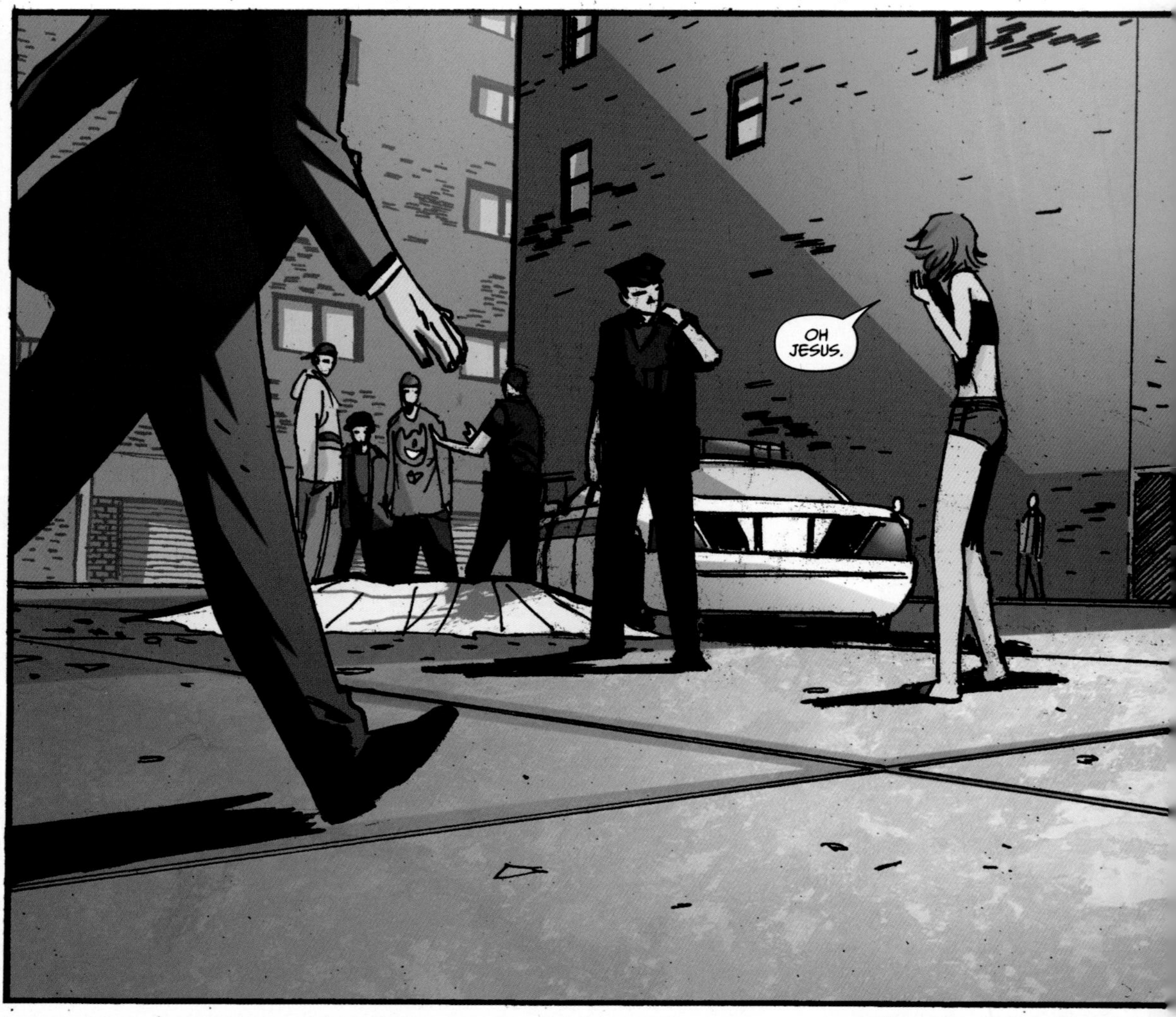
OH JESUS.

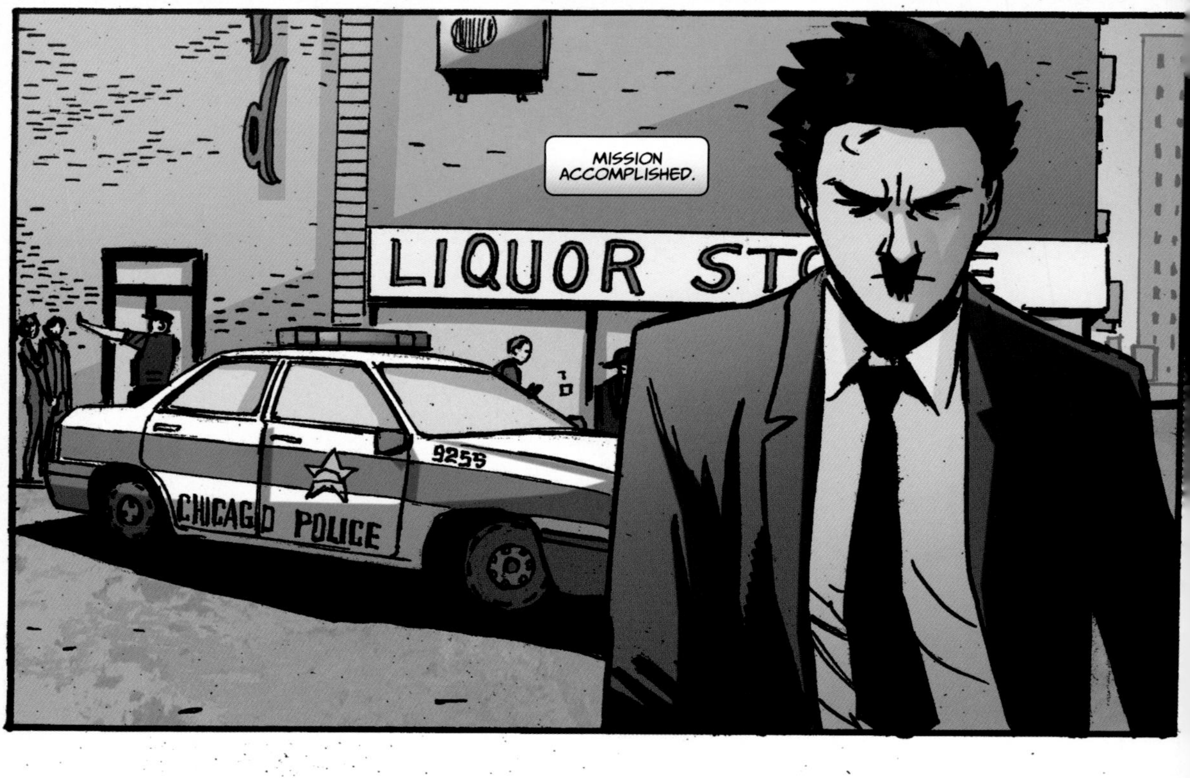
MISSION ACCOMPLISHED.
LIQUOR STO
9255
CHICAGO POLICE

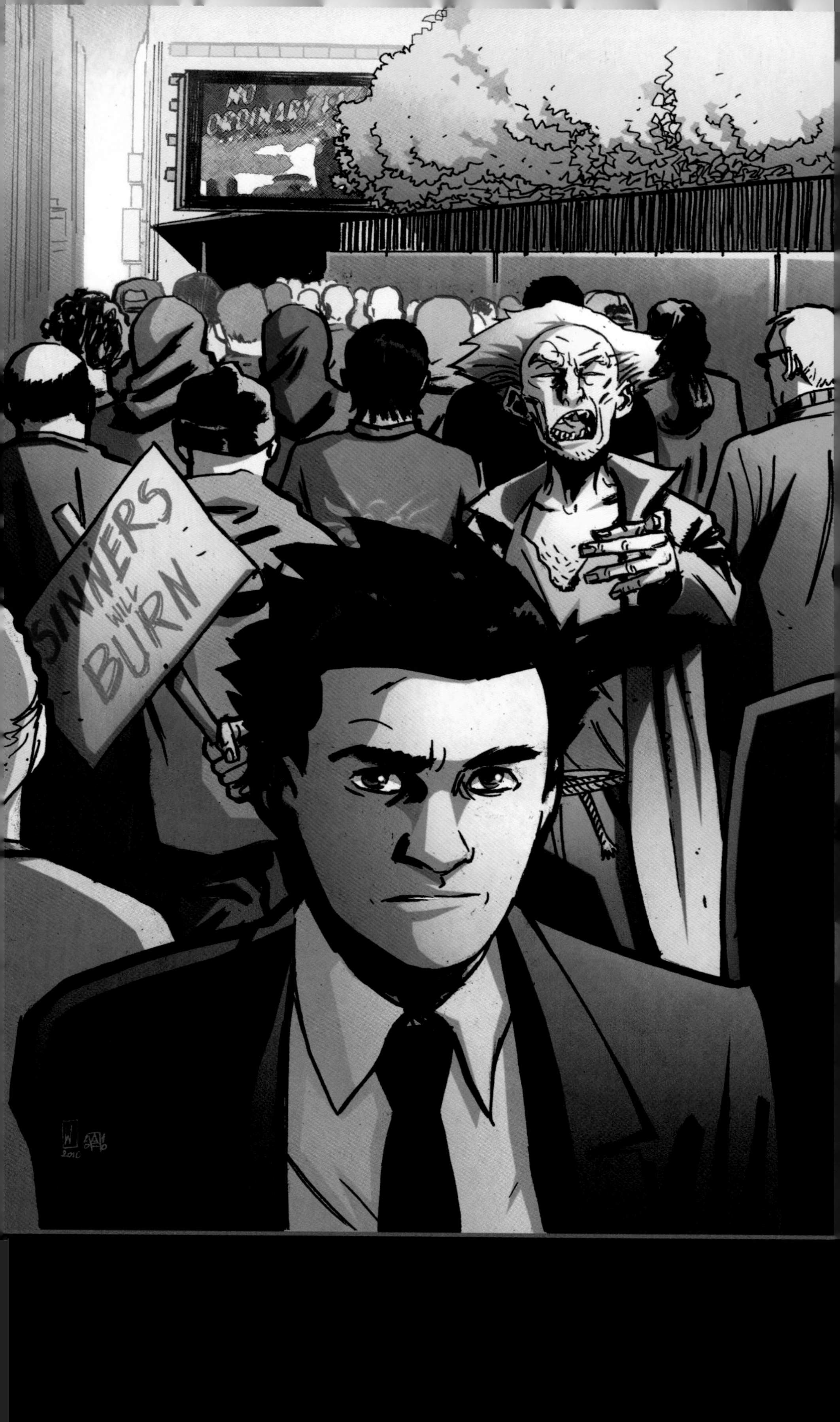
NO ORDINARY
SINNERS WILL BURN

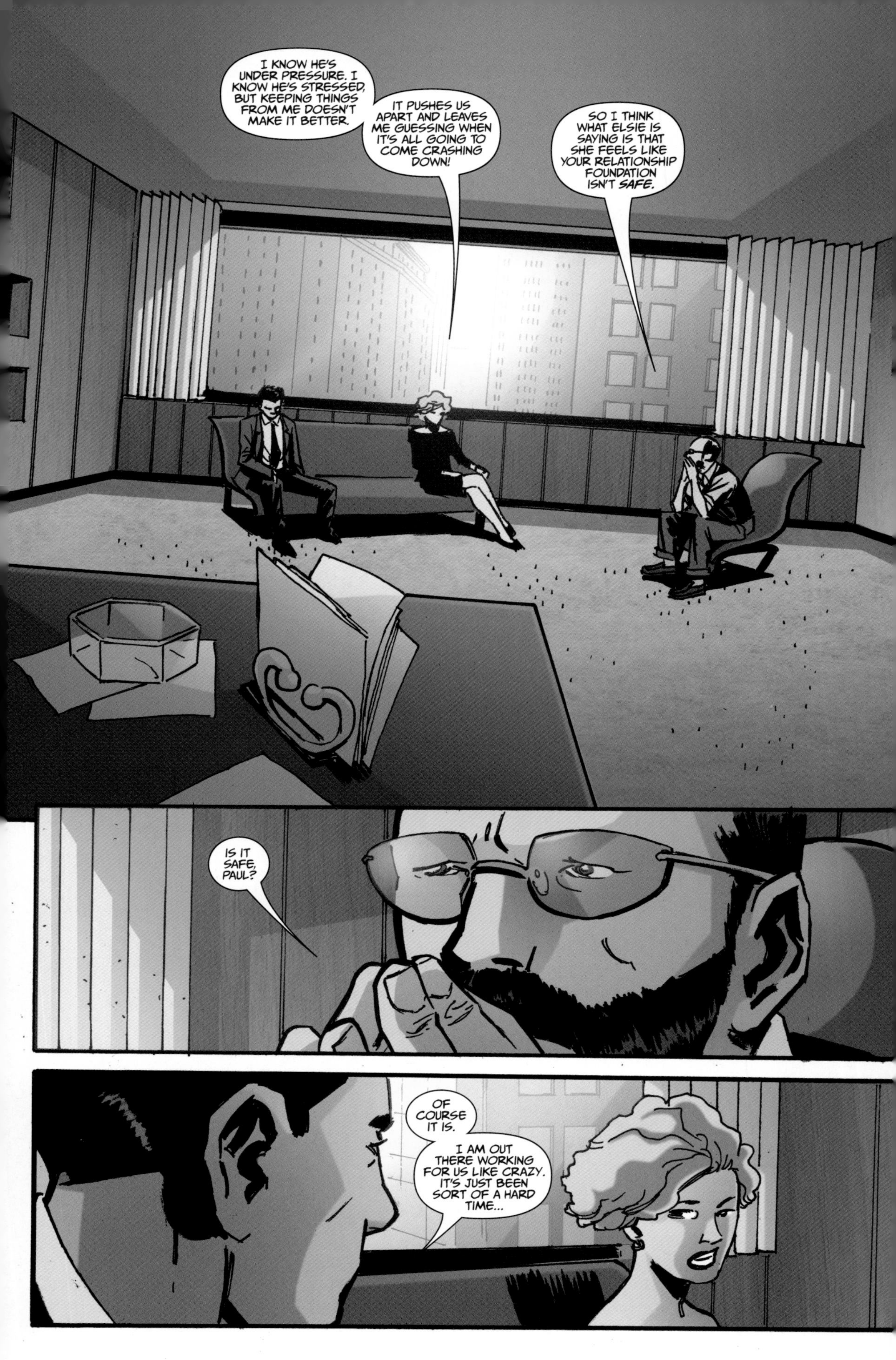
I KNOW HE'S UNDER PRESSURE. I KNOW HE'S STRESSED, BUT KEEPING THINGS FROM ME DOESN'T MAKE IT BETTER.
IT PUSHES US APART AND LEAVES ME GUESSING WHEN IT'S ALL GOING TO COME CRASHING DOWN!
SO I THINK WHAT ELSIE IS SAYING IS THAT SHE FEELS LIKE YOUR RELATIONSHIP FOUNDATION ISN'T *SAFE.*
IS IT SAFE, PAUL?
OF COURSE IT IS.
I AM OUT THERE WORKING FOR US LIKE CRAZY. IT'S JUST BEEN SORT OF A HARD TIME...

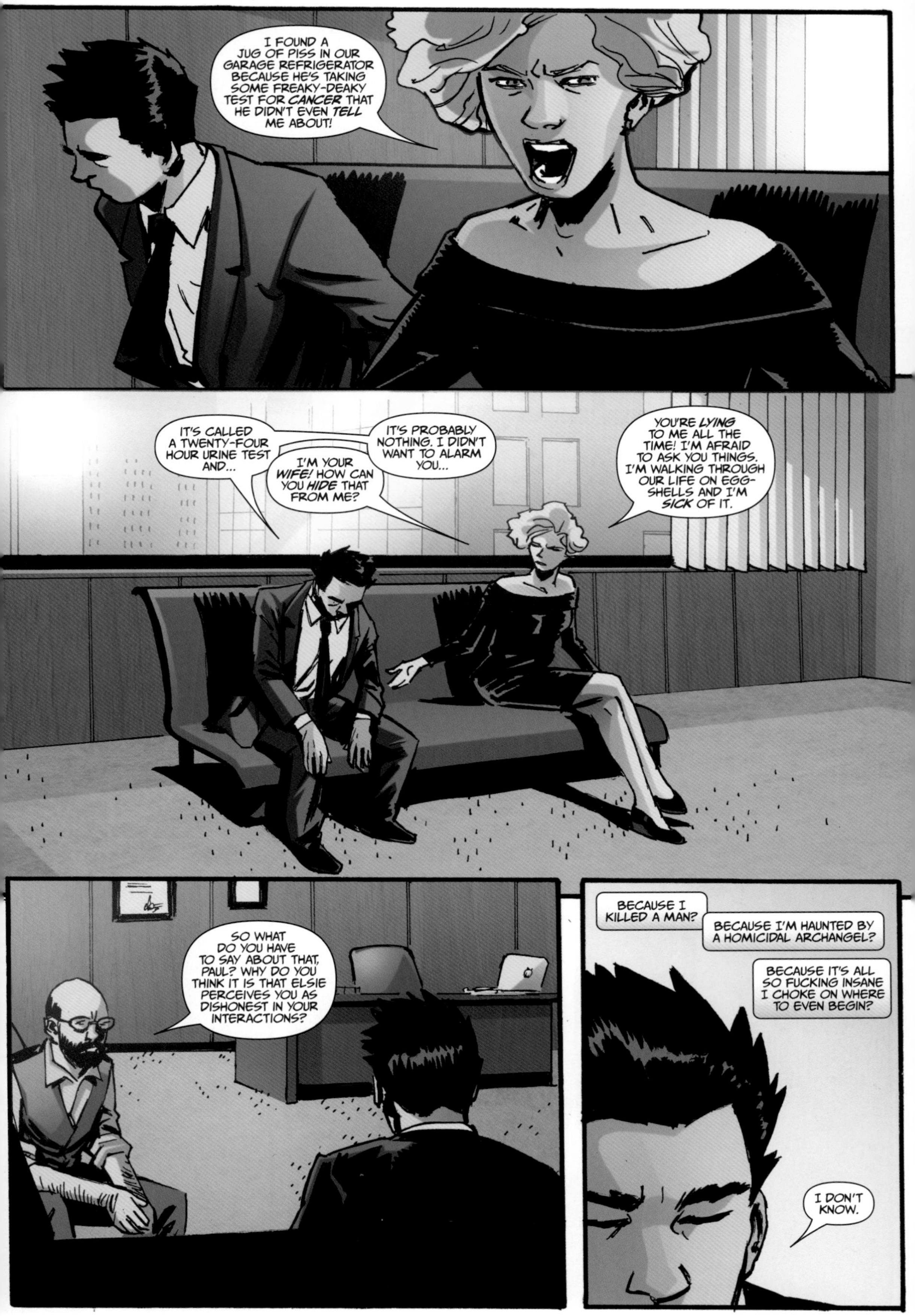
I FOUND A JUG OF PISS IN OUR GARAGE REFRIGERATOR BECAUSE HE'S TAKING SOME FREAKY-DEAKY TEST FOR CANCER THAT HE DIDN'T EVEN TELL ME ABOUT!
IT'S CALLED A TWENTY-FOUR HOUR URINE TEST AND...
IT'S PROBABLY NOTHING. I DIDN'T WANT TO ALARM YOU...
I'M YOUR WIFE! HOW CAN YOU HIDE THAT FROM ME?
YOU'RE LYING TO ME ALL THE TIME! I'M AFRAID TO ASK YOU THINGS. I'M WALKING THROUGH OUR LIFE ON EGG-SHELLS AND I'M SICK OF IT.
SO WHAT DO YOU HAVE TO SAY ABOUT THAT, PAUL? WHY DO YOU THINK IT IS THAT ELSIE PERCEIVES YOU AS DISHONEST IN YOUR INTERACTIONS?
BECAUSE I KILLED A MAN?
BECAUSE I'M HAUNTED BY A HOMICIDAL ARCHANGEL?
BECAUSE IT'S ALL SO FUCKING INSANE I CHOKE ON WHERE TO EVEN BEGIN?
I DON'T KNOW.

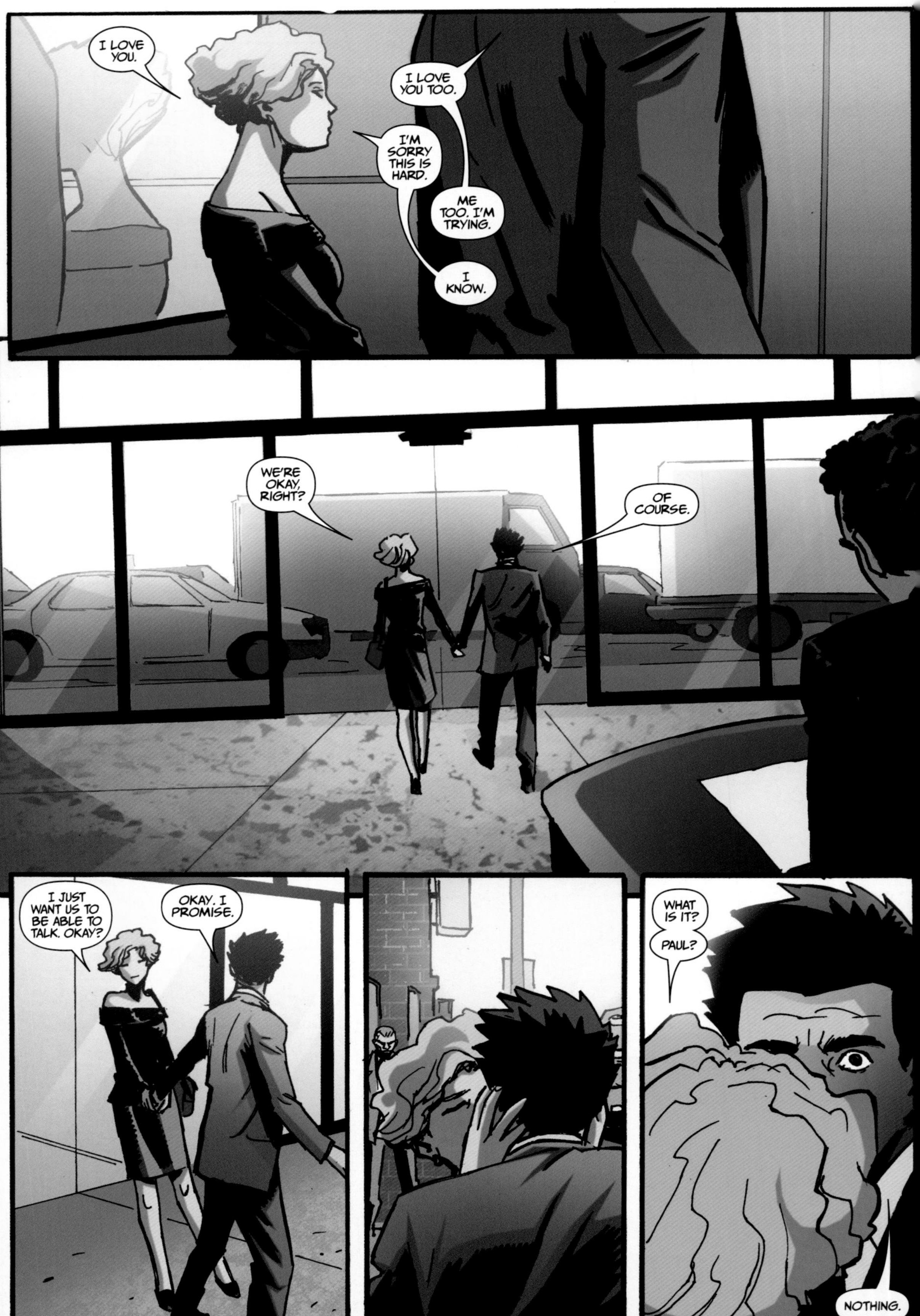
I LOVE YOU.
I LOVE YOU TOO.
I'M SORRY THIS IS HARD.
ME TOO. I'M TRYING.
I KNOW.
WE'RE OKAY, RIGHT?
OF COURSE.
I JUST WANT US TO BE ABLE TO TALK. OKAY?
OKAY. I PROMISE.
WHAT IS IT?
PAUL?
NOTHING.

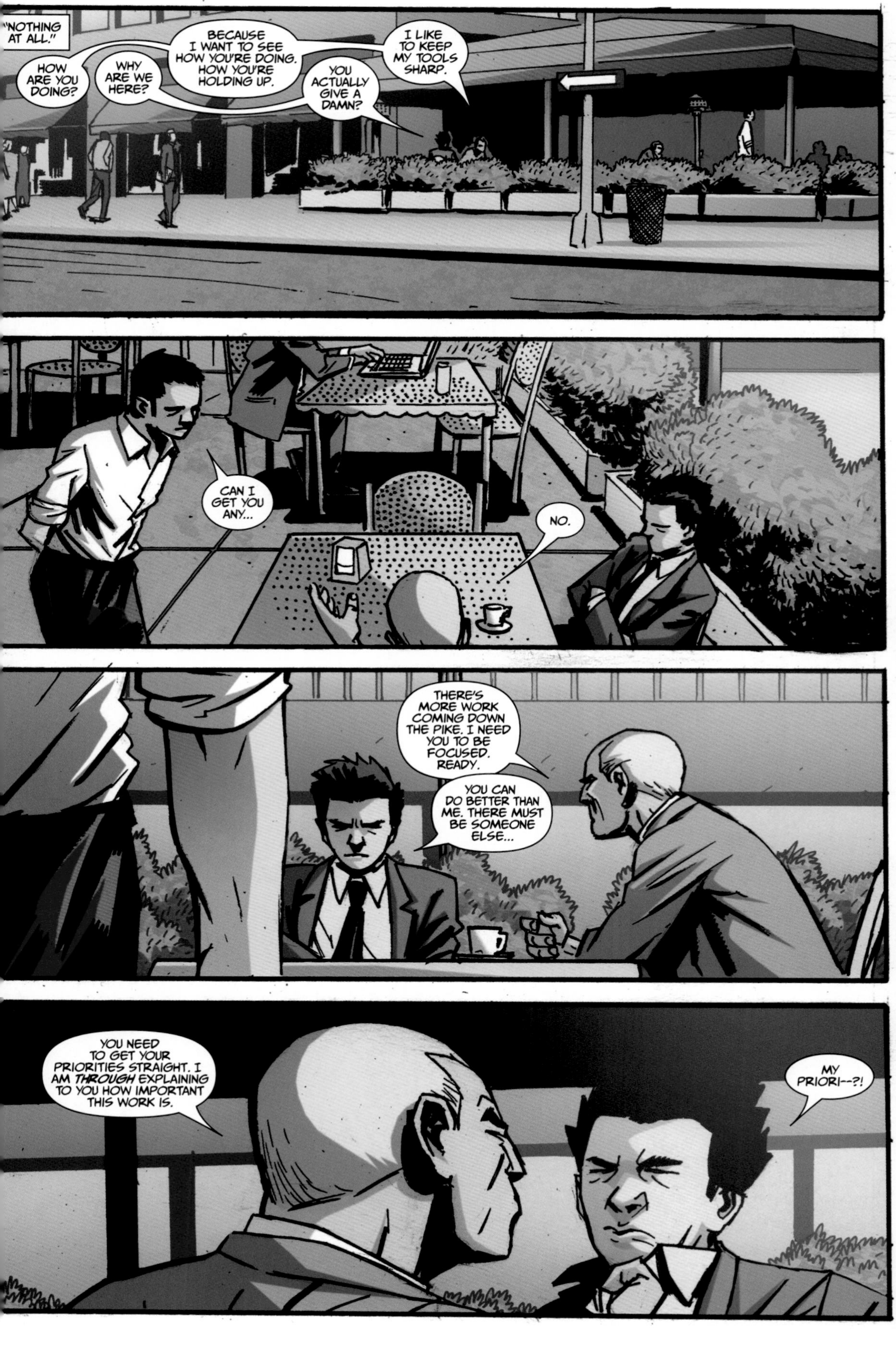
"NOTHING AT ALL."
HOW ARE YOU DOING?
BECAUSE I WANT TO SEE HOW YOU'RE DOING. HOW YOU'RE HOLDING UP.
WHY ARE WE HERE?
I LIKE TO KEEP MY TOOLS SHARP.
YOU ACTUALLY GIVE A DAMN?
CAN I GET YOU ANY...
NO.
THERE'S MORE WORK COMING DOWN THE PIKE. I NEED YOU TO BE FOCUSED. READY.
YOU CAN DO BETTER THAN ME. THERE MUST BE SOMEONE ELSE...
YOU NEED TO GET YOUR PRIORITIES STRAIGHT. I AM THROUGH EXPLAINING TO YOU HOW IMPORTANT THIS WORK IS.
MY PRIORI--?!

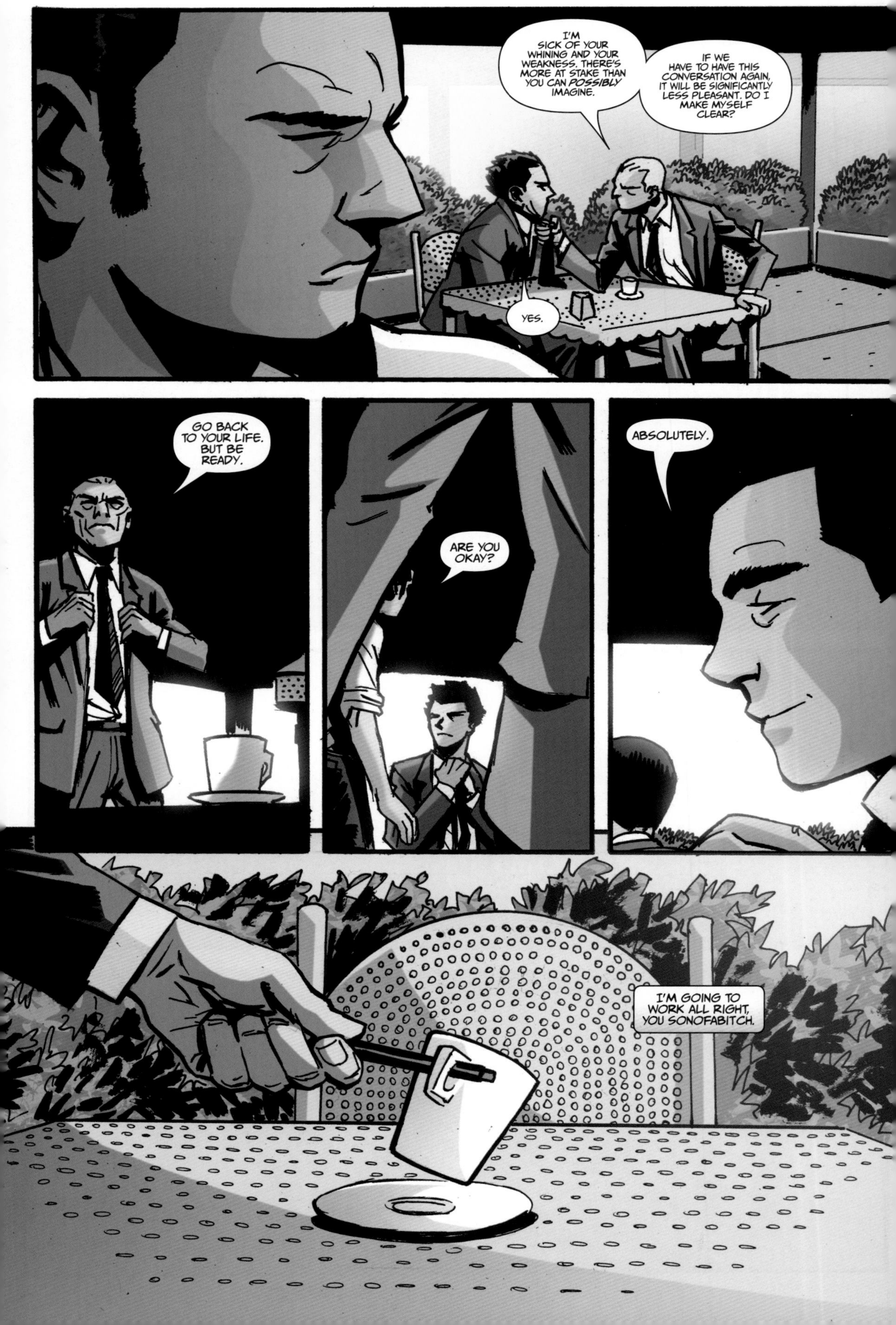
I'M SICK OF YOUR WHINING AND YOUR WEAKNESS. THERE'S MORE AT STAKE THAN YOU CAN *POSSIBLY* IMAGINE.
IF WE HAVE TO HAVE THIS CONVERSATION AGAIN, IT WILL BE SIGNIFICANTLY LESS PLEASANT. DO I MAKE MYSELF CLEAR?
YES.
GO BACK TO YOUR LIFE. BUT BE READY.
ARE YOU OKAY?
ABSOLUTELY.
I'M GOING TO WORK ALL RIGHT, YOU SONOFABITCH.

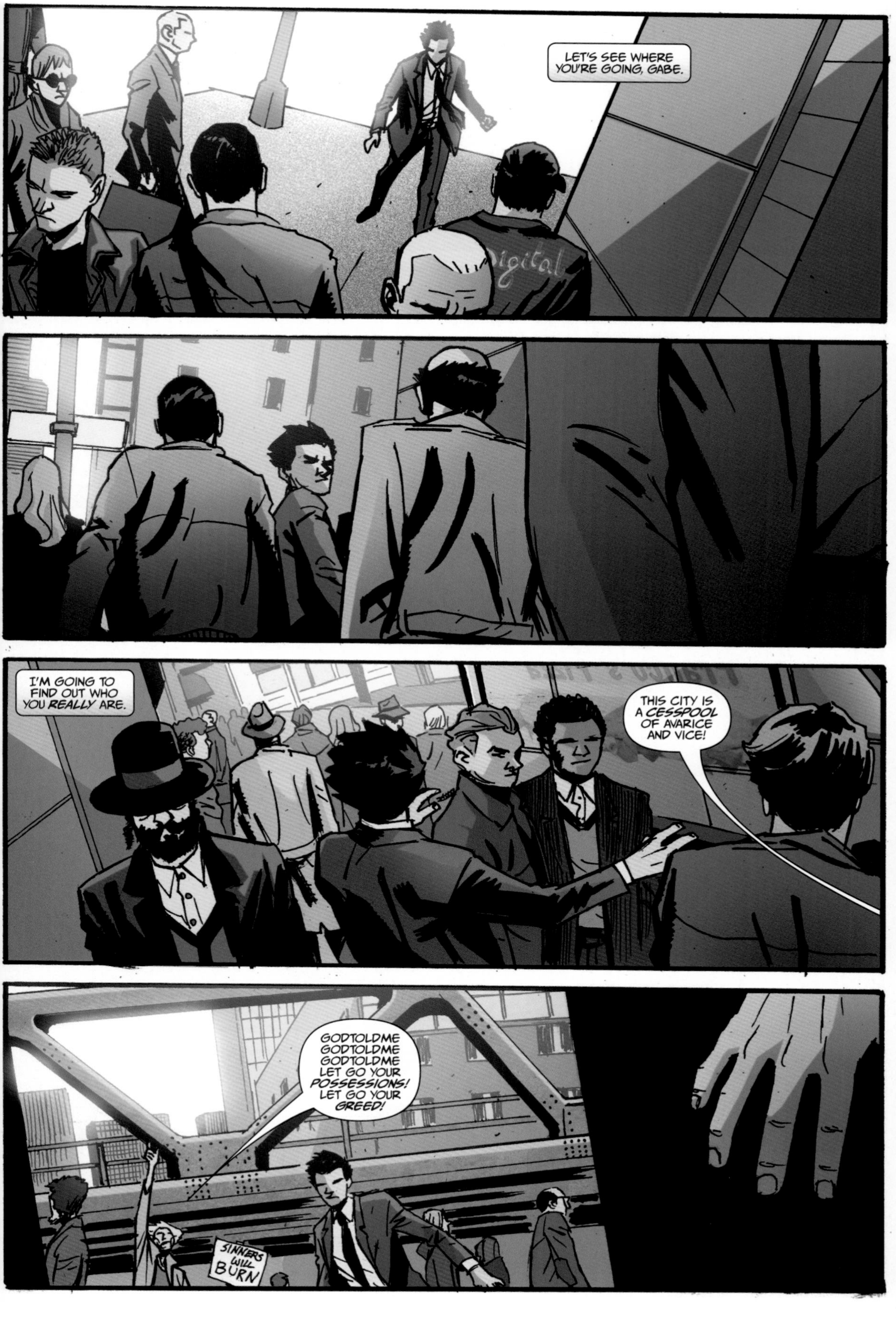
LET'S SEE WHERE YOU'RE GOING, GABE.
digital
I'M GOING TO FIND OUT WHO YOU *REALLY* ARE.
THIS CITY IS A *CESSPOOL* OF AVARICE AND VICE!
GODTOLDME GODTOLDME GODTOLDME LET GO YOUR *POSSESSIONS!* LET GO YOUR *GREED!*
SINNERS WILL BURN

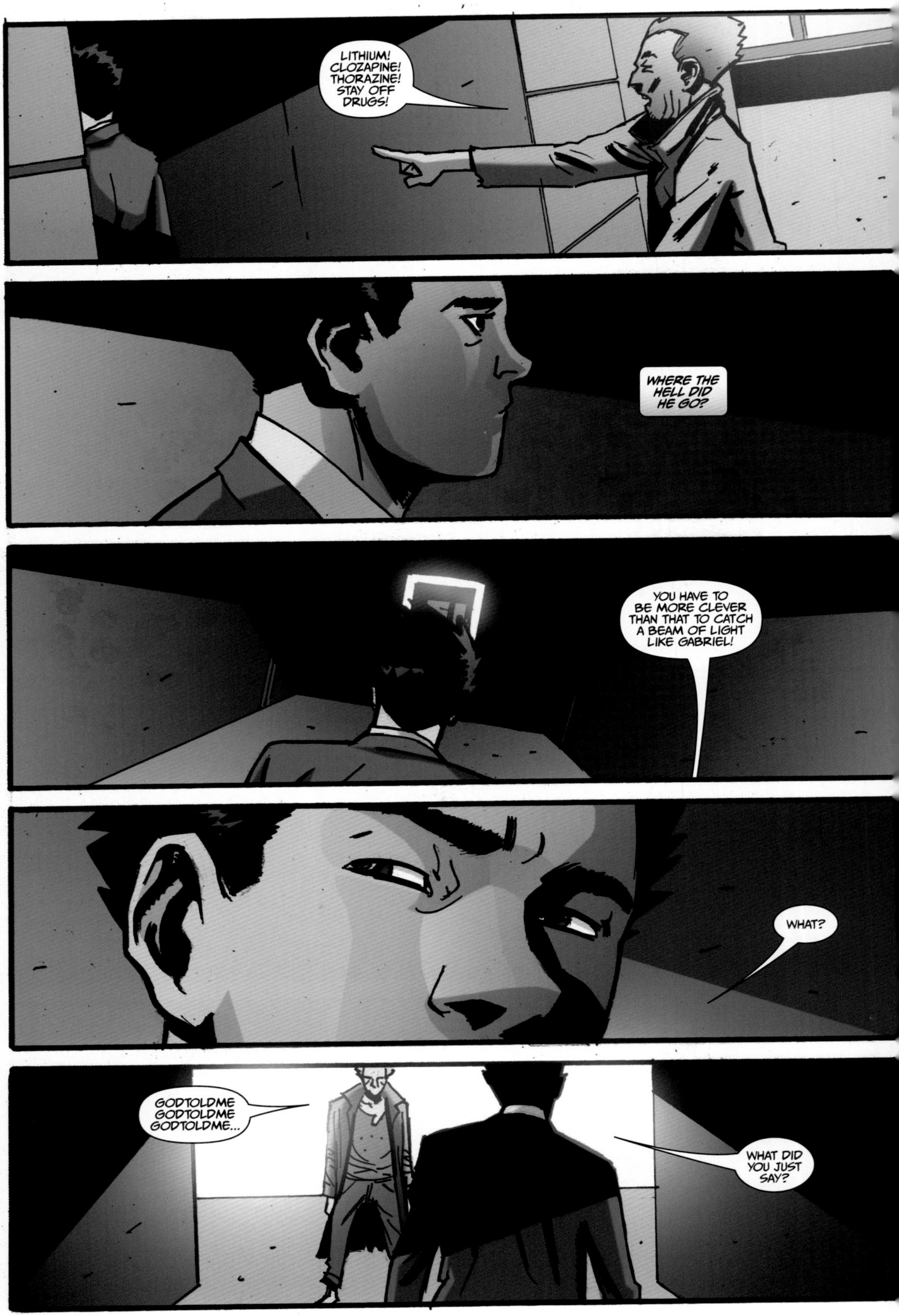
LITHIUM! CLOZAPINE! THORAZINE! STAY OFF DRUGS!
WHERE THE HELL DID HE GO?
YOU HAVE TO BE MORE CLEVER THAN THAT TO CATCH A BEAM OF LIGHT LIKE GABRIEL!
WHAT?
GODTOLDME GODTOLDME GODTOLDME...
WHAT DID YOU JUST SAY?

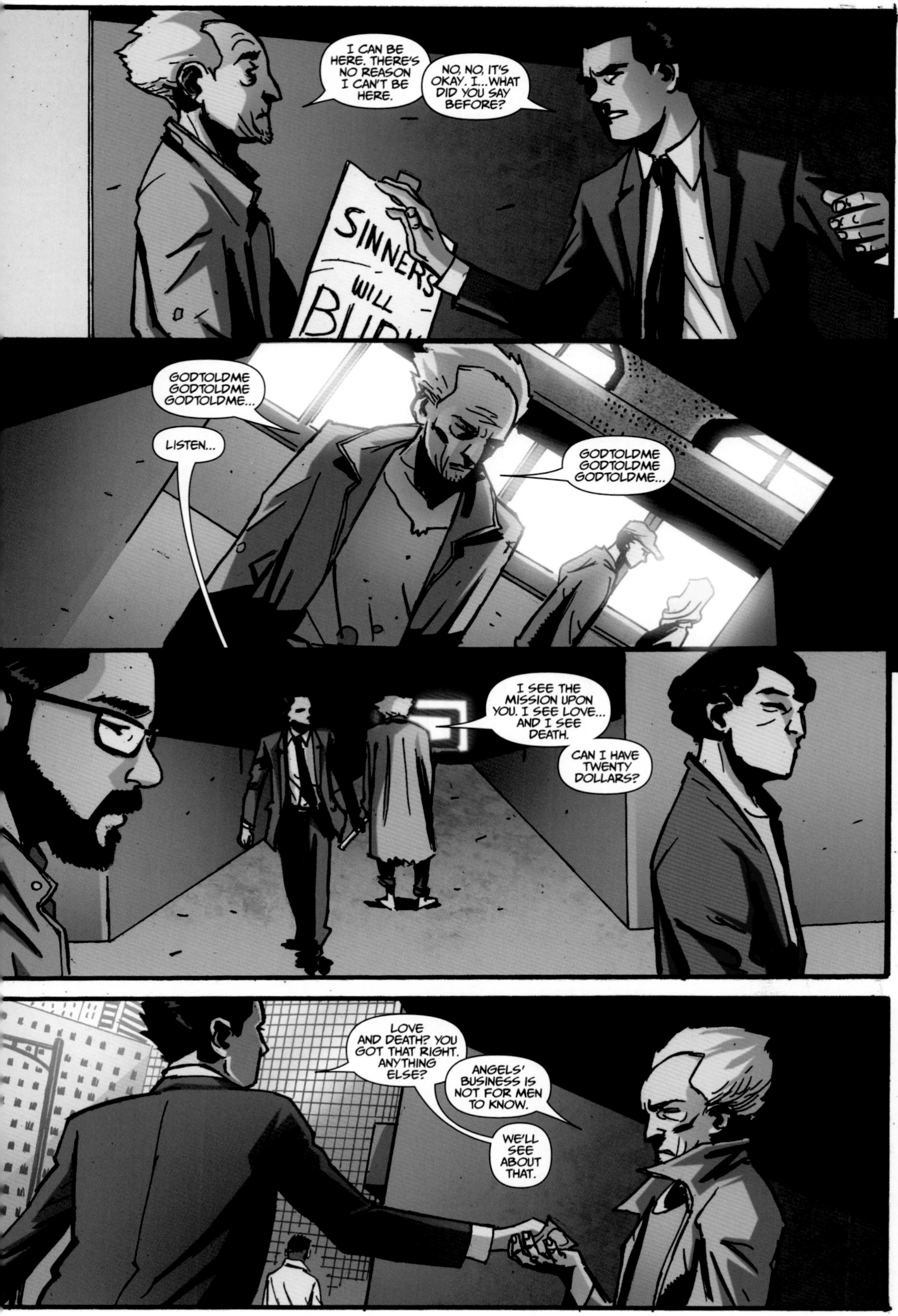
I CAN BE HERE. THERE'S NO REASON I CAN'T BE HERE.
NO, NO, IT'S OKAY. I...WHAT DID YOU SAY BEFORE?
SINNERS WILL BUR
GODTOLDME GODTOLDME GODTOLDME...
LISTEN...
GODTOLDME GODTOLDME GODTOLDME...
I SEE THE MISSION UPON YOU. I SEE LOVE... AND I SEE DEATH.
CAN I HAVE TWENTY DOLLARS?
LOVE AND DEATH? YOU GOT THAT RIGHT. ANYTHING ELSE?
ANGELS' BUSINESS IS NOT FOR MEN TO KNOW.
WE'LL SEE ABOUT THAT.

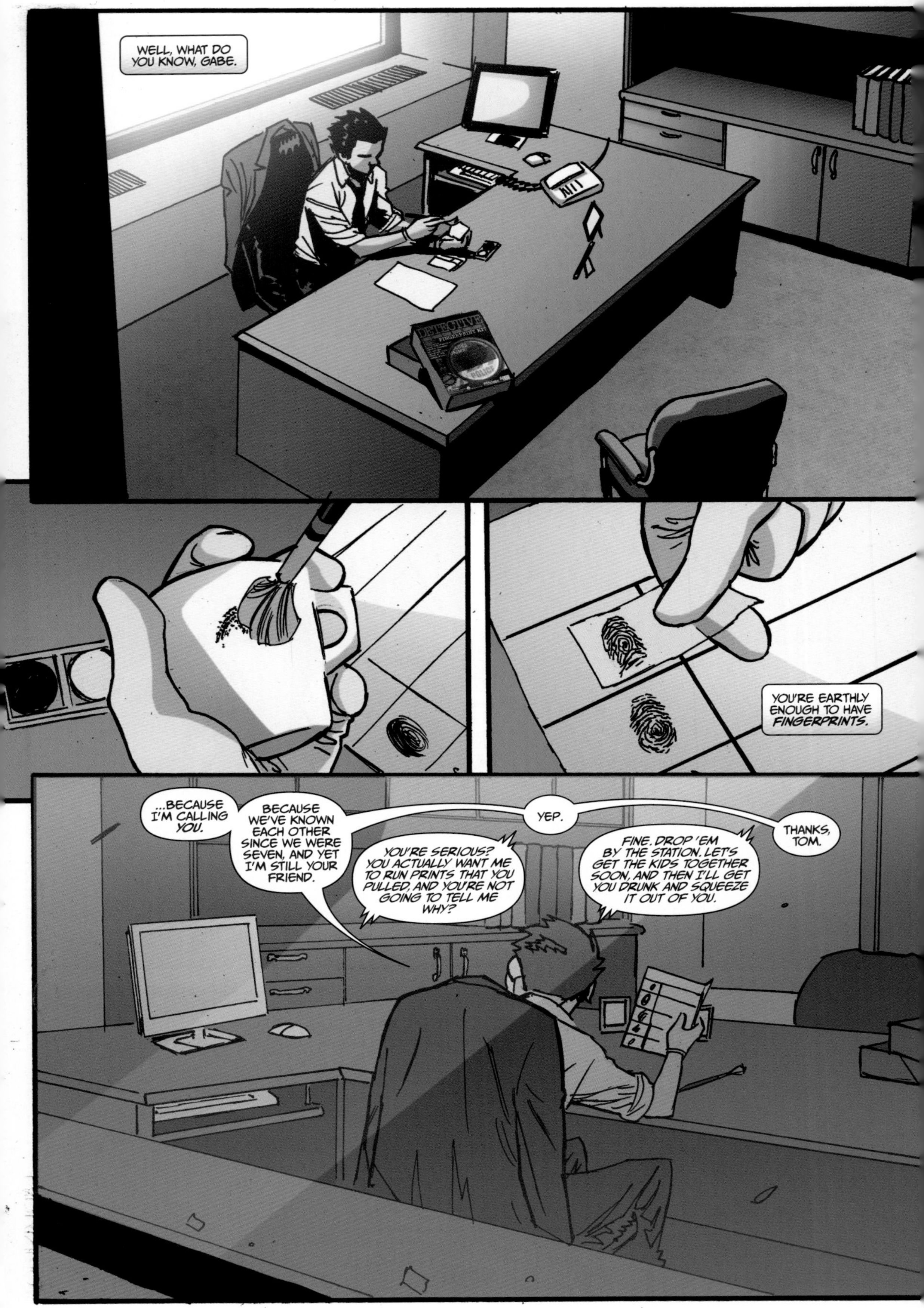
WELL, WHAT DO YOU KNOW, GABE.
DETECTIVE FINGERPRINT KIT
POLICE
YOU'RE EARTHLY ENOUGH TO HAVE FINGERPRINTS.
...BECAUSE I'M CALLING YOU.
BECAUSE WE'VE KNOWN EACH OTHER SINCE WE WERE SEVEN, AND YET I'M STILL YOUR FRIEND.
YOU'RE SERIOUS? YOU ACTUALLY WANT ME TO RUN PRINTS THAT YOU PULLED, AND YOU'RE NOT GOING TO TELL ME WHY?
YEP.
FINE. DROP 'EM BY THE STATION. LET'S GET THE KIDS TOGETHER SOON, AND THEN I'LL GET YOU DRUNK AND SQUEEZE IT OUT OF YOU.
THANKS, TOM.

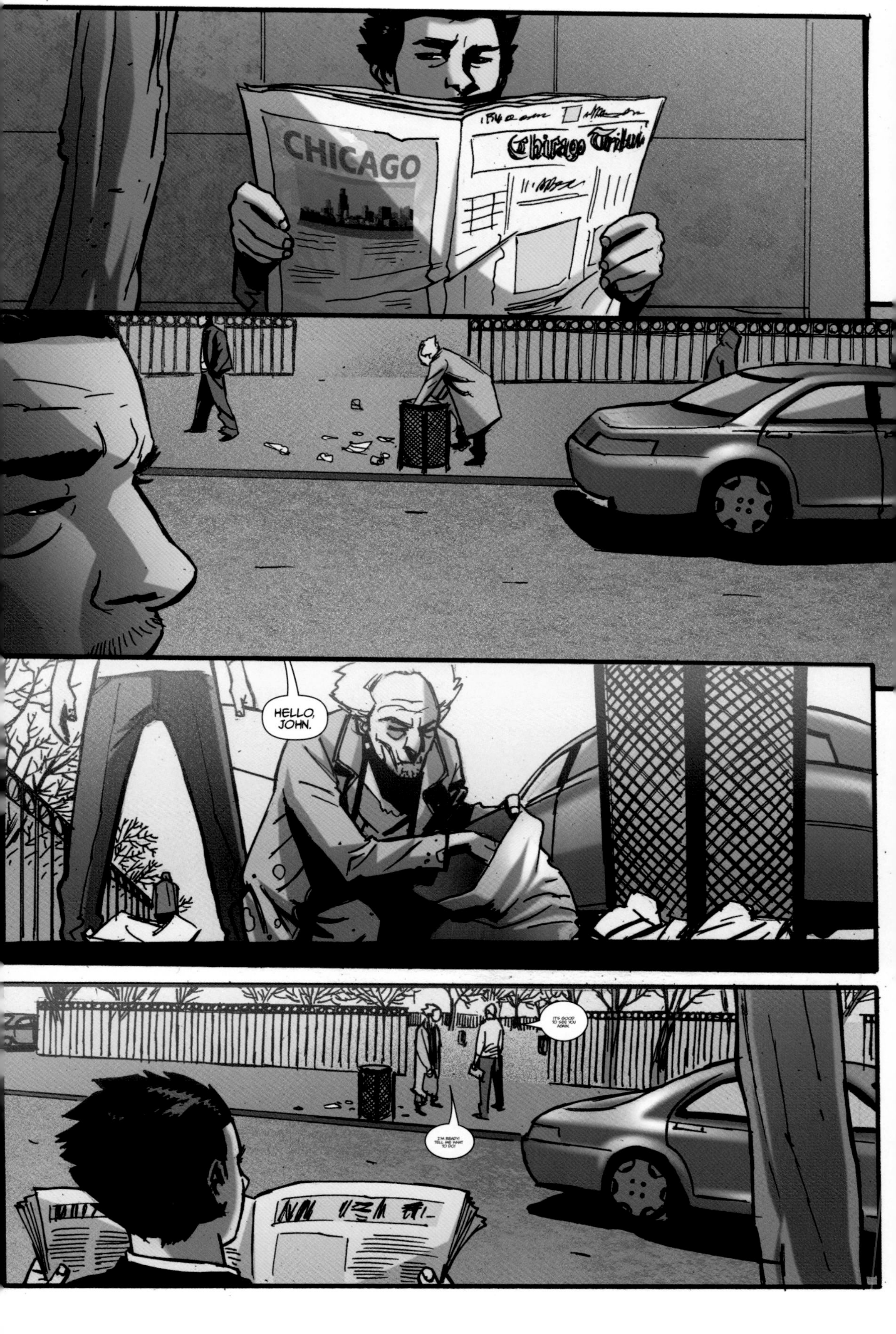
CHICAGO
HELLO, JOHN.
IT'S GOOD TO SEE YOU AGAIN.
I'M READY! TELL ME WHAT TO DO!

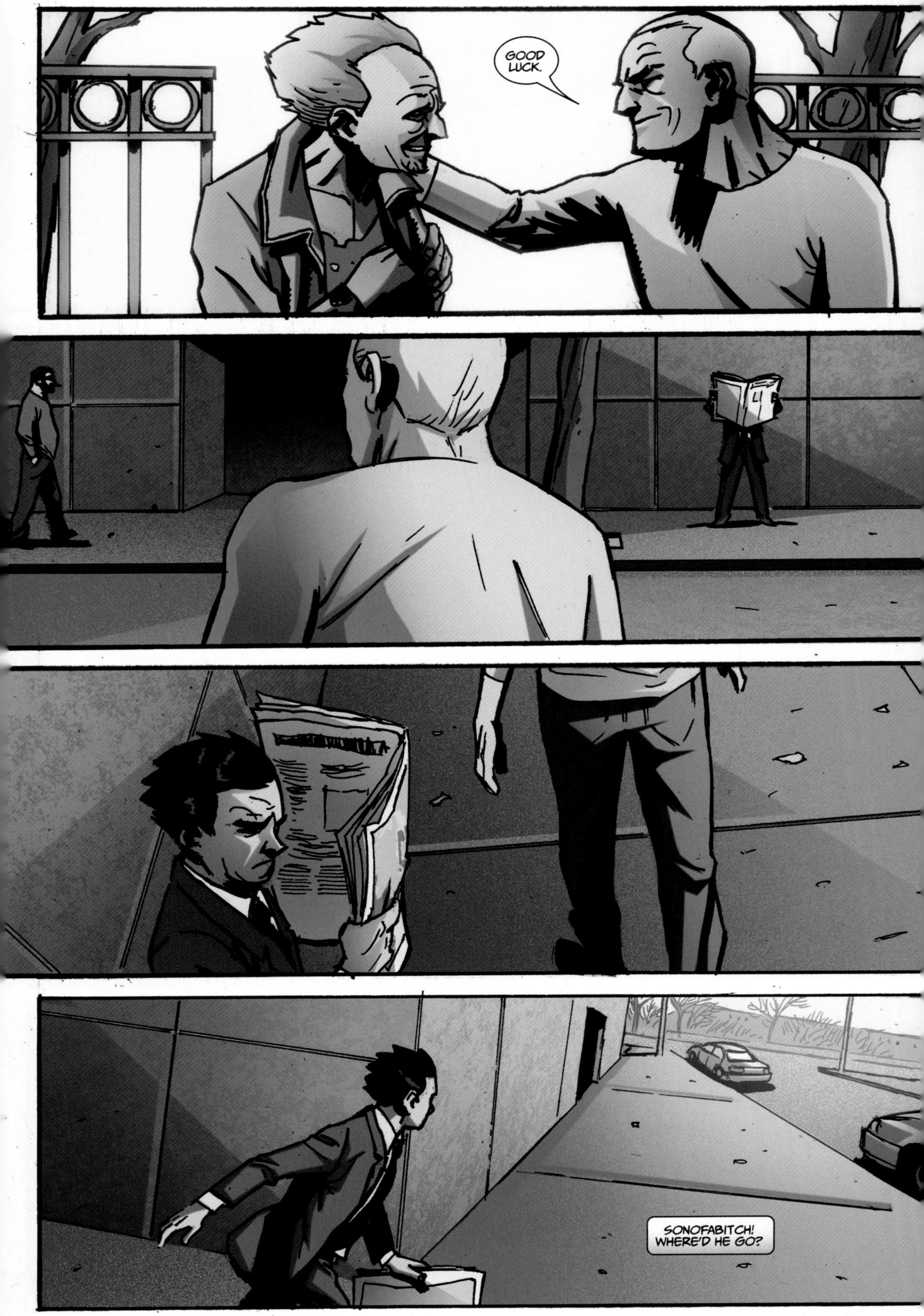
GOOD LUCK.
SONOFABITCH! WHERE'D HE GO?

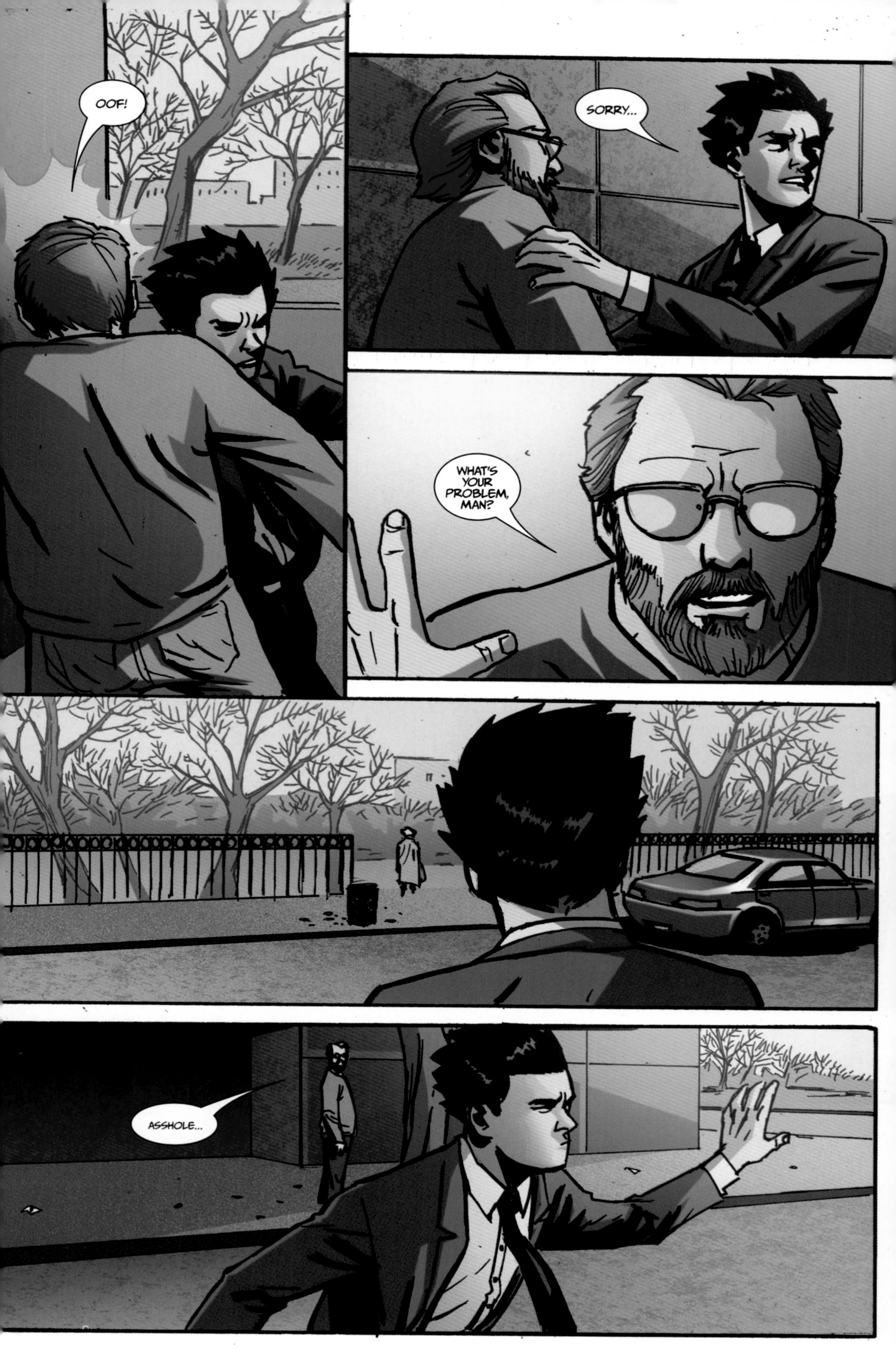
OOF!
SORRY...
WHAT'S YOUR PROBLEM, MAN?
ASSHOLE...

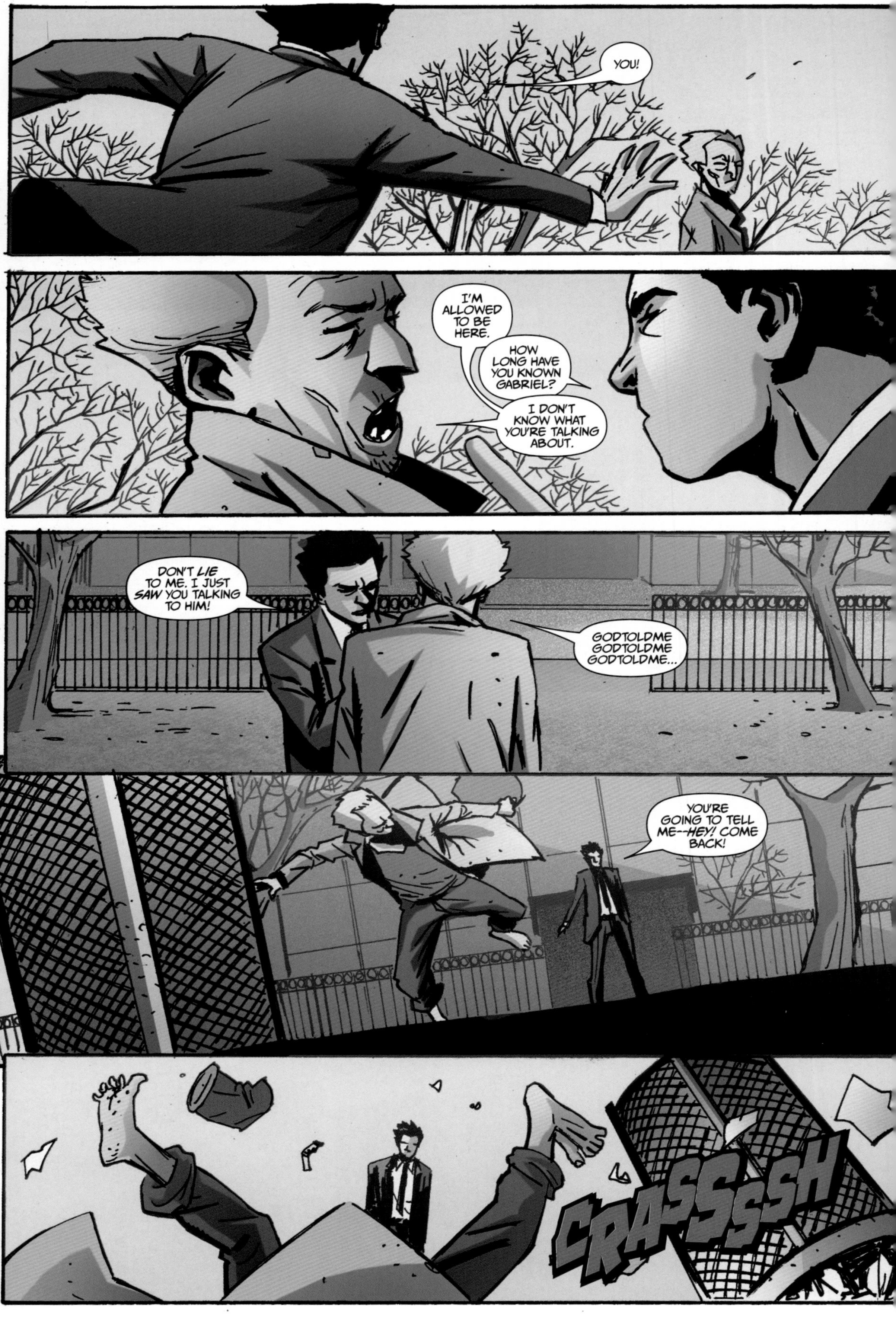
YOU!
I'M ALLOWED TO BE HERE.
HOW LONG HAVE YOU KNOWN GABRIEL?
I DON'T KNOW WHAT YOU'RE TALKING ABOUT.
DON'T *LIE* TO ME. I JUST *SAW* YOU TALKING TO HIM!
GODTOLDME GODTOLDME GODTOLDME...
YOU'RE GOING TO TELL ME--*HEY!* COME BACK!
CRASSSSH

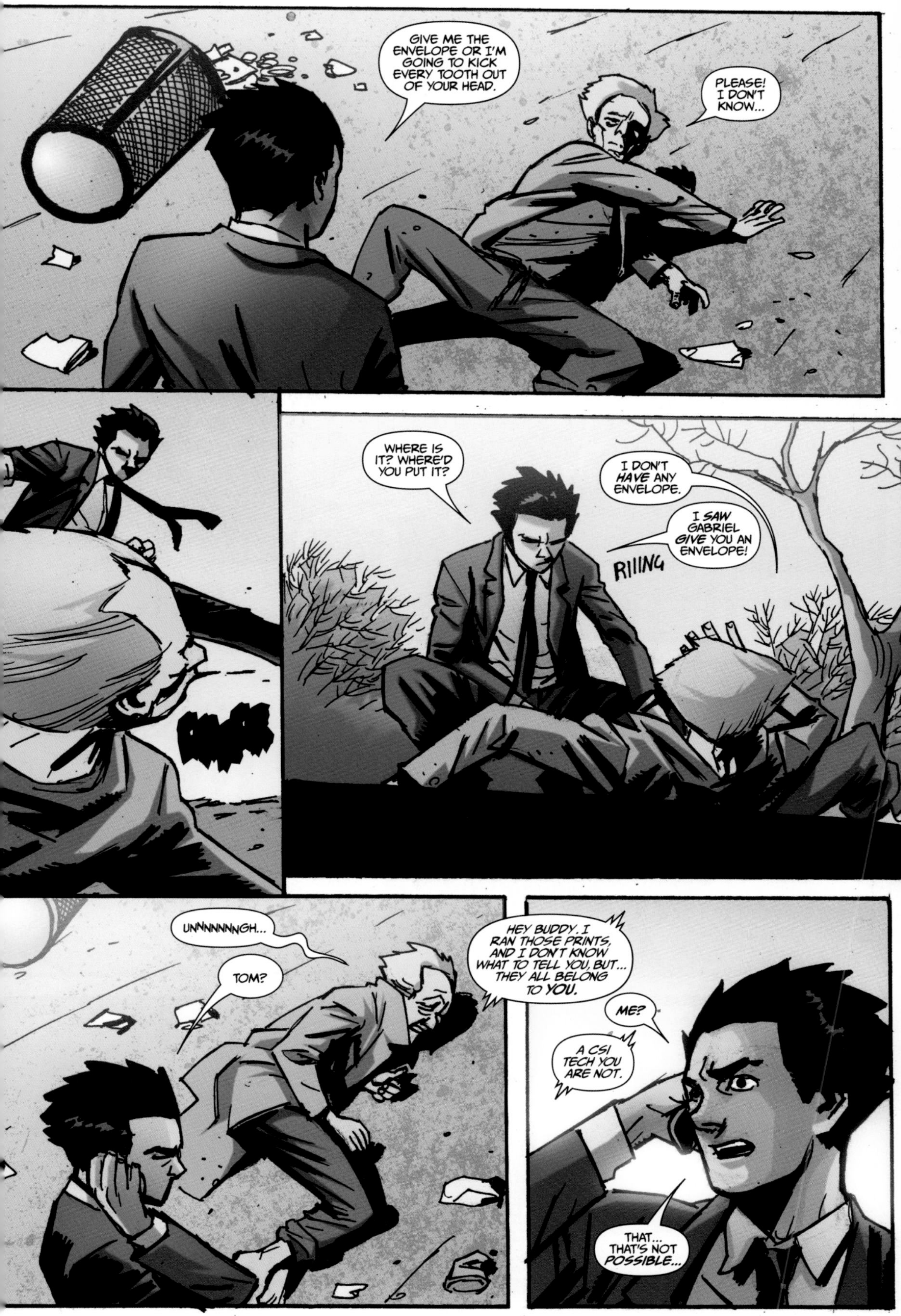
GIVE ME THE ENVELOPE OR I'M GOING TO KICK EVERY TOOTH OUT OF YOUR HEAD.
PLEASE! I DON'T KNOW...
WHERE IS IT? WHERE'D YOU PUT IT?
I DON'T HAVE ANY ENVELOPE.
I SAW GABRIEL GIVE YOU AN ENVELOPE!
RIIING
UNNNNNNNGH...
TOM?
HEY BUDDY. I RAN THOSE PRINTS, AND I DON'T KNOW WHAT TO TELL YOU, BUT... THEY ALL BELONG TO YOU.
ME?
A CSI TECH YOU ARE NOT.
THAT... THAT'S NOT POSSIBLE...

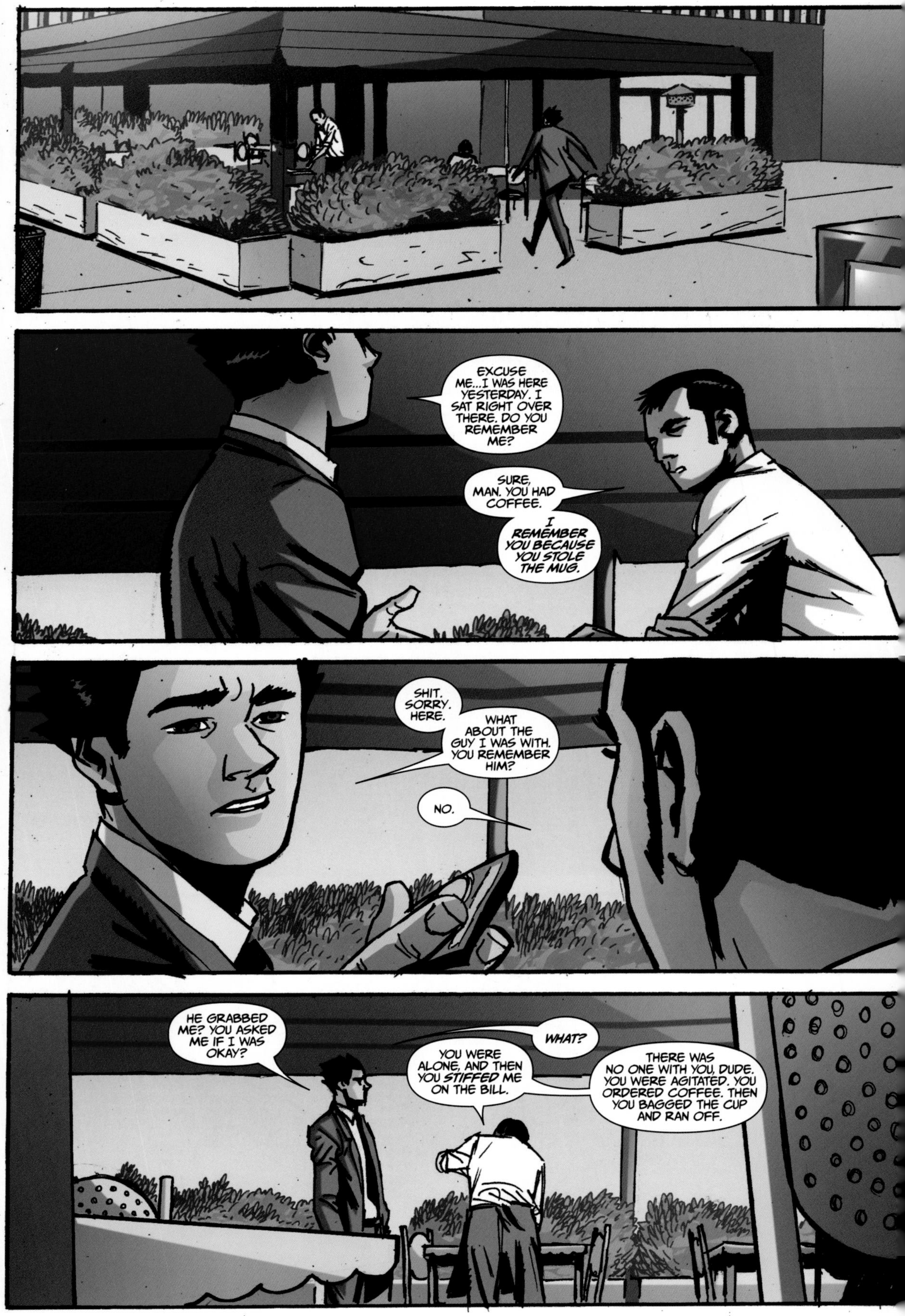
EXCUSE ME...I WAS HERE YESTERDAY. I SAT RIGHT OVER THERE. DO YOU REMEMBER ME?
SURE, MAN. YOU HAD COFFEE.
I *REMEMBER* *YOU BECAUSE* *YOU STOLE* *THE MUG.*
SHIT. SORRY. HERE.
WHAT ABOUT THE GUY I WAS WITH. YOU REMEMBER HIM?
NO.
WHAT?
YOU WERE ALONE, AND THEN YOU *STIFFED* ME ON THE BILL.
THERE WAS NO ONE WITH YOU, DUDE. YOU WERE AGITATED. YOU ORDERED COFFEE. THEN YOU BAGGED THE CUP AND RAN OFF.
HE GRABBED ME? YOU ASKED ME IF I WAS OKAY?

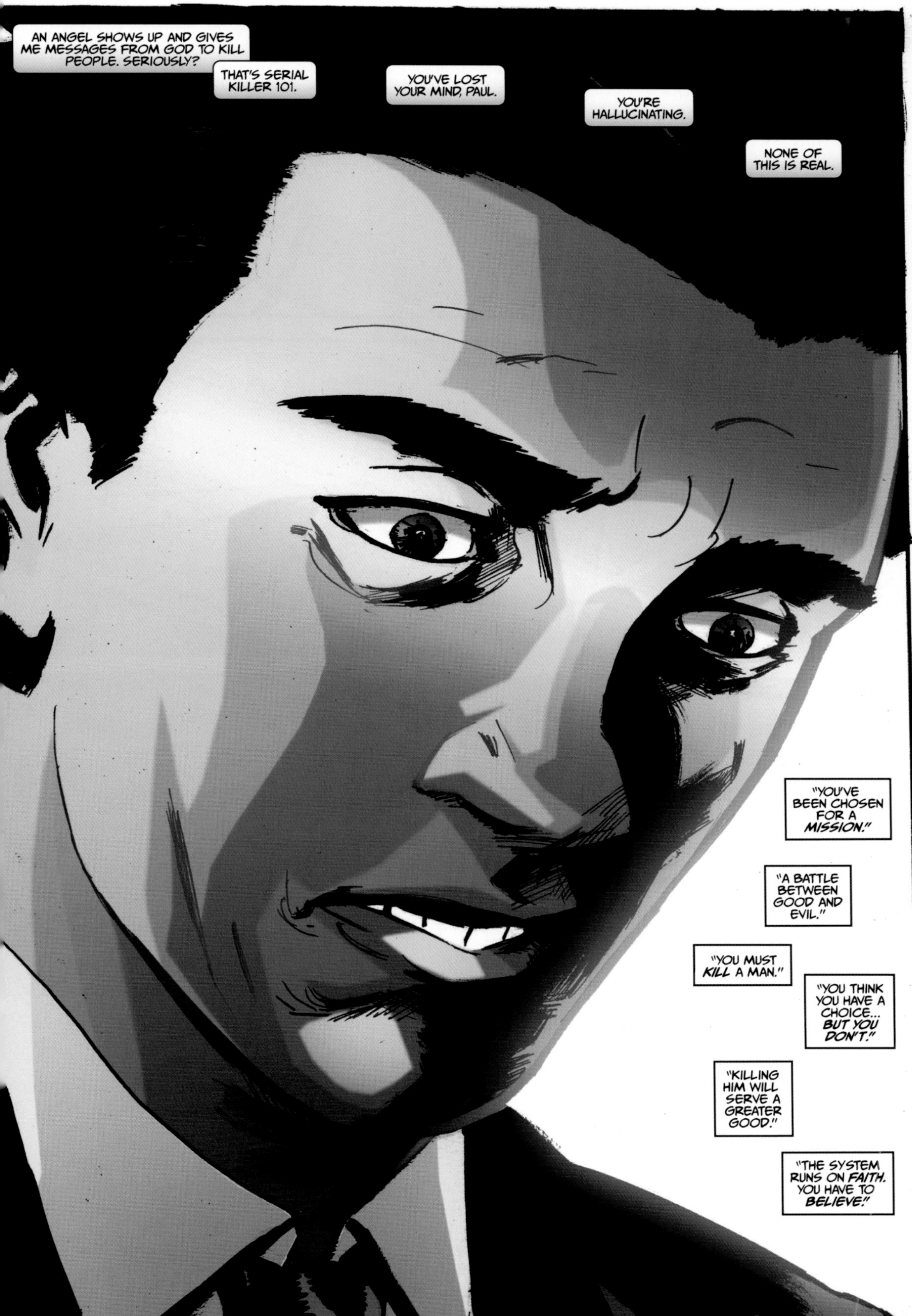
AN ANGEL SHOWS UP AND GIVES ME MESSAGES FROM GOD TO KILL PEOPLE. SERIOUSLY?
THAT'S SERIAL KILLER 101.
YOU'VE LOST YOUR MIND, PAUL.
YOU'RE HALLUCINATING.
NONE OF THIS IS REAL.
"YOU'VE BEEN CHOSEN FOR A *MISSION.*"
"A BATTLE BETWEEN GOOD AND EVIL."
"YOU MUST *KILL* A MAN."
"YOU THINK YOU HAVE A CHOICE... *BUT YOU DON'T.*"
"KILLING HIM WILL SERVE A GREATER GOOD."
"THE SYSTEM RUNS ON *FAITH.* YOU HAVE TO *BELIEVE!*"

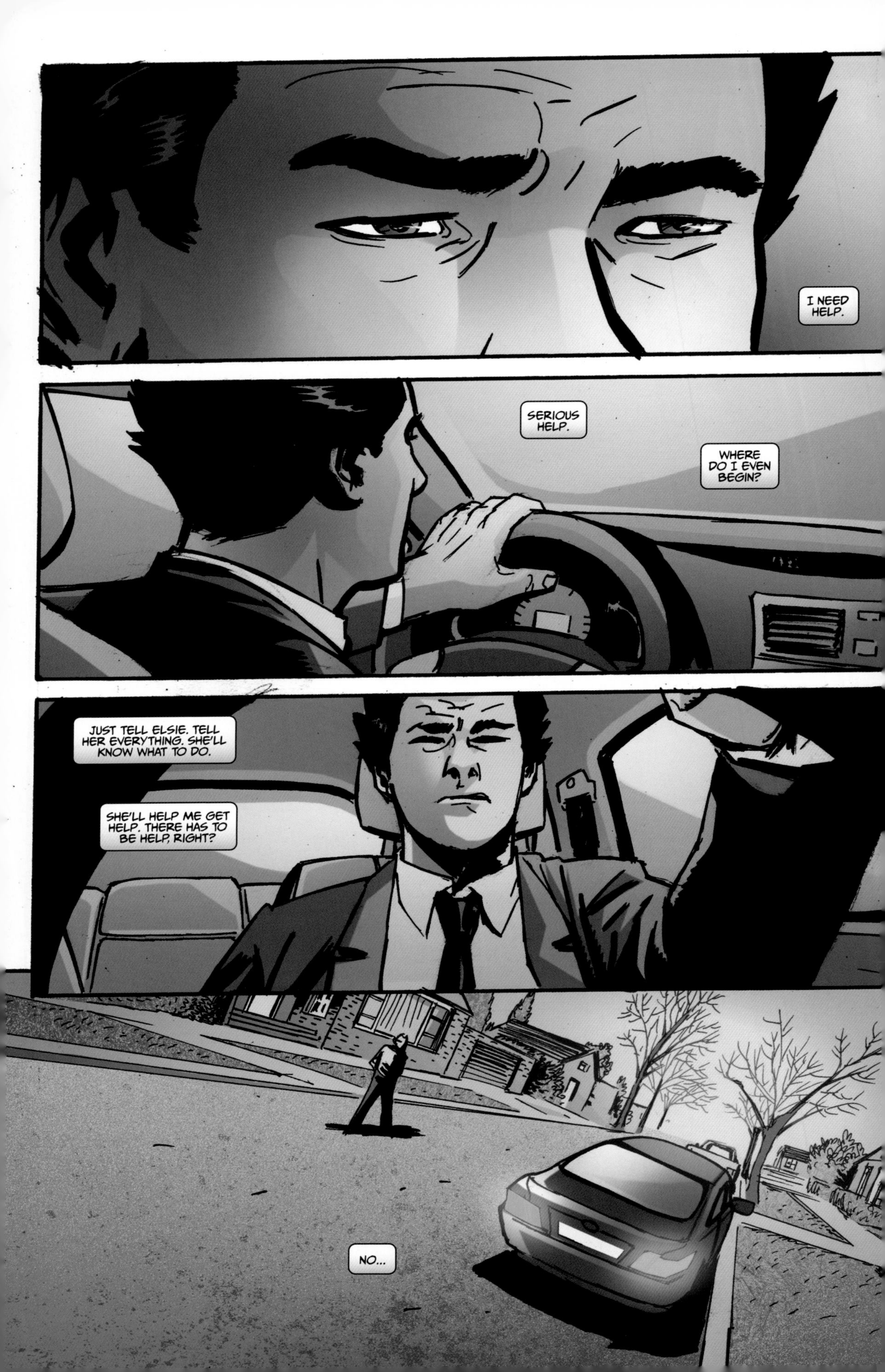
I NEED HELP.
SERIOUS HELP.
WHERE DO I EVEN BEGIN?
JUST TELL ELSIE. TELL HER EVERYTHING. SHE'LL KNOW WHAT TO DO.
SHE'LL HELP ME GET HELP. THERE HAS TO BE HELP, RIGHT?
NO...

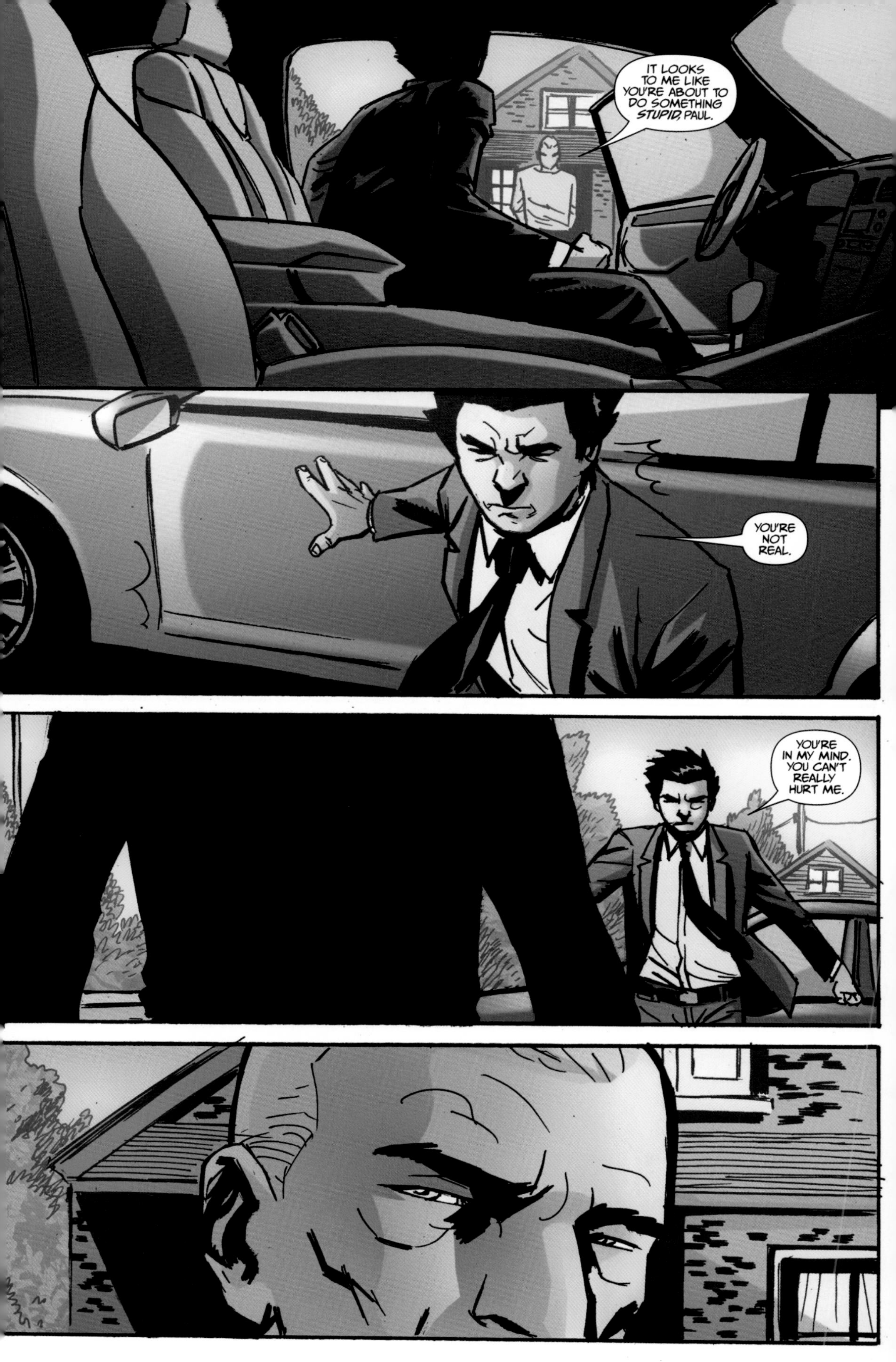
IT LOOKS TO ME LIKE YOU'RE ABOUT TO DO SOMETHING *STUPID*, PAUL.
YOU'RE NOT REAL.
YOU'RE IN MY MIND. YOU CAN'T REALLY HURT ME.

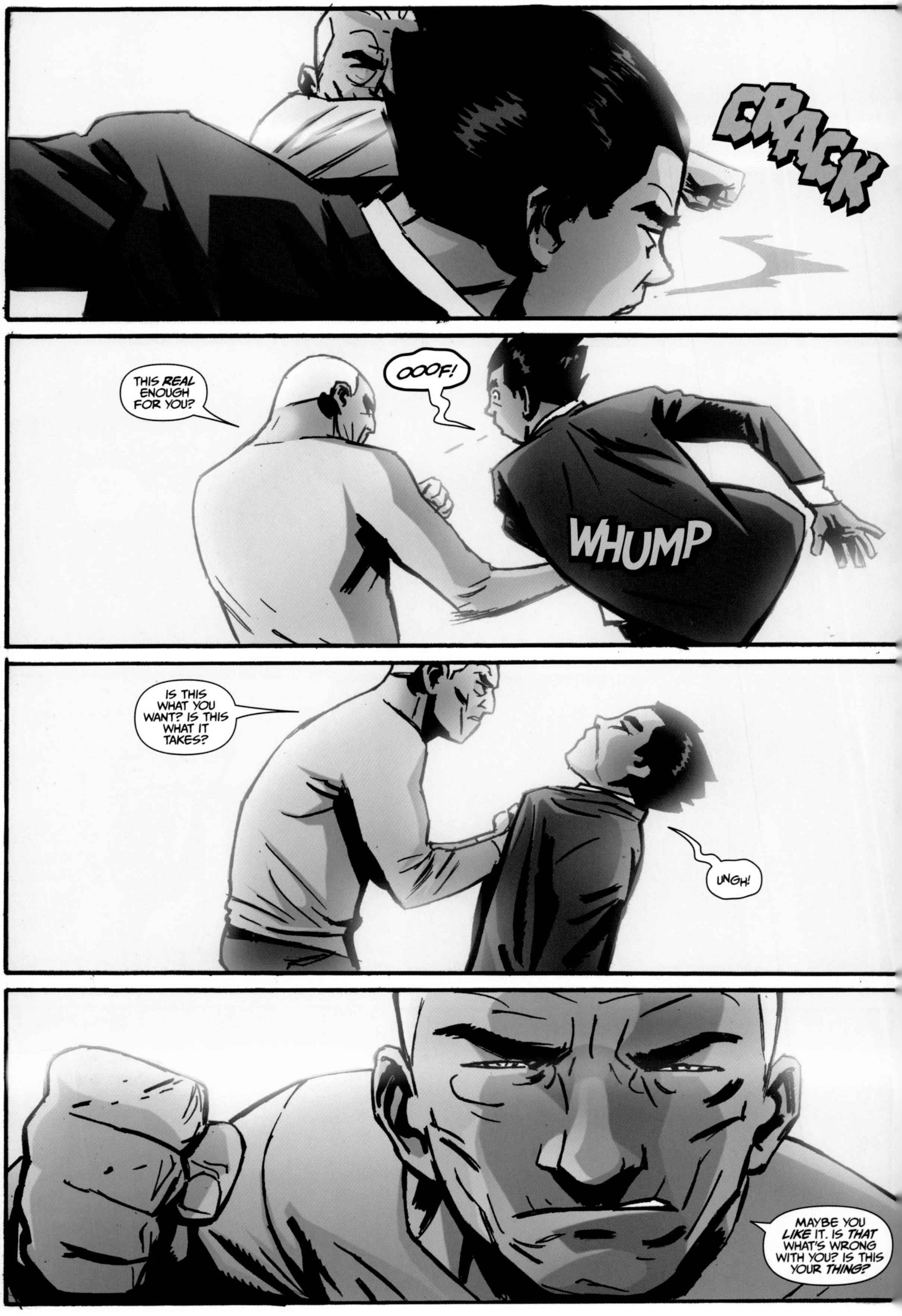
CRACK
THIS REAL ENOUGH FOR YOU?
OOOF!
WHUMP
IS THIS WHAT YOU WANT? IS THIS WHAT IT TAKES?
UNGH!
MAYBE YOU LIKE IT. IS THAT WHAT'S WRONG WITH YOU? IS THIS YOUR THING?

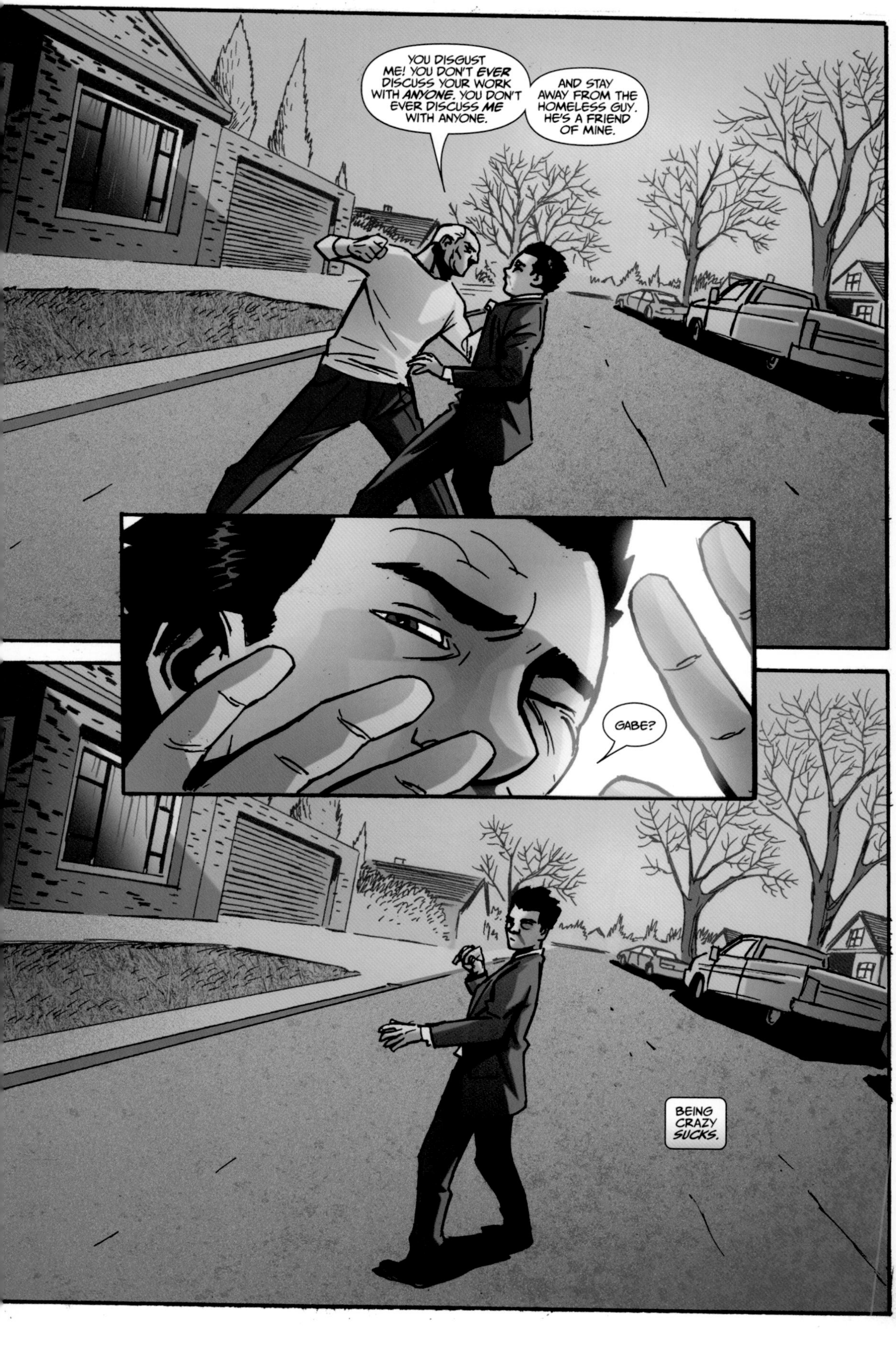
YOU DISGUST ME! YOU DON'T *EVER* DISCUSS YOUR WORK WITH *ANYONE*. YOU DON'T EVER DISCUSS *ME* WITH ANYONE.
AND STAY AWAY FROM THE HOMELESS GUY. HE'S A FRIEND OF MINE.
GABE?
BEING CRAZY *SUCKS*.

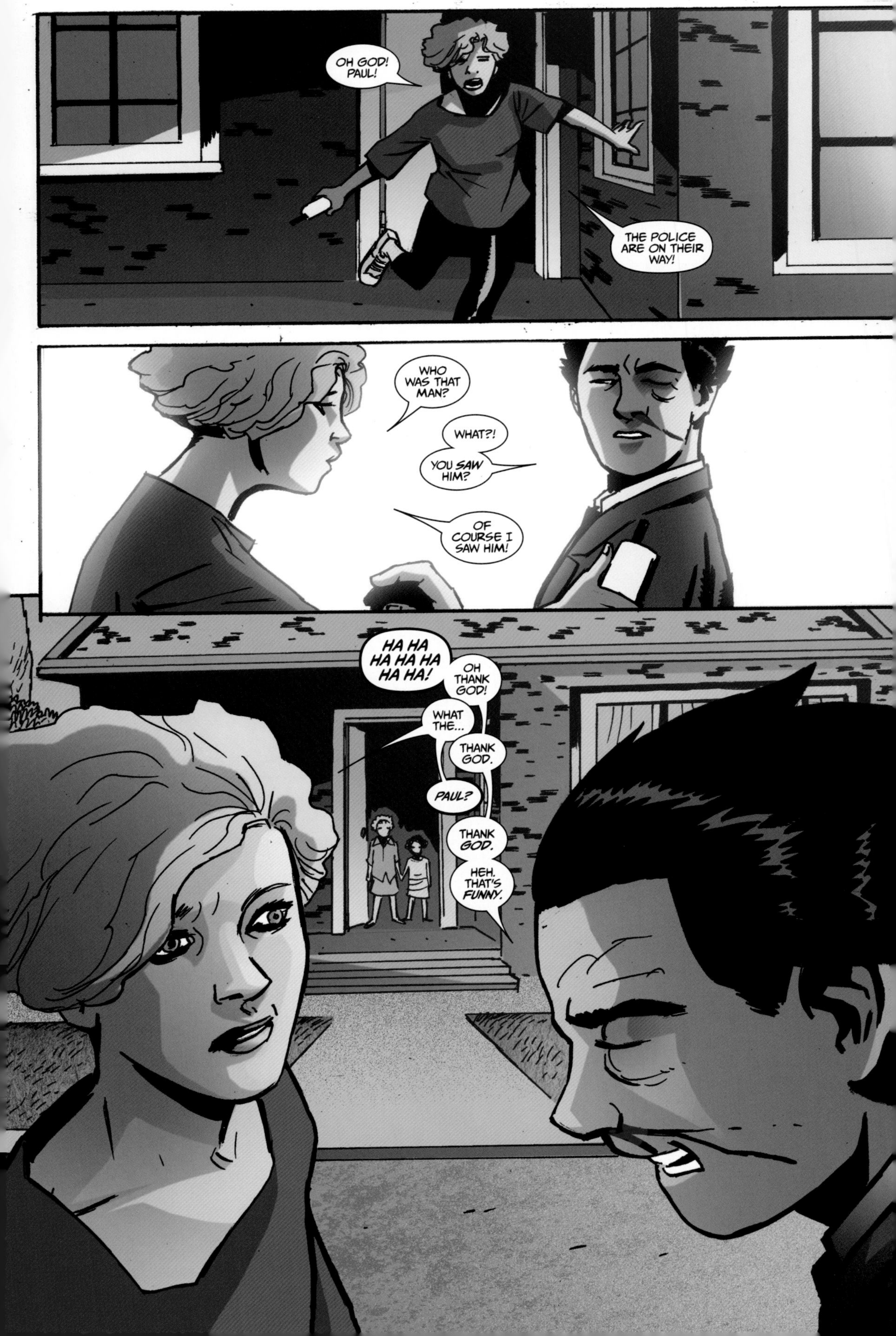
OH GOD! PAUL!
THE POLICE ARE ON THEIR WAY!
WHO WAS THAT MAN?
WHAT?!
YOU *SAW* HIM?
OF COURSE I SAW HIM!
HA HA HA HA HA HA HA!
OH THANK GOD!
WHAT THE...
THANK GOD.
PAUL?
THANK *GOD.*
HEH. THAT'S *FUNNY.*

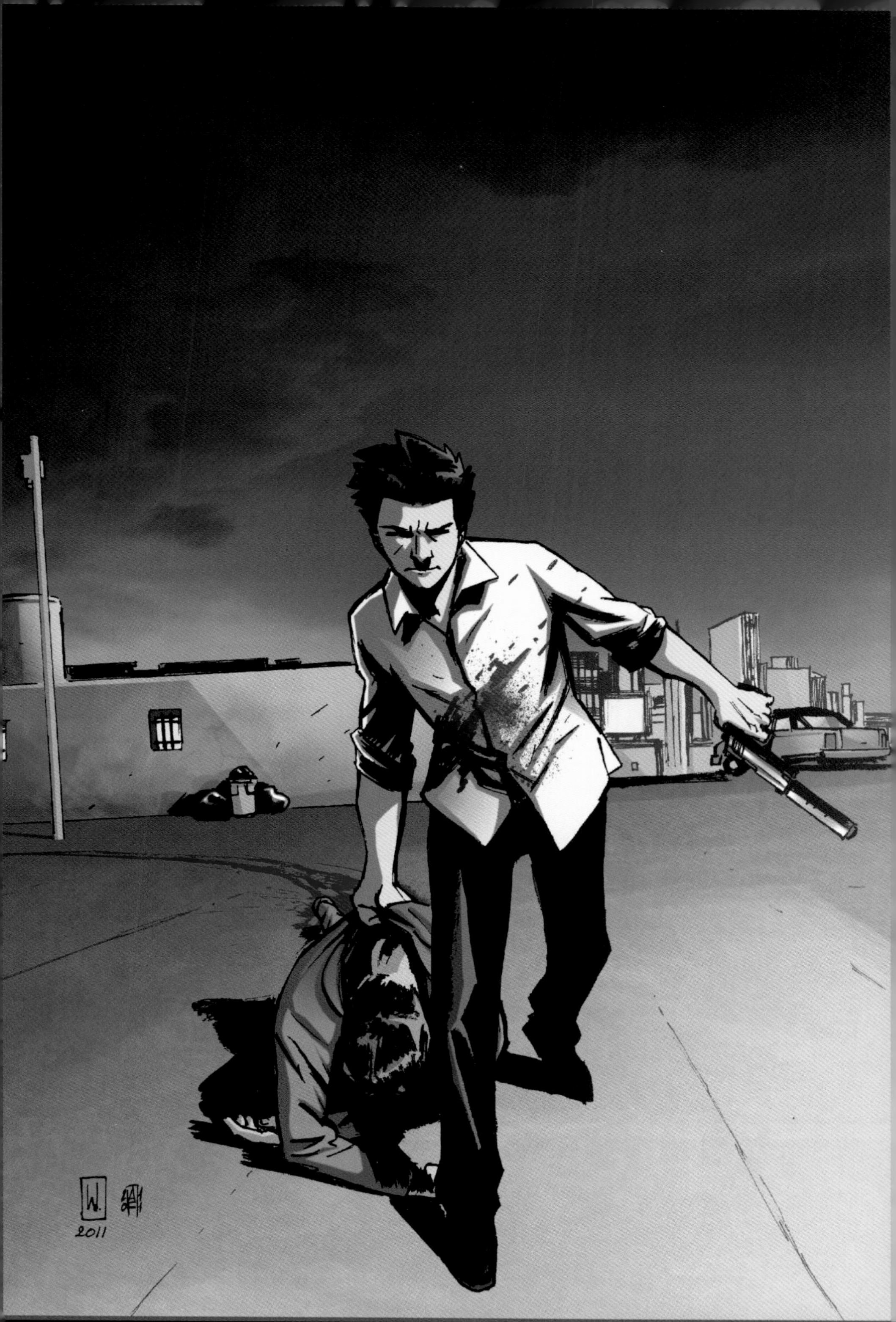
2011

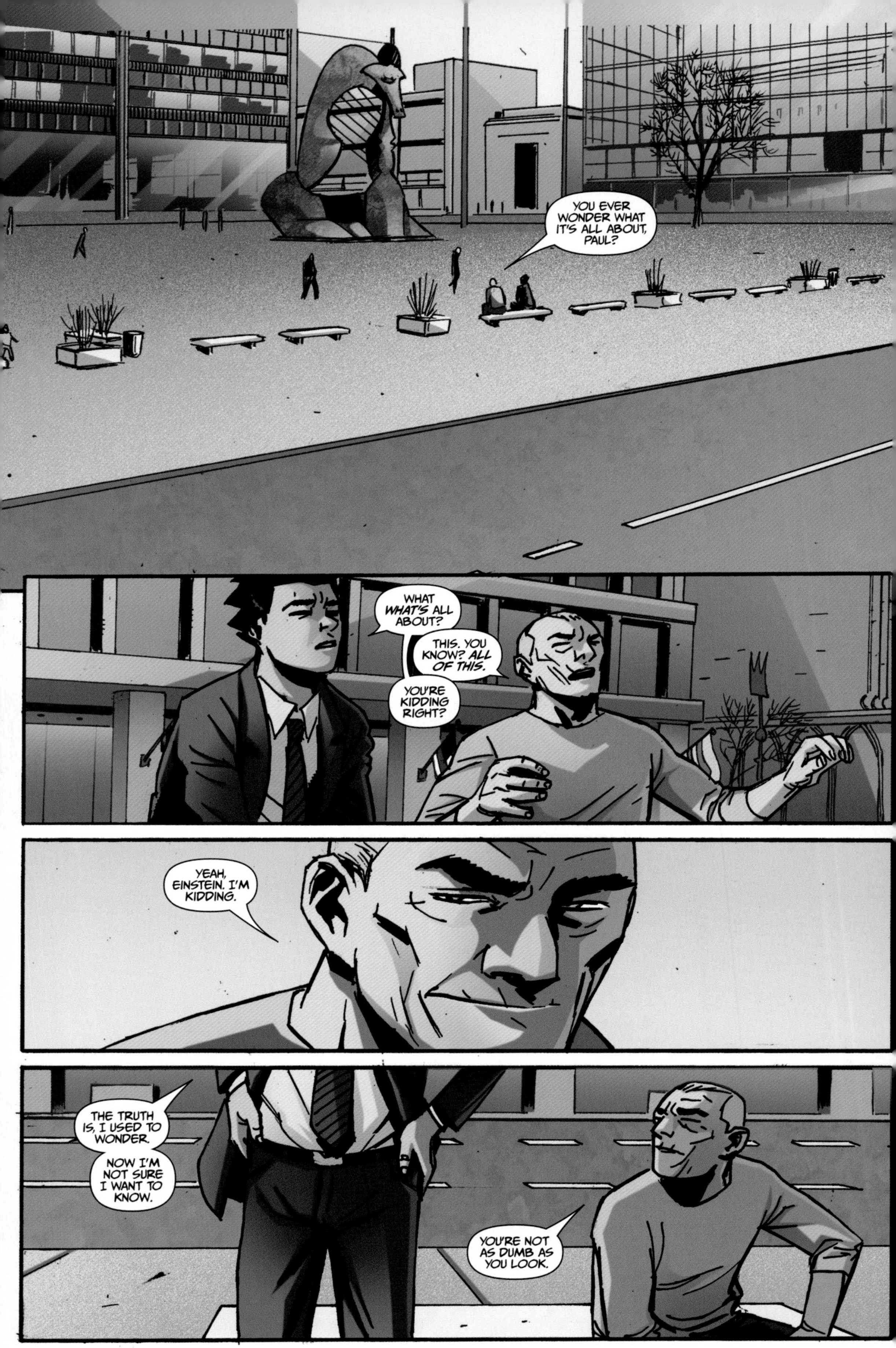
YOU EVER WONDER WHAT IT'S ALL ABOUT, PAUL?
WHAT *WHAT'S* ALL ABOUT?
THIS. YOU KNOW? *ALL OF THIS.*
YOU'RE KIDDING RIGHT?
YEAH, EINSTEIN. I'M KIDDING.
THE TRUTH IS, I USED TO WONDER.
NOW I'M NOT SURE I WANT TO KNOW.
YOU'RE NOT AS DUMB AS YOU LOOK.

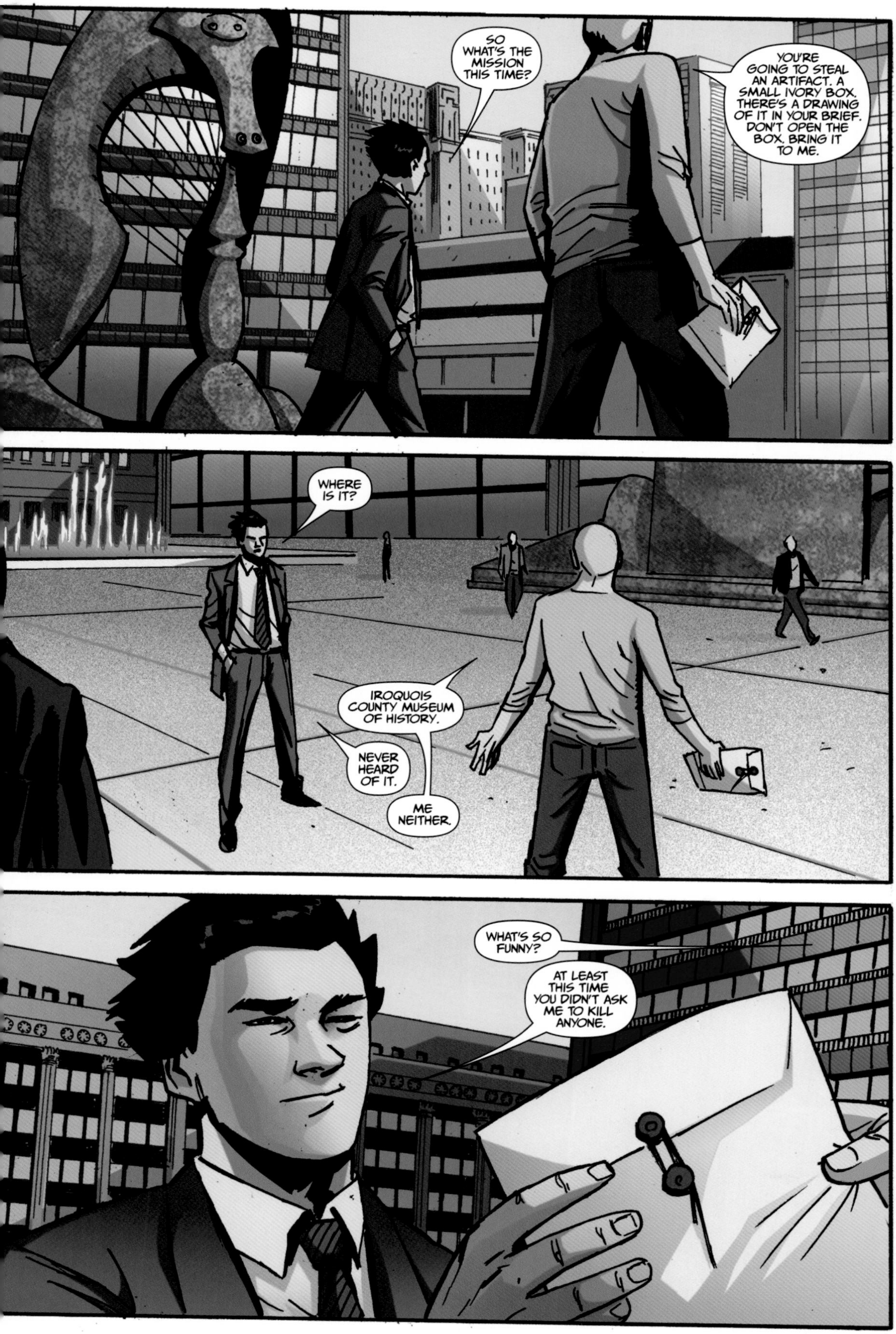
SO WHAT'S THE MISSION THIS TIME?
YOU'RE GOING TO STEAL AN ARTIFACT. A SMALL IVORY BOX. THERE'S A DRAWING OF IT IN YOUR BRIEF. DON'T OPEN THE BOX. BRING IT TO ME.
WHERE IS IT?
IROQUOIS COUNTY MUSEUM OF HISTORY.
NEVER HEARD OF IT.
ME NEITHER.
WHAT'S SO FUNNY?
AT LEAST THIS TIME YOU DIDN'T ASK ME TO KILL ANYONE.

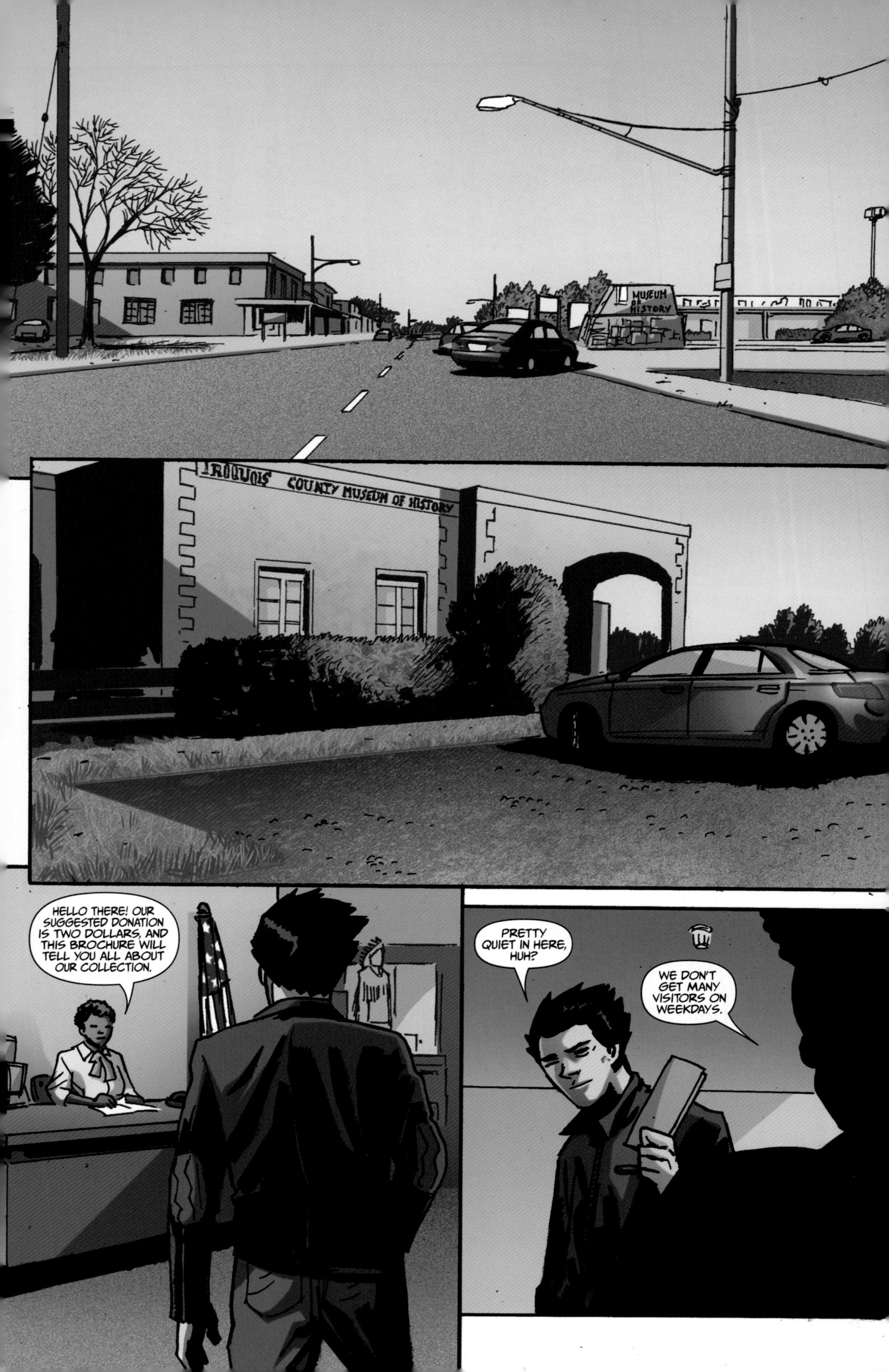
MUSEUM OF HISTORY
COUNTY MUSEUM OF HISTORY
HELLO THERE! OUR SUGGESTED DONATION IS TWO DOLLARS, AND THIS BROCHURE WILL TELL YOU ALL ABOUT OUR COLLECTION.
PRETTY QUIET IN HERE, HUH?
WE DON'T GET MANY VISITORS ON WEEKDAYS.

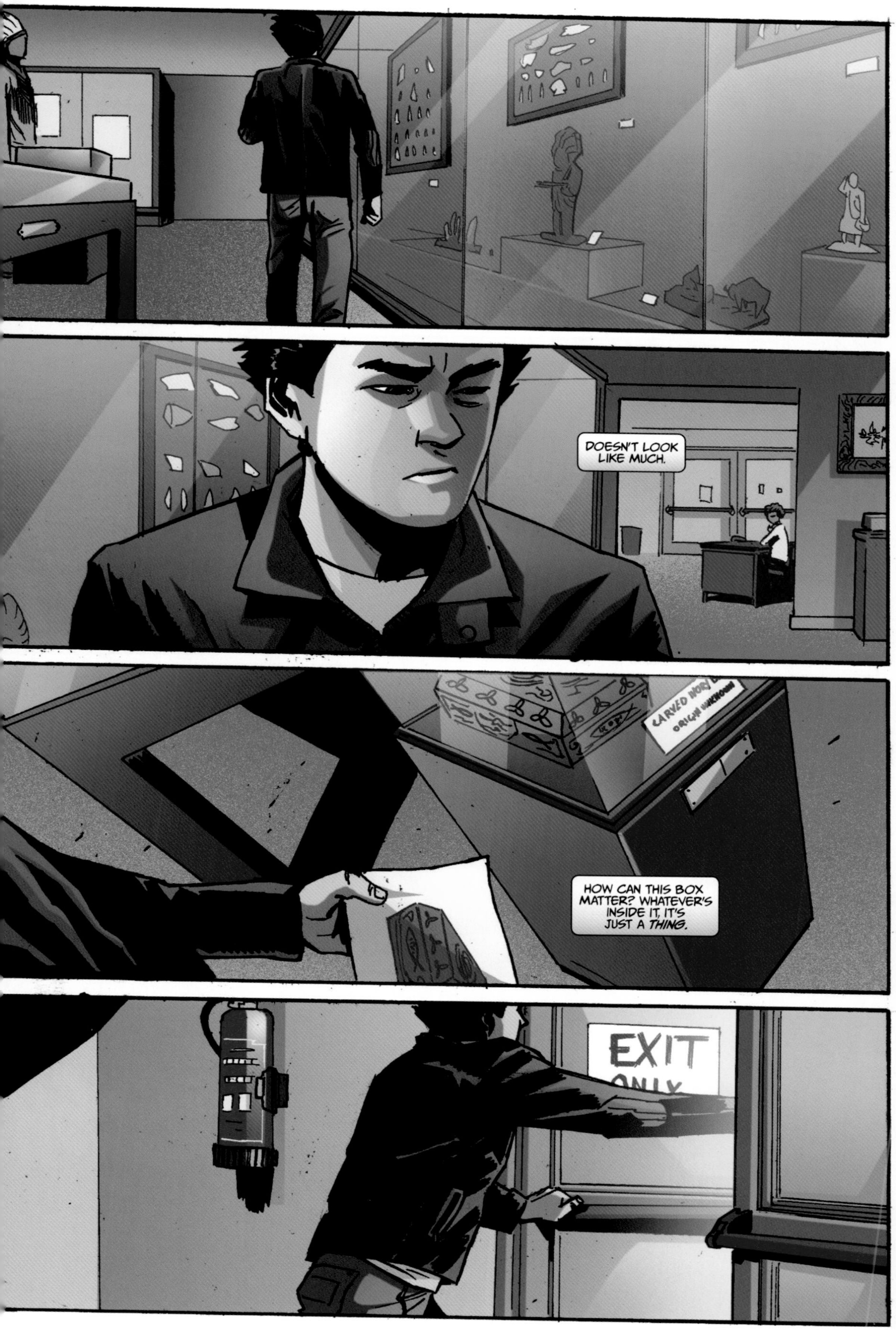
DOESN'T LOOK LIKE MUCH.
HOW CAN THIS BOX MATTER? WHATEVER'S INSIDE IT, IT'S JUST A *THING*.
EXIT

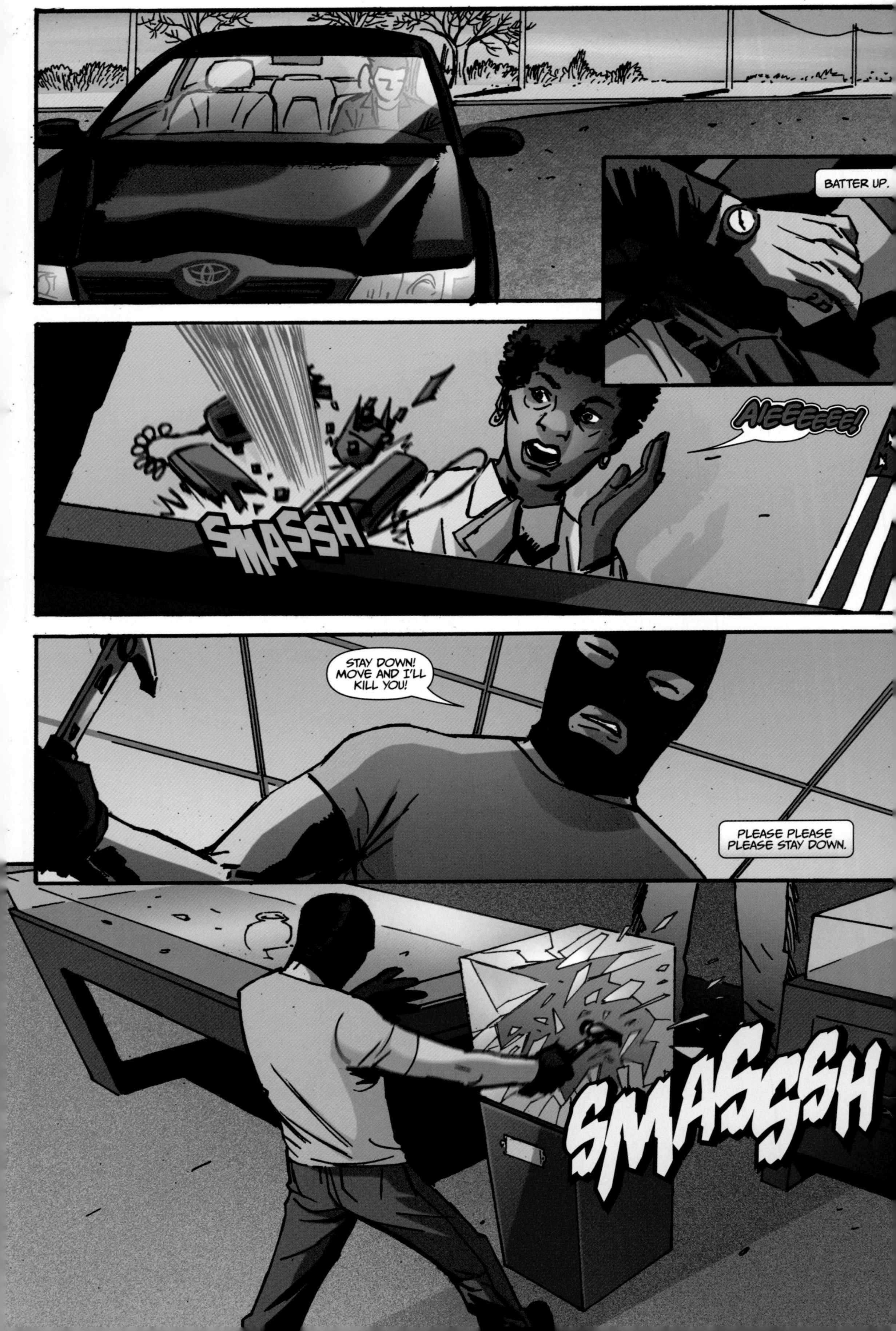
BATTER UP.
AIEEEEEEE!
SMASSH
STAY DOWN! MOVE AND I'LL KILL YOU!
PLEASE PLEASE PLEASE STAY DOWN.
SMASSSH

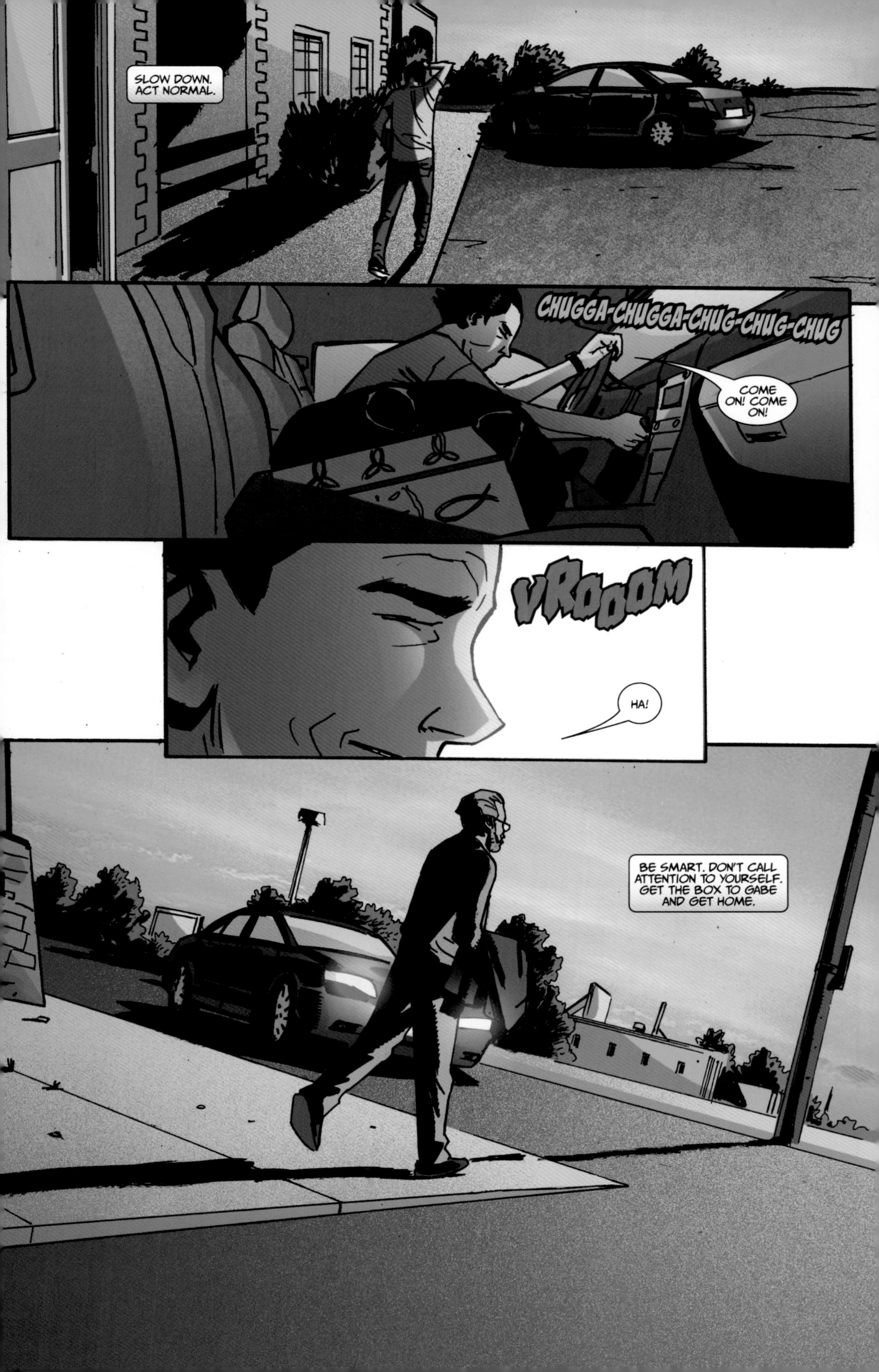

SLOW DOWN. ACT NORMAL.
CHUGGA-CHUGGA-CHUG-CHUG-CHUG
COME ON! COME ON!
VROOOM
HA!
BE SMART. DON'T CALL ATTENTION TO YOURSELF. GET THE BOX TO GABE AND GET HOME.

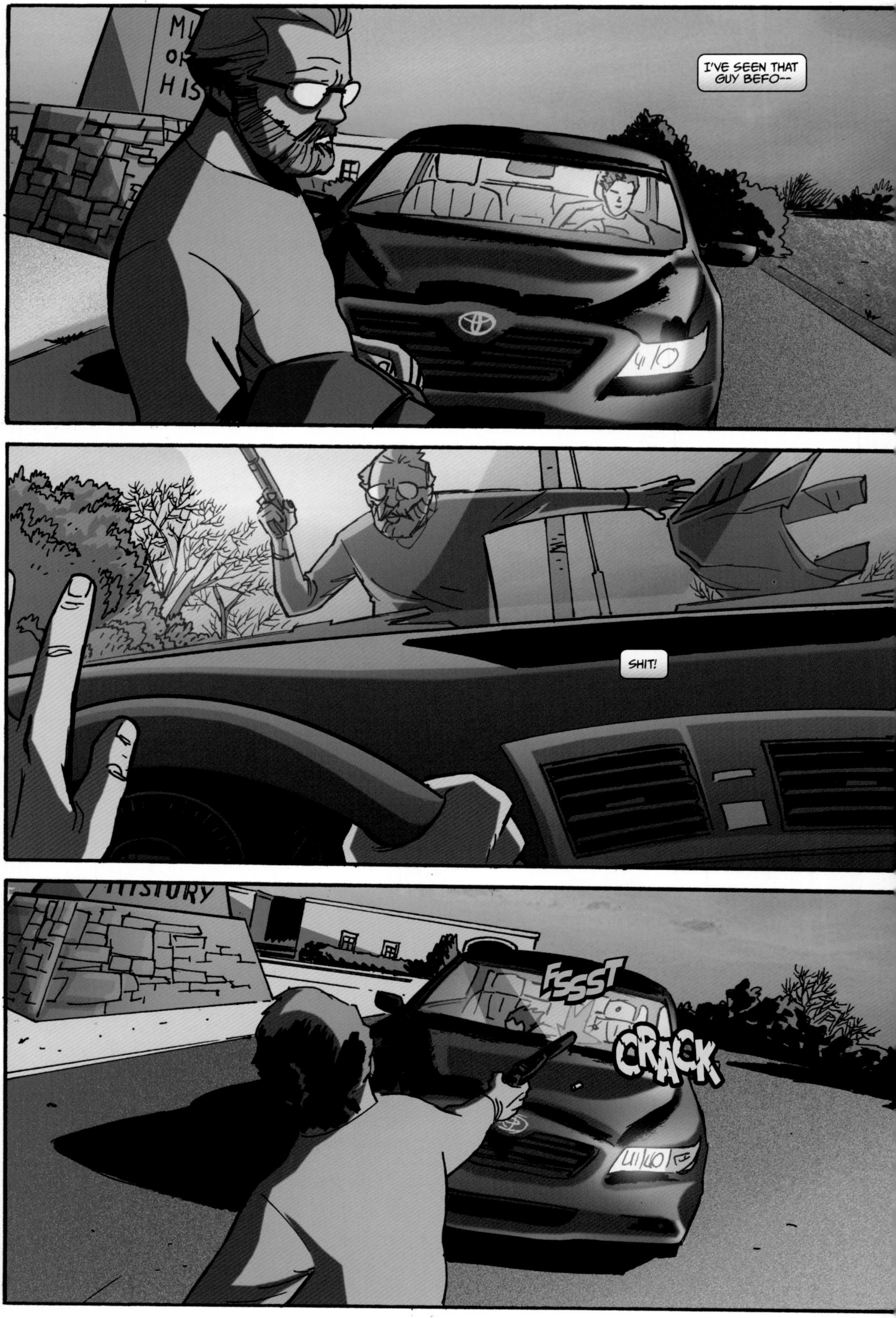
I'VE SEEN THAT GUY BEFO--
SHIT!
FSSST
CRACK

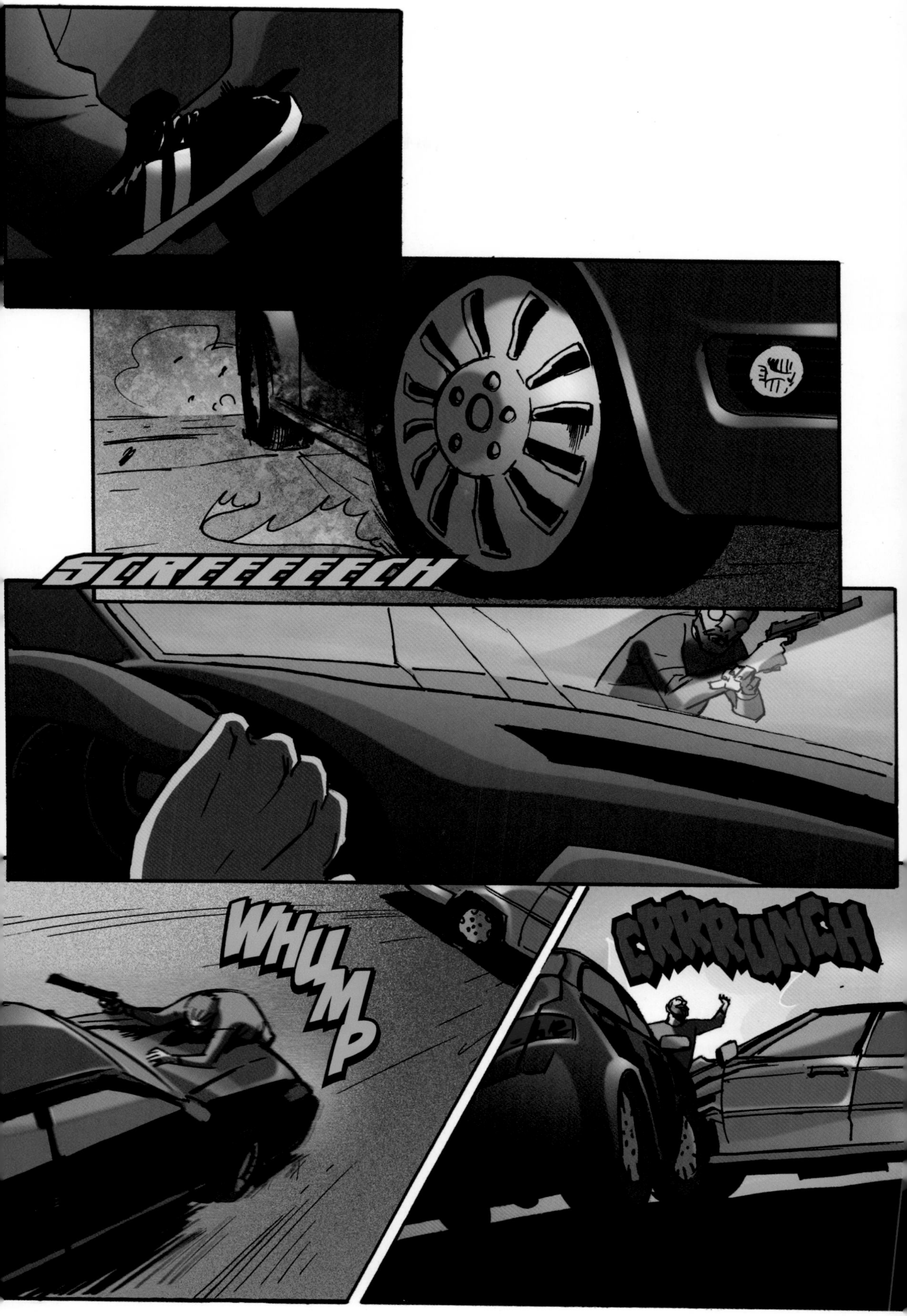
SCREEEEEEECH
WHUMP
CRRRUNCH

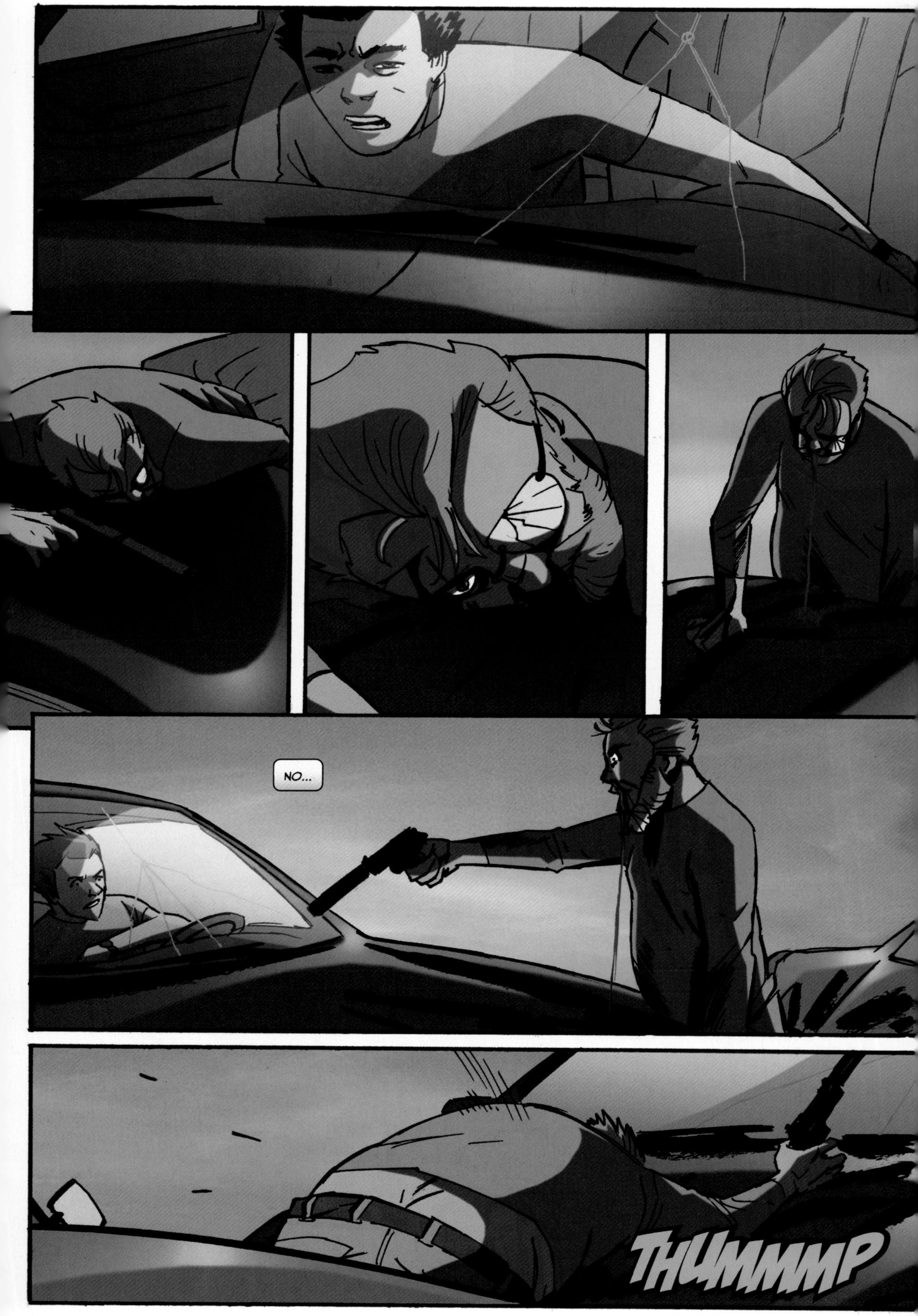
NO...
THUMMMP

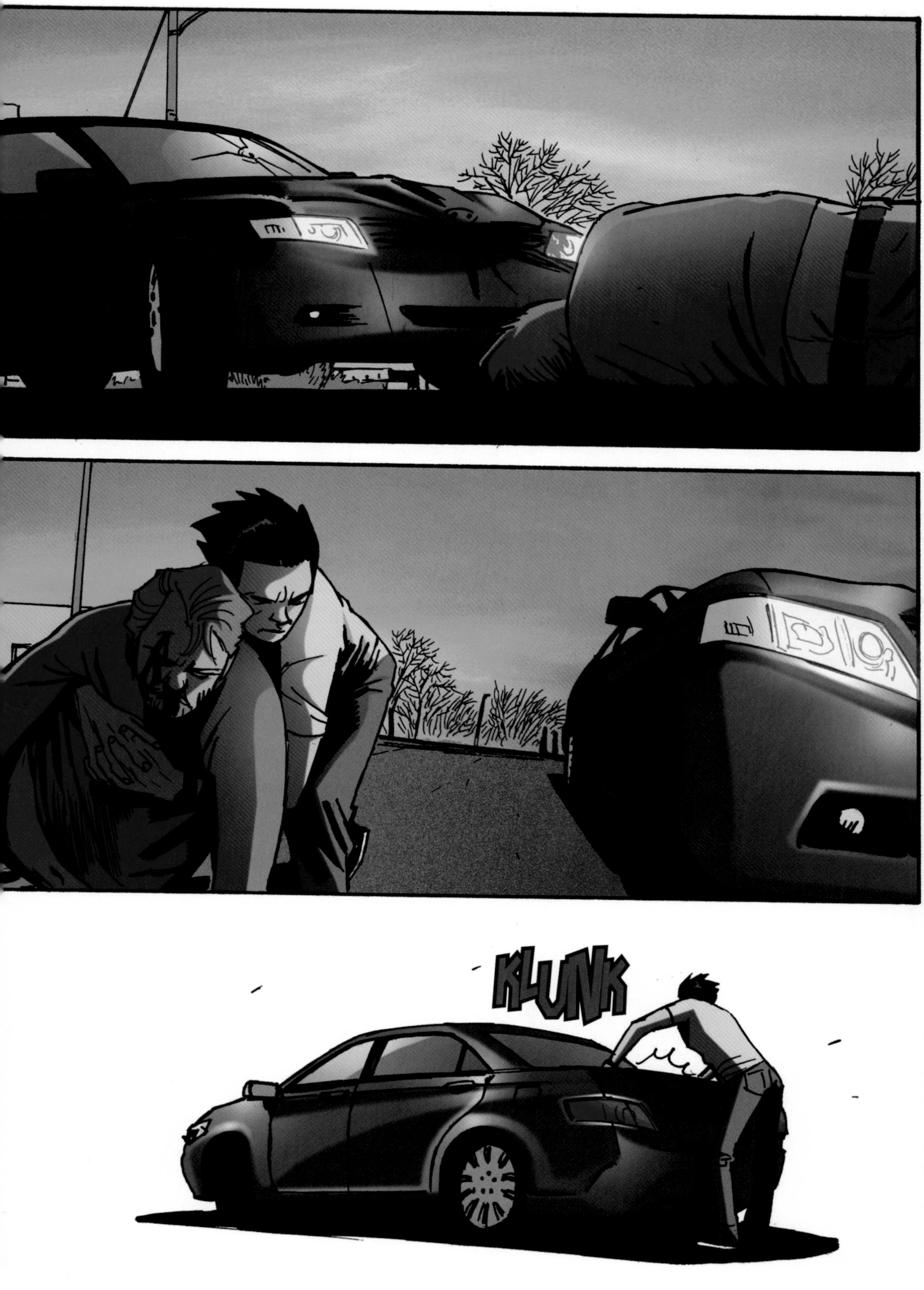
KLUNK

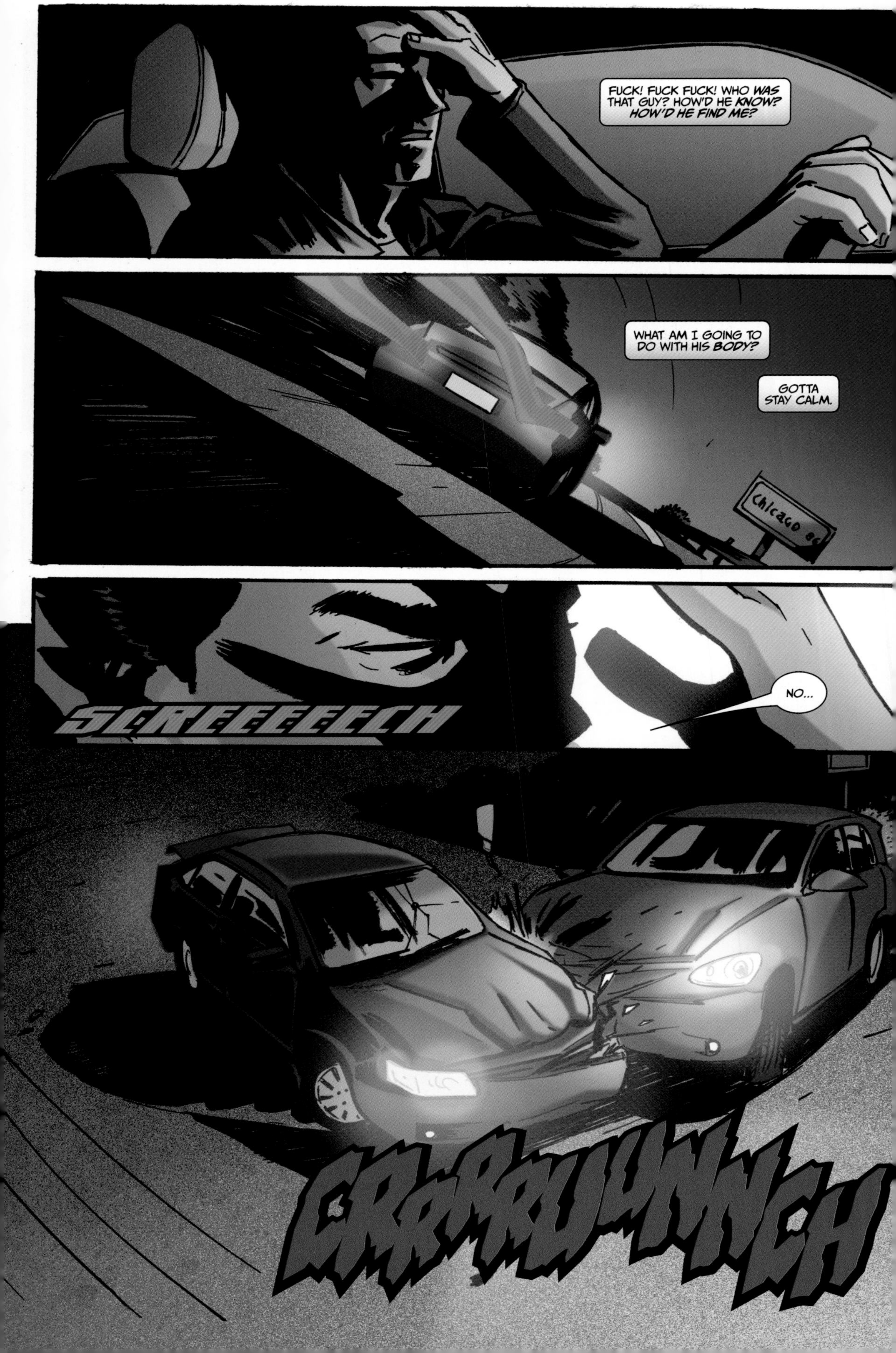
FUCK! FUCK FUCK! WHO WAS THAT GUY? HOW'D HE KNOW? HOW'D HE FIND ME?
WHAT AM I GOING TO DO WITH HIS BODY?
GOTTA STAY CALM.
CHICAGO 86
SCREEEEEECH
NO...
CRRRUUNNCH

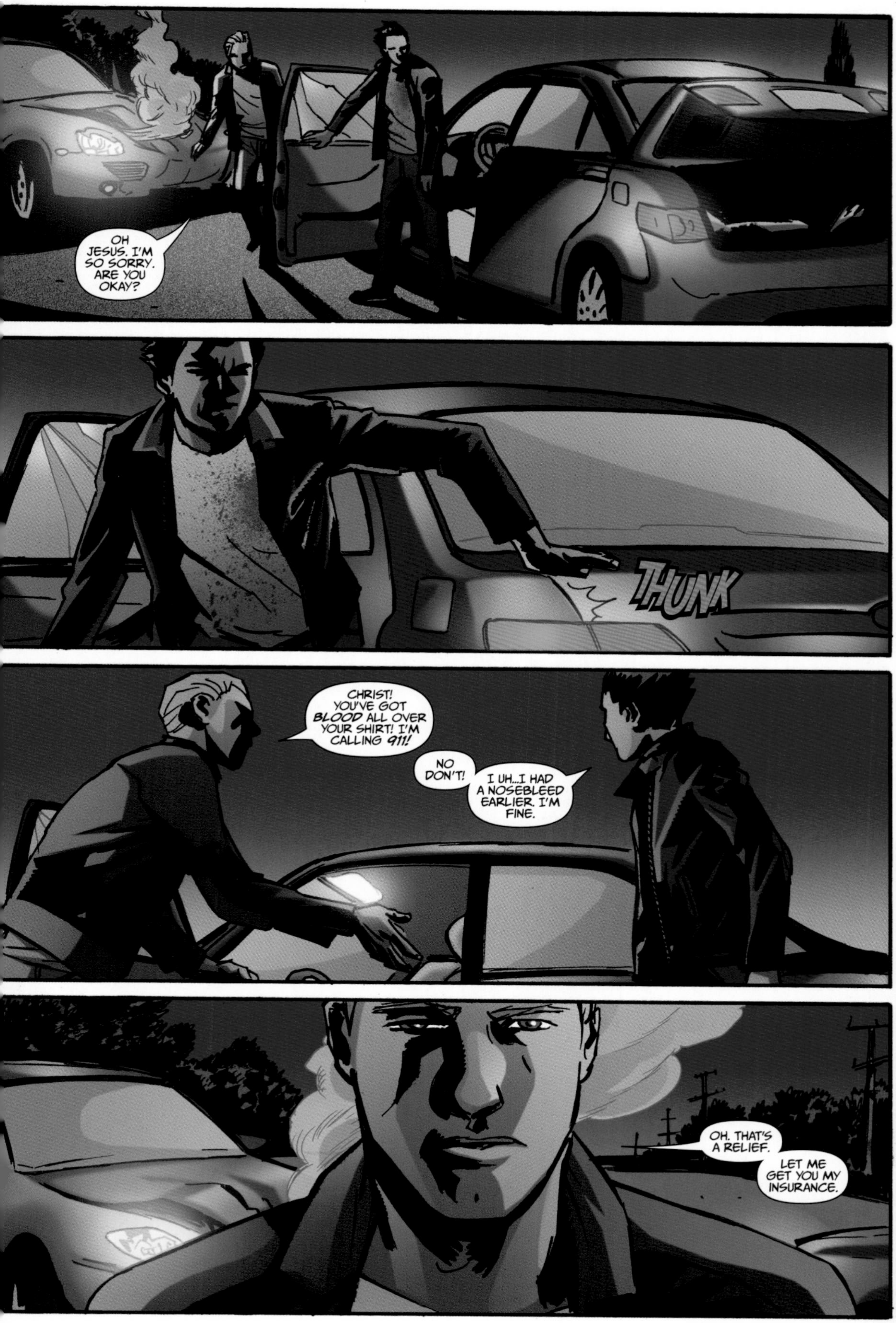
OH JESUS. I'M SO SORRY. ARE YOU OKAY?
THUNK
CHRIST! YOU'VE GOT BLOOD ALL OVER YOUR SHIRT! I'M CALLING 911!
NO DON'T!
I UH...I HAD A NOSEBLEED EARLIER. I'M FINE.
OH. THAT'S A RELIEF.
LET ME GET YOU MY INSURANCE.

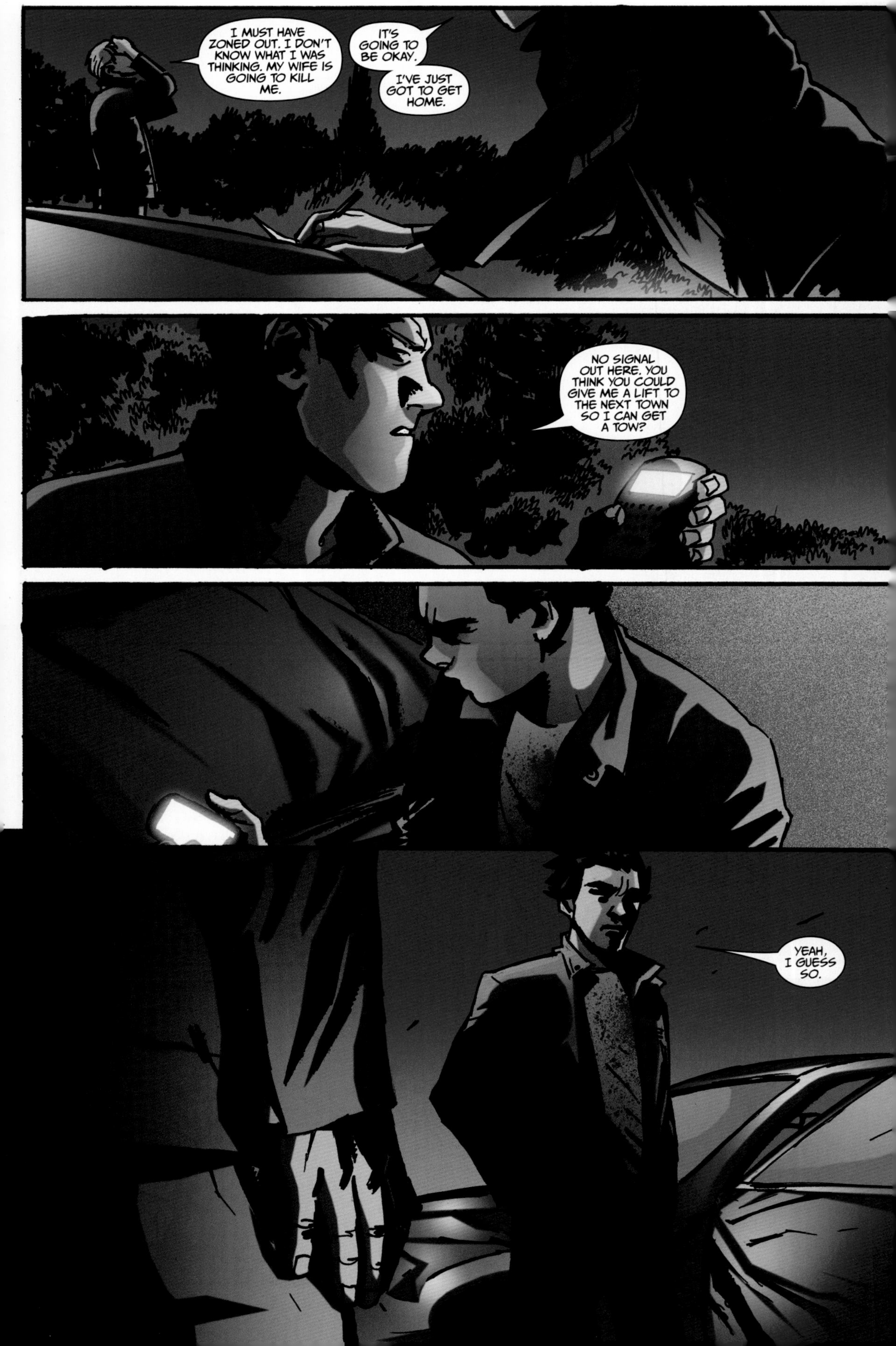
I MUST HAVE ZONED OUT. I DON'T KNOW WHAT I WAS THINKING. MY WIFE IS GOING TO KILL ME.
IT'S GOING TO BE OKAY.
I'VE JUST GOT TO GET HOME.
NO SIGNAL OUT HERE. YOU THINK YOU COULD GIVE ME A LIFT TO THE NEXT TOWN SO I CAN GET A TOW?
YEAH, I GUESS SO.

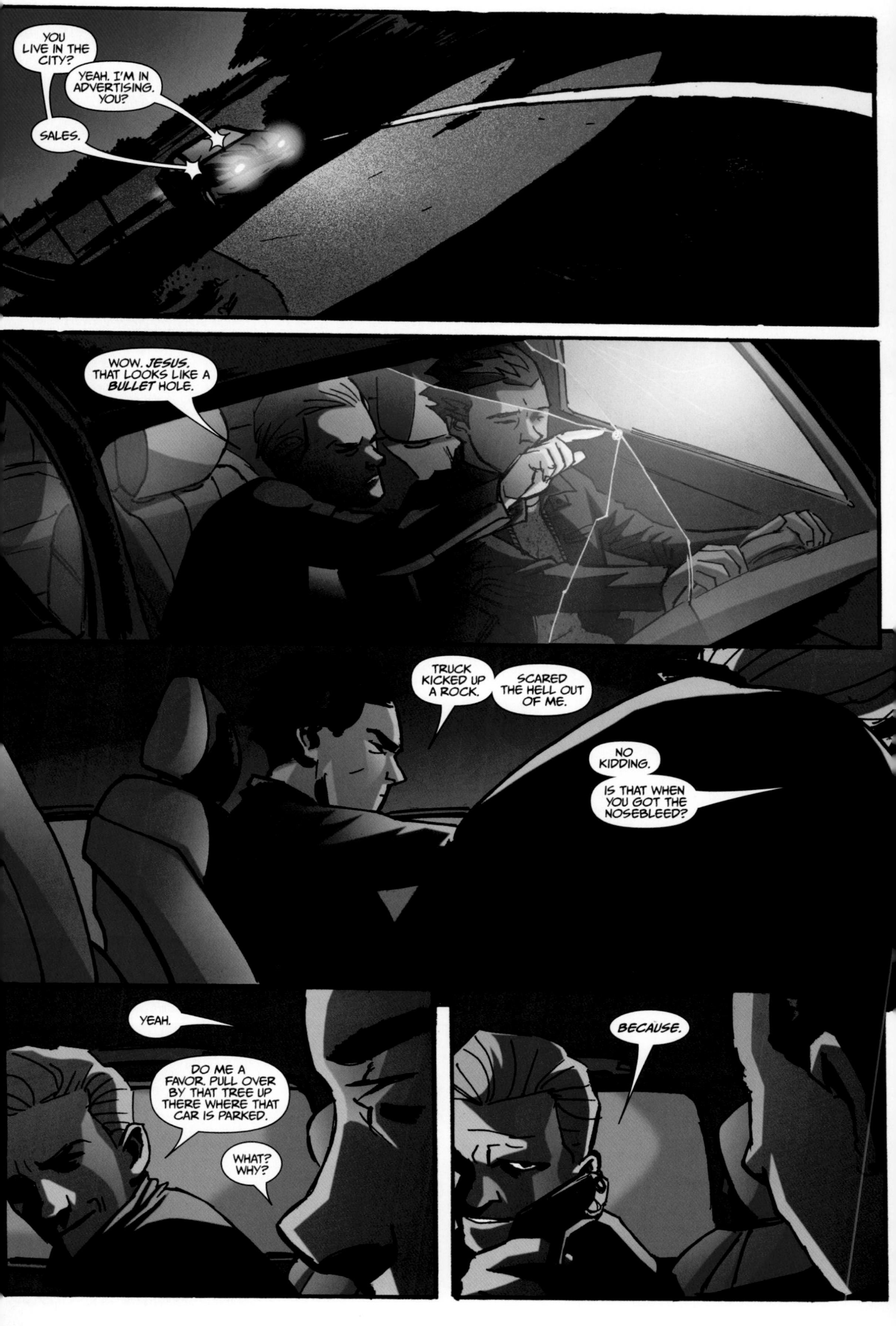
YOU LIVE IN THE CITY?
YEAH. I'M IN ADVERTISING. YOU?
SALES.
WOW. JESUS. THAT LOOKS LIKE A BULLET HOLE.
TRUCK KICKED UP A ROCK.
SCARED THE HELL OUT OF ME.
NO KIDDING.
IS THAT WHEN YOU GOT THE NOSEBLEED?
YEAH.
DO ME A FAVOR. PULL OVER BY THAT TREE UP THERE WHERE THAT CAR IS PARKED.
WHAT? WHY?
BECAUSE.

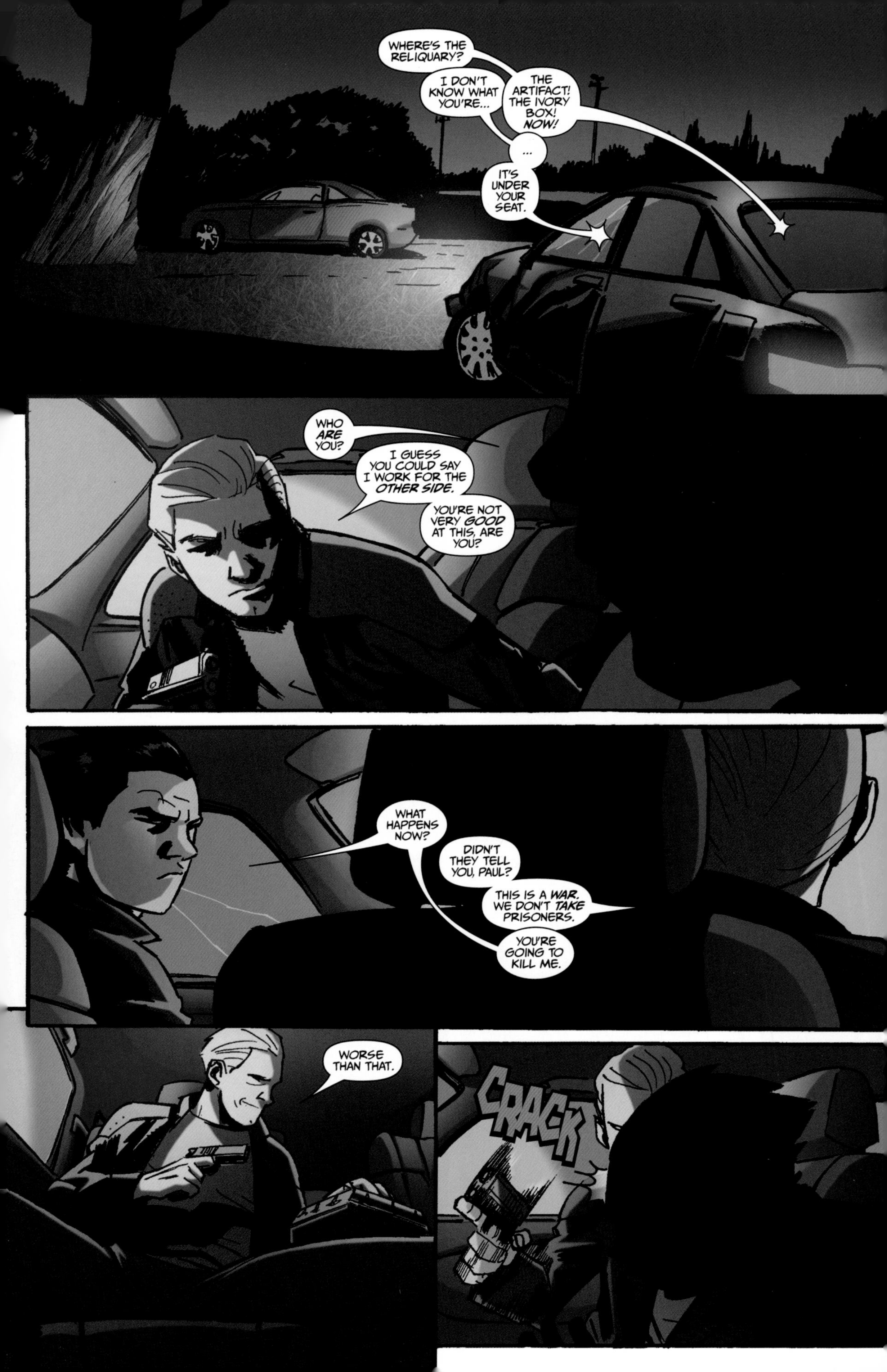
WHERE'S THE RELIQUARY?
I DON'T KNOW WHAT YOU'RE...
THE ARTIFACT! THE IVORY BOX! NOW!
...
IT'S UNDER YOUR SEAT.
WHO ARE YOU?
I GUESS YOU COULD SAY I WORK FOR THE OTHER SIDE.
YOU'RE NOT VERY GOOD AT THIS, ARE YOU?
WHAT HAPPENS NOW?
DIDN'T THEY TELL YOU, PAUL?
THIS IS A WAR. WE DON'T TAKE PRISONERS.
YOU'RE GOING TO KILL ME.
WORSE THAN THAT.
CRACK

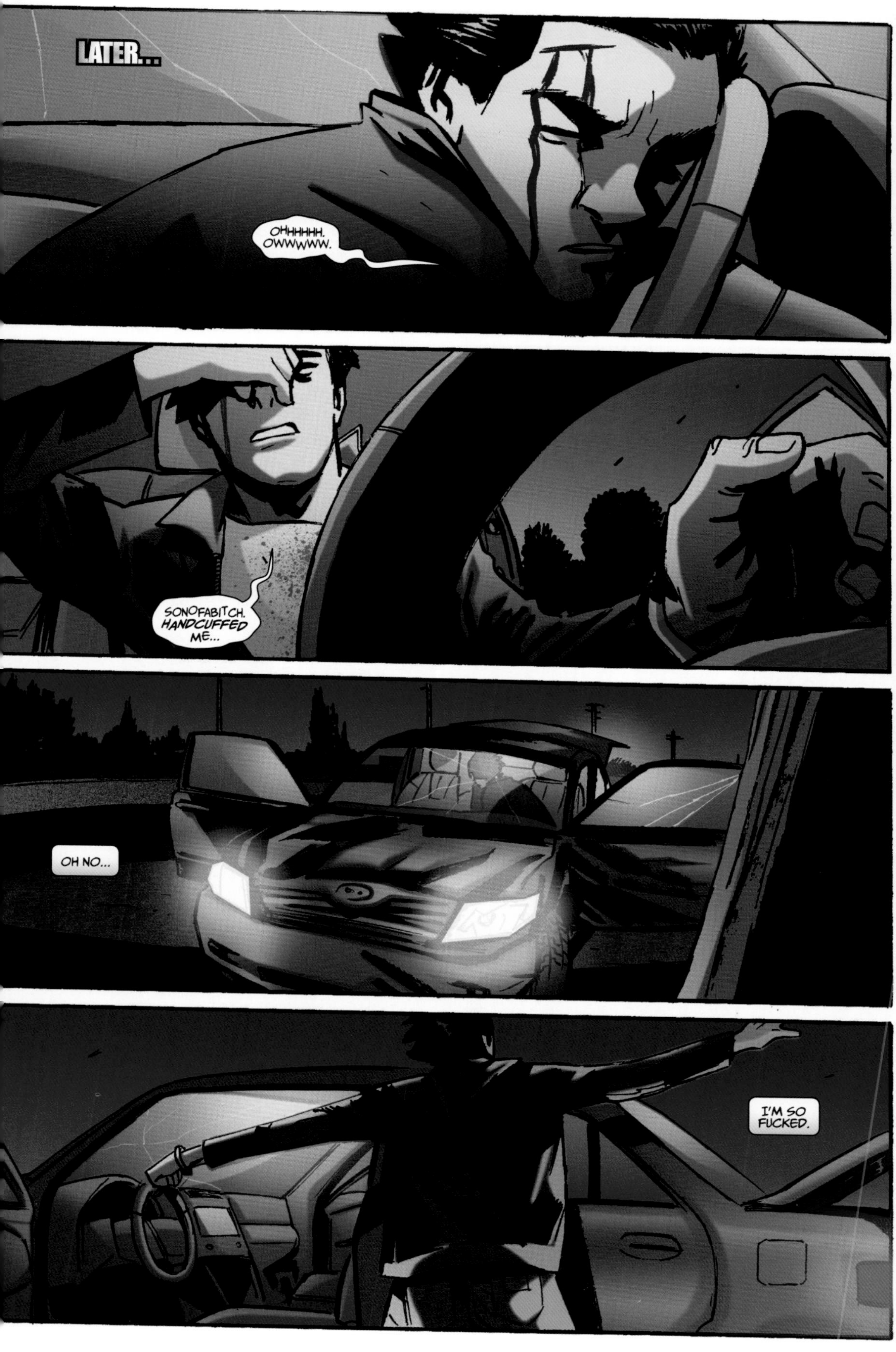
LATER...
OHHHHHH. OWWWWWW.
SONOFABITCH. HANDCUFFED ME...
OH NO...
I'M SO FUCKED.

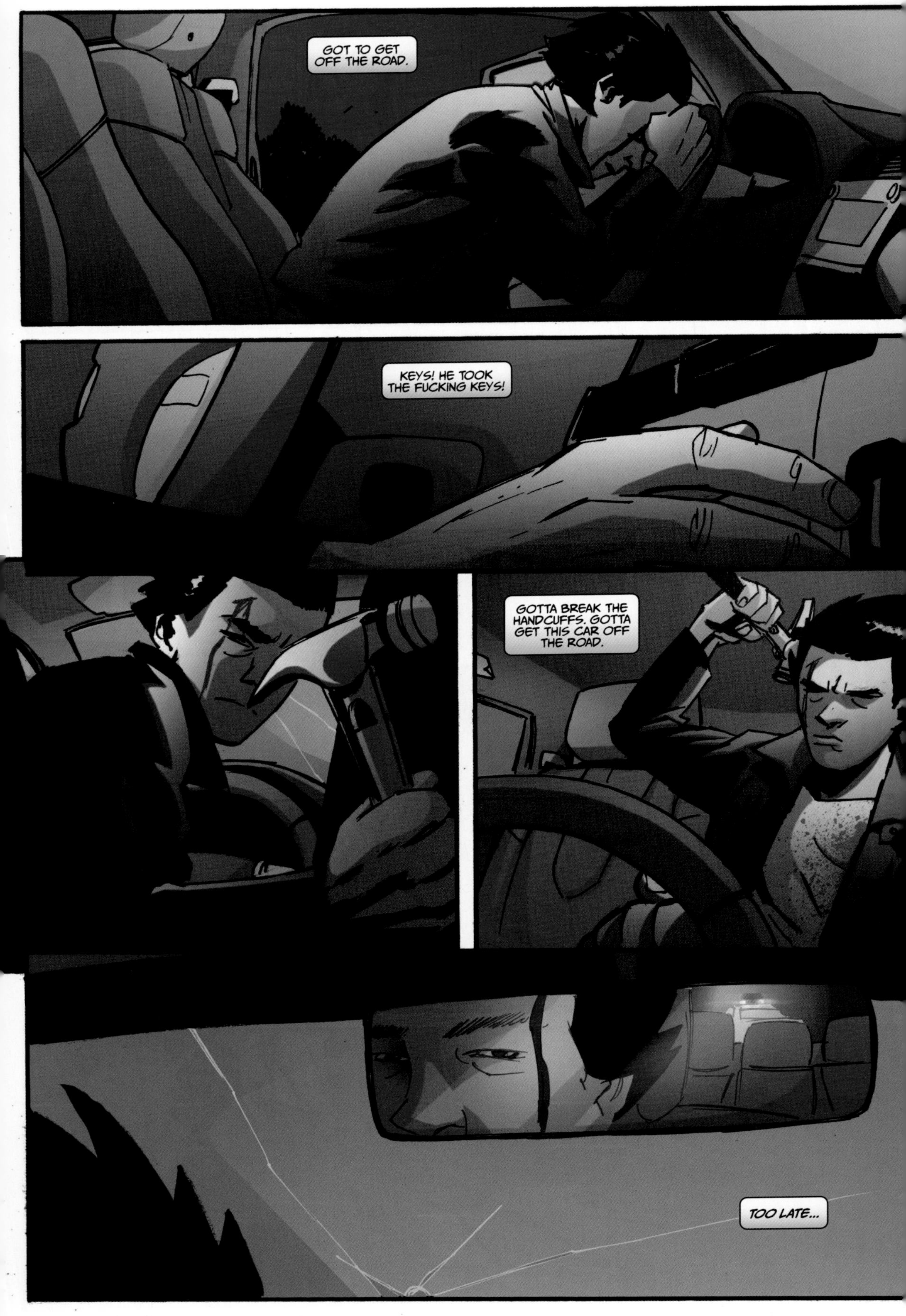
GOT TO GET OFF THE ROAD.
KEYS! HE TOOK THE FUCKING KEYS!
GOTTA BREAK THE HANDCUFFS. GOTTA GET THIS CAR OFF THE ROAD.
TOO LATE...

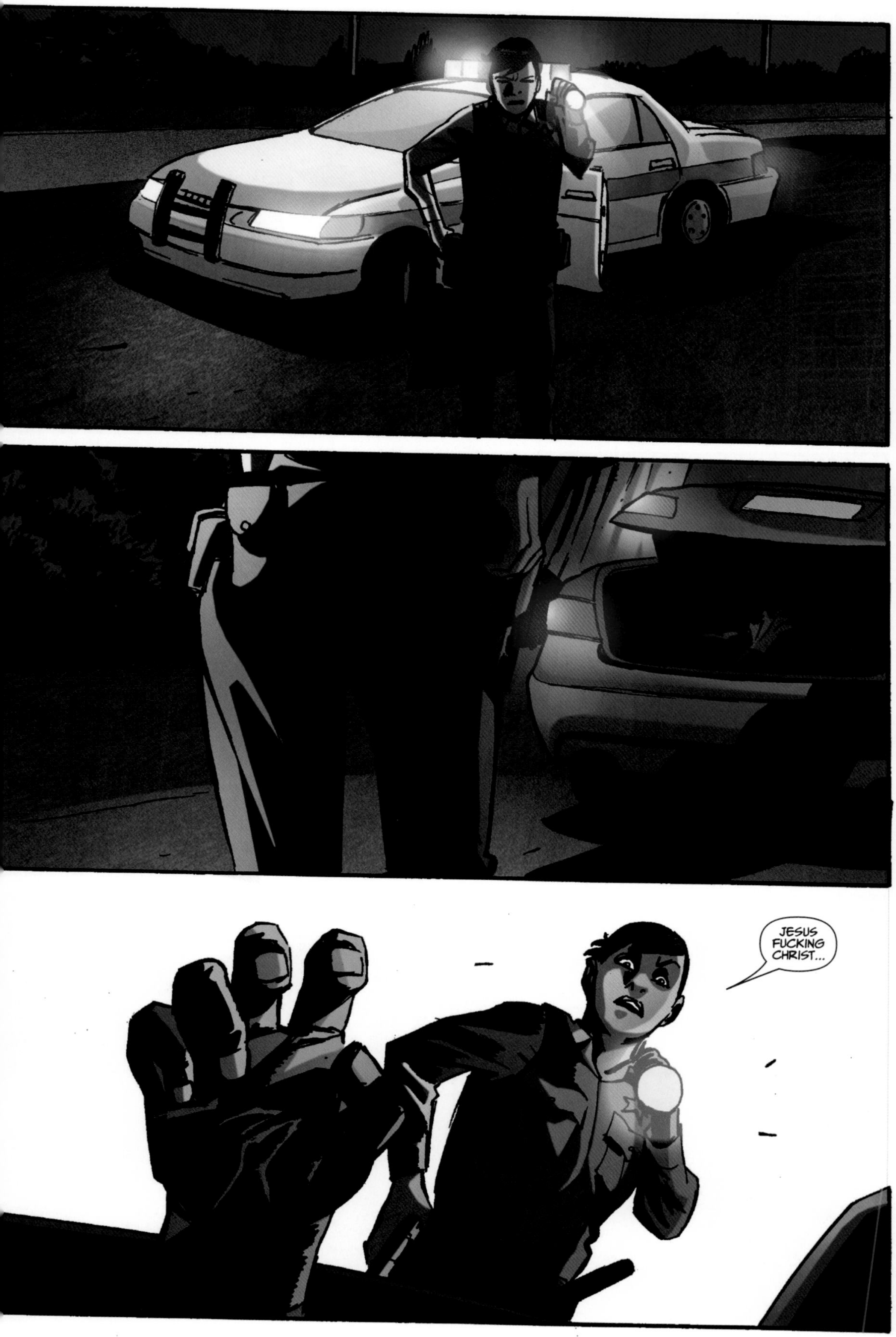
JESUS FUCKING CHRIST...

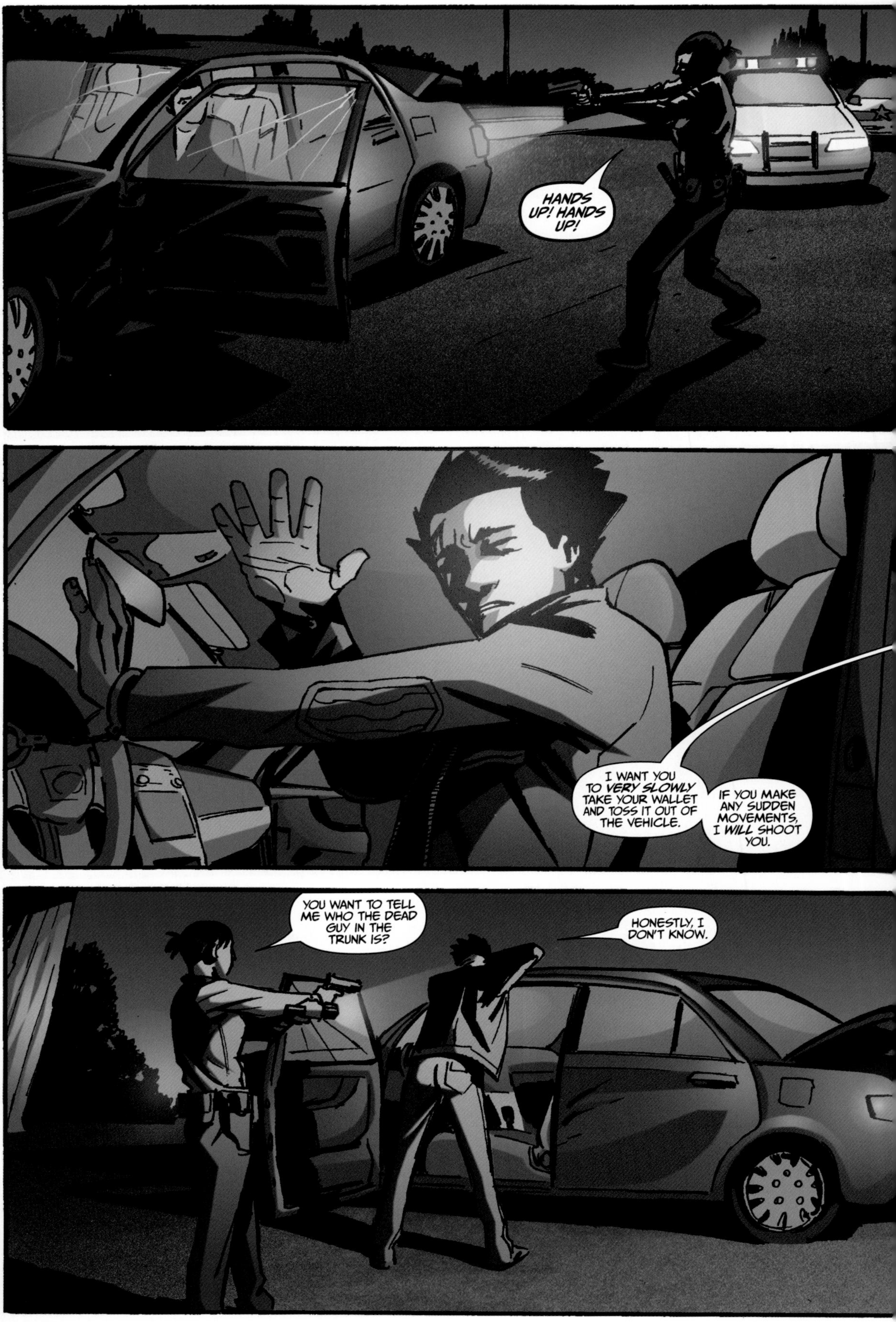
HANDS UP! HANDS UP!
I WANT YOU TO VERY SLOWLY TAKE YOUR WALLET AND TOSS IT OUT OF THE VEHICLE.
IF YOU MAKE ANY SUDDEN MOVEMENTS, I WILL SHOOT YOU.
YOU WANT TO TELL ME WHO THE DEAD GUY IN THE TRUNK IS?
HONESTLY, I DON'T KNOW.

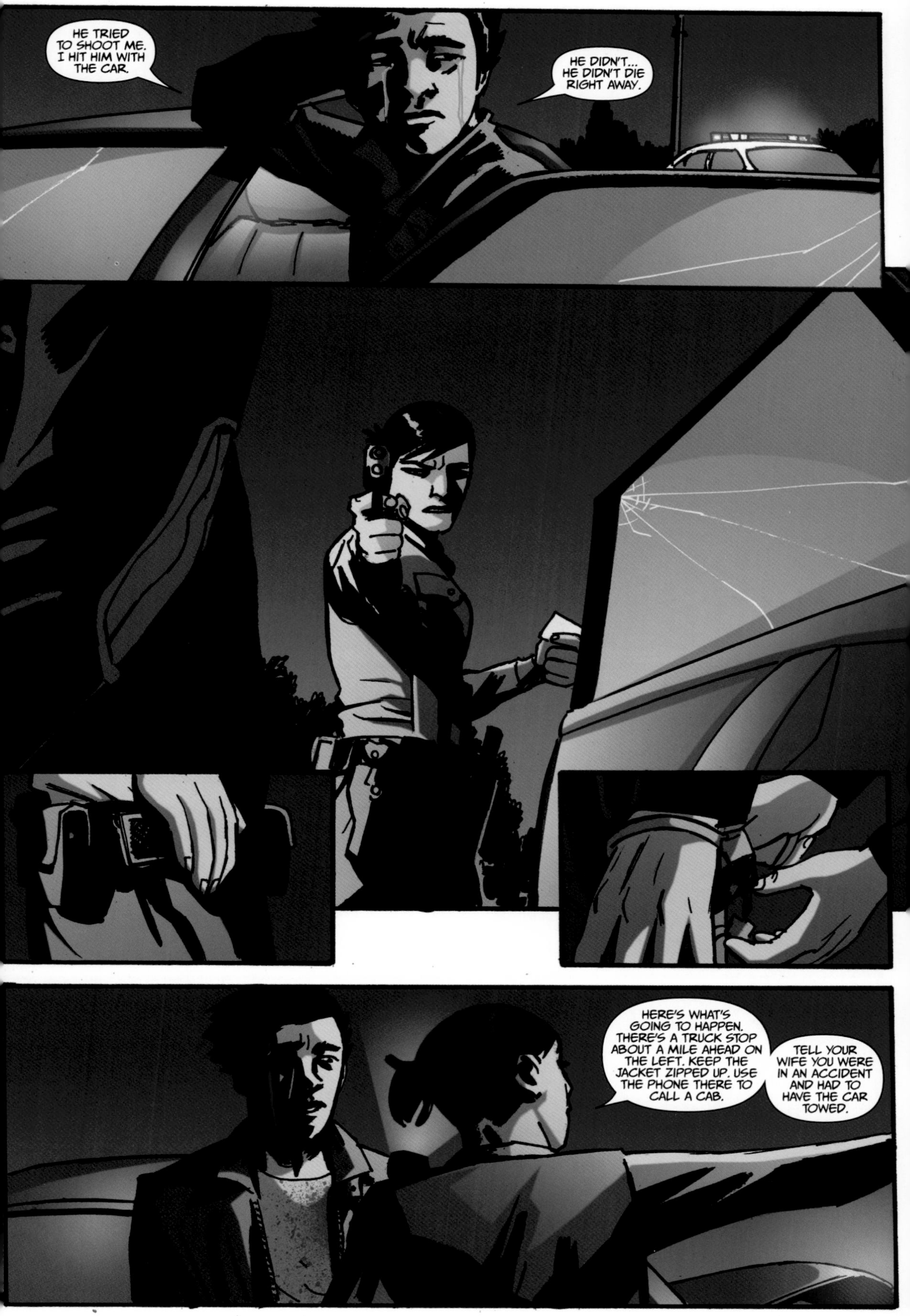
HE TRIED TO SHOOT ME. I HIT HIM WITH THE CAR.
HE DIDN'T... HE DIDN'T DIE RIGHT AWAY.
HERE'S WHAT'S GOING TO HAPPEN. THERE'S A TRUCK STOP ABOUT A MILE AHEAD ON THE LEFT. KEEP THE JACKET ZIPPED UP. USE THE PHONE THERE TO CALL A CAB.
TELL YOUR WIFE YOU WERE IN AN ACCIDENT AND HAD TO HAVE THE CAR TOWED.

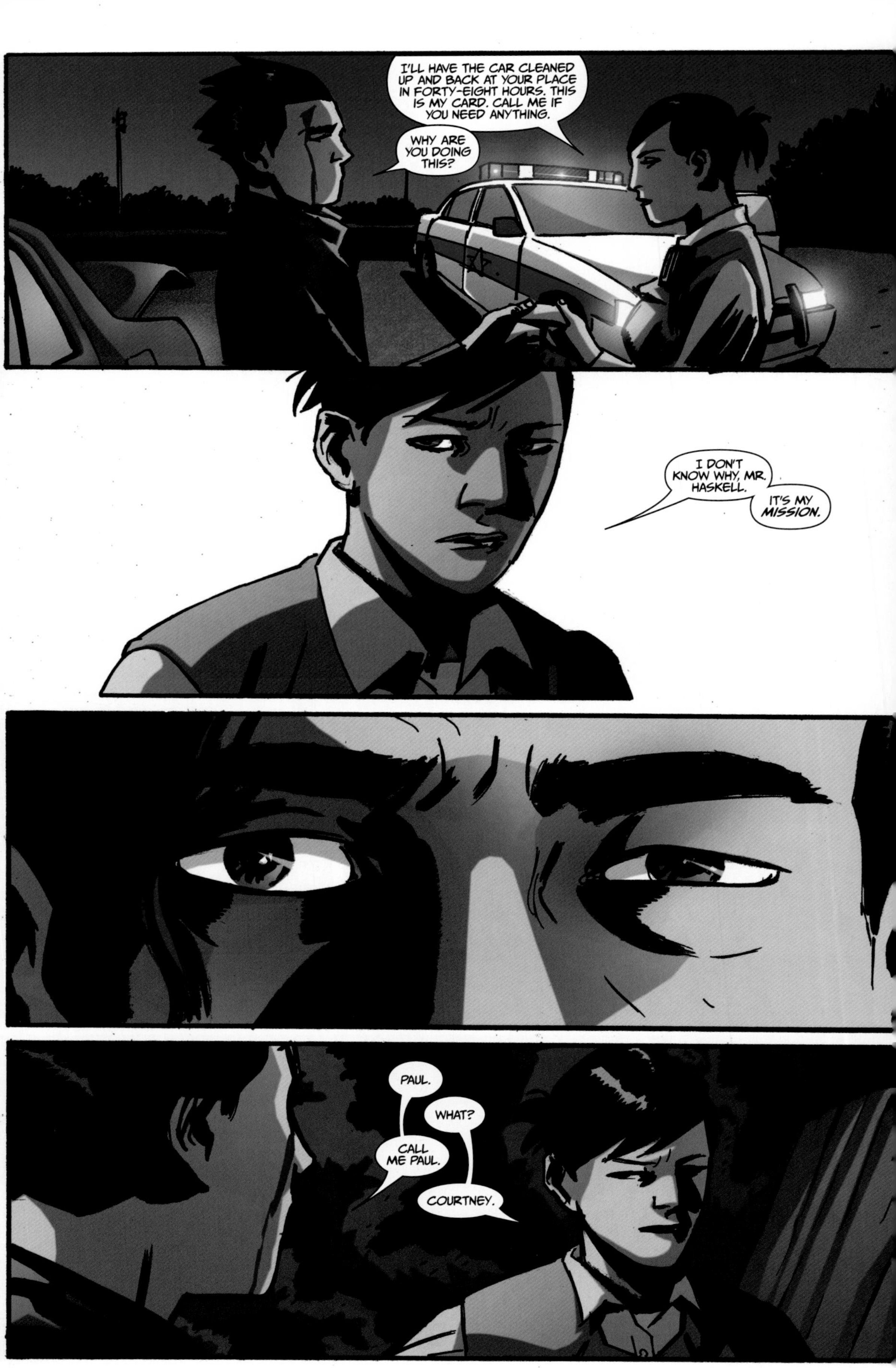

I'LL HAVE THE CAR CLEANED UP AND BACK AT YOUR PLACE IN FORTY-EIGHT HOURS. THIS IS MY CARD. CALL ME IF YOU NEED ANYTHING.
WHY ARE YOU DOING THIS?
I DON'T KNOW WHY, MR. HASKELL.
IT'S MY *MISSION*.
PAUL.
WHAT?
CALL ME PAUL.
COURTNEY.

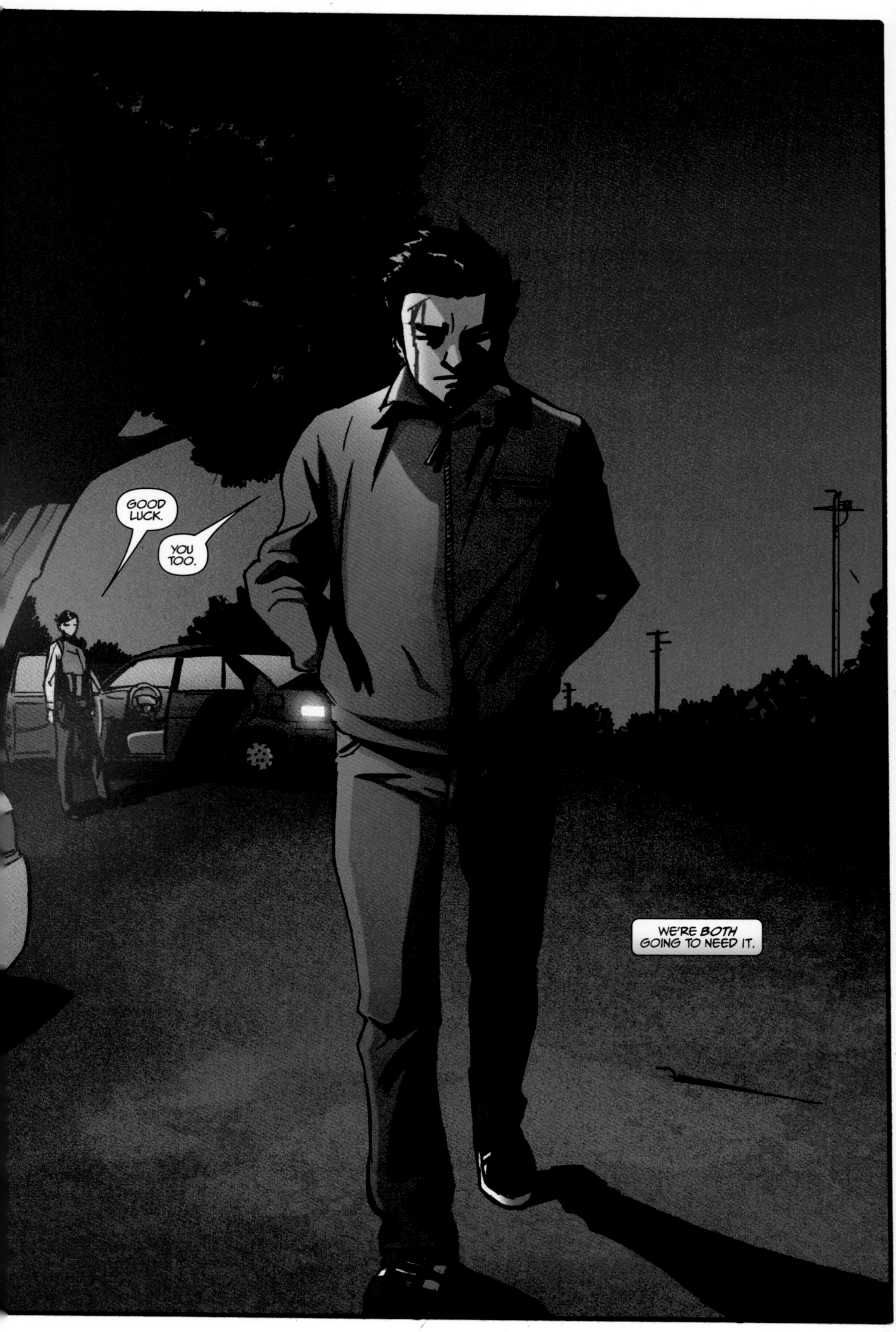
GOOD LUCK.
YOU TOO.
WE'RE *BOTH* GOING TO NEED IT.

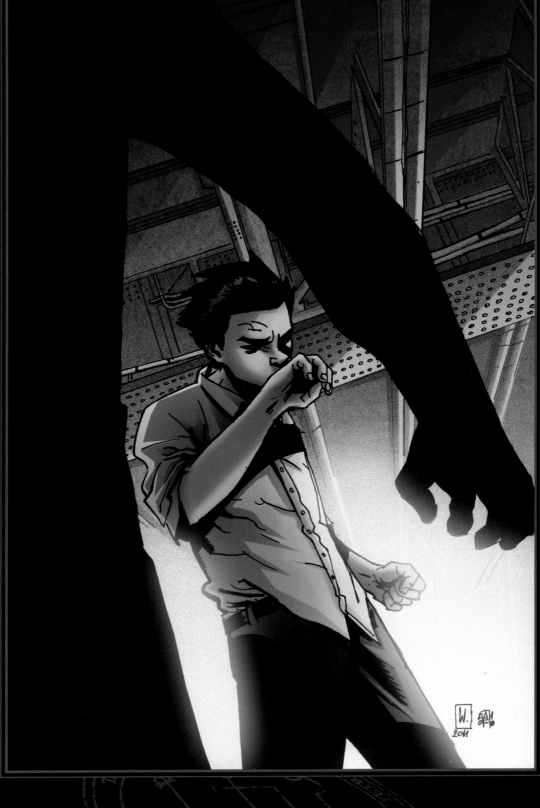

CHAPTER 5

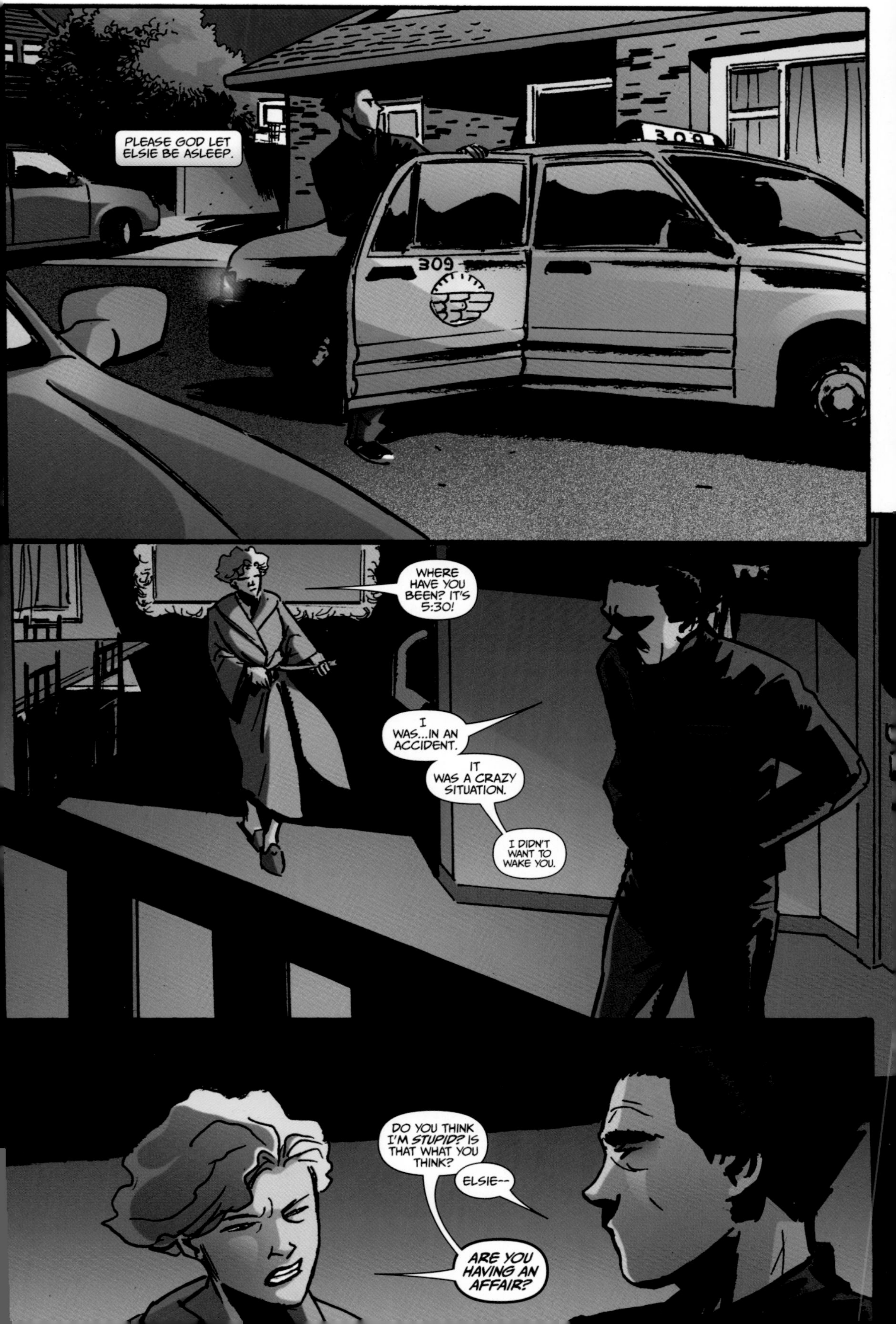

PLEASE GOD LET ELSIE BE ASLEEP.
309
309
WHERE HAVE YOU BEEN? IT'S 5:30!
I WAS...IN AN ACCIDENT.
IT WAS A CRAZY SITUATION.
I DIDN'T WANT TO WAKE YOU.
DO YOU THINK I'M *STUPID?* IS THAT WHAT YOU THINK?
ELSIE--
ARE YOU HAVING AN AFFAIR?

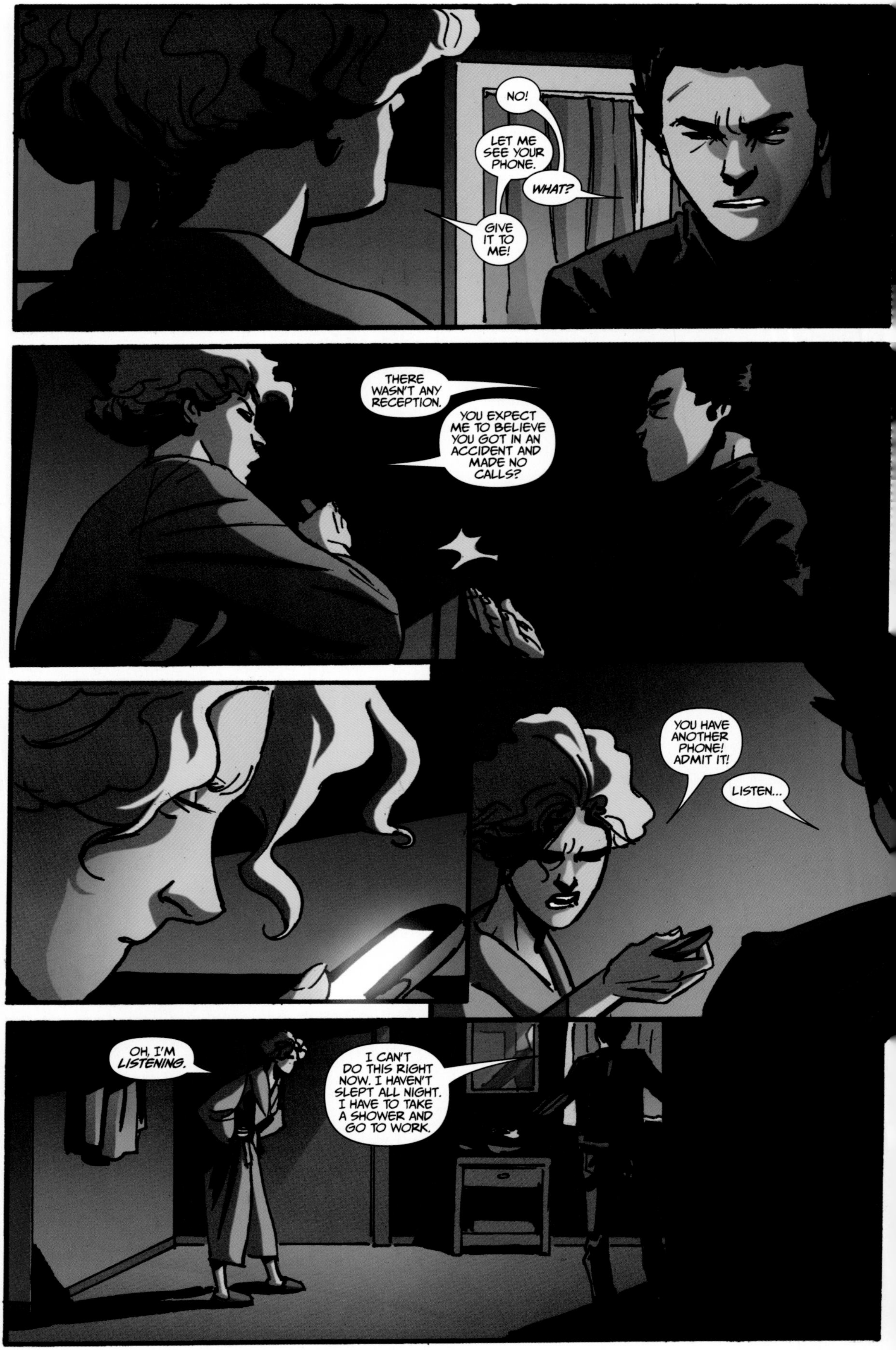
NO!
LET ME SEE YOUR PHONE.
WHAT?
GIVE IT TO ME!
THERE WASN'T ANY RECEPTION.
YOU EXPECT ME TO BELIEVE YOU GOT IN AN ACCIDENT AND MADE NO CALLS?
YOU HAVE ANOTHER PHONE! ADMIT IT!
LISTEN...
OH, I'M *LISTENING.*
I CAN'T DO THIS RIGHT NOW. I HAVEN'T SLEPT ALL NIGHT. I HAVE TO TAKE A SHOWER AND GO TO WORK.

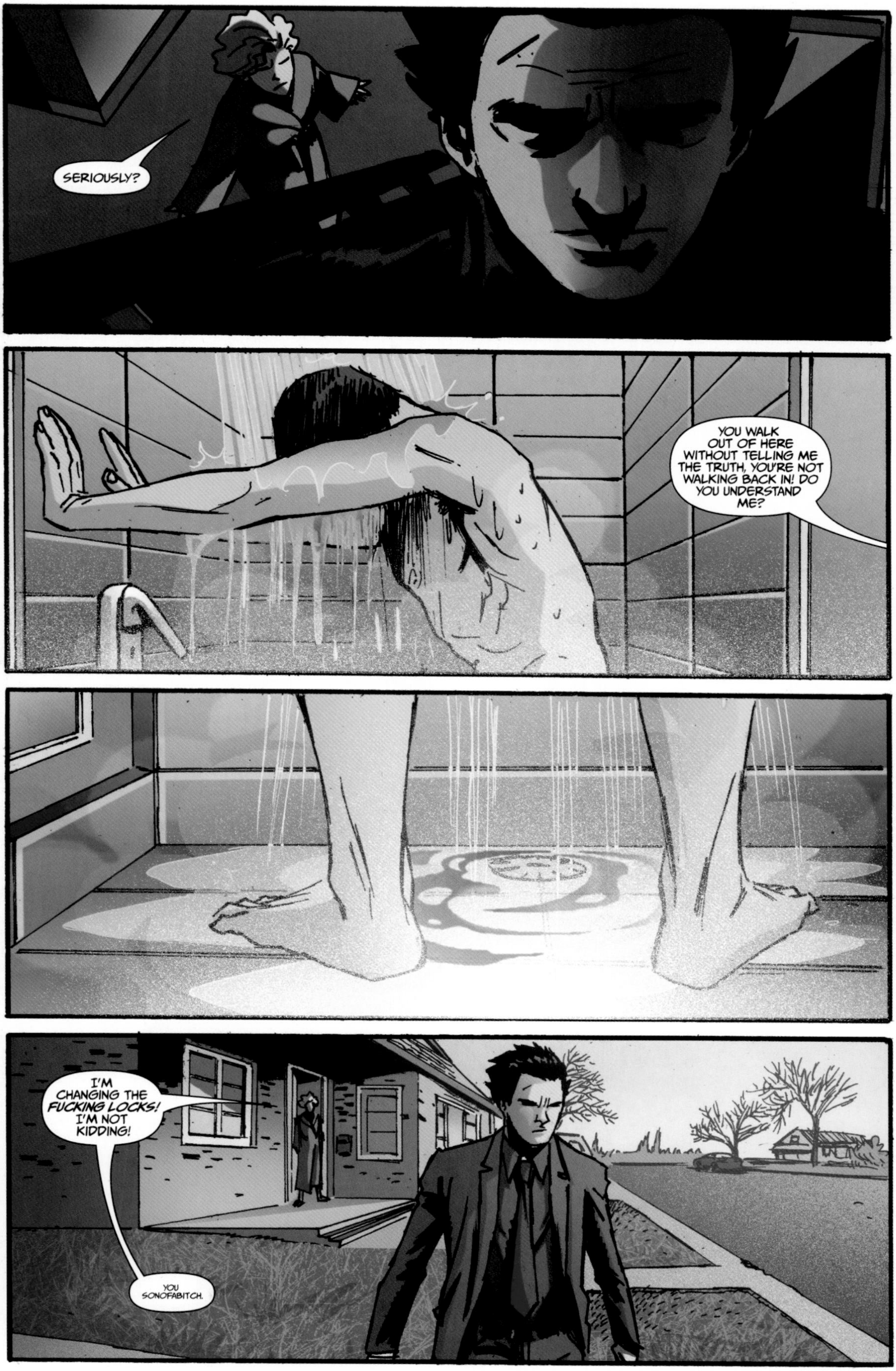
SERIOUSLY?
YOU WALK OUT OF HERE WITHOUT TELLING ME THE TRUTH, YOU'RE NOT WALKING BACK IN! DO YOU UNDERSTAND ME?
I'M CHANGING THE *FUCKING LOCKS!* I'M NOT KIDDING!
YOU SONOFABITCH.

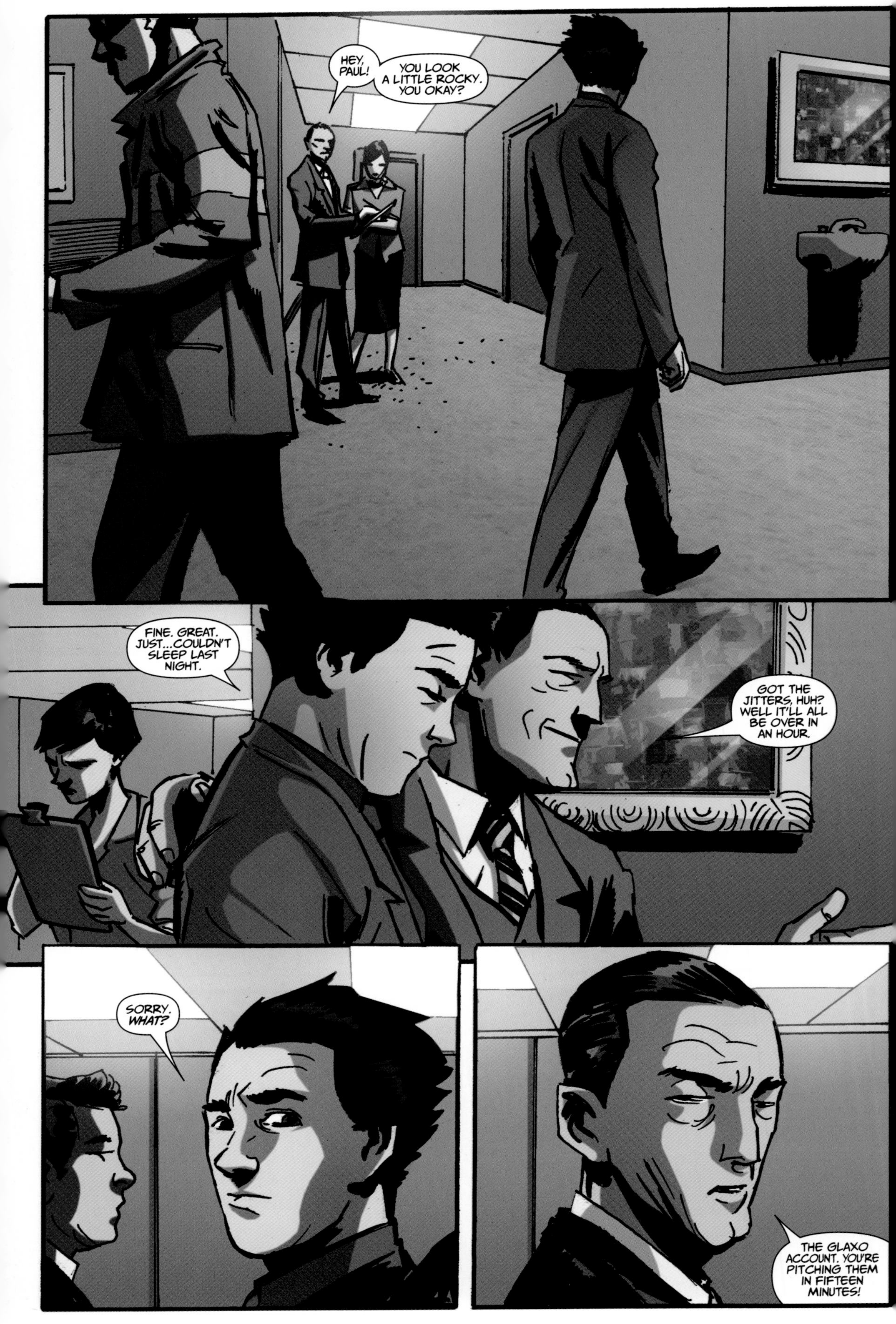
HEY, PAUL!
YOU LOOK A LITTLE ROCKY. YOU OKAY?
FINE. GREAT. JUST...COULDN'T SLEEP LAST NIGHT.
GOT THE JITTERS, HUH? WELL IT'LL ALL BE OVER IN AN HOUR.
SORRY. WHAT?
THE GLAXO ACCOUNT. YOU'RE PITCHING THEM IN FIFTEEN MINUTES!

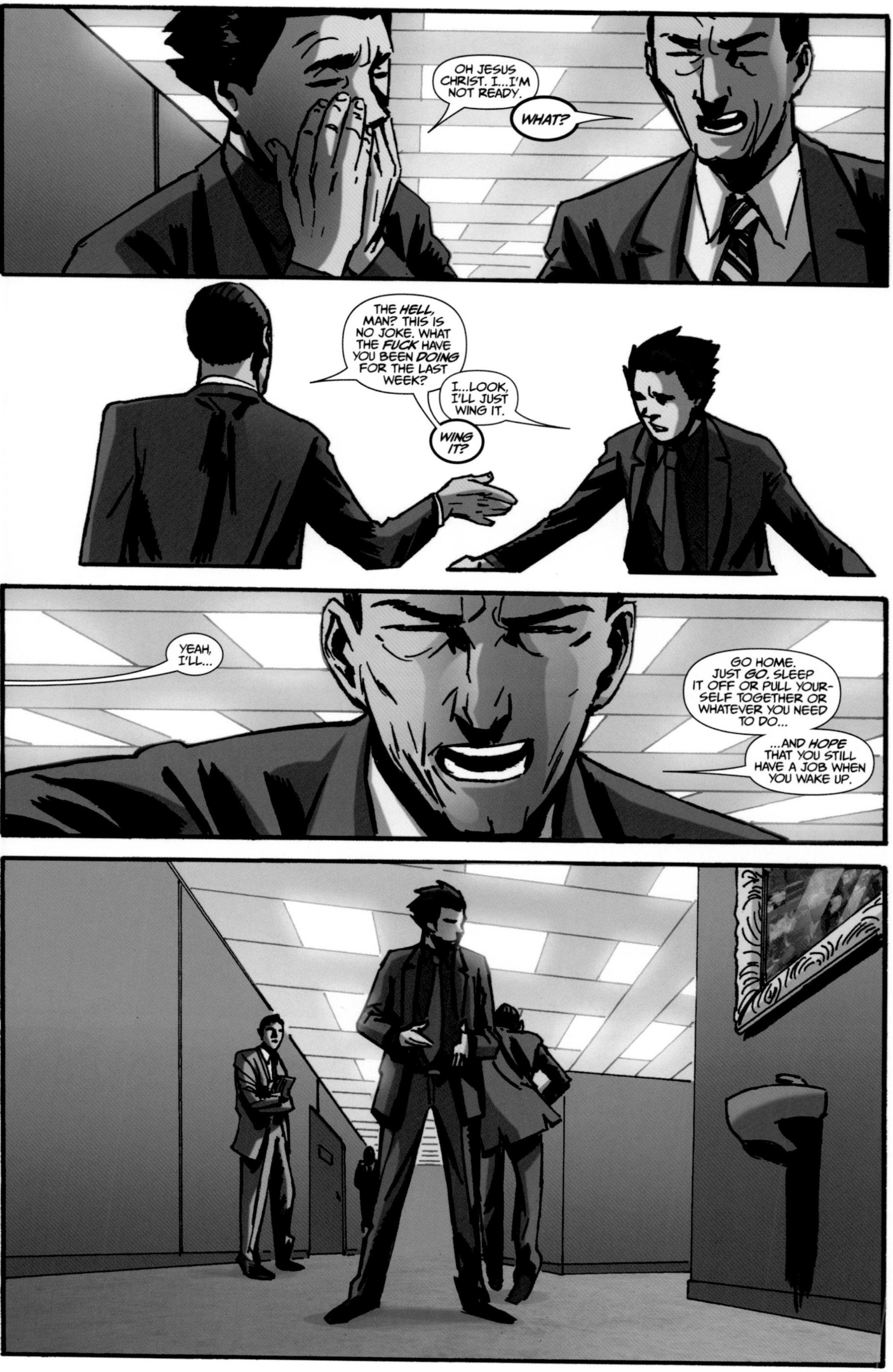
OH JESUS CHRIST. I...I'M NOT READY.
WHAT?
THE HELL, MAN? THIS IS NO JOKE. WHAT THE FUCK HAVE YOU BEEN DOING FOR THE LAST WEEK?
I...LOOK, I'LL JUST WING IT.
WING IT?
YEAH, I'LL...
GO HOME. JUST GO. SLEEP IT OFF OR PULL YOURSELF TOGETHER OR WHATEVER YOU NEED TO DO...
...AND HOPE THAT YOU STILL HAVE A JOB WHEN YOU WAKE UP.

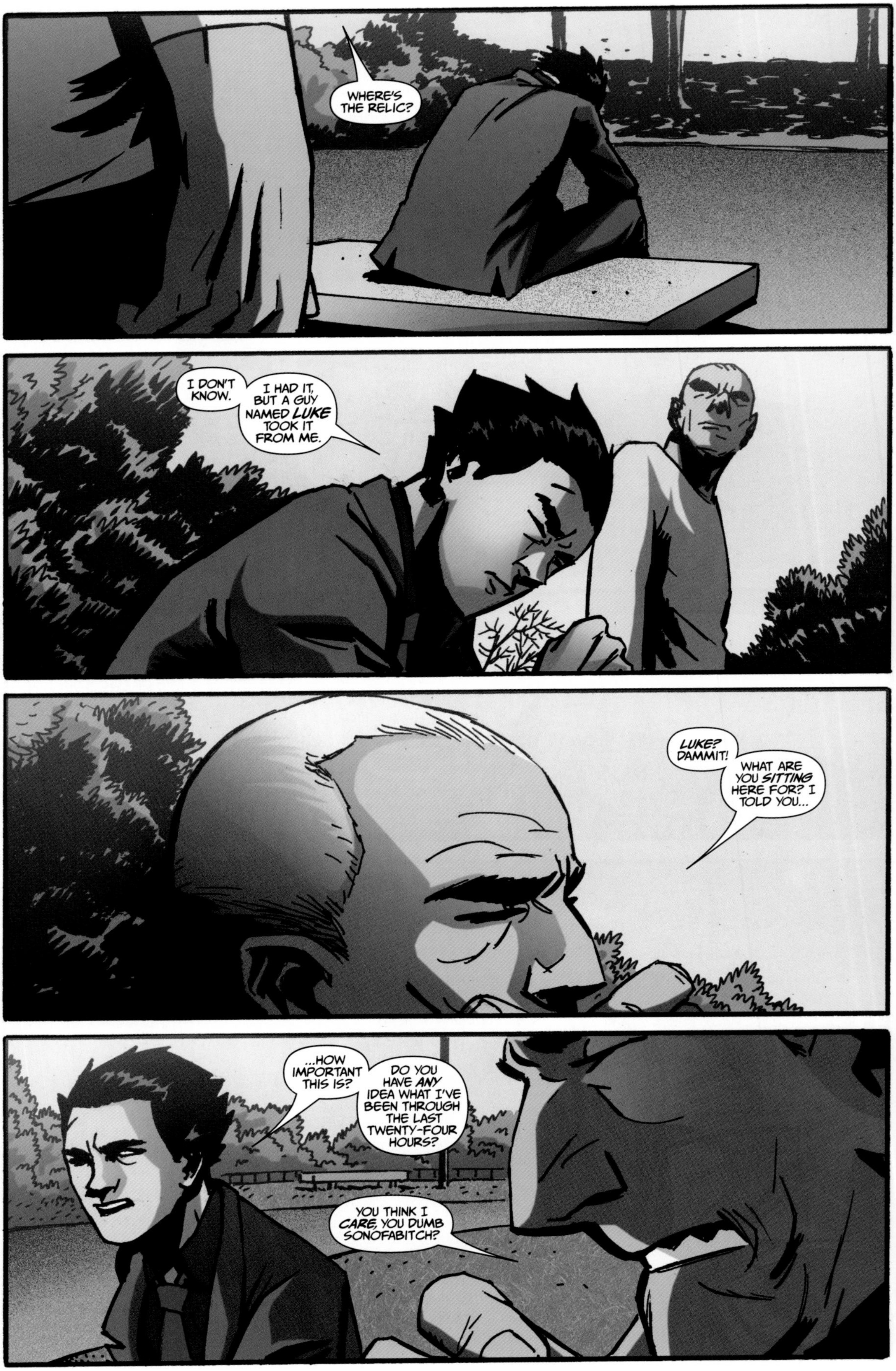
WHERE'S THE RELIC?
I DON'T KNOW.
BUT A GUY NAMED *LUKE* TOOK IT FROM ME.
LUKE? DAMMIT!
WHAT ARE YOU *SITTING* HERE FOR? I TOLD YOU...
DO YOU HAVE *ANY* IDEA WHAT I'VE BEEN THROUGH THE LAST TWENTY-FOUR HOURS?
...HOW IMPORTANT THIS IS?
YOU THINK I *CARE*, YOU DUMB SONOFABITCH?

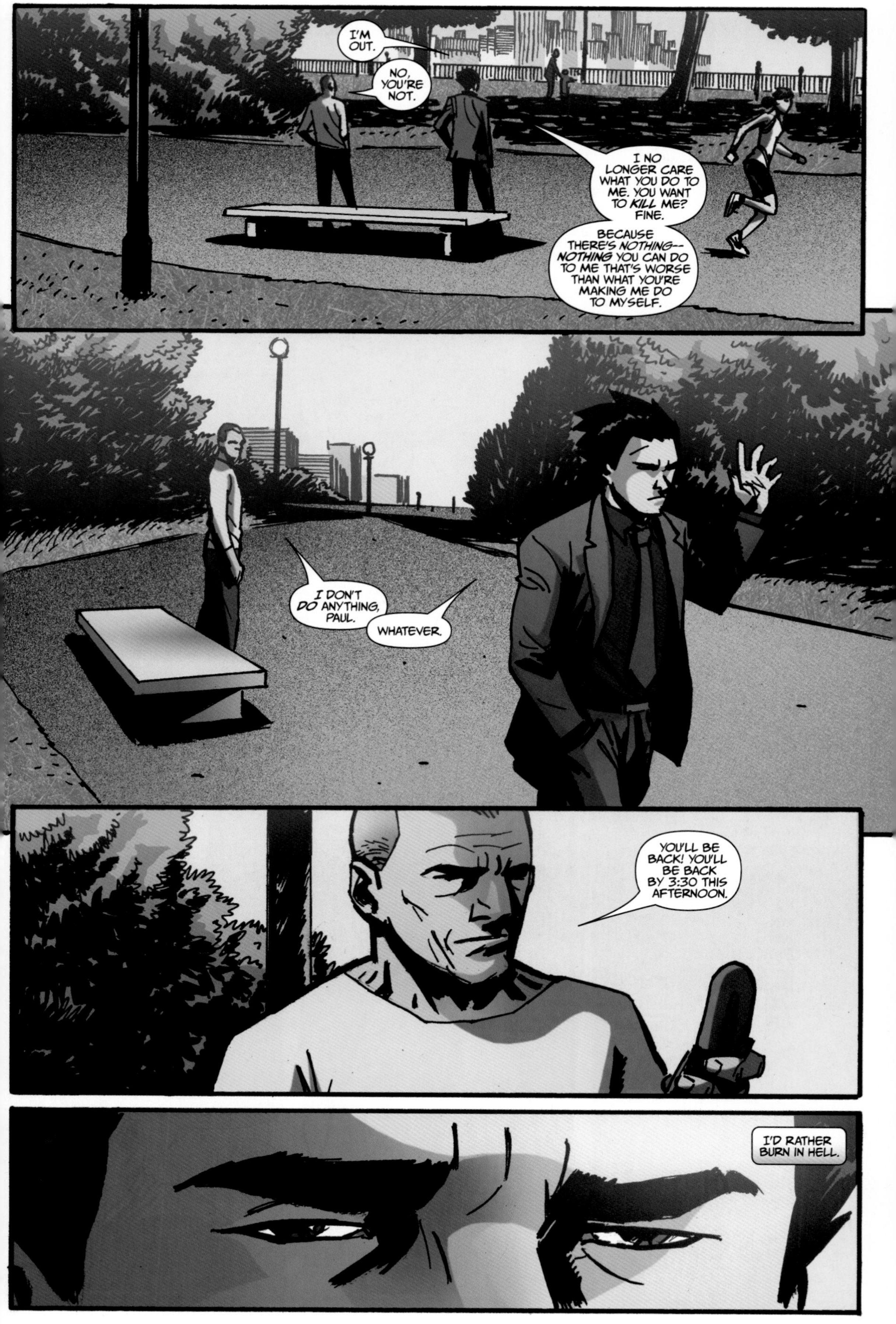
I'M OUT.
NO, YOU'RE NOT.
I NO LONGER CARE WHAT YOU DO TO ME. YOU WANT TO KILL ME? FINE.
BECAUSE THERE'S NOTHING-- NOTHING YOU CAN DO TO ME THAT'S WORSE THAN WHAT YOU'RE MAKING ME DO TO MYSELF.
I DON'T DO ANYTHING, PAUL.
WHATEVER.
YOU'LL BE BACK! YOU'LL BE BACK BY 3:30 THIS AFTERNOON.
I'D RATHER BURN IN HELL.

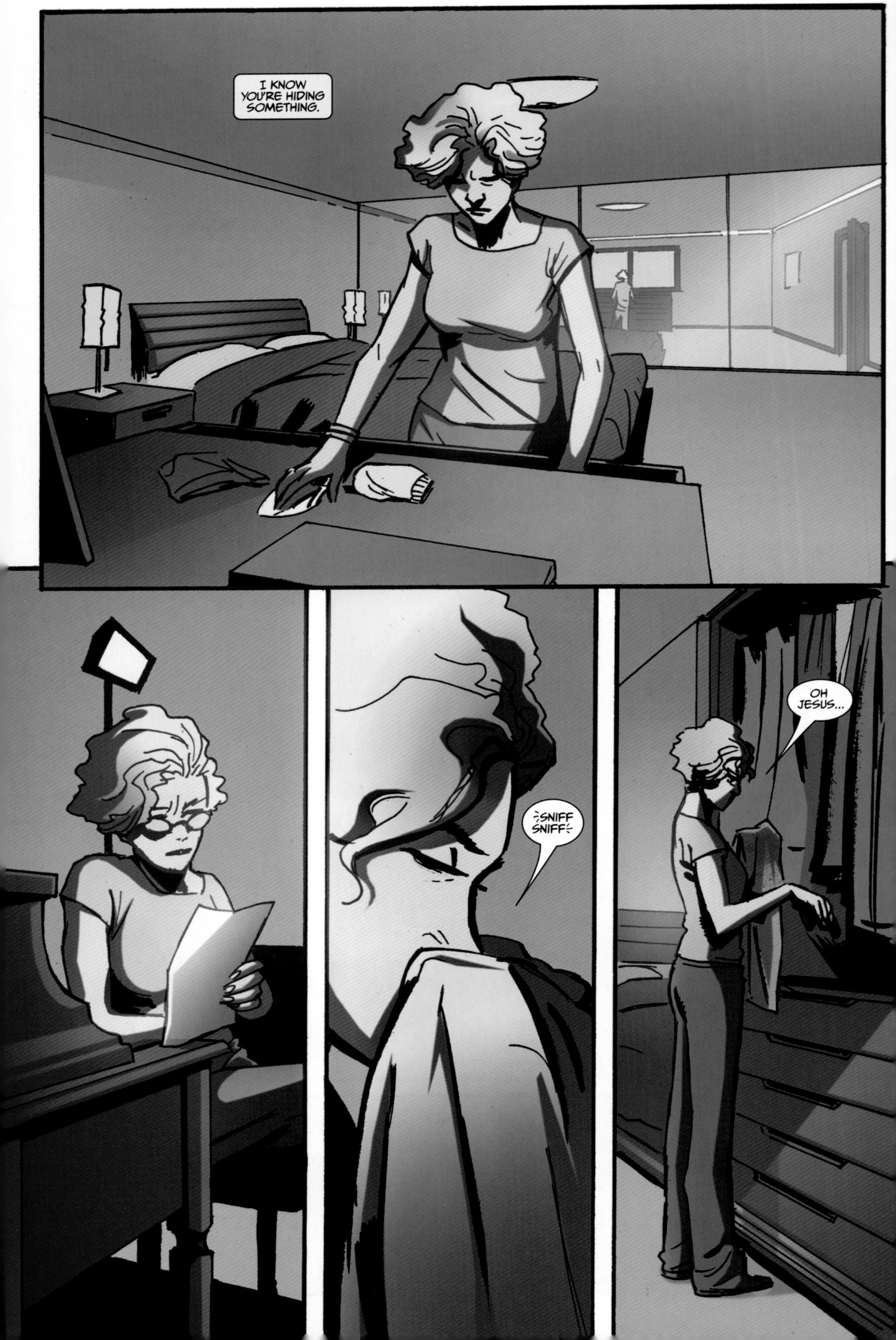

I KNOW YOU'RE HIDING SOMETHING.
SNIFF SNIFF
OH JESUS...

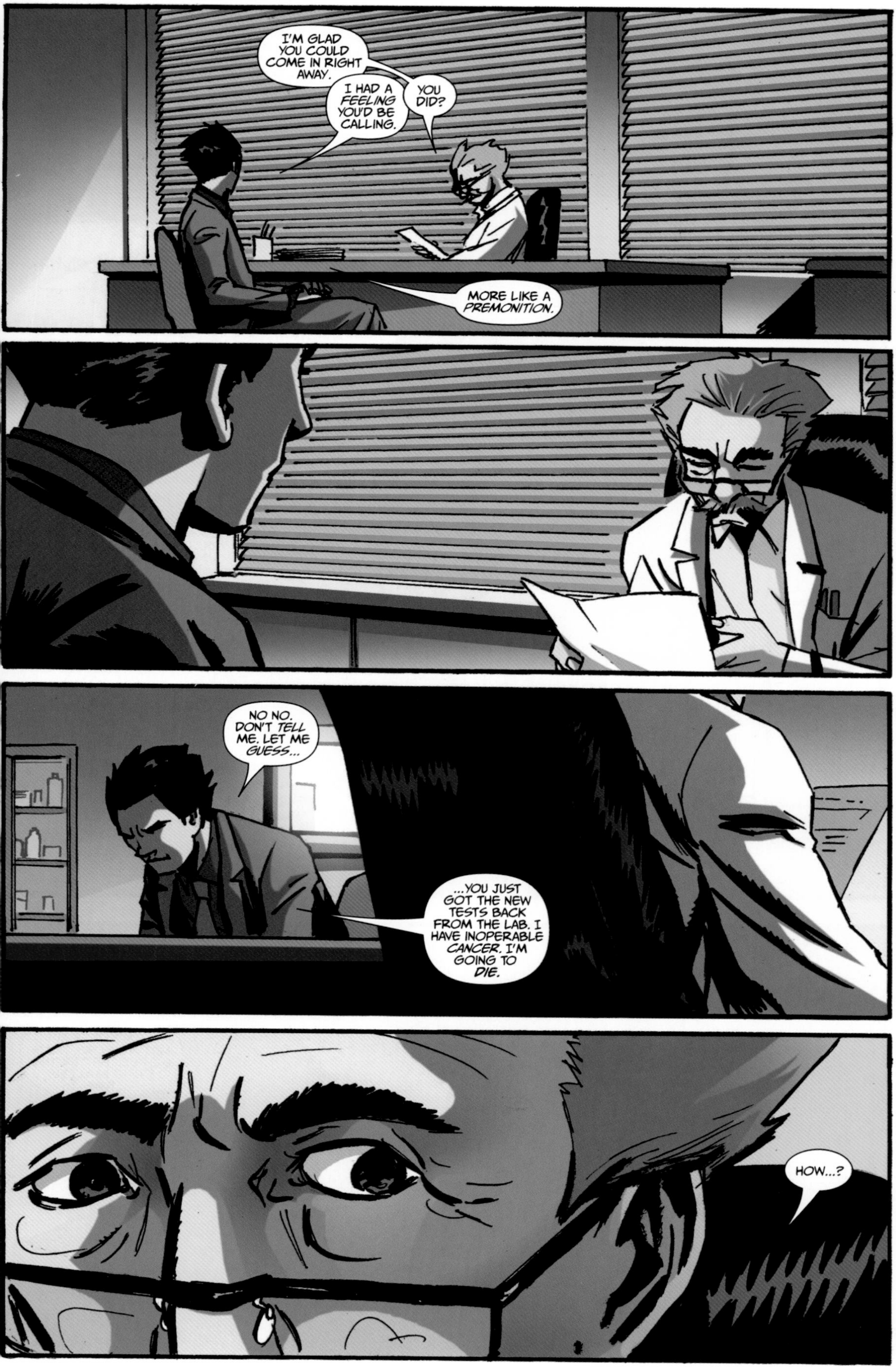
I'M GLAD YOU COULD COME IN RIGHT AWAY.
YOU DID?
I HAD A *FEELING* YOU'D BE CALLING.
MORE LIKE A *PREMONITION*.
NO NO. DON'T *TELL* ME. LET ME *GUESS*...
...YOU JUST GOT THE NEW TESTS BACK FROM THE LAB. I HAVE INOPERABLE *CANCER*. I'M GOING TO *DIE*.
HOW...?

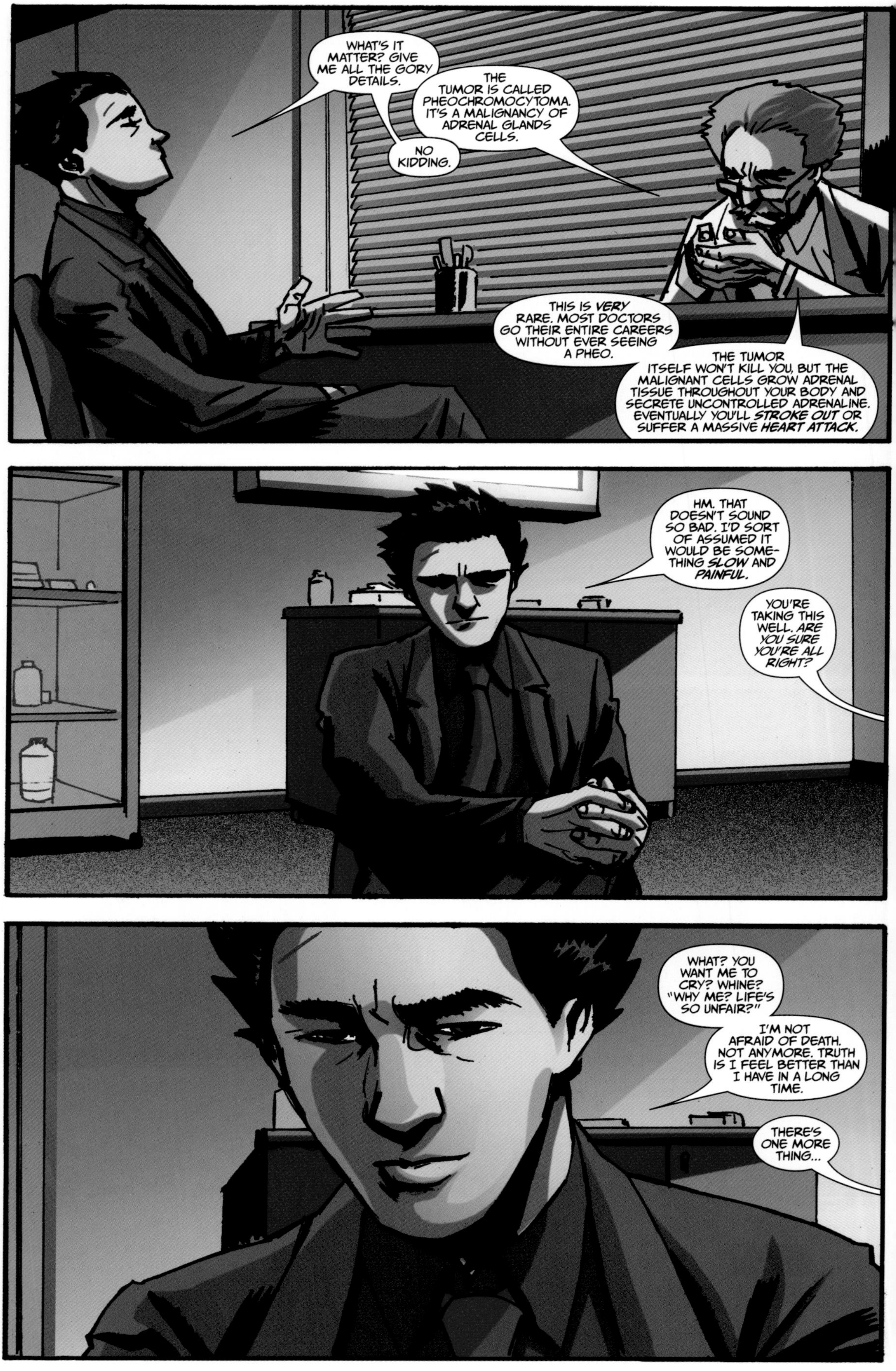
WHAT'S IT MATTER? GIVE ME ALL THE GORY DETAILS.
THE TUMOR IS CALLED PHEOCHROMOCYTOMA. IT'S A MALIGNANCY OF ADRENAL GLANDS CELLS.
NO KIDDING.
THIS IS VERY RARE. MOST DOCTORS GO THEIR ENTIRE CAREERS WITHOUT EVER SEEING A PHEO.
THE TUMOR ITSELF WON'T KILL YOU, BUT THE MALIGNANT CELLS GROW ADRENAL TISSUE THROUGHOUT YOUR BODY AND SECRETE UNCONTROLLED ADRENALINE. EVENTUALLY YOU'LL STROKE OUT OR SUFFER A MASSIVE HEART ATTACK.
HM. THAT DOESN'T SOUND SO BAD. I'D SORT OF ASSUMED IT WOULD BE SOMETHING SLOW AND PAINFUL.
YOU'RE TAKING THIS WELL. ARE YOU SURE YOU'RE ALL RIGHT?
WHAT? YOU WANT ME TO CRY? WHINE? "WHY ME? LIFE'S SO UNFAIR?"
I'M NOT AFRAID OF DEATH. NOT ANYMORE. TRUTH IS I FEEL BETTER THAN I HAVE IN A LONG TIME.
THERE'S ONE MORE THING...

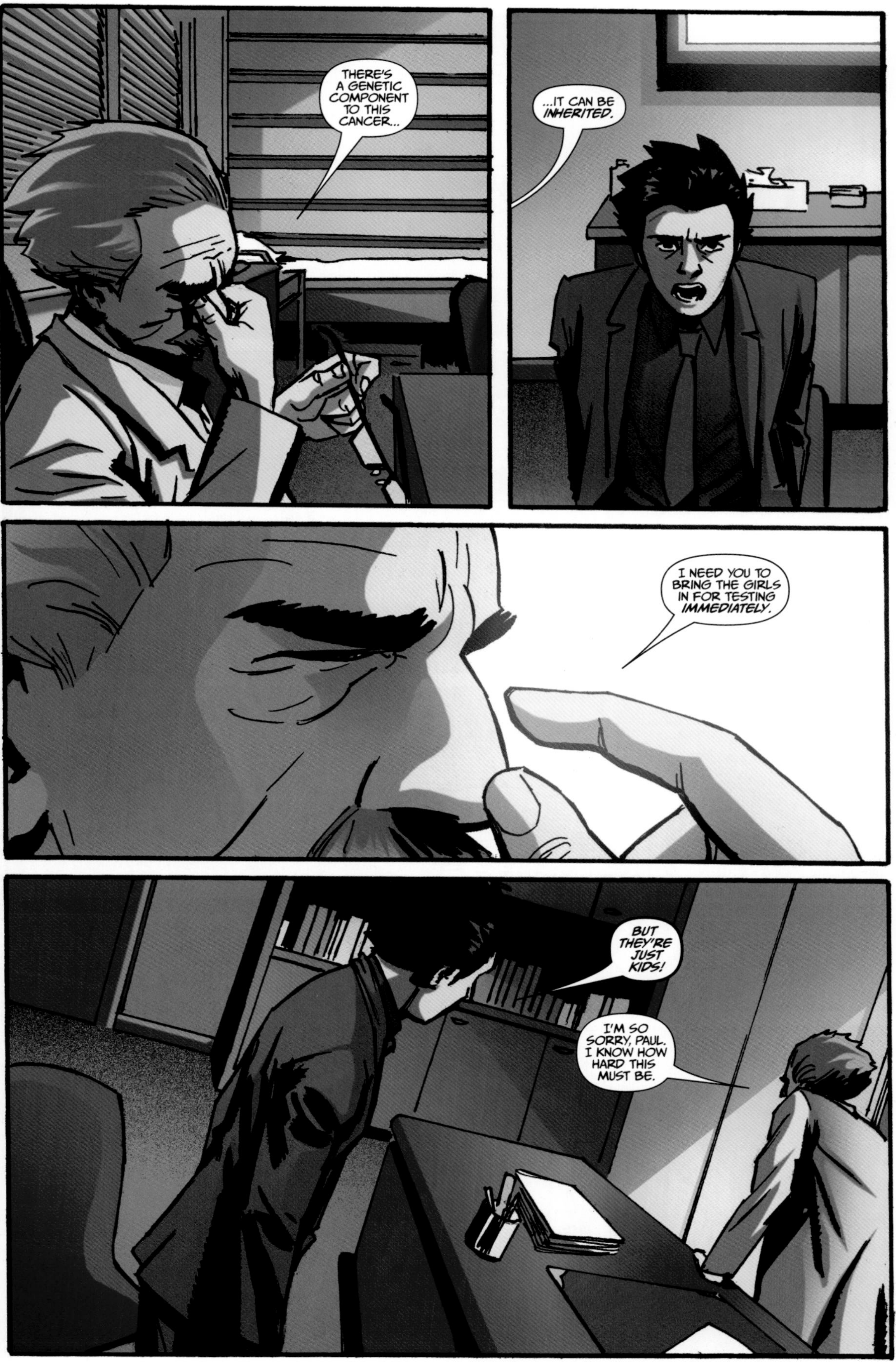
THERE'S A GENETIC COMPONENT TO THIS CANCER...
...IT CAN BE *INHERITED.*
I NEED YOU TO BRING THE GIRLS IN FOR TESTING *IMMEDIATELY.*
BUT THEY'RE JUST KIDS!
I'M SO SORRY, PAUL. I KNOW HOW HARD THIS MUST BE.

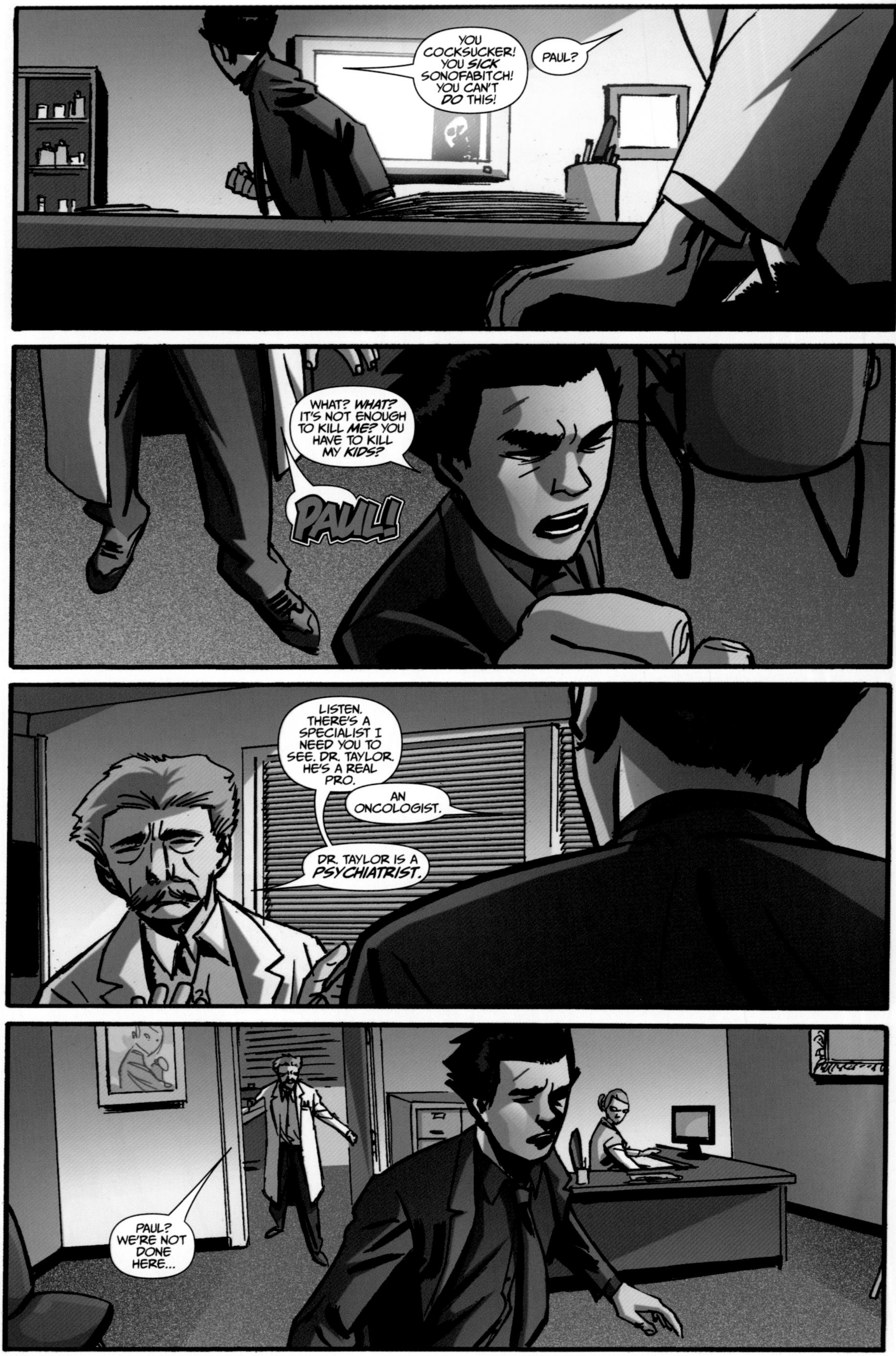
YOU COCKSUCKER! YOU SICK SONOFABITCH! YOU CAN'T DO THIS!
PAUL?
WHAT? WHAT? IT'S NOT ENOUGH TO KILL ME? YOU HAVE TO KILL MY KIDS?
PAUL!
LISTEN. THERE'S A SPECIALIST I NEED YOU TO SEE. DR. TAYLOR. HE'S A REAL PRO.
AN ONCOLOGIST.
DR. TAYLOR IS A PSYCHIATRIST.
PAUL? WE'RE NOT DONE HERE...

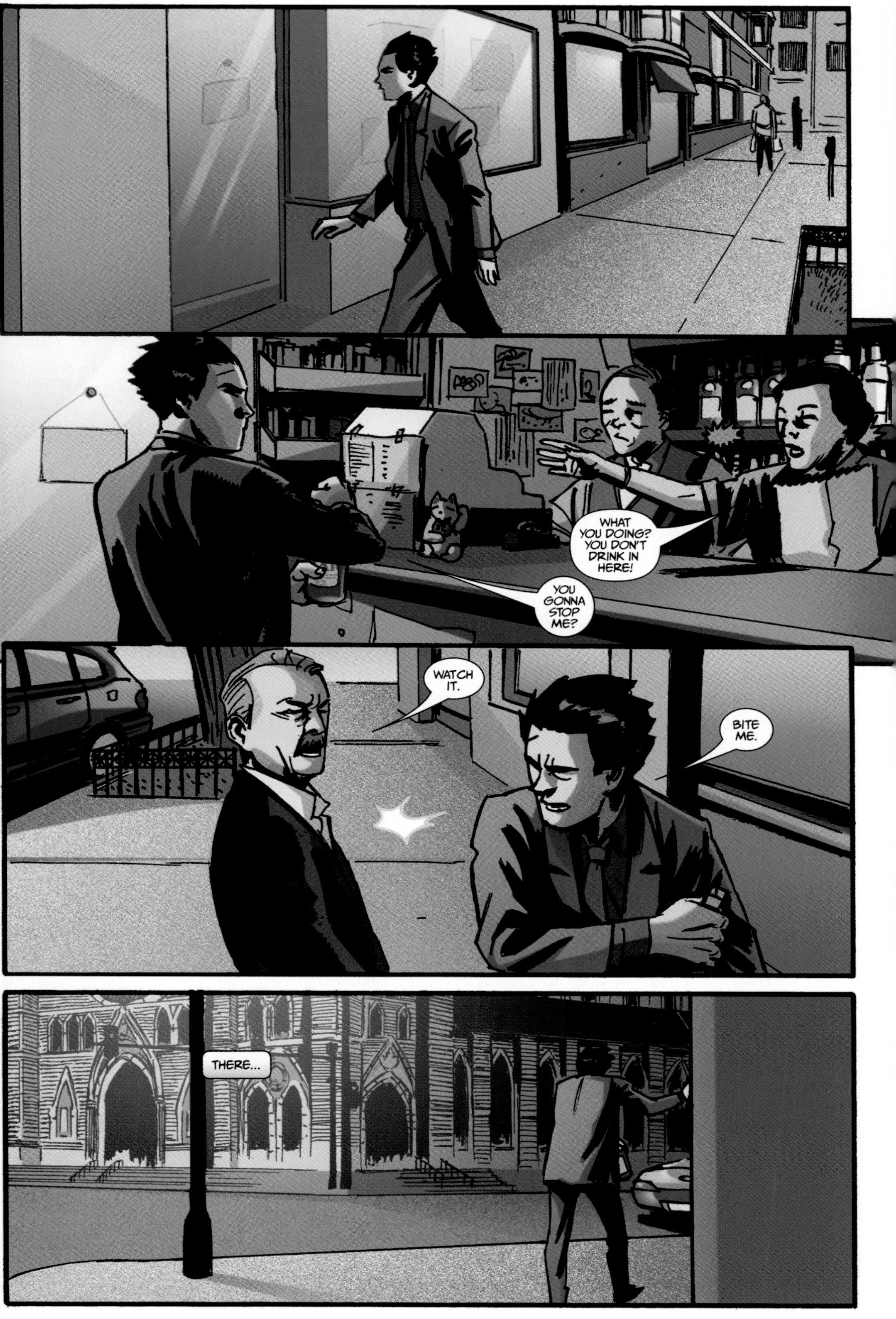
WHAT YOU DOING? YOU DON'T DRINK IN HERE!
YOU GONNA STOP ME?
WATCH IT.
BITE ME.
THERE...

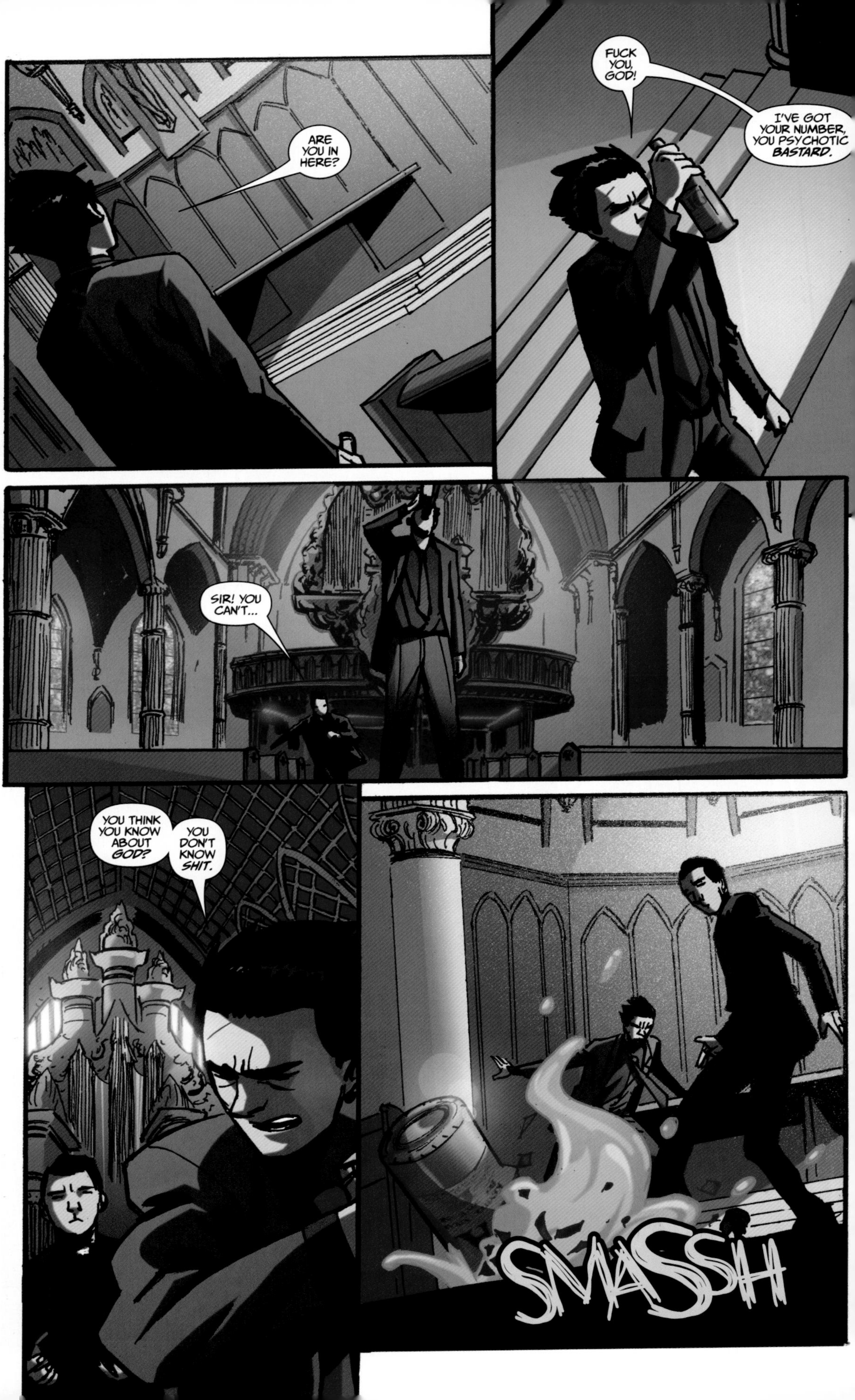
ARE YOU IN HERE?
FUCK YOU, GOD!
I'VE GOT YOUR NUMBER, YOU PSYCHOTIC BASTARD.
SIR! YOU CAN'T...
YOU THINK YOU KNOW ABOUT GOD?
YOU DON'T KNOW SHIT.
SMASSH

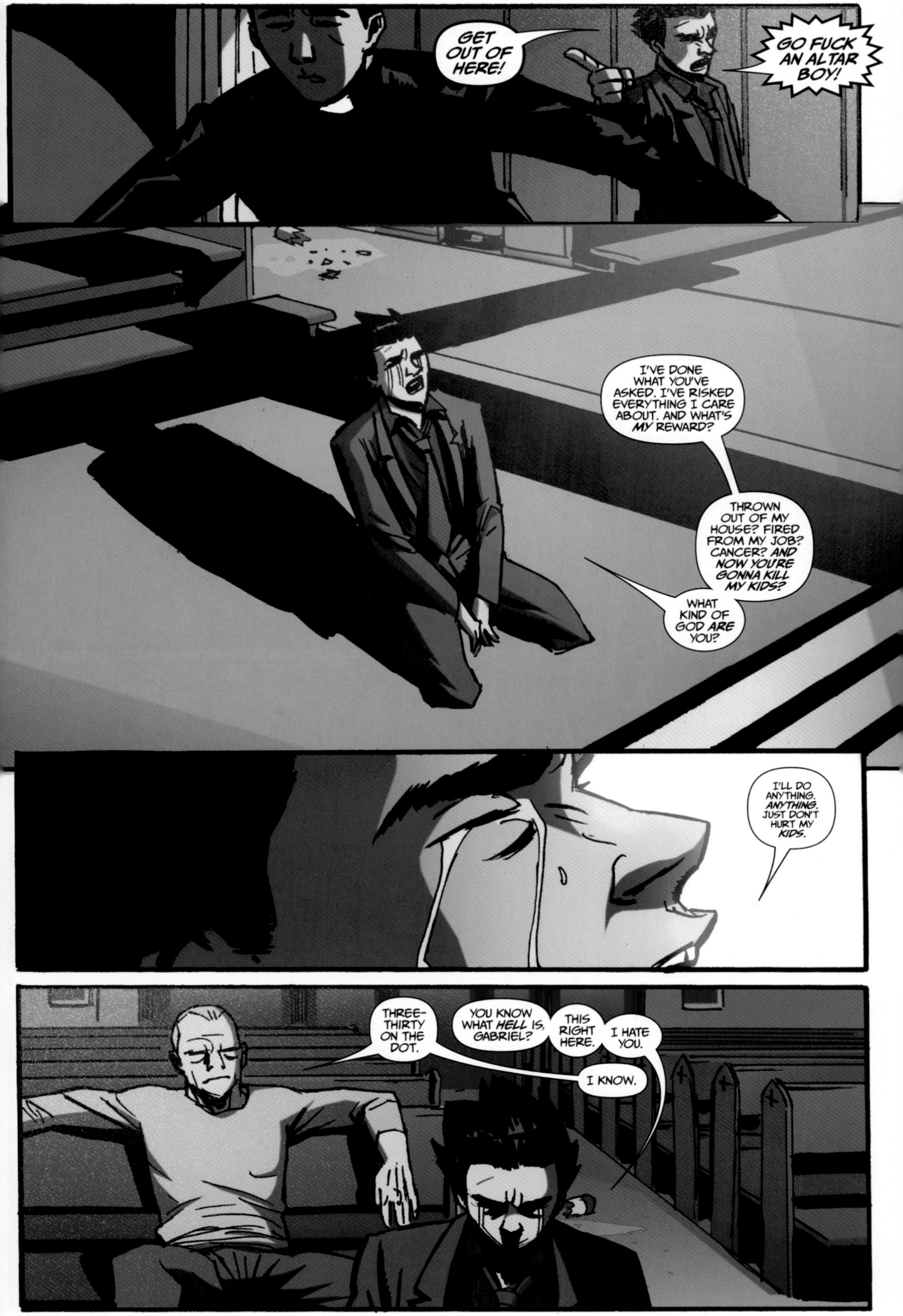
GET OUT OF HERE!
GO FUCK AN ALTAR BOY!
I'VE DONE WHAT YOU'VE ASKED. I'VE RISKED EVERYTHING I CARE ABOUT. AND WHAT'S MY REWARD?
THROWN OUT OF MY HOUSE? FIRED FROM MY JOB? CANCER? AND NOW YOU'RE GONNA KILL MY KIDS?
WHAT KIND OF GOD ARE YOU?
I'LL DO ANYTHING. ANYTHING. JUST DON'T HURT MY KIDS.
THREE-THIRTY ON THE DOT.
YOU KNOW WHAT HELL IS, GABRIEL?
THIS RIGHT HERE.
I HATE YOU.
I KNOW.

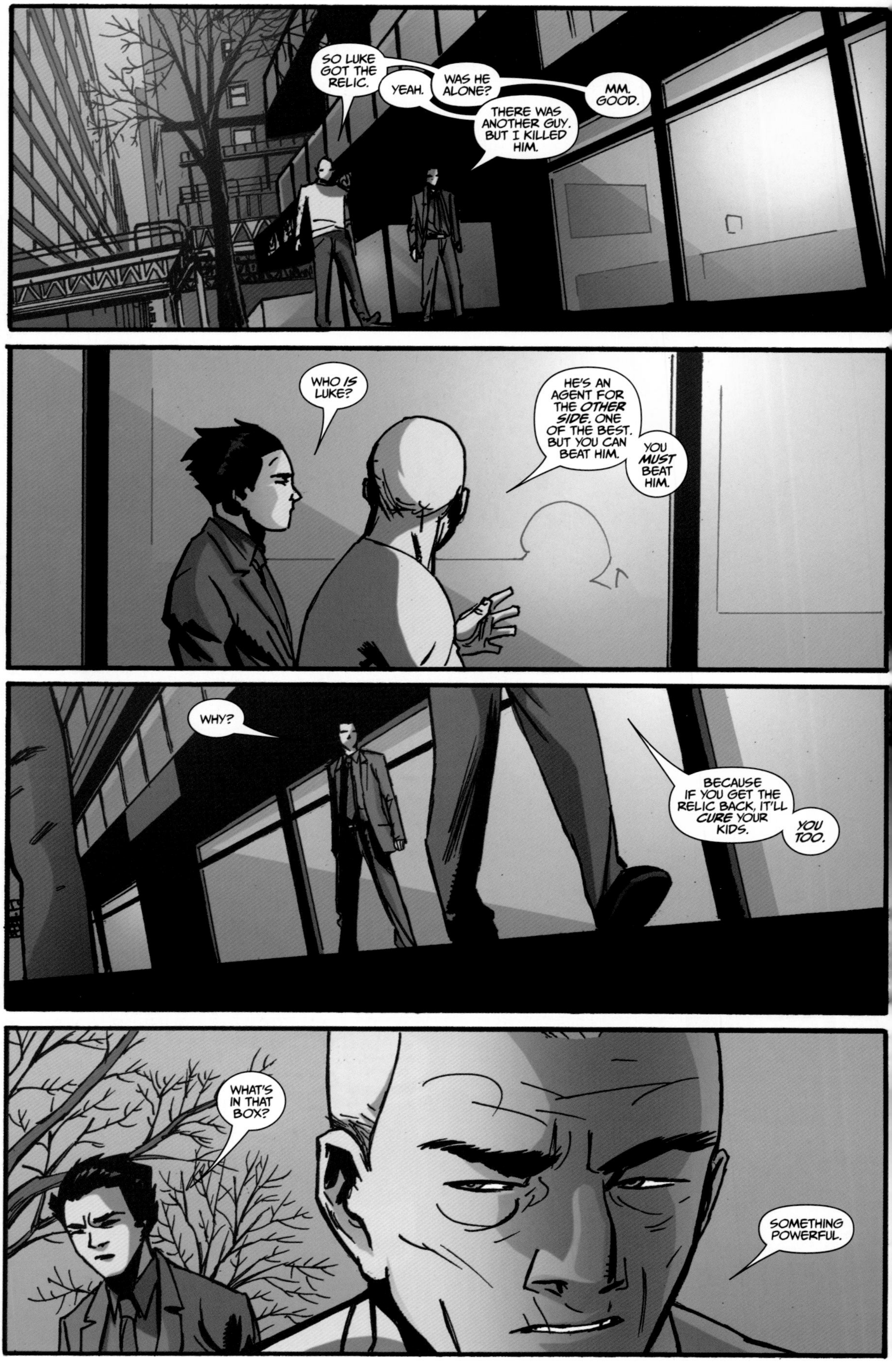

SO LUKE GOT THE RELIC.
YEAH.
WAS HE ALONE?
THERE WAS ANOTHER GUY. BUT I KILLED HIM.
MM. GOOD.
WHO *IS* LUKE?
HE'S AN AGENT FOR THE *OTHER SIDE*. ONE OF THE BEST. BUT YOU CAN BEAT HIM.
YOU *MUST* BEAT HIM.
WHY?
BECAUSE IF YOU GET THE RELIC BACK, IT'LL *CURE* YOUR KIDS.
YOU TOO.
WHAT'S IN THAT BOX?
SOMETHING POWERFUL.

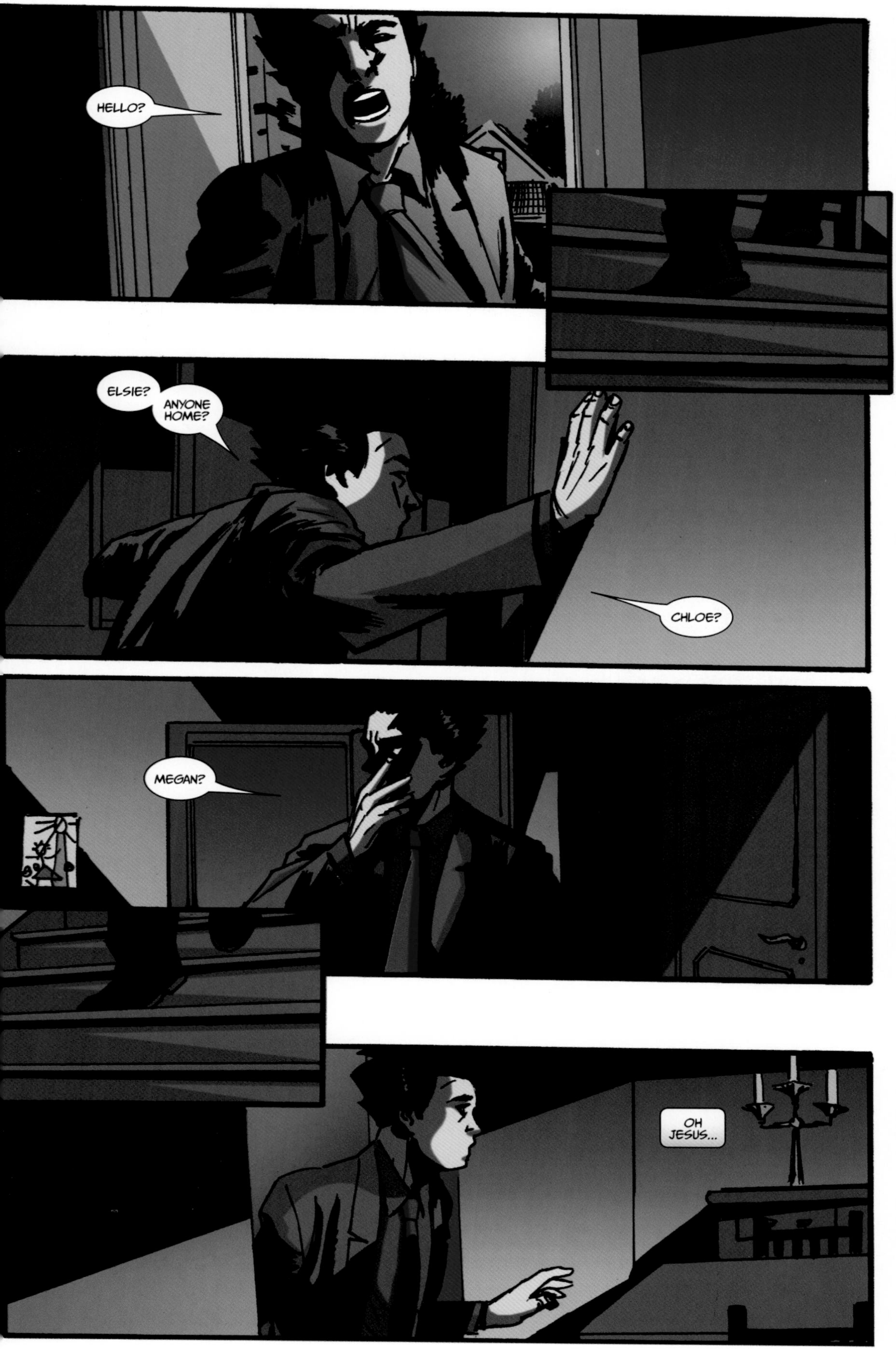
HELLO?
ELSIE?
ANYONE HOME?
CHLOE?
MEGAN?
OH JESUS...

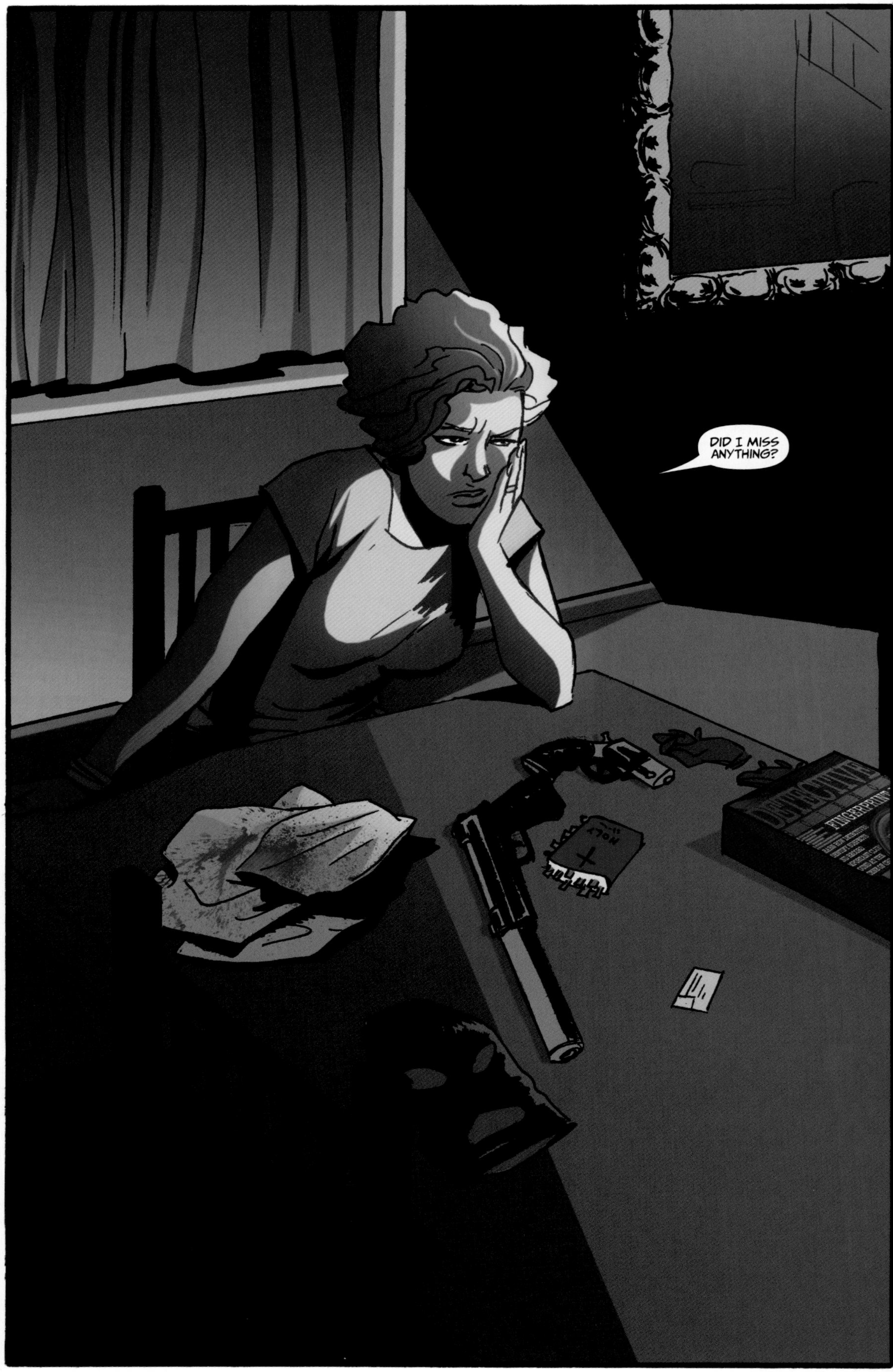
DID I MISS ANYTHING?

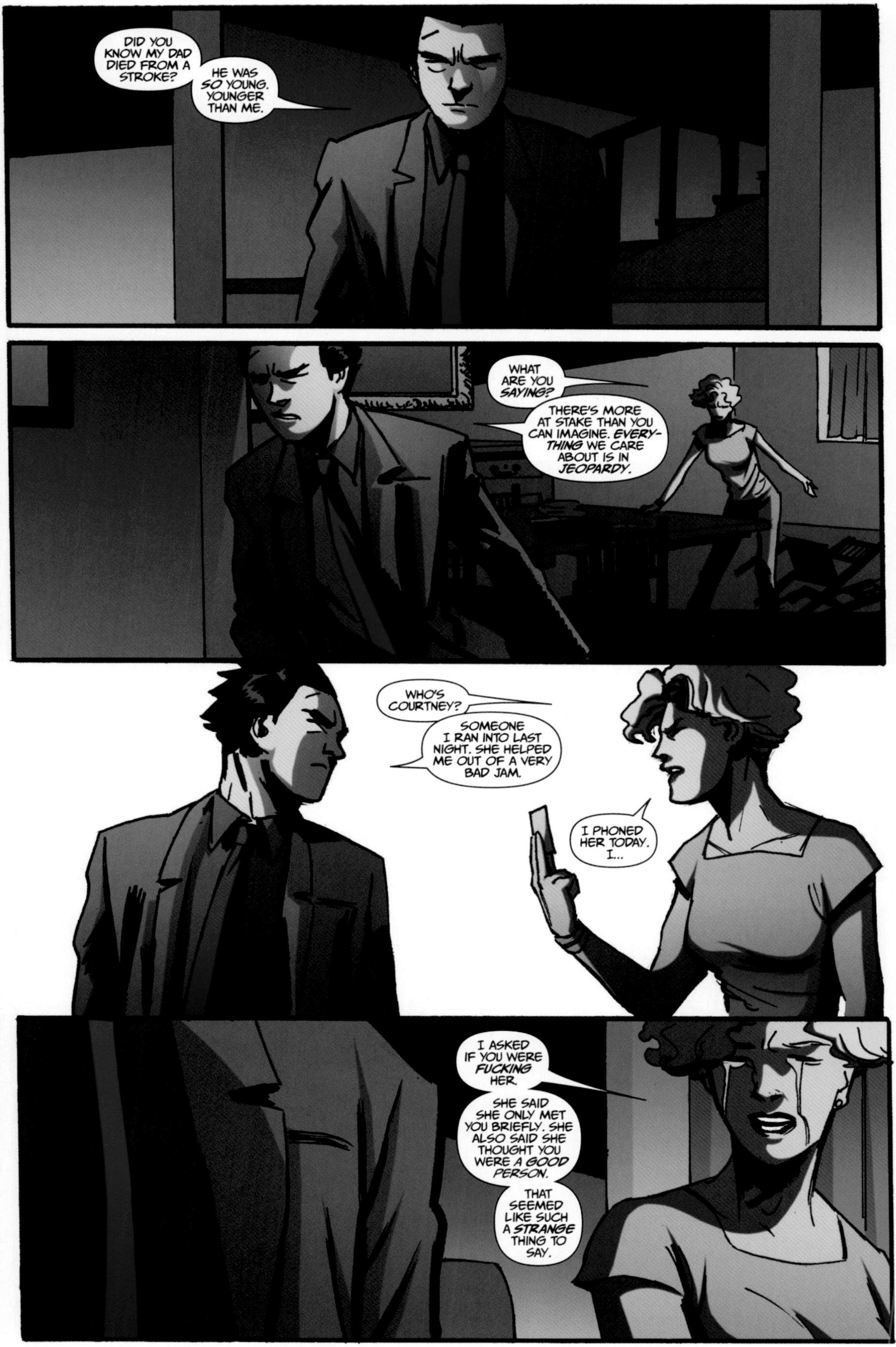
DID YOU KNOW MY DAD DIED FROM A STROKE?
HE WAS *SO* YOUNG. YOUNGER THAN ME.
WHAT ARE YOU *SAYING?*
THERE'S MORE AT STAKE THAN YOU CAN IMAGINE. *EVERYTHING* WE CARE ABOUT IS IN *JEOPARDY*.
WHO'S COURTNEY?
SOMEONE I RAN INTO LAST NIGHT. SHE HELPED ME OUT OF A VERY BAD JAM.
I PHONED HER TODAY. I...
I ASKED IF YOU WERE *FUCKING* HER.
SHE SAID SHE ONLY MET YOU BRIEFLY. SHE ALSO SAID SHE THOUGHT YOU WERE *A GOOD PERSON*.
THAT SEEMED LIKE SUCH A *STRANGE* THING TO SAY.

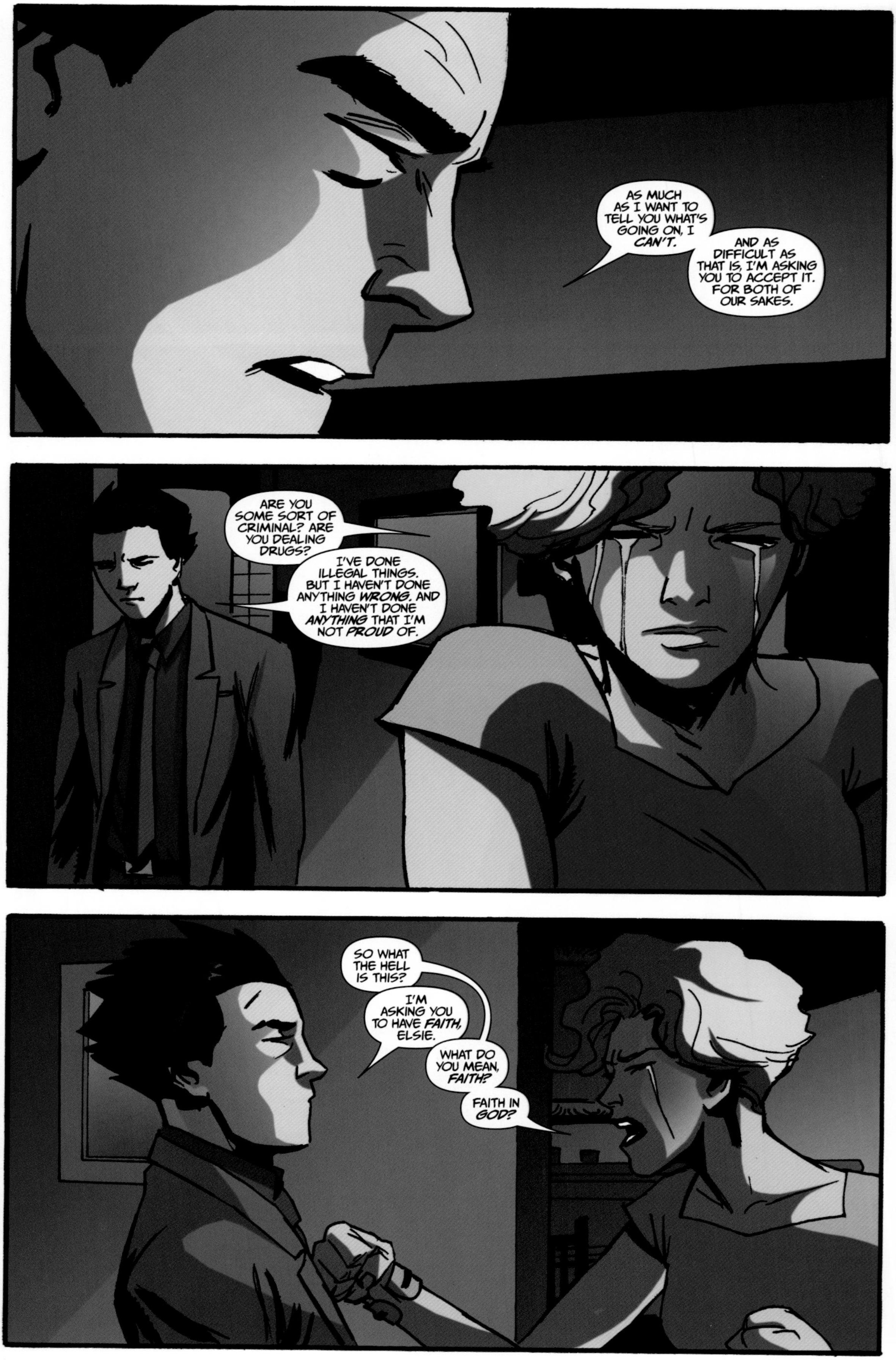
AS MUCH AS I WANT TO TELL YOU WHAT'S GOING ON, I *CAN'T.*
AND AS DIFFICULT AS THAT IS, I'M ASKING YOU TO ACCEPT IT. FOR BOTH OF OUR SAKES.
ARE YOU SOME SORT OF CRIMINAL? ARE YOU DEALING DRUGS?
I'VE DONE ILLEGAL THINGS. BUT I HAVEN'T DONE ANYTHING *WRONG.* AND I HAVEN'T DONE *ANYTHING* THAT I'M NOT *PROUD* OF.
SO WHAT THE HELL IS THIS?
I'M ASKING YOU TO HAVE *FAITH,* ELSIE.
WHAT DO YOU MEAN, *FAITH?*
FAITH IN *GOD?*

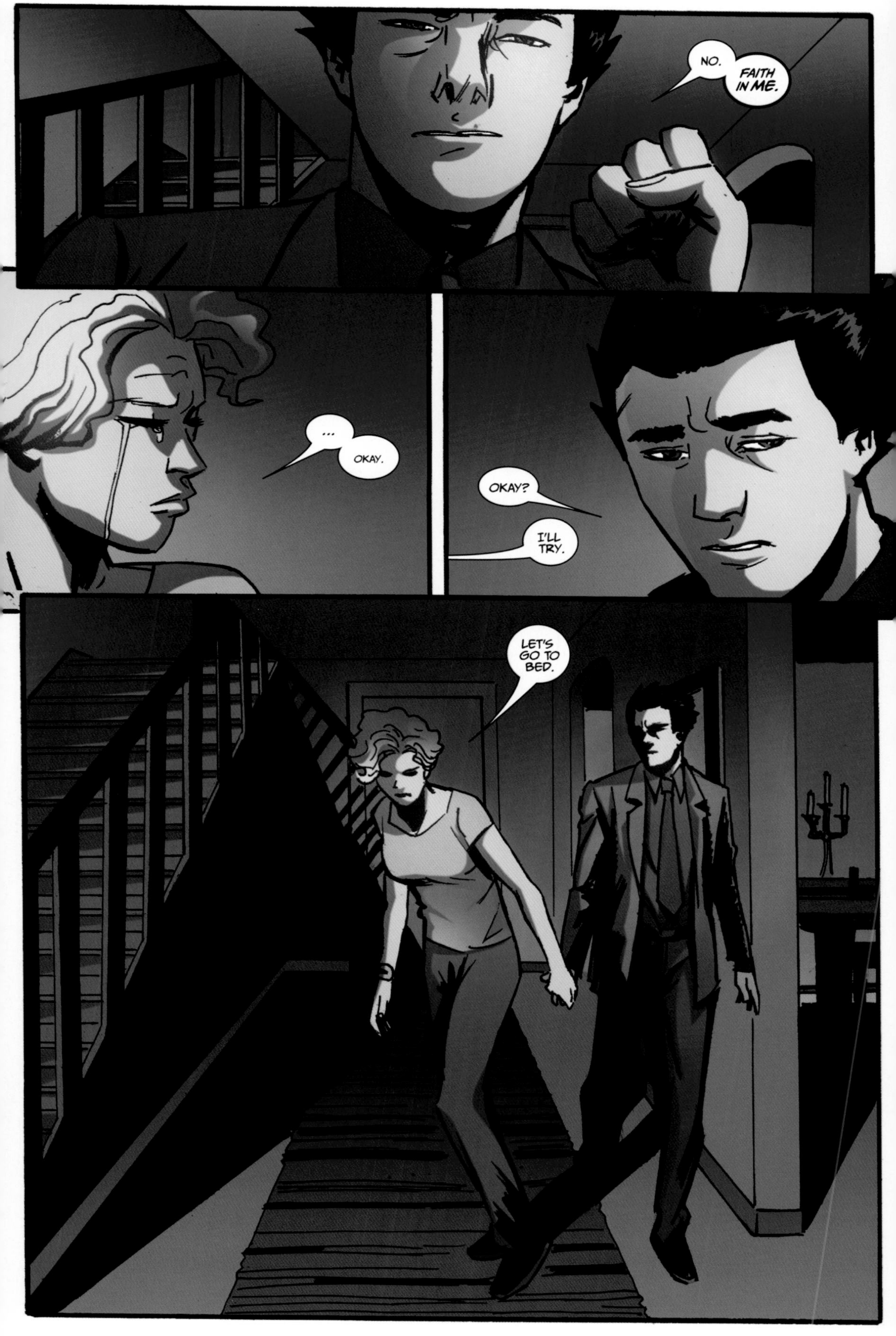
NO.
FAITH IN ME.
...
OKAY.
OKAY?
I'LL TRY.
LET'S GO TO BED.

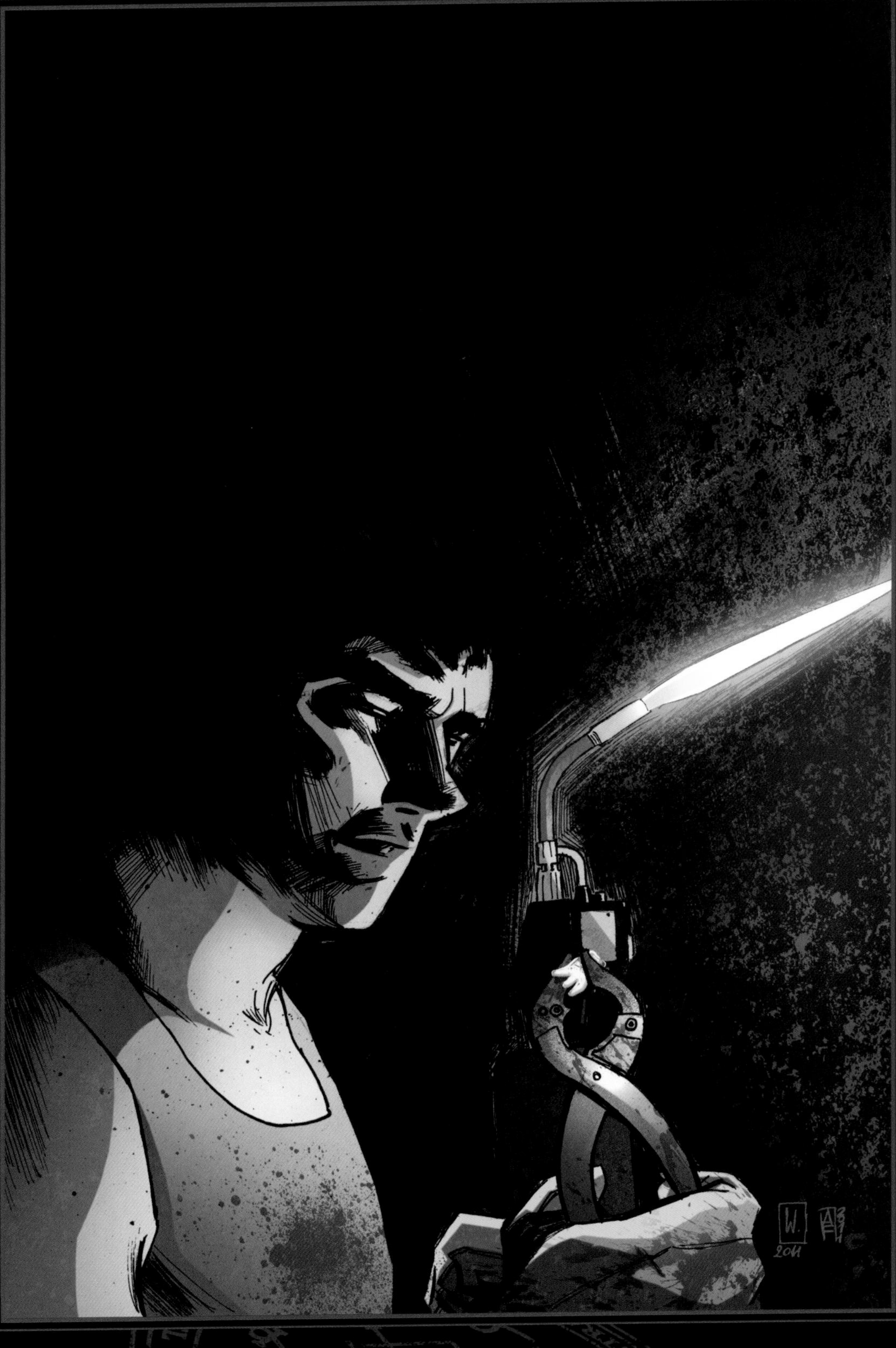
W.
2011

CHAPTER 6

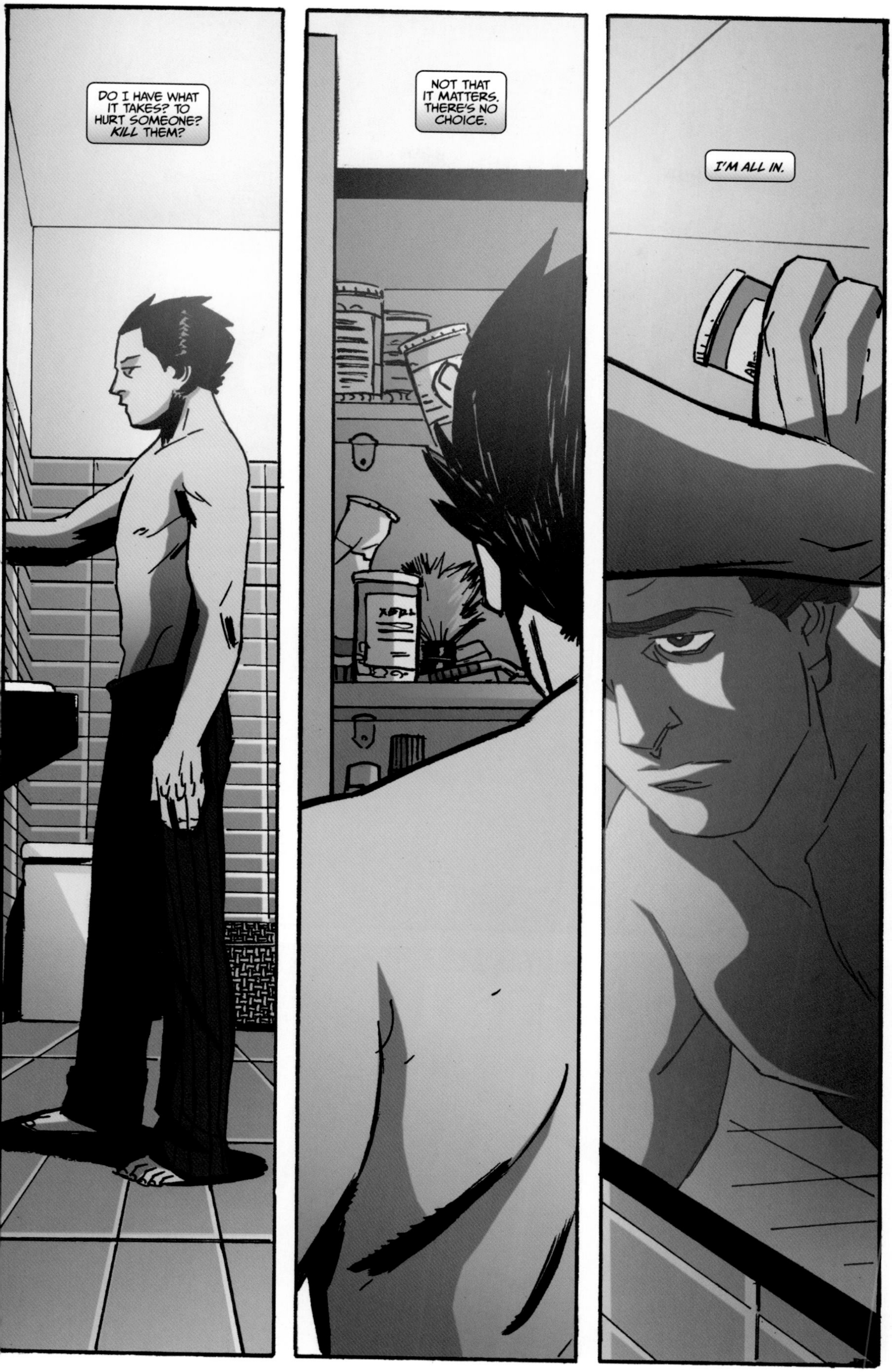
DO I HAVE WHAT IT TAKES? TO HURT SOMEONE? *KILL* THEM?
NOT THAT IT MATTERS. THERE'S NO CHOICE.
I'M ALL IN.

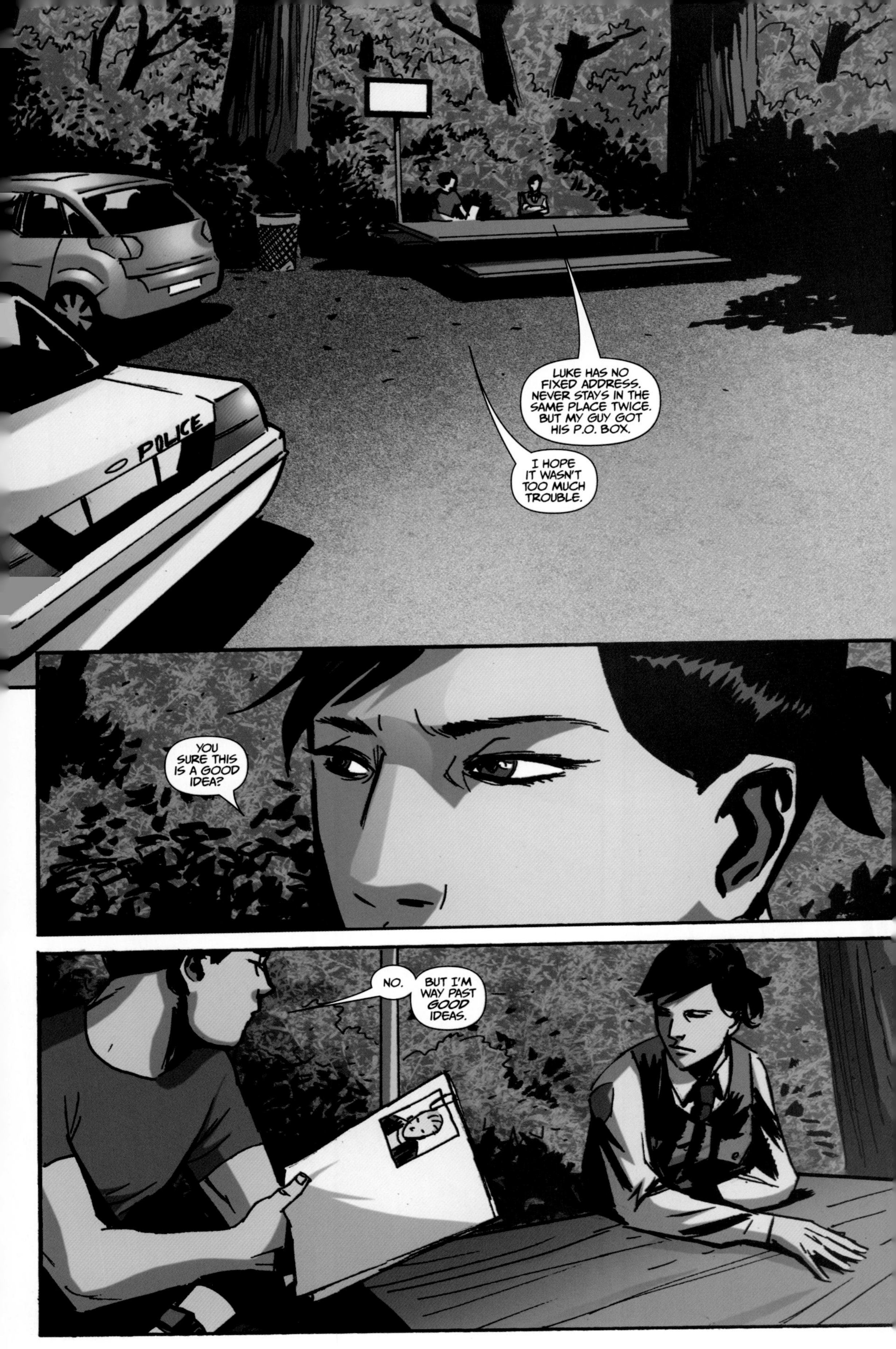
LUKE HAS NO FIXED ADDRESS. NEVER STAYS IN THE SAME PLACE TWICE. BUT MY GUY GOT HIS P.O. BOX.
POLICE
I HOPE IT WASN'T TOO MUCH TROUBLE.
YOU SURE THIS IS A GOOD IDEA?
NO.
BUT I'M WAY PAST GOOD IDEAS.

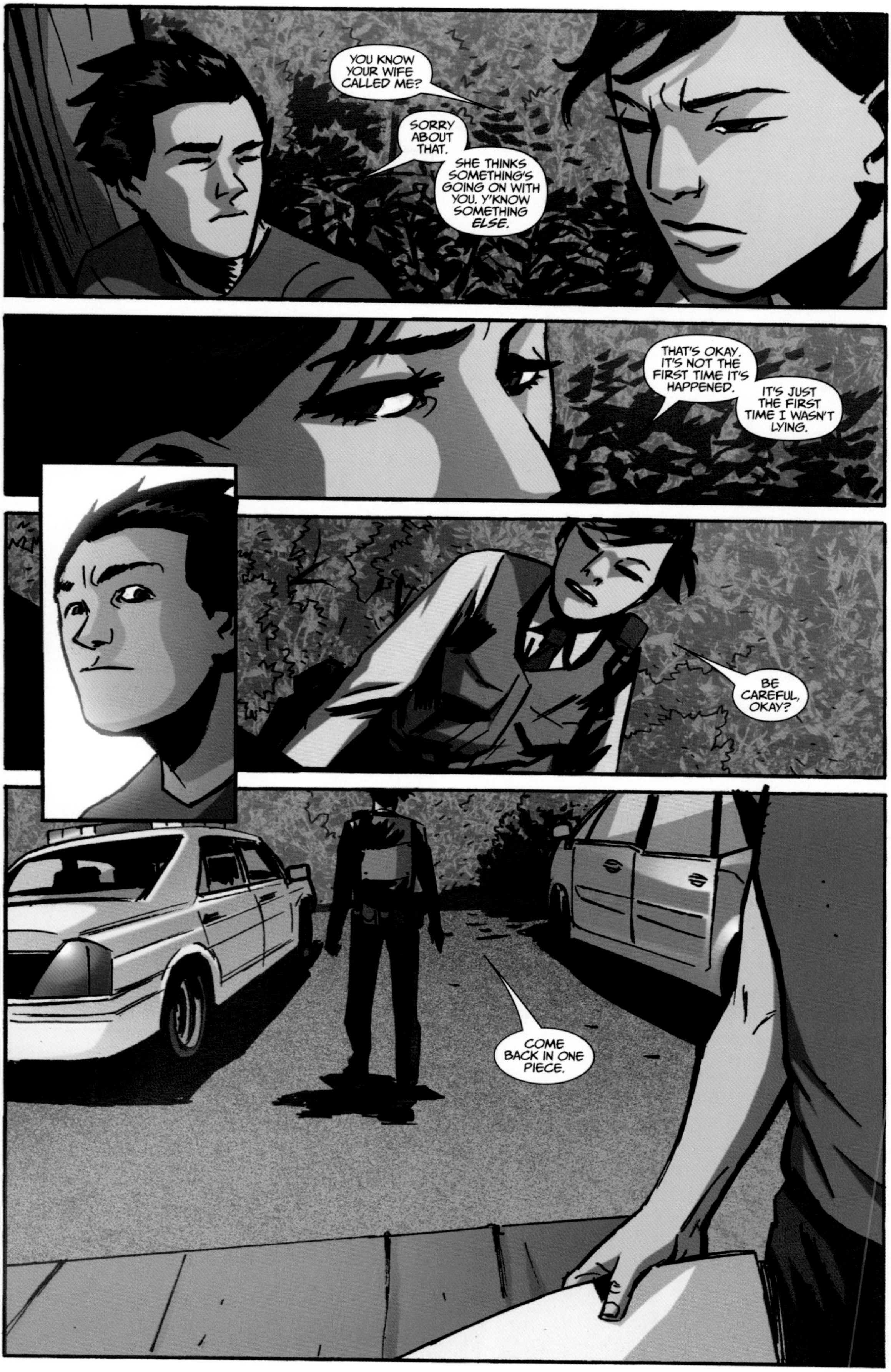
YOU KNOW YOUR WIFE CALLED ME?
SORRY ABOUT THAT.
SHE THINKS SOMETHING'S GOING ON WITH YOU. Y'KNOW SOMETHING *ELSE*.
THAT'S OKAY. IT'S NOT THE FIRST TIME IT'S HAPPENED.
IT'S JUST THE FIRST TIME I WASN'T LYING.
BE CAREFUL, OKAY?
COME BACK IN ONE PIECE.

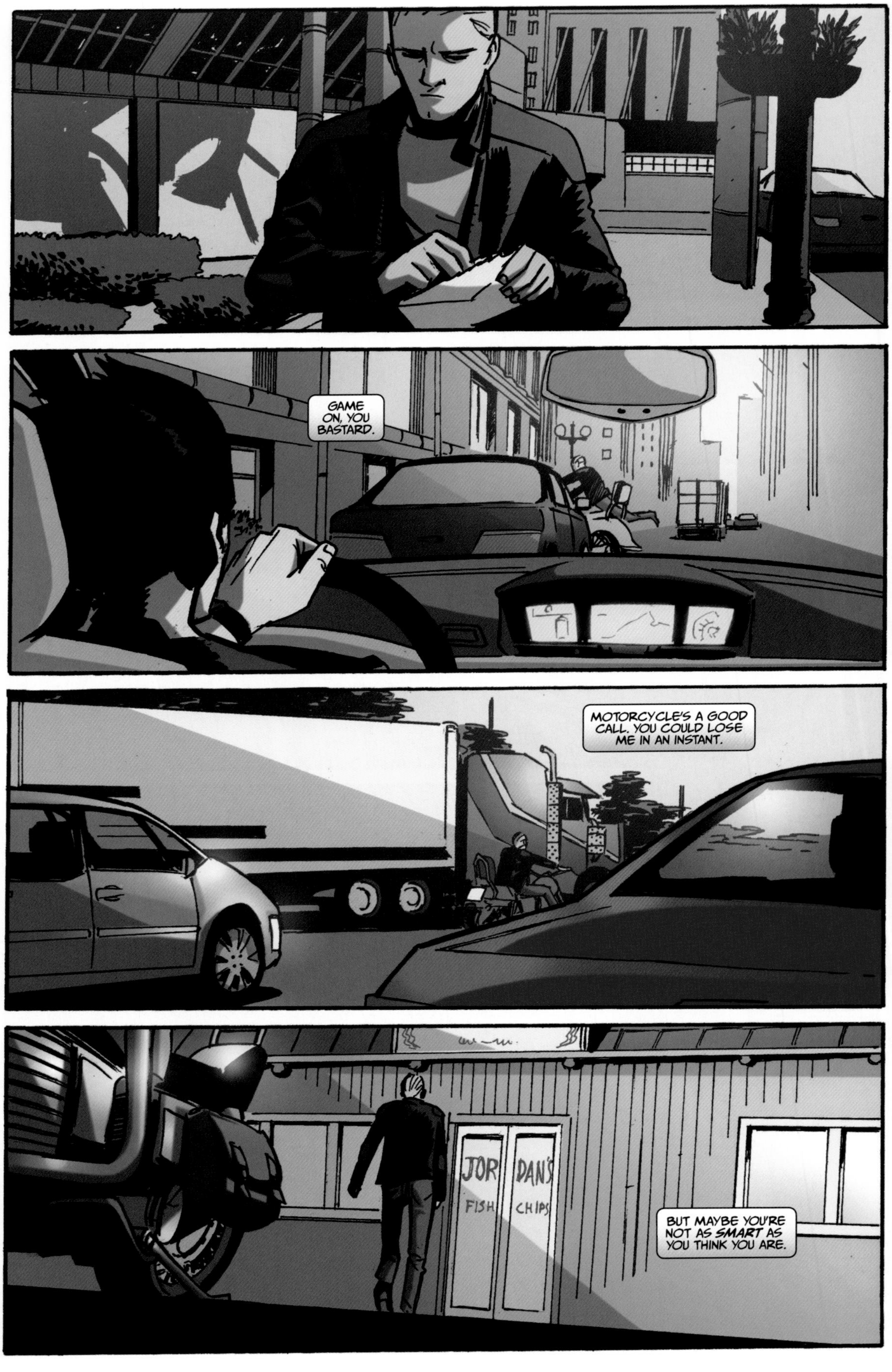
GAME ON, YOU BASTARD.
MOTORCYCLE'S A GOOD CALL. YOU COULD LOSE ME IN AN INSTANT.
JORDAN'S
FISH CHIPS
BUT MAYBE YOU'RE NOT AS SMART AS YOU THINK YOU ARE.

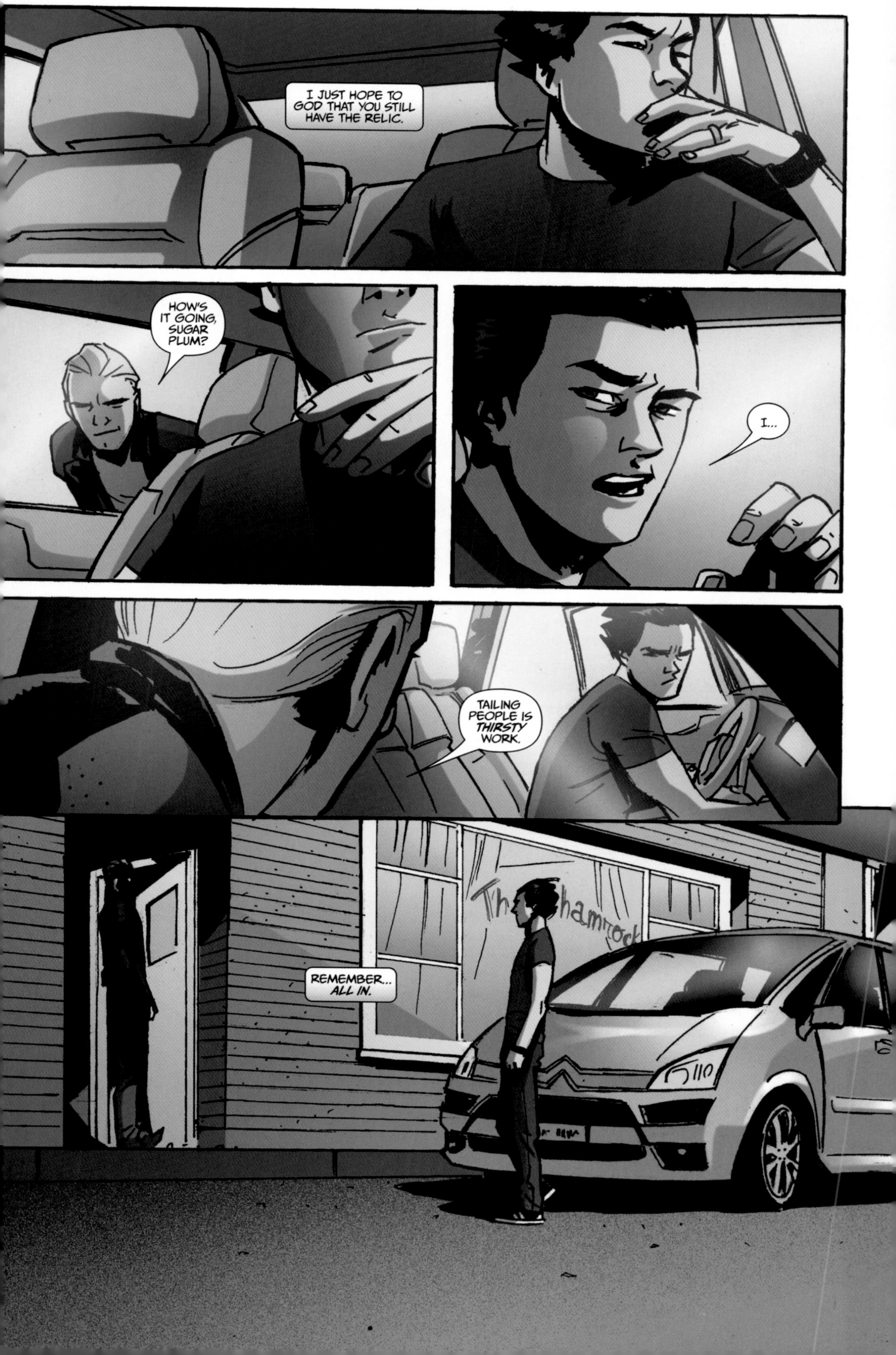
I JUST HOPE TO GOD THAT YOU STILL HAVE THE RELIC.
HOW'S IT GOING, SUGAR PLUM?
I...
TAILING PEOPLE IS *THIRSTY* WORK.
REMEMBER... *ALL IN.*

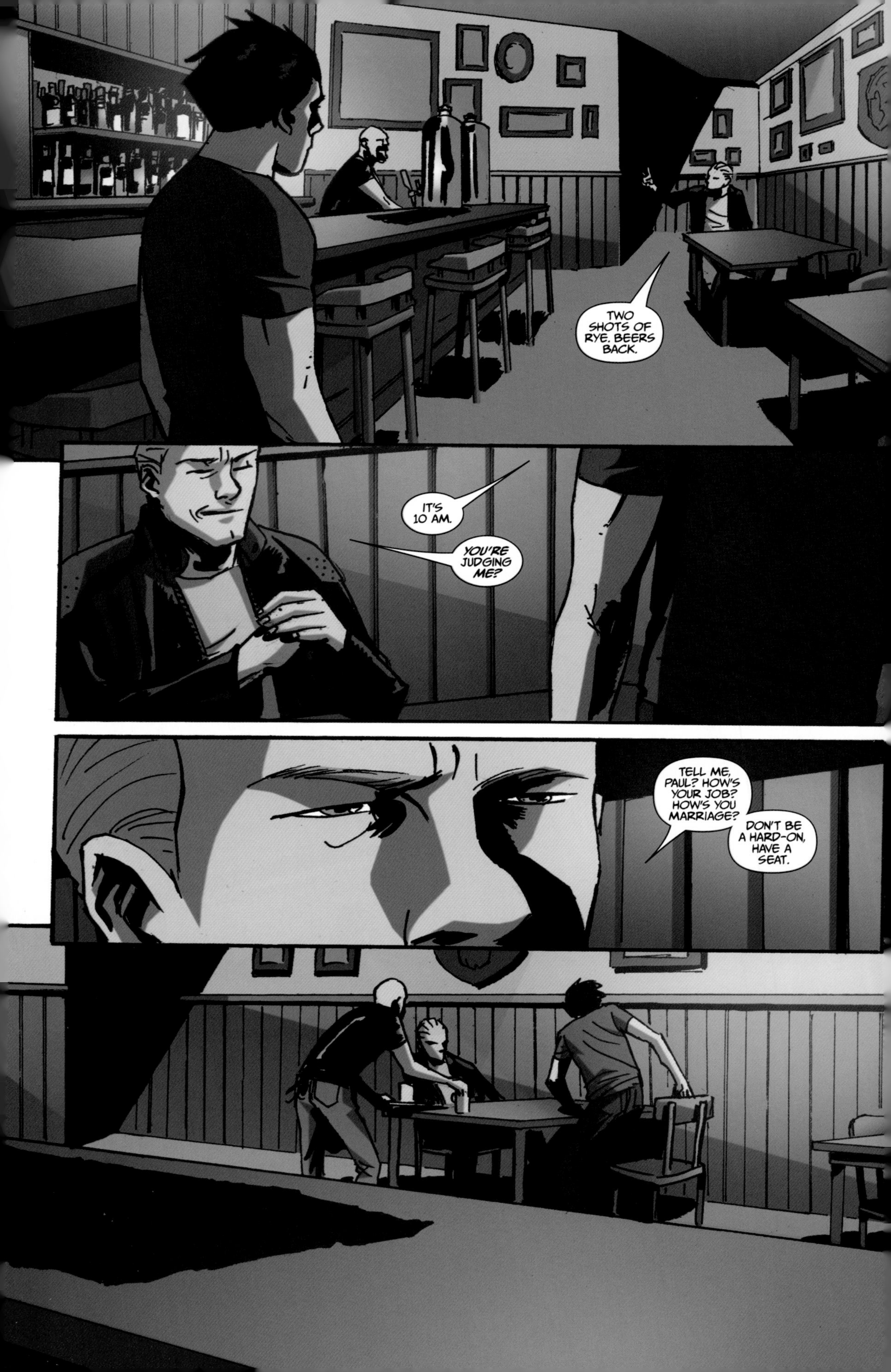
TWO SHOTS OF RYE. BEERS BACK.
IT'S 10 AM.
YOU'RE JUDGING ME?
TELL ME, PAUL? HOW'S YOUR JOB? HOW'S YOU MARRIAGE?
DON'T BE A HARD-ON, HAVE A SEAT.

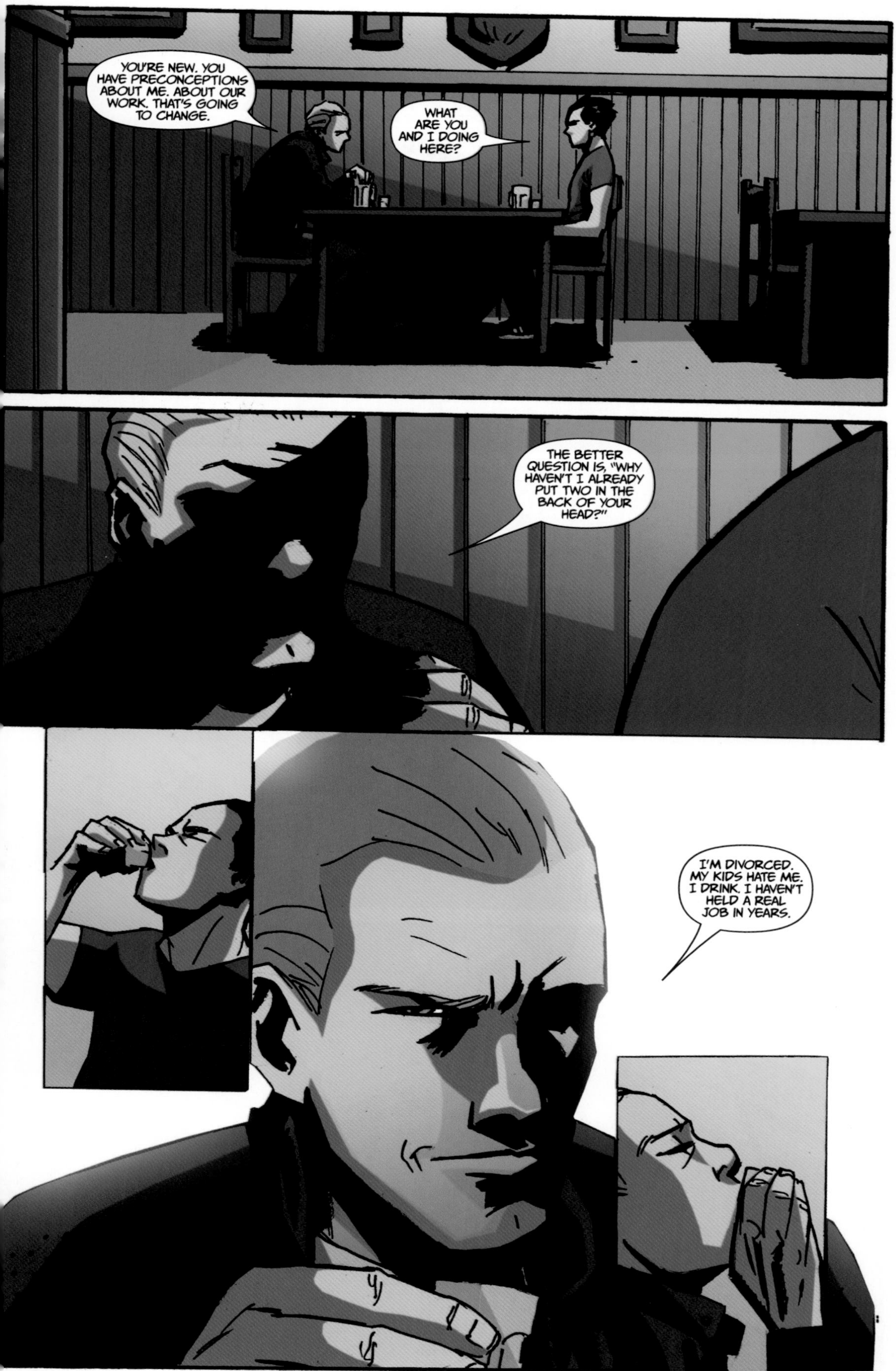
YOU'RE NEW. YOU HAVE PRECONCEPTIONS ABOUT ME. ABOUT OUR WORK. THAT'S GOING TO CHANGE.
WHAT ARE YOU AND I DOING HERE?
THE BETTER QUESTION IS, "WHY HAVEN'T I ALREADY PUT TWO IN THE BACK OF YOUR HEAD?"
I'M DIVORCED. MY KIDS HATE ME. I DRINK. I HAVEN'T HELD A REAL JOB IN YEARS.

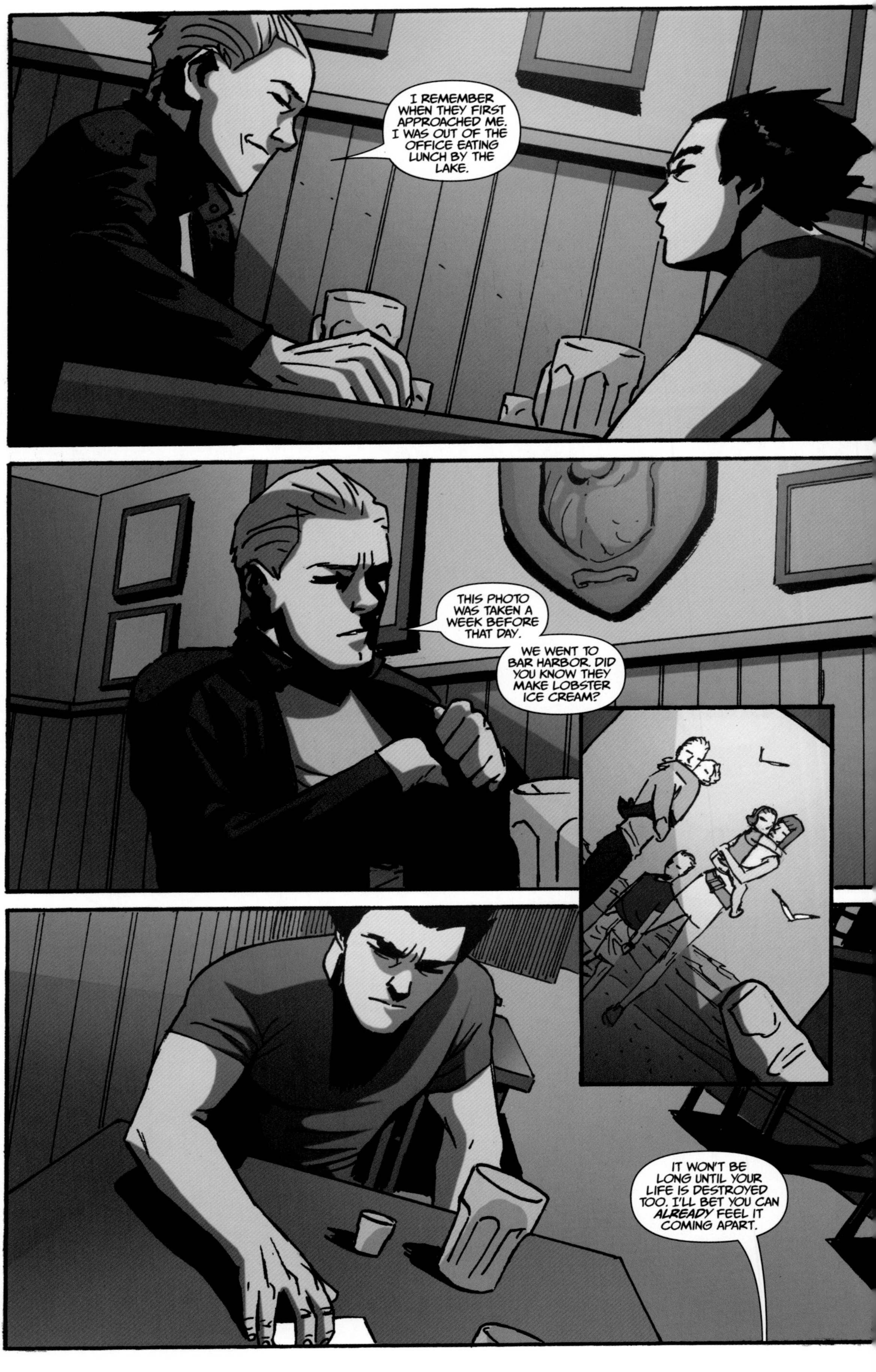
I REMEMBER WHEN THEY FIRST APPROACHED ME. I WAS OUT OF THE OFFICE EATING LUNCH BY THE LAKE.
THIS PHOTO WAS TAKEN A WEEK BEFORE THAT DAY.
WE WENT TO BAR HARBOR. DID YOU KNOW THEY MAKE LOBSTER ICE CREAM?
IT WON'T BE LONG UNTIL YOUR LIFE IS DESTROYED TOO. I'LL BET YOU CAN *ALREADY* FEEL IT COMING APART.

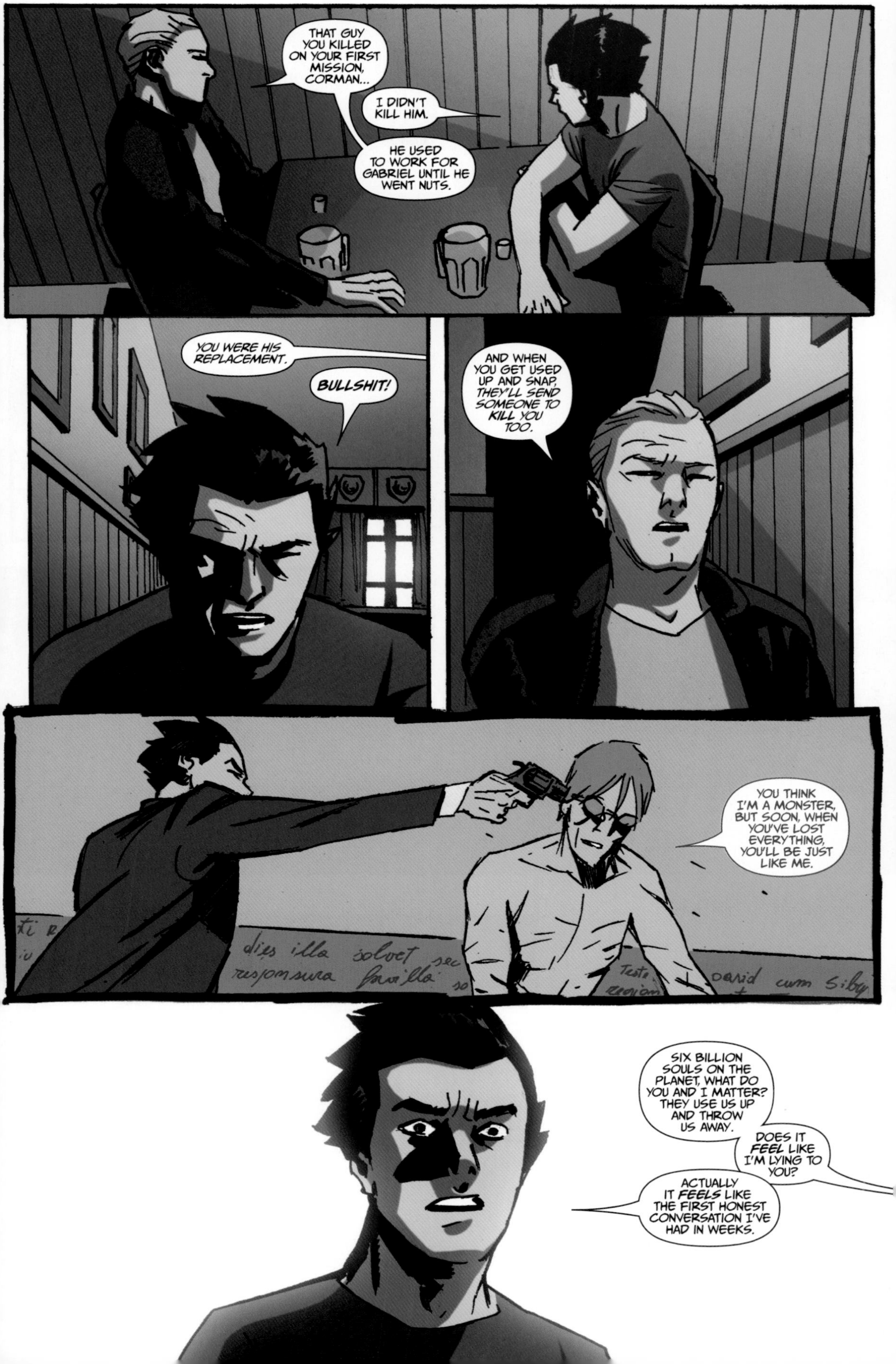
THAT GUY YOU KILLED ON YOUR FIRST MISSION, CORMAN...
I DIDN'T KILL HIM.
HE USED TO WORK FOR GABRIEL UNTIL HE WENT NUTS.
YOU WERE HIS REPLACEMENT.
BULLSHIT!
AND WHEN YOU GET USED UP AND SNAP, THEY'LL SEND SOMEONE TO KILL YOU TOO.
YOU THINK I'M A MONSTER, BUT SOON, WHEN YOU'VE LOST EVERYTHING, YOU'LL BE JUST LIKE ME.
SIX BILLION SOULS ON THE PLANET, WHAT DO YOU AND I MATTER? THEY USE US UP AND THROW US AWAY.
DOES IT FEEL LIKE I'M LYING TO YOU?
ACTUALLY IT FEELS LIKE THE FIRST HONEST CONVERSATION I'VE HAD IN WEEKS.

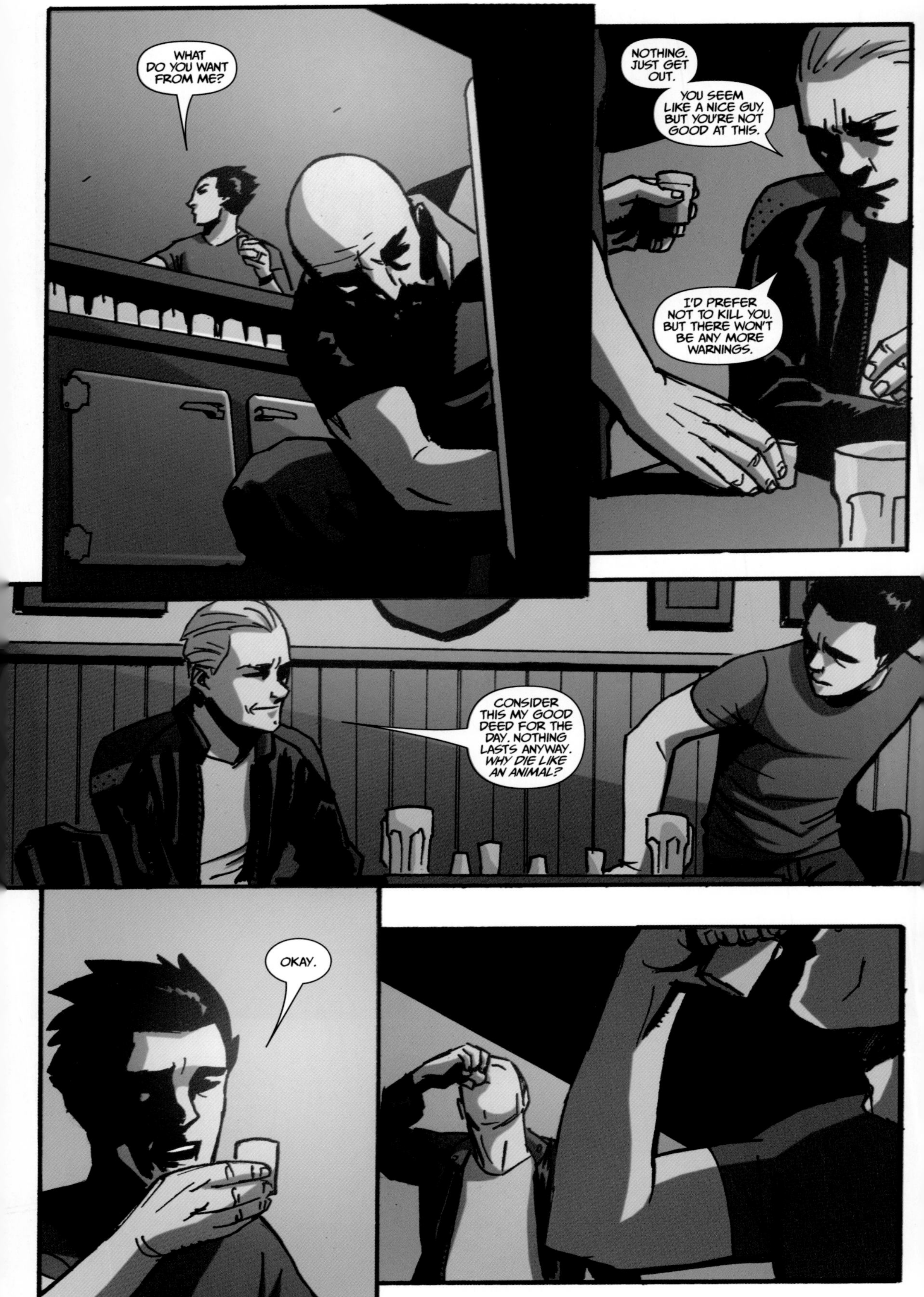
WHAT DO YOU WANT FROM ME?
NOTHING. JUST GET OUT.
YOU SEEM LIKE A NICE GUY, BUT YOU'RE NOT GOOD AT THIS.
I'D PREFER NOT TO KILL YOU. BUT THERE WON'T BE ANY MORE WARNINGS.
CONSIDER THIS MY GOOD DEED FOR THE DAY. NOTHING LASTS ANYWAY. *WHY DIE LIKE AN ANIMAL?*
OKAY.

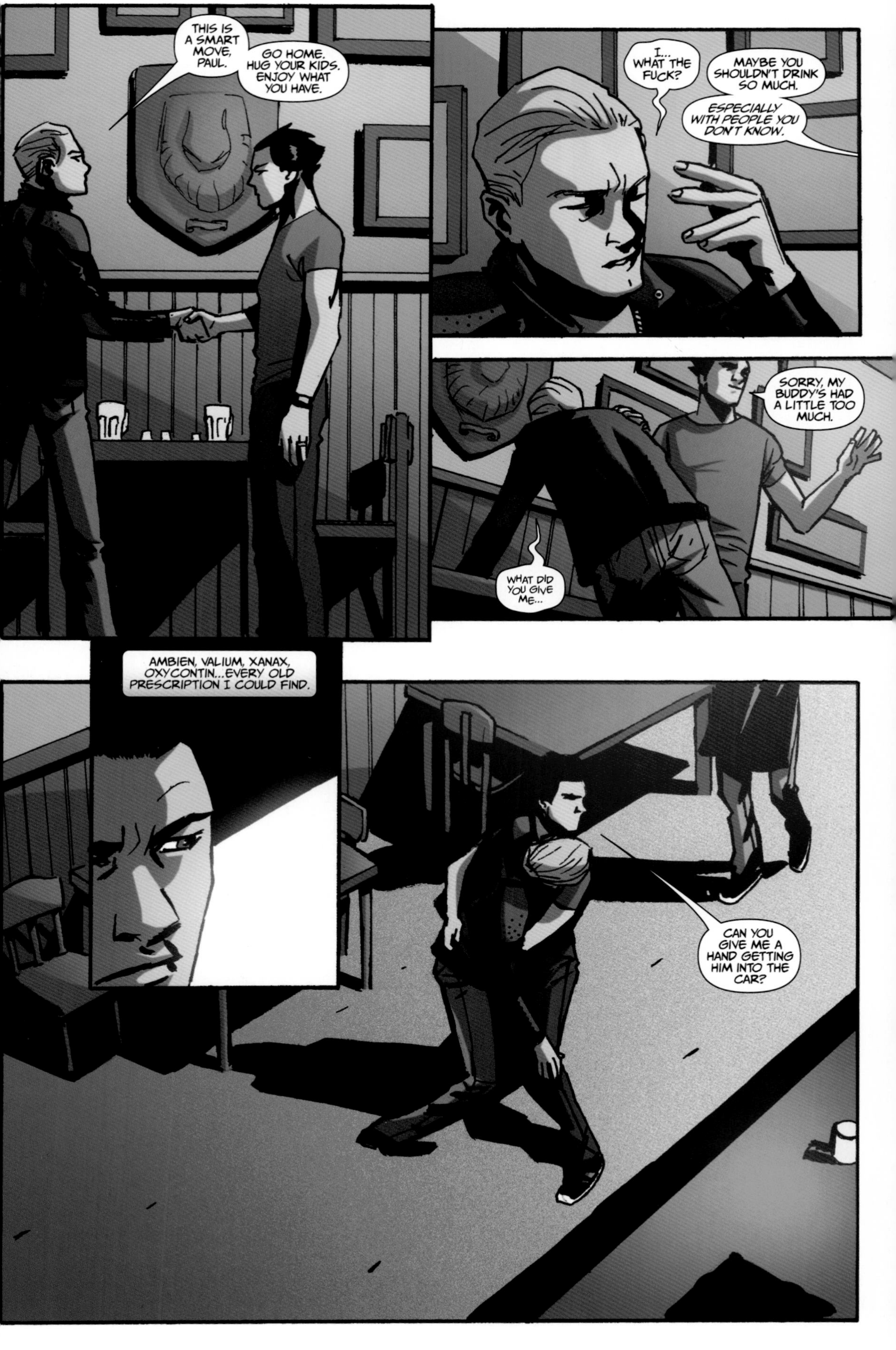
THIS IS A SMART MOVE, PAUL.
GO HOME. HUG YOUR KIDS. ENJOY WHAT YOU HAVE.
I... WHAT THE FUCK?
MAYBE YOU SHOULDN'T DRINK SO MUCH.
ESPECIALLY WITH PEOPLE YOU DON'T KNOW.
SORRY, MY BUDDY'S HAD A LITTLE TOO MUCH.
WHAT DID YOU GIVE ME...
AMBIEN, VALIUM, XANAX, OXYCONTIN...EVERY OLD PRESCRIPTION I COULD FIND.
CAN YOU GIVE ME A HAND GETTING HIM INTO THE CAR?

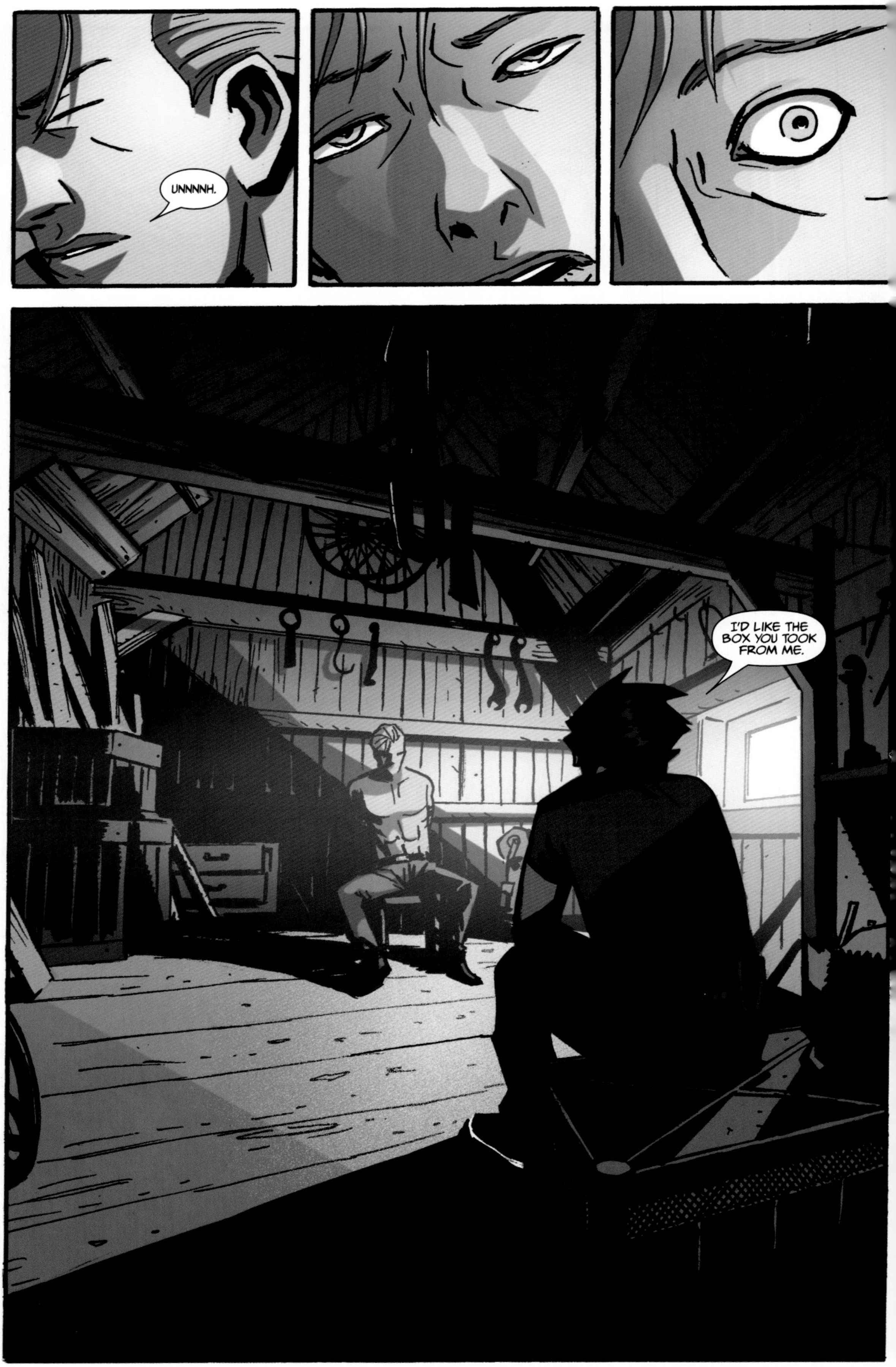
UNNNNH.
I'D LIKE THE BOX YOU TOOK FROM ME.

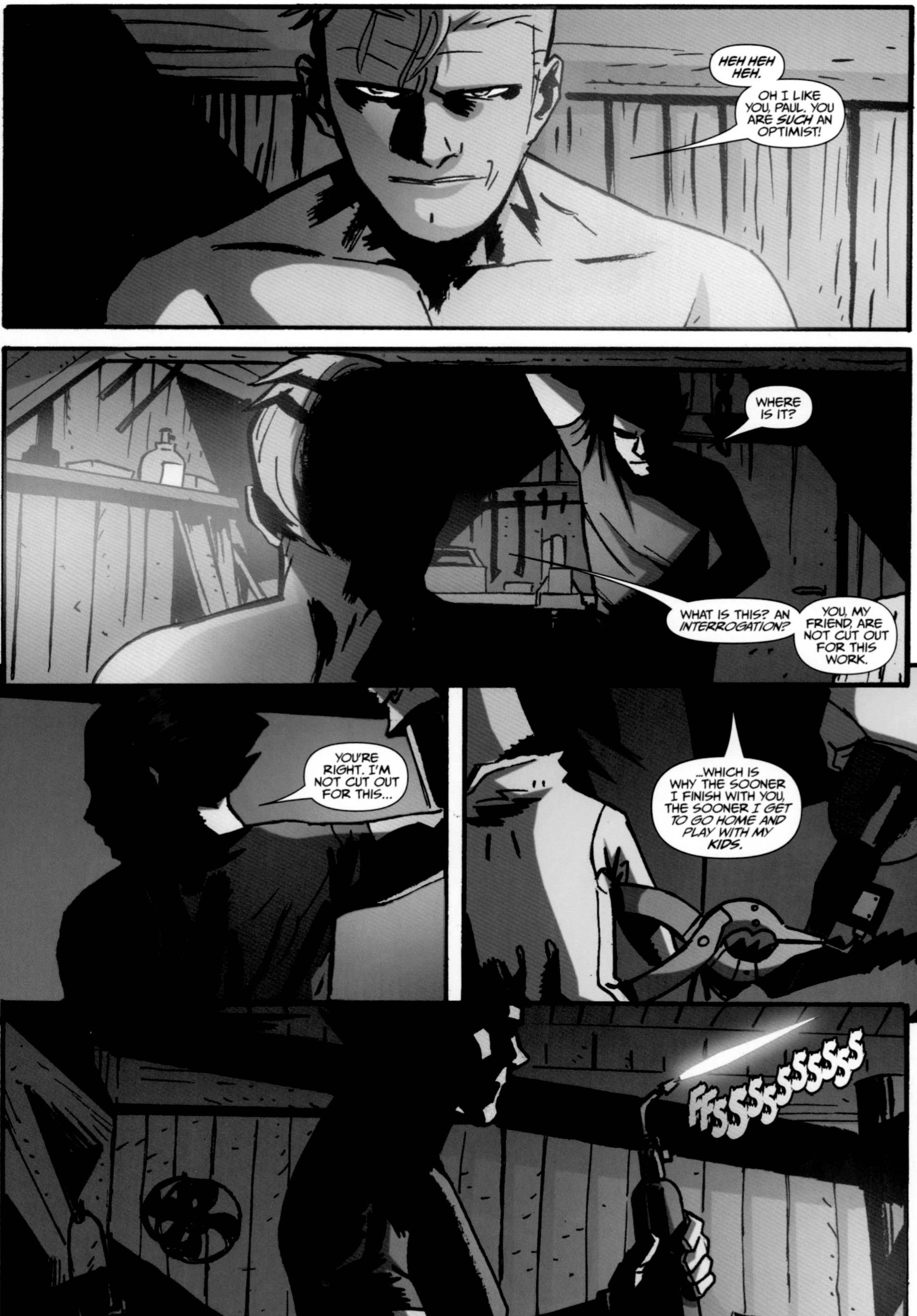
HEH HEH HEH.
OH I LIKE YOU, PAUL. YOU ARE SUCH AN OPTIMIST!
WHERE IS IT?
WHAT IS THIS? AN INTERROGATION?
YOU, MY FRIEND, ARE NOT CUT OUT FOR THIS WORK.
YOU'RE RIGHT. I'M NOT CUT OUT FOR THIS...
...WHICH IS WHY THE SOONER I FINISH WITH YOU, THE SOONER I GET TO GO HOME AND PLAY WITH MY KIDS.
FFSSSSSSSSSS

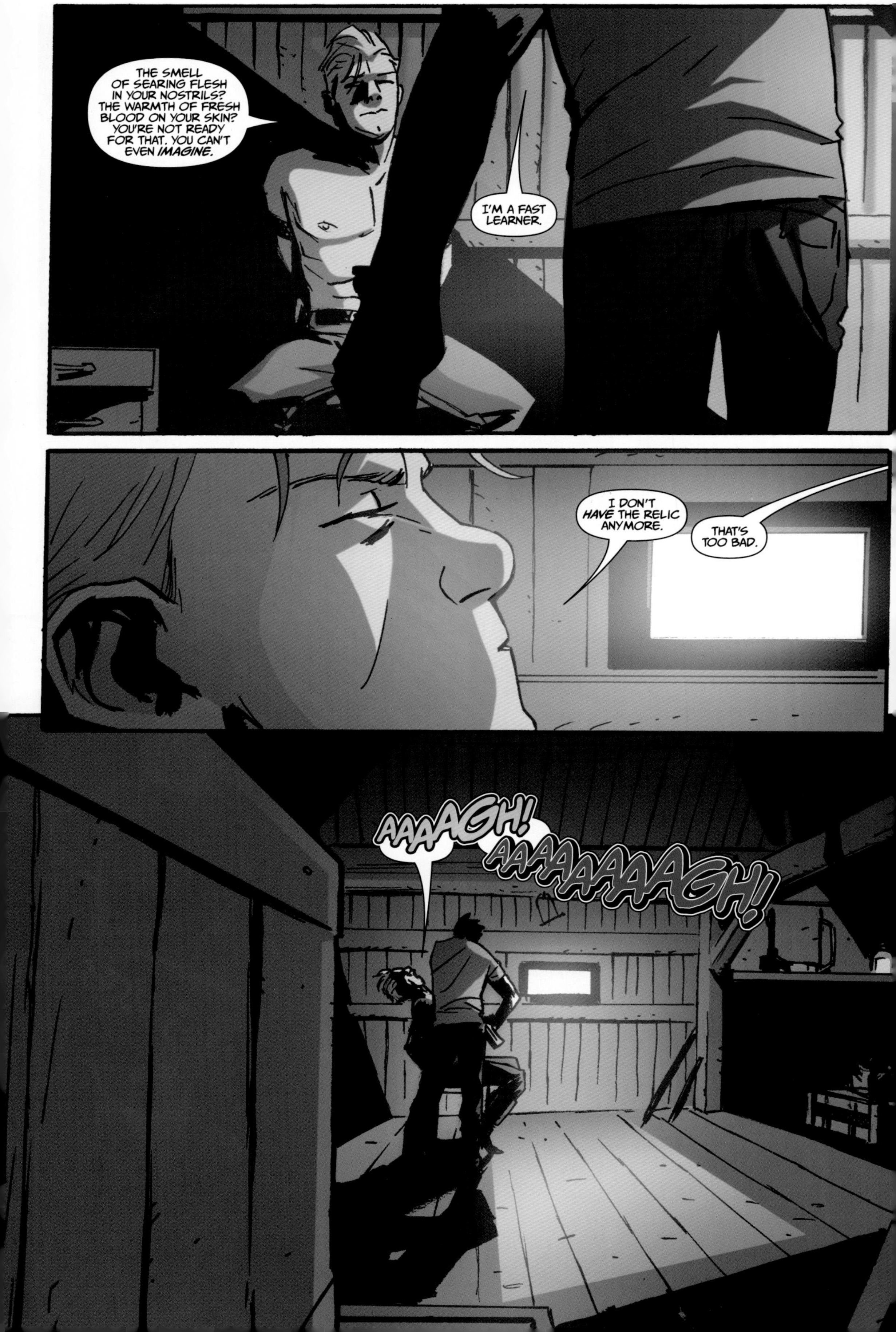

THE SMELL OF SEARING FLESH IN YOUR NOSTRILS? THE WARMTH OF FRESH BLOOD ON YOUR SKIN? YOU'RE NOT READY FOR THAT. YOU CAN'T EVEN *IMAGINE.*
I'M A FAST LEARNER.
I DON'T *HAVE* THE RELIC ANYMORE.
THAT'S TOO BAD.
AAAAGH!
AAAAAAAAAGH!

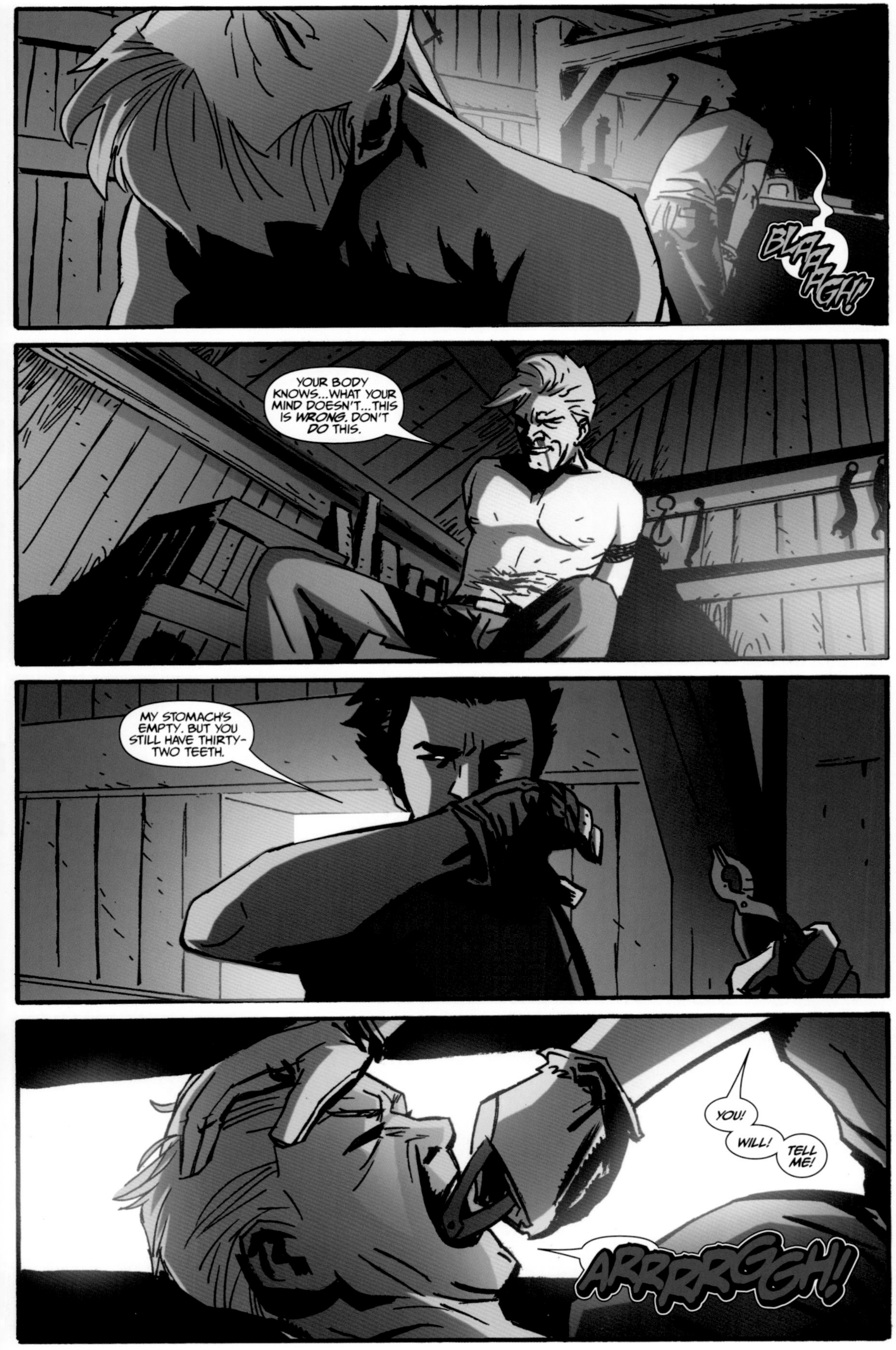
BLAAAGH!
YOUR BODY KNOWS...WHAT YOUR MIND DOESN'T...THIS IS *WRONG*. DON'T *DO* THIS.
MY STOMACH'S EMPTY. BUT YOU STILL HAVE THIRTY-TWO TEETH.
YOU!
WILL!
TELL ME!
ARRRRGGH!

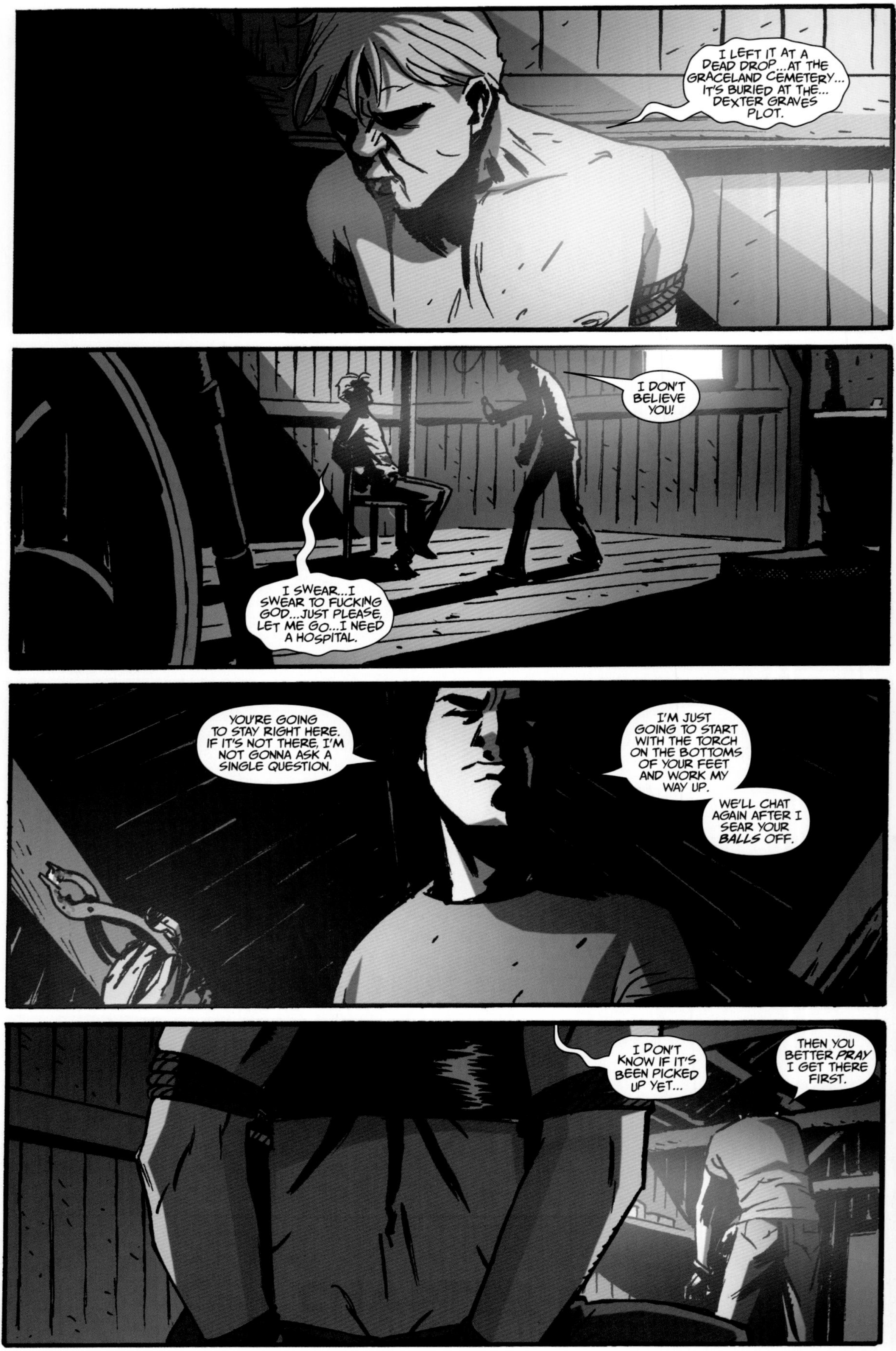
I LEFT IT AT A DEAD DROP...AT THE GRACELAND CEMETERY... IT'S BURIED AT THE... DEXTER GRAVES PLOT.
I DON'T BELIEVE YOU!
I SWEAR...I SWEAR TO FUCKING GOD...JUST PLEASE, LET ME GO...I NEED A HOSPITAL.
YOU'RE GOING TO STAY RIGHT HERE. IF IT'S NOT THERE, I'M NOT GONNA ASK A SINGLE QUESTION.
I'M JUST GOING TO START ON THE TORCH ON THE BOTTOMS OF YOUR FEET AND WORK MY WAY UP.
WE'LL CHAT AGAIN AFTER I SEAR YOUR *BALLS* OFF.
I DON'T KNOW IF IT'S BEEN PICKED UP YET...
THEN YOU BETTER *PRAY* I GET THERE FIRST.

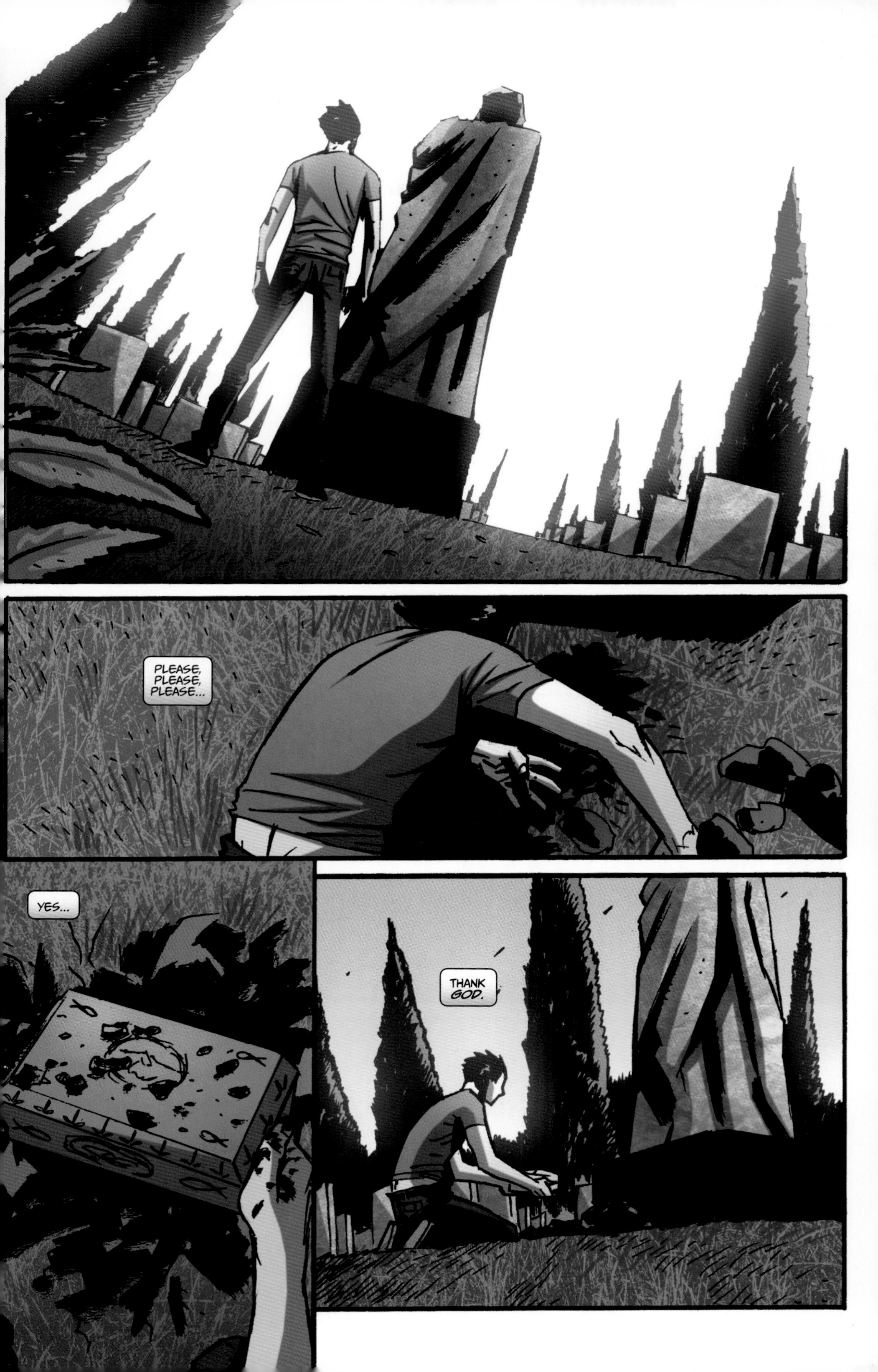
PLEASE, PLEASE, PLEASE...
YES...
THANK GOD.

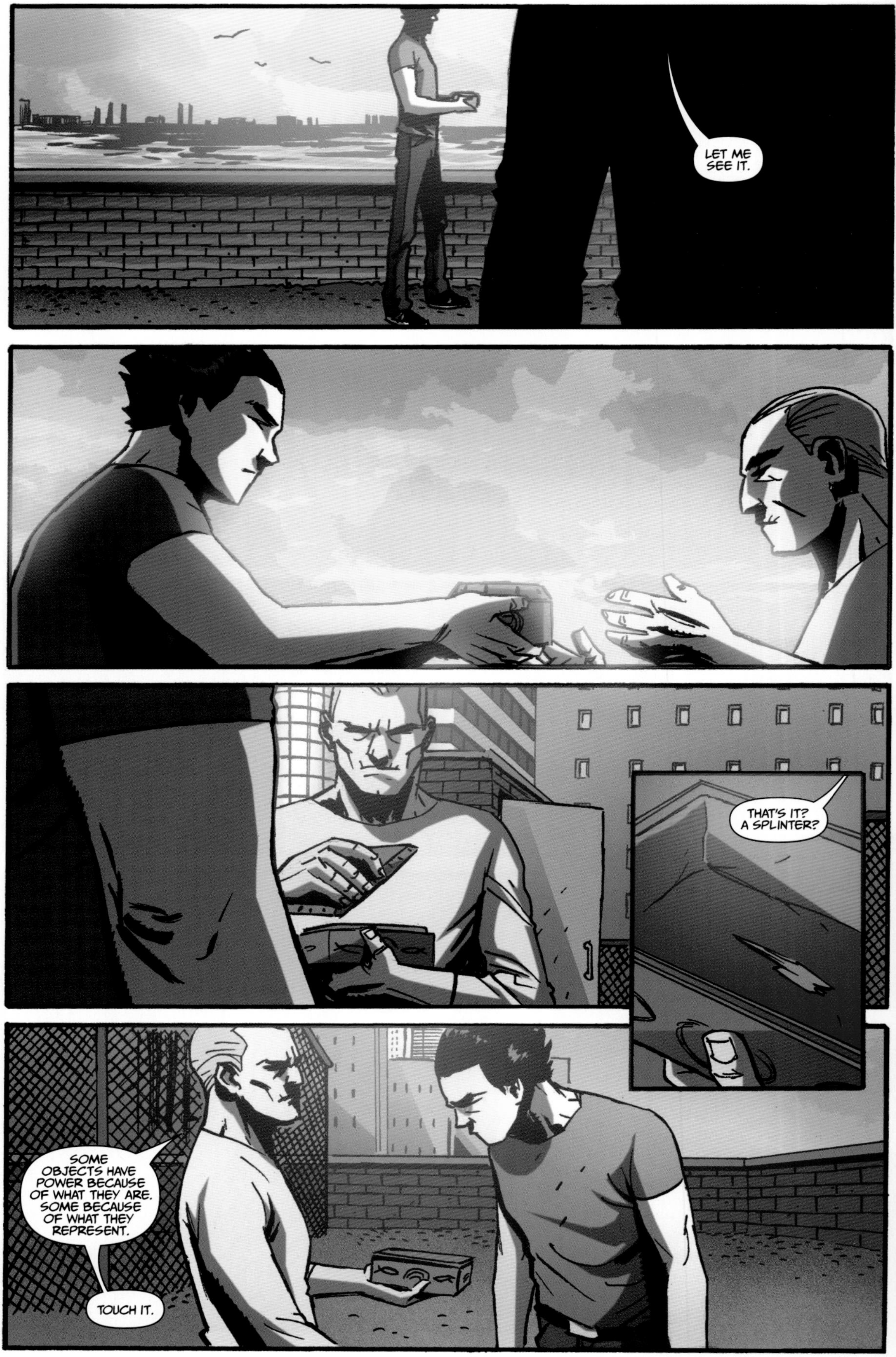
LET ME SEE IT.
THAT'S IT? A SPLINTER?
SOME OBJECTS HAVE POWER BECAUSE OF WHAT THEY ARE. SOME BECAUSE OF WHAT THEY REPRESENT.
TOUCH IT.

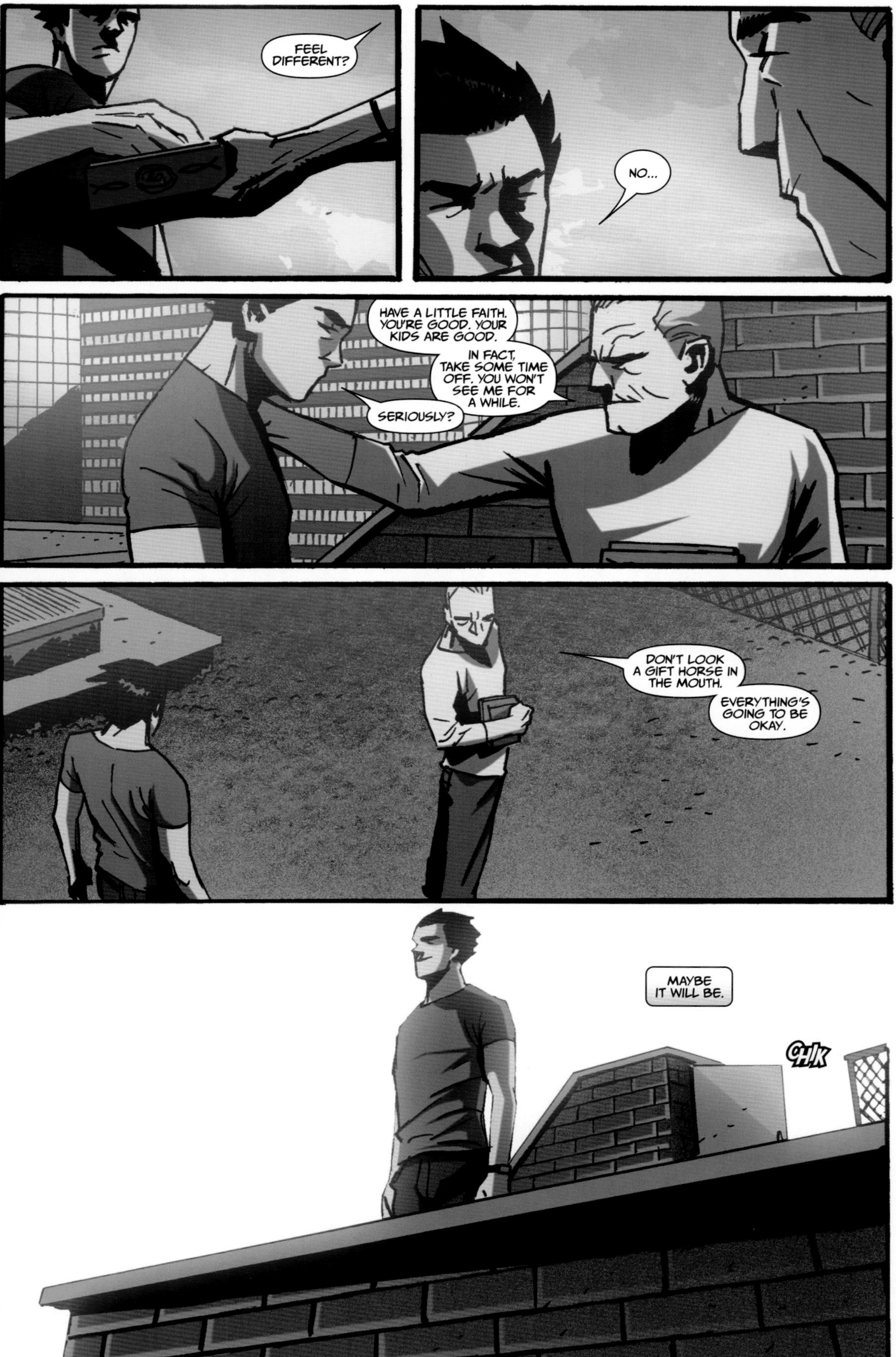
FEEL DIFFERENT?
NO...
HAVE A LITTLE FAITH. YOU'RE GOOD. YOUR KIDS ARE GOOD.
SERIOUSLY?
IN FACT, TAKE SOME TIME OFF. YOU WON'T SEE ME FOR A WHILE.
DON'T LOOK A GIFT HORSE IN THE MOUTH.
EVERYTHING'S GOING TO BE OKAY.
MAYBE IT WILL BE.
CHIK

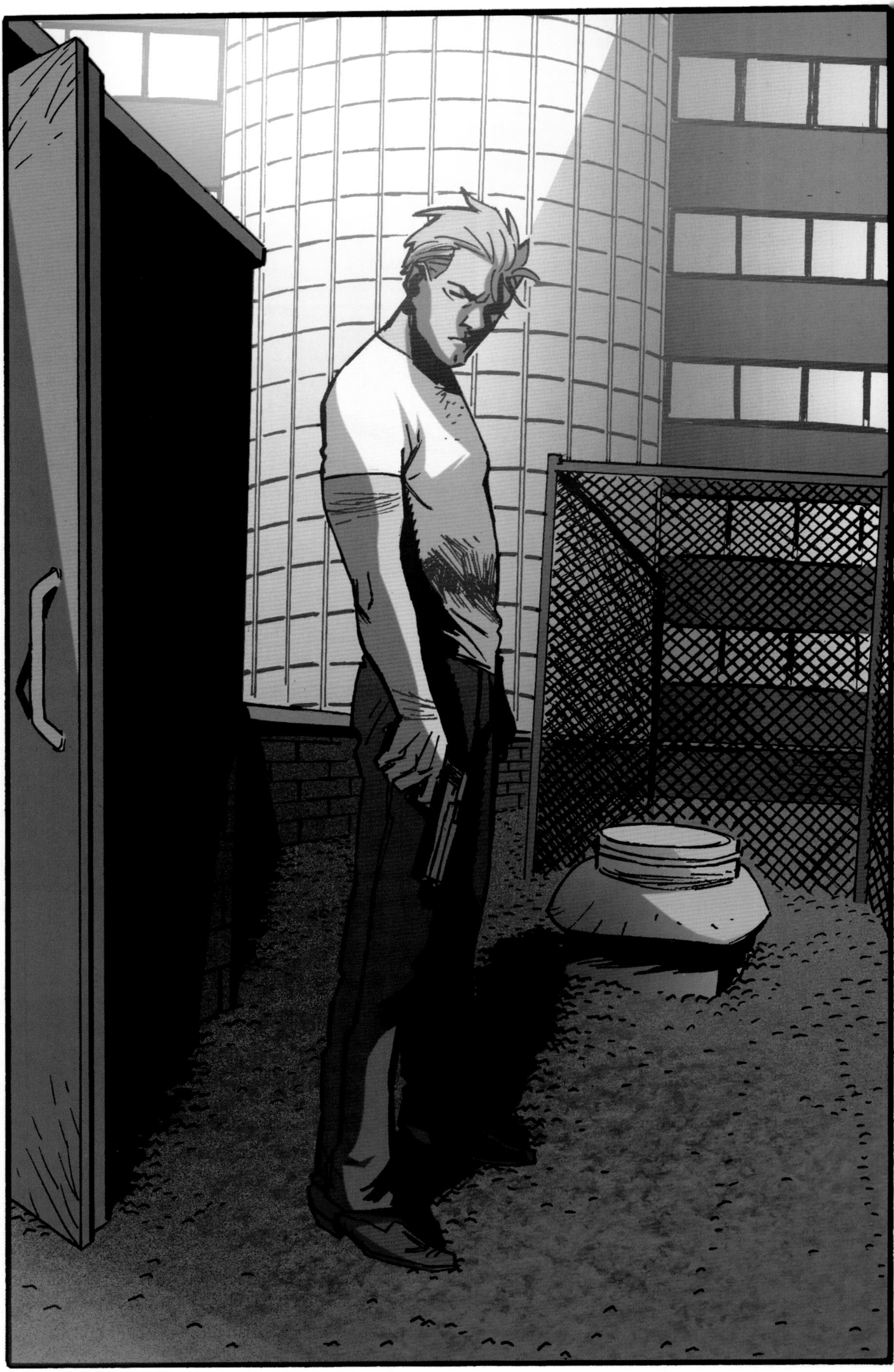

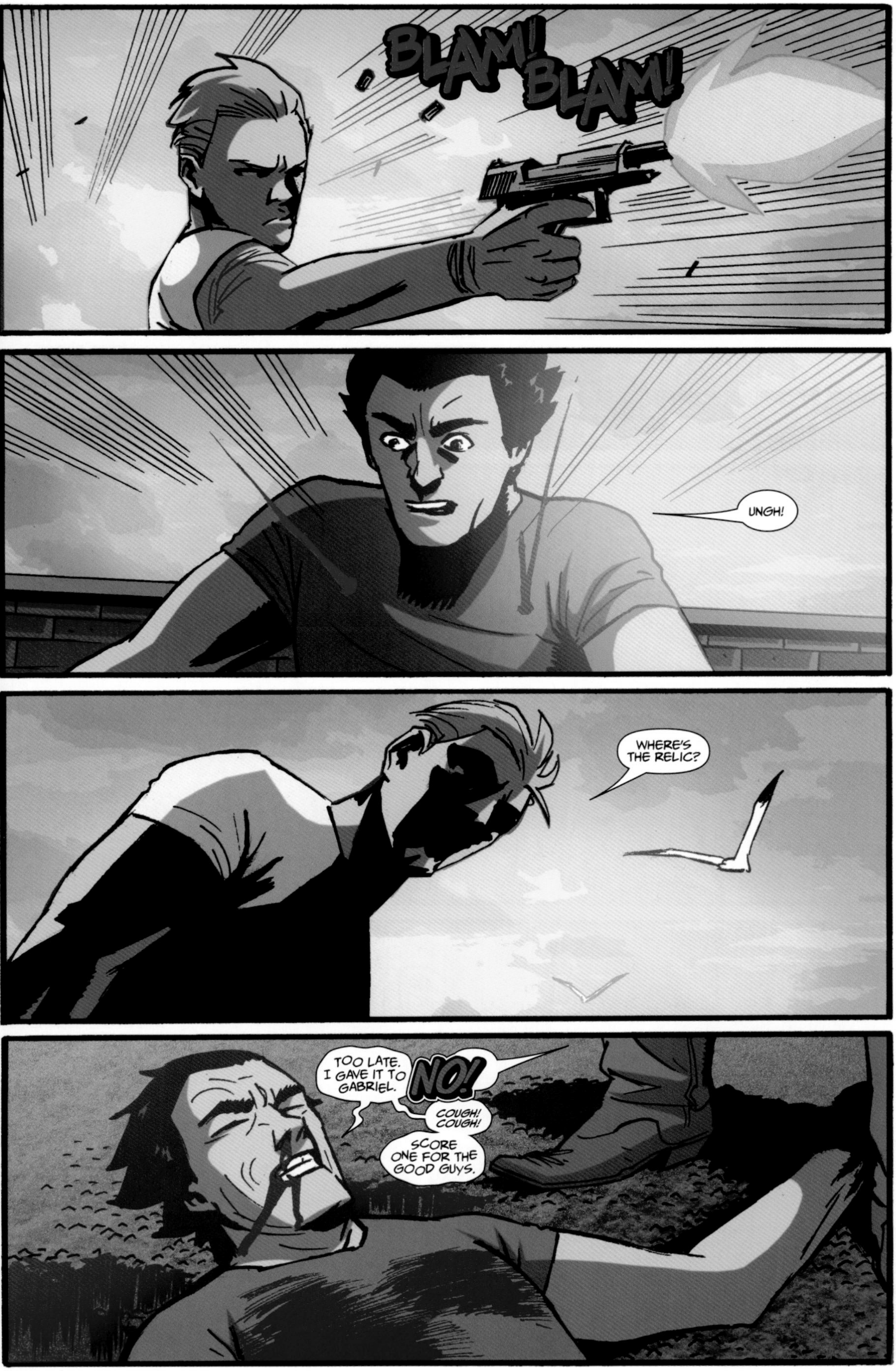
BLAM! BLAM!
UNGH!
WHERE'S THE RELIC?
TOO LATE. I GAVE IT TO GABRIEL.
NO!
COUGH! COUGH!
SCORE ONE FOR THE GOOD GUYS.

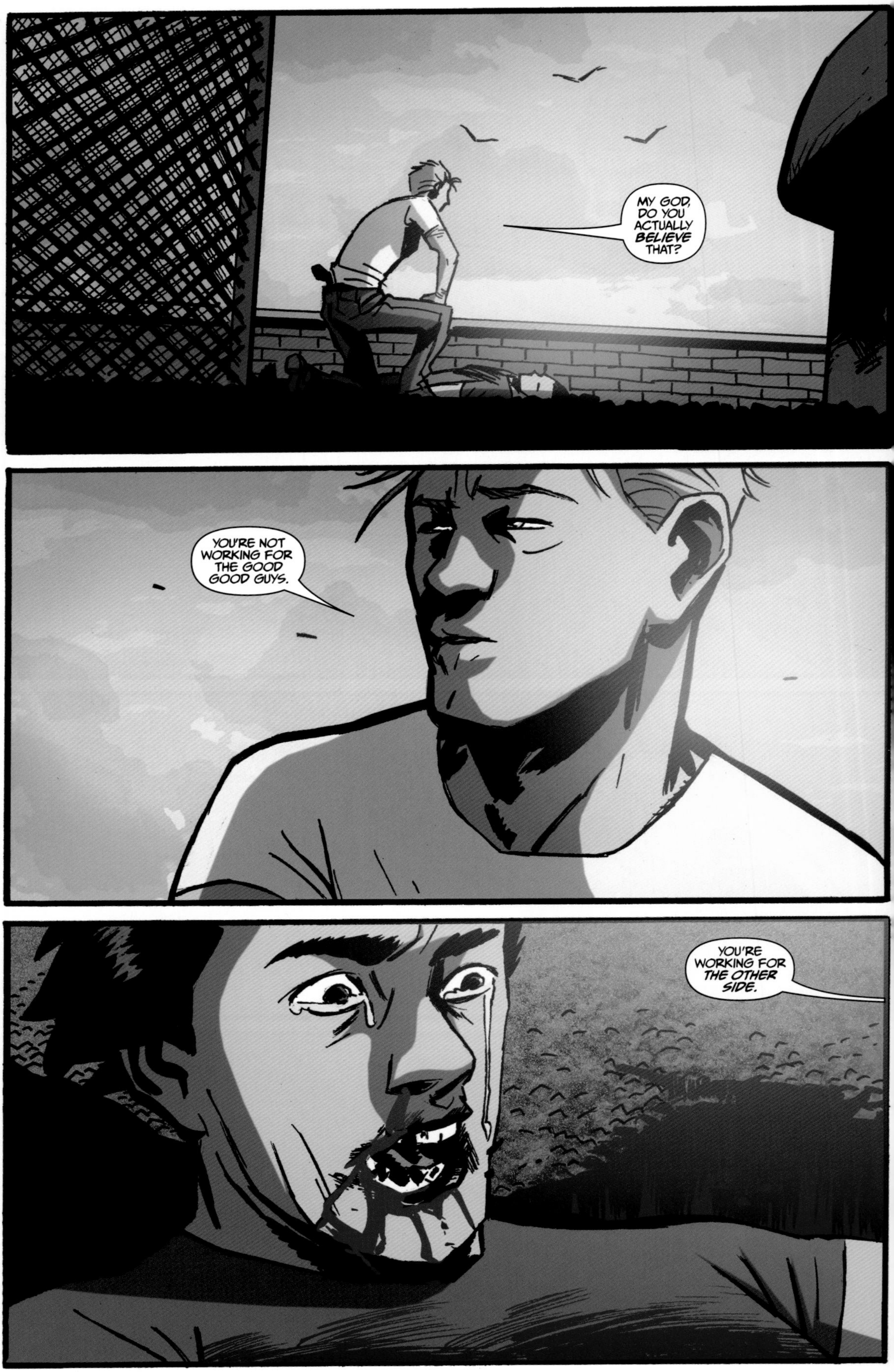
MY GOD, DO YOU ACTUALLY *BELIEVE* THAT?
YOU'RE NOT WORKING FOR THE GOOD GOOD GUYS.
YOU'RE WORKING FOR *THE OTHER SIDE.*

ABOUT THE MISSION

This was a story we'd wanted to explore for a long time. We've always been intrigued by people with extreme beliefs. On one hand, most of us would assume that a guy who actually believed that an angel had told him to kill must be a lunatic. And yet perfectly sane suicide bombers blow themselves up all the time for reasons that don't seem all that different. Such is the power of belief that from an outside perspective it's indistinguishable from madness — so much so that the question of what is actually real and true may start to feel inconsequential. In this ambiguous world, we wanted to take a character and see how far we could push him. Like a latter-day Job, how much could we hurt him? How much could we strip away? It's often said that you can't really know yourself until you've been truly tested. When you've lost everything, does your belief evaporate, or do you double-down on it? These six issues take the first steps down that road.

Some *thank you*s are in order. First and foremost, to Werther Dell'Edera, who created all the incredible artwork for this book. He's been a truly amazing creative partner. Thanks also to Arianna Florean, who continually surprised us with her smart and startling color choices. We'd seriously have been up a creek without a paddle if not for our talented and tireless editor Aubrey Sitterson. And finally a very special thanks to Marc Guggenheim and Alisa Tager who heard our idea for this book and without further ado, set out to make it a reality.

Erich Hoeber & Jon Hoeber
Santa Monica, 2011

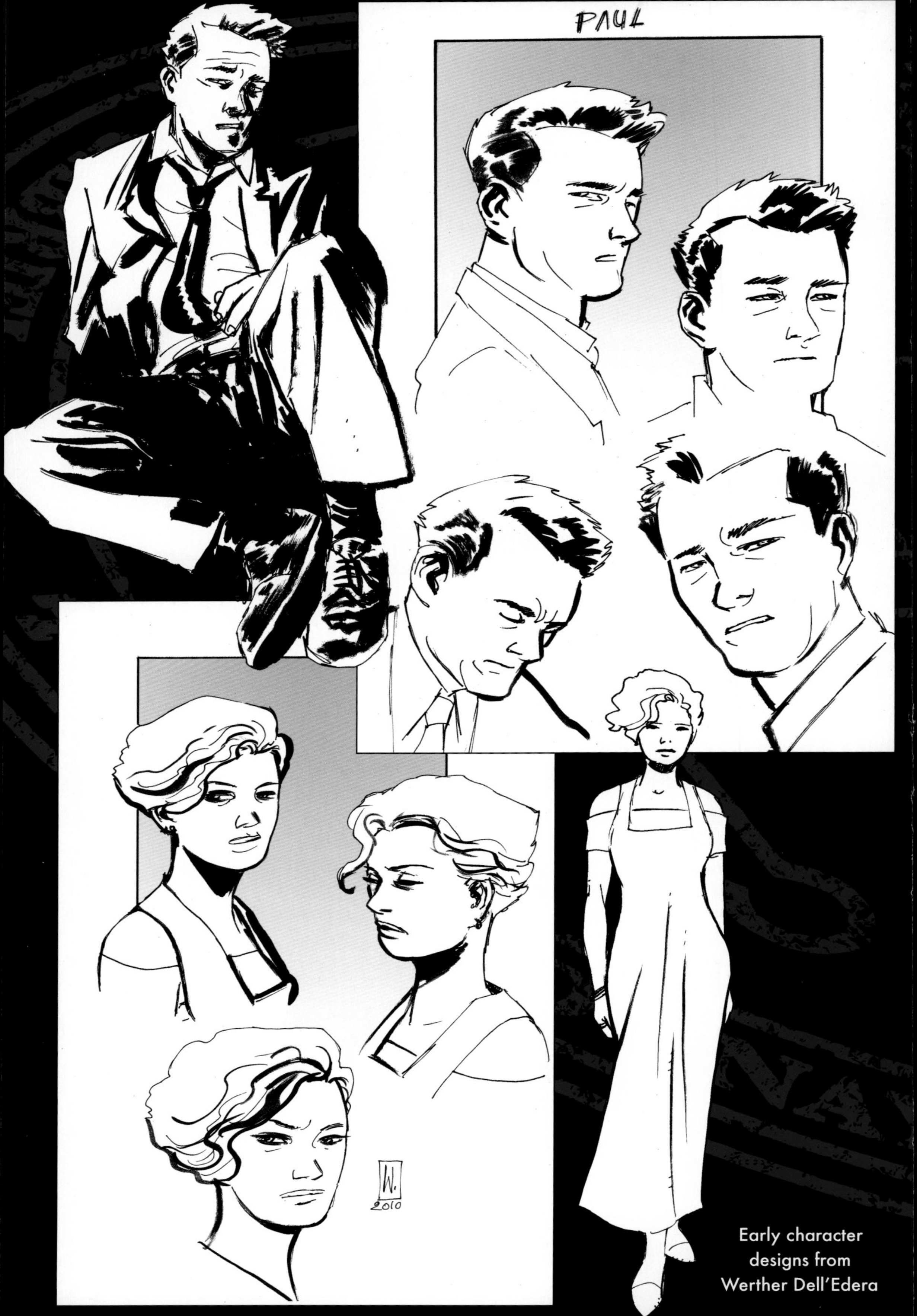
PAUL
W.
2010

Early character
designs from
Werther Dell'Edera

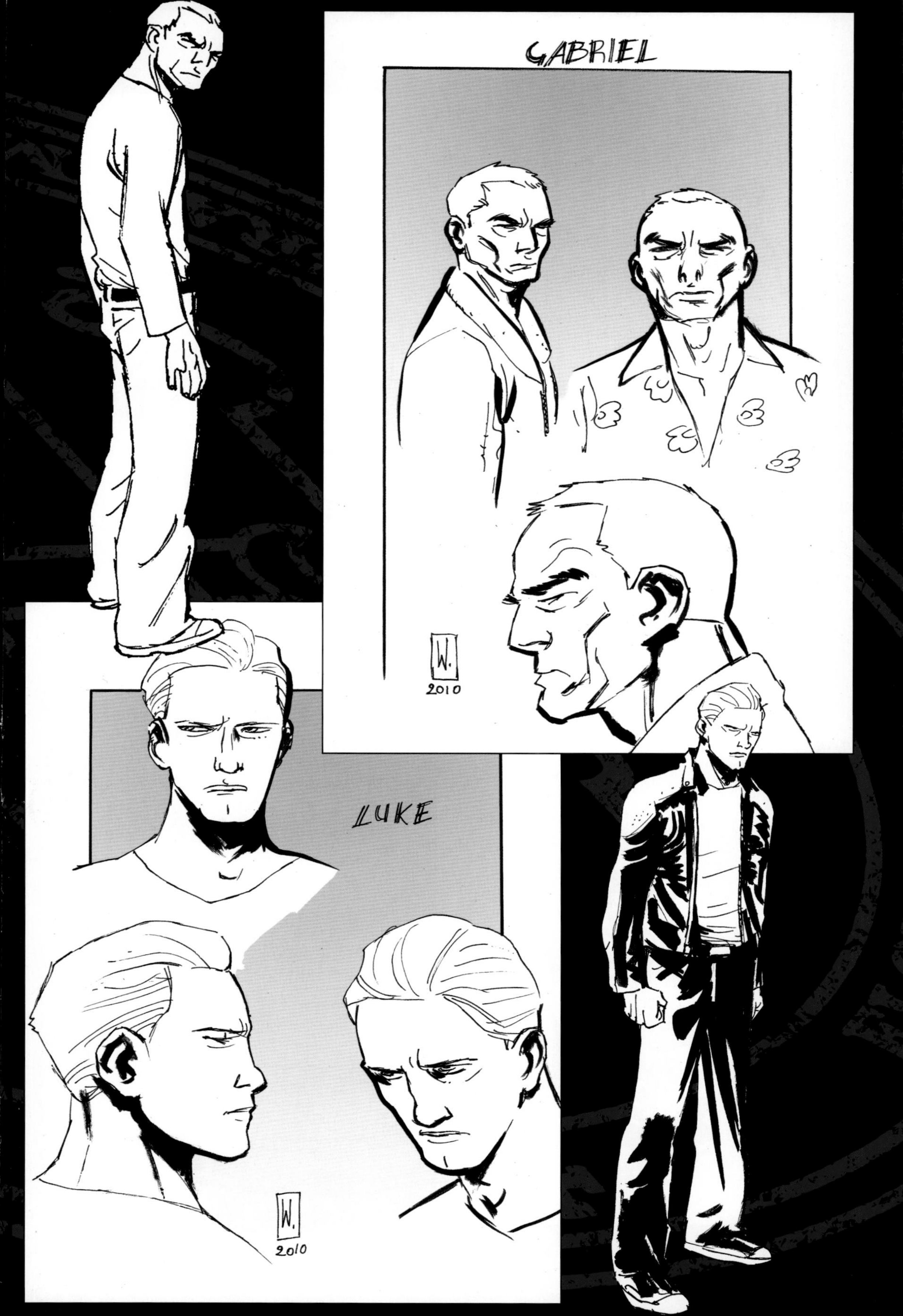
GABRIEL
W.
2010
LUKE
W.
2010

Cover development